Andrea Tompa

First published in 2024 by Istros Books
London, United Kingdom
www.istrosbooks.com

Cover image: Greg Curtis
Design and layout: pikavejica.com

Printed by CMP, Poole, Dorset, UK

ISBN: 978-1-912545-38-4

The publishers would like to express their thanks for the financial support that made the publication of this book possible:

English PEN

Petőfi Literary Fund

Hungarian Translators' House, Balatonfüred

Jelen mű kiadása a Petőfi Literary Fund (www.plf.hu) magyar irodalmat népszerűsítő célkitűzése szerinti együttműködés keretén belül valósult meg. The publication of this work was carried out within the framework of the cooperation according to the objective of the Petőfi Literary Fund (www.plf.hu) promoting Hungarian literature.

Supported using public funding by

ARTS COUNCIL ENGLAND

This book has been selected to receive financial assistance from English PEN's PEN Translates programme, supported by Arts Council England. English PEN exists to promote literature and our understanding of it, to uphold writers' freedoms around the world, to campaign against the persecution and imprisonment of writers for stating their views, and to promote the friendly co-operation of writers and the free exchange of ideas.
www.englishpen.org

Home

Andrea Tompa

Translated
from the Hungarian by
Jozefina Komporaly

Translator's Note:

Words/lines in italics are in English in the Hungarian text. American spelling is preserved wherever this is the case in the original. Phrases in French and Russian are also retained, also in italics, in the translation.

The landscape appears out of focus, with no clear outlines and solid forms. Its edges are dissolving; parts are fading into one another. The view is fuzzy, blurred, details are impossible to make out, only vast unities are visible to the naked eye. A grey cube-shaped building, myriads of parked cars in every colour, the sky smeared with clouds, on the horizon, an arc of trees or perhaps a forest.

Our protagonist is contemplating the landscape through the lense of reading glasses, from behind the steering wheel. The low, windowless cube is a shopping centre with a huge car park, while further away, there's a bleak airport. The grimness is softened by being viewed through glasses. There is no vanishing point, no sharp lines, no perspective. Sky and land merge together on the horizon, without conveying a sense of depth. Even the light is more muted.

Heading into the sun has lost its charm.

This airport is the grimmest place our protagonist has ever seen, but the plus lenses in her glasses makes even concrete and metal appear somewhat softer. This time, it isn't her turn to fly, only to wait for someone, which brings a sense of relief. Where's that former self who was so keen on airports? When did this change? Is it possible to have seen enough, once and for all?

There was a time when just standing there, waiting, tied to a spot, would have seemed impossible – the very act of stopping would have been a sign of defeat. When did that former passion for travel vanish? Even this present journey was a torture. Where's the person who used to grab every single opportunity to get going, keen to take possession of the whole wide world? Where's that inner Hannibal who crosses the Alps in a snowstorm, just as Turner painted it, commemorating the dark stormy sky, menacing like a wave, and the cascading avalanche, rather than the minor historical hero: Turner knew how we must always struggle with landscape, and not with people and foreign tribes. In the distance, there's sunshine and the promising warm lights of Rome, while at the forefront, Hannibal fights the elements by way of a snowstorm. These two contrasting weathers perhaps can't even co-exist in actual time and in such proximity, in a shared moment, that is to say in the so-called 'real', but only in the painter's dreams.

What has our protagonist gained or conquered while going round the world?

In the autumn, there'll be another flight to undertake though. Wouldn't it be somehow possible to just get there without embarking on an actual journey? When agreeing to this prospective travel to a small Northern town, barely traceable on the map, the unknown landscape and foreign climate had some mysterious lure. The invitation was to attend a conference called *A guest in your country*. They had discussed the meaning of the title at length, and what the person who formulated this phrase might have had in mind. 'Does this mean that you invited immigrants?' was the prospective speaker's abrupt response. 'Oh, no, not at all...' the reassuring elderly man of letters who organised the event hastened to reply and then attended to all subsequent questions, such as '*Why me?*, Why me in particular?', aimed at ensuring that it wasn't some misunderstanding that led to our protagonist's irrevocable presence as a non-guest, a victim of an error, who had arrived at a new homeland and was now an eternal winner.

In their correspondence, that commenced the previous winter, the Finnish organiser kept to a slow pace, adopting a relaxed tempo despite the promise around this *little low profile conference*. Perhaps the Northern light could illuminate things anew. Besides, two editors had recommended our protagonist, a writer, for the guest in your country topic, so she too ended up responding at a slow pace, confirming that the term *guest*, or *гость* was indeed correct, in response to which the cheerful Finnish organiser immediately prided himself with speaking some Russian. Funny how the English as well as the Russian word is also used to refer to the host, she thought: wouldn't that constitute a great conference topic for a linguist? How is it possible for both the guest and the host to be one and the same? However, after a bit of research, it emerged that the term *hostis* was in fact referring to the 'enemy'. Does this mean that guests are enemies? This realisation made her give up on the unwarranted peeling back of words in correspondence, aware of her own deficit in the field. Perhaps it would be best not to get to the bottom of words because at the bottom of things there are unimaginable vortexes that can pull you in.

Still, as the imminent journey and the presentation for the Finnish event approached, it conjured up the memory of a talk she was invited to attend in which Anne Bogart, a tall and well-built American director, suggested that one should either get really close to things or contemplate them from a distance. Perhaps Bogart meant that from close-up, details, complex structures, unresolvable correlations and intricate systems are visible to the naked eye, while from a distance, one can sense the greater picture for a split second, akin to the moment when giant cyclops lift their heavy heads and take a look around. What's in-between? The *medium view* is basically nothing, grey death, where everything is reassuringly familiar and knowable.

Yet the Finns, or to be precise this easy-going elderly gentleman by the name of Mikko, who calls himself a philosopher, tend to just go on holiday for two to three weeks. Mikko mentioned this in his latest letter, in which he also gave ample details about the various *berries* that were in season up North and the particular kinds he'd be harvesting in that distant forest where there were hardly any inhabitants left because they had all moved away to the nearby towns. The two of them continued to exchange long letters in which the *little conference* no longer got a mention. As the Finnish philosopher, literary scholar, translator and berry-expert noted, he was spending a lot of time in the woods, being *a regular guest of these forests*. He even rounded off one of his letters by stating that although he wasn't a writer as such, he could pen a book about berries and might actually proceed with this plan one day. He also shared his difficulties with translating the names of Finnish berries into English, and that he'd never agree to simply using the same English term, even as a compound, for the multiple words available in his mother tongue for the many different kinds of fruit ranging from black to red and blue varieties: 'How could anyone translate anything in such circumstances? *Berries don't migrate, do they?*'

As it happens, the Finnish gentleman wasn't interested in a 'tailored response', *not a personal perspective*, and would leave it up to the panellists to decide what to say about the topic. '*Well, we are all guests in this world, aren't we?*' he brought his letter to a close reassuringly, continuing on this persuasive tone even though the invitation had long been accepted. 'By the way, there won't be a large audience in this small town for our *little conference*, so there's no need to worry about too much *publicity*.' This is as inviting as it gets, she concluded and purchased her flight tickets.

Still, the presentation needed preparing, with the trip and the menacing flight suddenly pressing two months ahead of schedule. The distant unknown place suddenly became attractive, but the topic still rather repelling and besides, there were no suitable words to describe it anyway. The presentation that needs writing for the conference, summed up by the organiser as '*just a small comment you could give*', suddenly grips her on the left shoulder, like any other missed task, and turns into a stiff muscle-knot, a nodule, a painful bundle that makes even her neck dead stiff.

Fortunately, the talk will be in English. It's reassuring to avoid the traps of one's mother tongue, with its exceedingly complicated twists and endless ramifications. Instead, there's an opportunity to proceed in English, as if navigating a safer and less busy dual carriageway, where things can be named a lot easier because they already have names in foreign languages. No need to be afraid, foreignness is a safe shield. A major language is a particularly solid defence, great to lean against, and in the light of which it's comforting to bask.

In summary, she bought the said plane ticket. Yet, while waiting in the vicinity of the airport and surveying the washed-out building through reading glasses, this now feels like a mistake. To hell with flights.

To top it all, this time it's her turn to take other passengers and do the driving in the wake of a successfully passed test. If only it could be over already, if only this class reunion were cancelled, and the world had come to an end...

She can't really recall when this journey ended up resembling a frightful final separation, a small death, and hence needing to be avoided. Life, a writer's life, doesn't consist of shifts and turns but of periodic swerves rather than fateful steps, as mountaineers also slip out of their harnesses and ropes, they slip off their path because there is no actual demarcated path and, more specifically, there is no goal. Perhaps this is the biggest problem, the lack of a dedicated path, as there are only actions without any guidance or goal. Even though meaning is constantly being sought by a diligent gaze, one can only slip out of the old and into the new, moving from one event to the next, and all this is just as lifeless and ill-defined as a sight viewed through the lens of reading glasses.

Each time she purchased a plane ticket this conjured up the long queues, the X-rays, the complicated routine of unpacking and re-packing belongings, the endless wait and tense surveillance of time, avoiding slipping out of the as-yet-unknown plan. It increasingly appeared a mistake to have even started, and she could only hope that it wasn't a fatal error and that there was a way back, a return to the point of departure and of respite. And that there was a way to return home.

On this occasion, however, it was reassuring to simply wait in the stationary car for Ágó, even if the plane was delayed, as she had learned from the electronic display board when arriving on time for the early morning flight. We won't be flying today, hallelujah, just waiting instead and then driving back home together.

Who's this we, by the way? And how about this business with home?

She drove over to a nearby shopping centre because parking was cheaper there according to an inbuilt device in the car, a small bubble instantly popping up on the screen, with an invisible helper asking in a confidential voice: 'Would you like to find cheaper parking?' Then, as if guiding a person with sight loss, it directed the driver, who wouldn't have managed otherwise, through the complicated overpass-system and there it was: half-price parking indeed. Couldn't this small device, capable of talking and of coming up with just about anything, also guide one towards a better life?

When checking the arrival time of Ágó's flight on the phone, it emerged that they added another hour to the delay. How can a plane be delayed with further hours and hours once it had taken off from New York? Had anything happened? Always does. Ágó is coming, or to be precise, they are coming because both Ágó and Susan are on the same flight, just unaware of each other at present, for even our protagonist only learned about Susan last night.

For driving, it's important to wear glasses to correct short-sightedness. They are the same prescription as the ones recommended when she had come of age. As if time had stood still in the eyes and saw just as far as before. It's only the frames that kept changing, getting more attractive, expensive and fashionable, whereas the focus stayed the same. Despite this, she keeps returning to the optician every year or so, explaining that perhaps these glasses are no longer good, they can't facilitate a clear enough vision to see things properly from either a close-up or afar. Then they prescribe the exact same lenses, and, for the last few years, reading glasses, too. She has never made a habit of using either of these, not feeling the need to see everything particularly sharply, doubting the possibility of it anyway, since things can never be seen entirely clearly. Besides, wholeness doesn't emerge in this way, either. Of course, glasses will be needed for driving, but the car is still stationary and there are another sixty minutes until the arrival of the plane. At this point, she is looking into the distance while still wearing reading glasses and gazing up from a book, thus witnessing a fragmented and flat landscape where things are fragmented, incomprehensibly blurring into one another.

Still, what if she just went for it right now? It would be a great avenue for escape. Having every single justification. Always having had every single justification. To avoid what's still lying ahead, to make herself explode if the world doesn't want to explode by itself, and just vanish.

This thought lingers on for a while, and then retracts to where it has come from. Left shoulder, knot.

The view gets sharper as she puts on a new pair of light-sensitivity glasses, which help with an even sharper and deeper vision while the car comes closer to the entrance of the shopping centre. The walls of the building with a flat roof have been decorated with soothing multicolour rectangles and squares. On the left-hand side, there is a fully paved parking area, with a row of evenly planted trees in the background, a concrete field of empty access roads. A transient landscape, that isn't home to anyone. She spends two to three hours here before heading home. Mind you, can anything be found there of the entity called 'home', anything at all?

She stops in front of a stationery shop, having just remembered a favourite Russian expression: *от нечего делать*, meaning idleness. The reason for going into the shop is simply to use up excess time. The shop isn't too large, it's just the right size. Being a writer, she comes to a halt in front of some hardback notebooks: Strong white paper that can cope with ink without blotching. Hard and sturdy cover, without any labels or branding, capable of safeguarding any manner of serious stuff in the future. This is exactly what a serious author needs. This author would have needed such stuff once, too. A composition notebook, because the glued ones fall apart from being used year in, year out. This one has a ridiculous price, 'pornographically expensive', as an acquaintance had once referred to the price of tickets at the Bayreuth Opera House. Next, she chooses a pen to go with the notebook, one that is thick enough yet still light, so writing shouldn't come as an effort. Shouldn't come? If she were to sequence life as manically as her once favourite author Nabokov, who had broken everything down to twenty-year cycles, then this would already be the third and final sequence. Final? What sort of knowledge could she possibly possess about finality?

In this final phase, she can afford to purchase anything but has everything already. First phase: 'everything is out of reach', wanting everything and unable to afford anything. Second phase: the phase of reachability, when still needing certain objects and carefully acquiring some. And then there is the present. Could this be the end? Dried out? Indifferent? Bored? Cynical? This is the phase of *je suis un homme fini*, I'm finished, in the words of Andrei Bolkonsky.

A person whose journey is completed, concluded, who can only have questions that cannot be clarified and asked anymore. What could the French language have meant to Prince Andrei, seeing that he made this claim as a Russian in a Russian book, addressing this serious statement about himself to his closest friend, in French. *Un homme fini*, he declares about himself at a point when there are another 1,500 pages left of the book the protagonist of which he becomes. *Я человек конченный*, it can be read in the footnotes of the Russian edition, though it is unlikely that Tolstoy needed to translate these words as contemporary readers would have understood them. *Я человек конченный* places the accent on the first syllable. How much more exhilarating it is for anyone to declare about themselves that they are finished in French, English, even Russian, rather than their mother tongue. Because in one's mother tongue it seems as if one was indeed truly finished. To Andrei's comment, Pierre responds, also in French, that he is a child born out of wedlock: *Je suis un bâtard!* In our mother tongue, it would be offensive, perhaps even fatal, to label ourselves in this way. That said, is there another language available for telling the truth?

The longing for sturdy notebooks, pens and colours is nothing but the memory of longing. How could one manage to fill a notebook once again, fuelled by genuine excitement? How could one write one's very first book? Perhaps, this wait, and fire, should be the start of a new beginning, or the end of everything for good, seeing that we are dealing with an *homme fini*.

Does the above also mean that humans are finite in French as well? I'm a finite man, the prince would say about himself. In a matter-of-fact fashion, in the indicative. I. And everyone else.

But what does Prince Andrei, this *homme fini*, do here, after all, he will be given the chance to live on, with passion and sorrow and fire. And where does this desire stem from anyway, for none other than Andrei Bolkonsky to fill the arid gap between waiting, returning home, the first international driving spree and the oppressive obligation of a looming class reunion? Wouldn't it be a great relief to just read *War and Peace* instead of attending a class reunion and spending three days at a rental accommodation with some obscure acquaintances, driving on dangerous roads, not to mention being responsible for other passengers in the car? Getting immersed in a book, where the protagonists love, suffer and live. Returning to the house, back home, locking herself away and just reading, reading, as in the summers of yesteryear, there, everywhere, in the garden, in the house, on the shores of lakes, with a book. Running away, into a book.

'I'm sorry', Brecht muses with a thick cigar between his teeth: 'art is no compensation for a life not lived'. She's standing in the stationery shop in front of a shelf laden with water colours, acrylic paints, brushes, needle-sharp pencils and fine rubbers. Happy are those who are in no need of language. They receive colours and shapes in exchange, fight with them instead. She nearly forgets to pay for the insanely expensive sturdy notebook and the pen in the basket, nearly walks out of the shop and only realizes this in front of the alarmed gate. This isn't absent-mindedness, but the sense of entitlement of someone to whom everything the world can offer is at arm's length and payment is a mere convention. It's time to turn back from the door with a sense of surprise and pay. She will write words yet again into a notebook, and dream about a book, a story, the end of which is yet unknown.

This is what I do, an American author, indifferent to success, replied once dryly to the question as to why he was writing. There is no cause only effect. 'This is what I do', the author, a good one at that, concluded. She is also a good writer but not great. Perhaps not even good enough to deserve peace like the Master, that one who couldn't obtain light only peace. This was the verdict in this regard, the most disquieting verdict in *The Master and Margarita*: the Master isn't entitled to light, only peace. He literally hasn't earned it, in other words, he hasn't deserved it. *Он не заслужил света, он заслужил покой.* Matthew Levi then communicates the verdict: he didn't deserve the light. But he did deserve peace. Only someone stupid would think that Light can be deserved. It can't. Whoever makes a judgement and takes a decision about the Master is Light itself.

Peace, however, would be a really big deal.

As for her, she hasn't yet deserved anything, certainly not peace, so can only be an average author at best, if that is considered to be a service at all. Standing on the verge of this so-called homecoming, wedged into nothingness and waiting for the New York flight to land with the long-awaited Ágó, who's so tired and sleepy throughout the entire journey that all hopes connected to catching up vanish as soon as she gets into the car and places her travel pillow around her neck. Yet our writer was really hoping to ask Ágó a question impossible to articulate: what is returning home like for her? Like a cup of tea? Too sweet? Or too hot? A topic for the discussion of which language will turn out to be inadequate. *How do you feel about this?* She might ask in the language in which everything can be discussed by virtue of the fact that it isn't one's own. Instead, there'll be this chattering Susan, a proper American, who doesn't yet know that the person about to pick her up from the airport in lieu of her mother will be a stranger, on her first drive carrying a passenger after passing her test, and on her first stomach-churning trip back home.

Susan has only been back home before as a little kid, while Ágó comes every three to four years, inasmuch as she still uses this word 'home'. Our protagonist, however, goes more often. And now they are all equally wedged into nothingness, into this nearly three-hour wait, and in this thirty-year-long insertion, this intermediate state in which nothing is granted – neither returning, nor arriving without looking back, nor ultimately – this ultimately is the ultimate trash word – finding peace. Especially now when it has emerged that our protagonist is an *homme fini*, overwhelmed by the fear of death, for the articulation of which one's mother tongue is entirely inadequate. Nonetheless, she does not and will not have the courage to give up on the supremacy of the mother tongue by way of a single radical shift and thus either prevent or fully accomplish linguistic suicide, like that Irish author with a creased face, by the name of Beckett. Who is to say that it's impossible to break away? This entire linguistic narcissism could have been left behind, in the manner of Beckett, all these elaborate ornaments, literary friezes and tympans, which she has also juggled with as a writer and garnered admiration for, despite the fact that this circus-style magic with one's maternal tongue can only conceal dead bodies, the unnameable. In what language can one possibly articulate the truth?

Stuck between two worlds, no longer at home but not yet back home either, overwhelmed with fear because something has definitely come to an end, at least temporarily, while something else cannot yet commence. In other words, this place called home and obtained at the cost of tremendous effort, has to be left behind in order to depart from home to (another) home, the latter without loved ones or a house to call one's own, only with some sort of a shared past, yet still experiencing the sensation that there must be something there for the articulation of which she is unsuitable.

At this point, the Son's brief message pops up on the screen: 'When are you coming home?' Well, I haven't even started off yet. To go home. She is dictating this to the machine – having settled for such a function because it's not possible to write while driving. These words sound muffled and empty in the car's inner space.

'Shall I wait for you regarding Somlyó?' The gadget pings again. 'By all means'.

'How's it going?', the next question follows. The Son has been driving for a lot longer, he's more self-confident and calmer, having obtained his licence before even turning eighteen. 'Lamely', is the reply, without mentioning that they are still loitering in the vicinity of the airport. Perhaps the Son is getting concerned and that's why he's asking these questions. Next to the bubble, a picture of the Son pops up – taken years ago, when he was still an awkward teenager, his hair hanging in his eyes, ashamed of his spots, large nose and slim, asymmetrical face.

'Lamely'. This is repeated twice. Initially, as if just addressed to the Son, the first syllable can be barely heard, so the device fails to understand and turns it into letters. Then again, this time slowly and articulately. LAME-LY. This is a conspiratorial word. A shared word. It was the Son who started to use it when he was small. For everything. To talk about himself, his mother, his father. Then she also began to make use of it, applying it ever so gently and forgivingly to oneself. This complicit word heats up the space.

One is only allowed to utter complicit words. Words that connect, and invigorate. As if we were locking eyes with words.

By this point, she's no longer planning to flee, doesn't want to commit suicide, is no longer an *homme fini*. It's time to start the engine.

The fear that has moved into her is localised in the left shoulder. She casts a glance in that direction and a greeting. 'Let's get going. The plane is about to land.' It's much more manageable now that the bird of death is only perching on her left shoulder. *This is what I do*, she starts off on this journey, like someone who has come to terms with the fact that it is what it is: having promised two years ago to attend this class reunion, in other words, to go home. 'You'll come home, won't you?' – 'Sure.' Despite having just started to refrain from the use of this word. The device dictates where to go, without it she'd be lost in space while driving, seeing that all these overpasses, interconnected and exit roads that are impossible to make sense of. The Son doesn't use any devices while driving, he just happens to know where he is and where is North and South. He seems to have an in-built map in his head. He is familiar with space and can orientate in it. He's come to take possession of it.

'Have a safe journey', another bubble pops up as she has just made a turn towards the airport. The following minute, the next bubble says 'Map'. This is a compound of 'mama' and 'papa' that somehow stuck when the Son had suddenly started to speak with great enthusiasm and conjoined the names of his parents. Later, this turned into map, aka muppet, as in the Muppet Show's two croaking oldies who are watching the proceedings from their box and keep offering a rolling commentary on a sour tone, disapproving of everything. According to the Son, our protagonist is just like these two croaking oldies, critical of everything and exasperated by the happiness of others.

She's trying to start the car but finds it hard to get used to the immobilizer, so the engine stalls. Checking the screen, there are no new messages after the LAME, that shared and complicit word. 'Your book is lame', the Son claims as they walk past a bookshop and she proudly points out her latest publication. He was in the middle of a tantrum, walking ahead in anger, while she slowed down to stare at this foreign object. This was the first time she saw this pale green thick book in a bookshop: was it a touch too turquoise-covered perhaps? She was ready to give the boy a hug now, which he repelled, ready now to give him those two scoops of ice cream or that extra topping or whatever, no matter the cost, only to put an end to the tantrum and the coldness. This coldness and foreignness were unbearable along with his recalcitrance, those eyes like daggers. From then on, she'd always make sure to ask: 'Will you come to the launch of my lame book?'

She starts the car again and it finally works, the device urging 'to turn left' and then 'head East'. Where's East, you idiot? The dictation function is still on, so the machine transcribes this question and sends it. 'Not you', she adds quickly, and the Son must be laughing at this from afar, too, knowing that Map is struggling with orientation. In the end, the correct road is found though.

Destination: the airport.

'What... earth'*?* she asks, pausing for a second between the two words.

A huge spot of colour emerges in front of the plane's right wing, breaking the monotonous steel grey shades of the water's surface. It looks quite near when viewed from above, almost tangible. An almost floating green land. A piece of land or an island. It emerges from the nothingness of the ocean. *Earth* turns out to be an inadequate word, this has become obvious even before getting here, in fact, her linguistic incompetence has been apparent from the very start. *Earth* is the Planet one has never seen for real, a globe the astonishing rotundity of which can only be visible from up here at eight thousand metres, though from here this green spot seems to be within reach. So far, this roundness was taken for granted despite not being seen, and it was of no real concern. The Earth is positively huge, round and endless.

Earth – new language, new gods. Those who have left and continue to go away, who don't even look back, who are scattered in the world, take up new languages and cling on to new gods.

What could that be in the near distance, what could that astonishing green be, she muses staring out of the window.

The question, awkwardly phrased and too soft, is addressed to a flight attendant leafing through a women's magazine. *People*, it says on the cover. People?

What kind of land is this?

'Sorry,' she leans over to be noticed by the woman, 'what earth?' asking again a little louder, to break through the humming grey engine noise, even raising a hand and pointing at the window splashed with drops of water. 'That,' with an added emphasis, realising that earth turned out to be an inadequate term.

The woman looks tired. The passengers have only been travelling for about four to five hours, but the flight attendants appear to have been journeying for decades. What time zone can this be? In-between time.

She addresses her question to the black flight attendant out of the two staff members sitting opposite each other, as she looks more approachable; aged around sixty, she seems uncomfortable in her worn-out footwear and regulation fuchsia uniform. Right now, the two of them are strikingly different – the passenger is young and supple, and much too alert despite the long journey. This is her very first flight, at half the age of the flight attendant, and this word doesn't yet mean anything unutterable or conceptually precarious.

Thirty years later, such a journey will be more problematic to undertake for her, based on the assumption that all journeys which have ever been in store have already been travelled, carrying restless work, unbridgeable time, *jetlag*, from here to there and back in a much heavier body. On the way back it takes longer to readjust, time falls apart and it takes ages to place it back together. There is even an explanation for why it's harder to fight jetlag in the direction of the rising sun. This term is so alien that the mother tongue can't even find an equivalent word for it, only four combined together: time-zone-change-syndrome. Homecoming is not the only explanation, yet while flying from West to East, the body is struggling and less obedient to time, as if it was something that no longer wants to adapt and go anywhere. It simply doesn't want another time zone only one and the same for good. Just to be home somewhere. It is slower and harder to adjust to *jetlag* flying from West to East, she reads with interest thirty years later. When travelling West, one's rhythm, body clock, the circadian circle ticking in the human body can be stretched and expanded, adding hours to the day. Yet strangely enough, time cannot be compressed, which is exactly what would need to happen when travelling towards the East. One's own time cannot be shortened only expanded.

That said, learning about time is light years away. Now, it's the turn of space. The first American trip.

She will end up reading the article about circadian circles three decades later, while navigating the dark waters of sleeplessness. Right now, time and the time within is of no interest. There is an infinite supply of this at the moment, seeing that she has only been alive for less than a quarter of a century. Space is the only source of excitement, that big round Globe. To indulge, acquire and conquer. Not even looking back but heading to battle. Odysseus comes to fight and to win. Not to return home. This is the start of craving-for-miles, there is no tiredness only a thirsty and unappeasable drive to travel.

'What earth?'

The flight attendant's face betrays decades of sleep deprivation and exhaustion, akin to someone who's never to be found in their own time but fluttering between different time zones. Two decades after this moment of being the passenger, our protagonist will also let out a sigh: 'Good god, how I hate flying, I hate it and fear it, I'm afraid of death to be honest, afraid of what's within arm's reach.' What arm, whose arm? The hugging arm of death. Three decades later, it will be a major effort to persuade herself to fly. 'This isn't the way I want to die', she would like to prepare for it, asking for more time to acknowledge death, 'grant me my own death, let's neither compress nor expand time, just grant me what I'm due'.

'What's the time here, in what time and space are we?' Another question could be, '*What time zone is this right now?*', a phrase she has already prepared and polished like someone who may need it in that large country with so many simultaneous time zones. UTC. This is the one that begins at the start of the flight, *Universal Time*.

This is her first trip by air, the very first stage in transforming into a mile-engulfing dragon, whose hunger, as in the fairy tales, just grows with every mile that it swallows. How many more decades are left of this insatiable craving?

The flight attendant looks up before parting her surprisingly red lips. She is the first black person our passenger on this transatlantic fight has ever spoken to. It was precisely this kind of foreignness that the latter wanted to connect with, this was fuelling her craving.

Nearly three decades later, when travelling home from home on a short and busy morning flight, two students are talking in a loud voice nearby. A sparkly young woman, without a single wrinkle or skin flaw, just the soft rosy skin of a twenty-something girl. Our protagonist keeps staring at the girl's hands while overhearing this incredible sentence: 'I'm so enjoying this flight, why is it so short', even replaying it in her head, to ensure that these were the actual words of the girl who may only be around twenty. The girl's light summer skirt slips up a bit and reveals her smooth thighs. Her body is hot and new, of someone who is marvelling at the world, flying above the clouds in the glittering sun. Under her eyes, even the most revealing areas are still soft and well rested, as if she was still a child. Casting a glance at the girl, this image lingers in front of our protagonist's eyes as the cruel beginning of irreversible time. This age-ring is part of the latter's make-up, too, this enthusiasm for the journey, for flying. The other girl sitting in the middle, who occupies most of the narrow space with her bag kept on her lap, agrees at once: 'Oh, yeah, me, too.' They stop talking, and just look out of the window, soaring above the blanket of clouds in a silver glaze. Girls heading into battle that they are.

Every departure is a battle, and our passenger's has already taken place.

Homer either omitted to write about this or didn't think it important, or he had simply nothing to say about whether Odysseus had any desire to go on another journey after he had finally returned home the hard way after two decades. Whether he was interested in travel, relocation or displacement at all after he had returned to his grown-up children he had abandoned for the sake of war. It is possible that the great sailor was longing to be on the move, but didn't want to take another risk. Because after his endless journey that just kept promising the return home without fulfilling this promise, he eventually made it home, unrecognised, and had reasons to believe that he was the favourite of the gods and that the gods would always stay with him. Pallas Athene would always be right next to him disguised as an old man, a bird or a nymph and look after him and talk to him, as Odysseus would talk to her. But perhaps he had exploited this privilege already. Perhaps it would be best not to put the gods to the test, though this is exactly what a hero likes to do the most, or what their very task is: to put the gods to the test.

Should she, as our protagonist, even accept being named as the hero, this won't lead to the confirmation of anything apart from sitting on a cliff, head held low, not even hearing the sound of the sea only that inner grey noise, the absence of silence. Where to go and where to be? Desire is no longer lifting her on its wings, only acting as a source of torment.

Now, it's crystal clear for her that returning home is much, much more tiresome than going away. Going away is easy: the two of them, that is the hero and the god, or to be precise the goddess, have been chattering, whispering and talking to each other like any other happy individuals on their way to war: the god is gently relocating the wayfarer from one place to another, where yet another victory is in wait. The hero, who's perhaps rattling with this very inexplicable desire, this desire for being underway, even after having arrived, and who's struggling in the merger of these two states, impossible to be named because this can only have a story and not a name. There are no words, only stories. The hero will also hide behind the name 'Nobody' on the way home, saying *Outis*, ουτις to the cyclops. 'Back home, I'm Nobody.' Since then, *outis* is the moniker of the artist.

'What earth?' she asks therefore, arms held out, knowing that this language is inadequate because neither earth nor country are the right words to use up here, there is no language, or perhaps there is for others, elsewhere, but not in this time and space impossible to grasp in-between languages and time zones.

'Greenland,' the woman replies, barely looking up. 'Isn't that splendid?' she adds. 'What lovely weather we're having, so fortunately it can be seen, *lucky you*, yesterday it couldn't...', she continues at the pace of flight attendants, which is a touch slower and with clearer articulation, coupled with a part official part personal smile. 'The top of the world.' She then loses herself again in the colourful pages of *People* magazine.

What yesterday, which yesterday, what weather, she seems

confused, translating the above to herself, just to make sense of them. This means that this distant bright green spot was also there yesterday, it existed a week ago, in their childhood as well as the childhood of their grandmothers, in all times, in fact. And yet, time seems to be just beginning, with this long-awaited, much desired and well-deserved overseas flight.

The flight attendant's tone is gently didactic, indicative of someone who had heard this question not only a thousand but ten thousand times, this stammering question of excitement on the tip of everyone's tongue. For a moment, it's quite difficult to identify the word she used because our protagonist, being a first-time passenger on such a journey, had never heard it before; this word had never been uttered, a word which isn't a country as such, like Germany or China or Canada. A word that is unrecognisable to the ear at first and needs translating, but as translation occurs, the word just falls apart because the woman wasn't talking about *Grönland*, that ice-cold nothingness and distant emptiness, that rocky unpopulated winter, dead space or the failure of nature. She was talking about *Greenland*: a green spot shining somewhere quite near to us, at arm's length, it's here and yet unreachably far but for real, a breathing, that is breath-taking, untouchable beauty. Cape Verde? No, that's not it, come on, where are the Cape Verde Islands actually? Wouldn't it have been wise to study some more geography and physics, to learn about time and space so we can be at home in them since our language has made us homeless to such an extent? Is there a world in which Greenland is a real thing? If so, then this was Ithaca, I have seen it and now I know where the hero is longing to be, she looks back, delighted with this recognition, because within minutes they've left it behind under the plane's right wing. The impossible set for a possible homecoming. What a trap one's mother tongue can be! It conceals the world instead of opening it up. This here is Greenland.

Still, what are they doing above Greenland? She looks up to the large screen tracking the slow progress of the tiny plane above the huge globe of the world. What's this curvature, where are they and why are they going this way? No idea. Is this really the way there?

The top of the world. Could it be that they have really seen the top of the world?

The subject known as geography was taught until year eight at school, and then it was discontinued. For some reason, they stopped teaching anything about the unknown and unpromising planet named Earth, with the gradual approach of adulthood, knowledge about Earth was deemed pointless, if not dangerous, seeing that a much larger world, voiced by the sirens, might tempt impressionable young souls. It's much better to chain passengers to the ship, cover their ears with wax, and in the worst case, throw them into the sea. To be fair, she had often looked aside during geography lessons, staring out of the window and dreaming of clouds. Rummaging for memories beyond the mere name of this subject, she can only find emptiness without any visual connections. The only thing that has persisted of these lessons delivered without any passion is the smell of the classroom in the warm autumn sun, the scent of the floor polished with kerosene and the evaporation of the oil paint with which the benches had been coated. And that head, turned to one side and looking out of the grated ground floor window. This is the whole wide world. And it had never come to light, not even in lessons called 'literature' and grammar', whether a hero called Abel[1] had ever managed to make it to America. To America, from where he later returned, because there is such a thing as a comeback according to the author, who had also returned home, in death, albeit with a regrettable detour.

Odysseus also returns in the end, but first, he has to keep sitting on a rock for ages, sobbing and crying.

'Howbeit if in thy heart thou knewest all the measure of woe
it is thy fate to fulfil before thou comest to thy native land...'[2]

A hero can never know how much sorrow they'll have to endure. The journey home will be ever so long.

She glances back at this new and striking cinnabar green land, of which she had been previously unaware. The top of the world is at arm's length. She can actually see the top of the world.

Jamaica, NY

Local time at departure / Local time at destination – the various screens keep informing the passengers, yet they are still unable to capture the actual passage of time while moving from one time zone to another, no matter how hard they focus: wrist watches persist in showing something that hasn't been accurate for at least four or five hours. When they arrive at their destination, it's finally time for everyone to get off the plane, and it becomes obvious just how many objects everyone has brought along, including her, with her assortment of books, notebooks, small dictionary, water bottle, pencil case, tissues, eye mask, ear plugs (much better ear plugs than the ones distributed on the plane, thanks). In addition, there's some hand cream, sweets, an elasticated folder with printouts of all the major destinations and hotel names, and at the bottom, an envelope with six green banknotes that haven't made it into the main wallet because, as yet, they haven't arrived at the place where these fairy tale banknotes are actual, legal tender. Soon enough, it will emerge that these banknotes are barely in use at the destination either, at least in such large denominations. A sea of objects, with which travellers cling on to their own existence on this long journey only manageable by plane, during which time stands on its head. As they get off the plane, with a tough day in their wake, she is left with the sensation of a lost night and the blurring of night and day, while departure and arrival times still chase one another.

It's a mystery how the awaiting car finds her, or the other way round, following the collection of a medium-sized suitcase labelled with a NY LGA tag. There is no signage or branding on this car, the black driver just silently grabs the suitcase: somehow, they recognise each other, and the driver is holding up a small hand-written sheet with our protagonist's misspelt and misgendered name.

'*Jamaica, yeah*?' he asks, seeking her approving nod in the rearview mirror. In the yellow car, the front and rear seats are separated by plexiglass, with only a small hole allowing a hand to fit through.

'Just a second,' comes her response, swiftly checking the first page in the folder. The first page is no good, that's the arrival which has already happened in principle, they have landed, her body has landed at NY LGA airport. This means that the second page is needed, with the details of the first accommodation.

'Hotel Old Castle,' comes the self-assured announcement.

The driver reaches back and takes the piece of paper from his passenger's hand without a word, he doesn't really pay attention to the journey, just keeps on driving. The passenger has been informed that there is no need to pay as the organiser has already settled the bill, but a certain anxiety is lingering on regardless whenever money matters tend to come up. It's impossible to appreciate the value of these banknotes, the unavoidable expenses lying ahead, there's an ongoing urge to think through, calculate, convert and assess each and every expense.

'How far is it?' she asks, awkwardly.

'Don't know. Nine miles maybe.'

Old Castle is a large new concrete building. She checks in, goes up to the room and throws the suitcase on the huge bed. It would be premature and dangerous to sit on the bed. The time: *The local time at destination* is 18:00, at home – well, that doesn't really matter, now the body has to adjust to this: Hotel Old Castle, Jamaica, New York. Home has simply ceased to exist, home time has ceased to exist, everything that used to be, has come to an end. It is what it is now, but still, what is this actually? From now on, the body always adjusting, or at least the body has to adjust to *local time at the destination.*

Hungry, not hungry, she's trying to probe time, when was the last meal, at home, this would be a good time to eat, needless to say, even this hypothesis is pointless, seeing that there was more than enough food during the journey, during the flight that is, a snack, then a main meal followed by another snack, with plenty of orange juice in-between, yet another snack if one went to ask the flight attendant, she has gobbled up everything that was handed out, so can't be hungry, or just a little perhaps, as always, after all it's comforting to eat, eating is a great way of measuring time. Eating is a great way to calm babies, from then on, they'll always want to eat when they grow up, she doesn't want to calm down though, that's not why she has come to the other side of the world. Calm wasn't the reason why she has now travelled to this desperately desired place. Which isn't Jamaica. How to express the fact that she's been desperately longing to come here? *Strongly? Deadly?* This is the extent of her vocabulary, which is no treasure trove but a dusty antiquities shop, flea market, bric-a-brac shop, state-owned department store, excavations around the dead languages of a low-performing school. It would be great to eat something, eating is familiar while everything else is foreign. Still, it's impossible to go to a restaurant or even buy something at a canteen, the whole thing is unmanageable - *Sports Bar* - what on earth can this be?

Having a couple of beers would help with calming down, but who wants to calm down, that's not why she has come here, two beers would instantly knock her out like a right hook.

'*Stay organized*', the invitation stressed. No beer. It's too risky to go into a shop, where are these shops anyway, what are they called, how can one tell a grocery store around here, what kind of shops are there, what do they sell, can one recognise anything at all? One would have to spend hours in front of the shelves to identify anything. Let's leave this business with eating, comes the decision, and go to sleep on an empty stomach - but it's not empty, she has gulfed down everything that was given to eat on the plane, comes the reminder, one should at least reclaim the body, so it's open to perception and one can sense time within. Yet the body has fallen out between time zones, it's tired and numb, feels like jelly and is unable to send messages.

She crosses out the first page in the folder, all that has already happened, and places it under the bunch of paper. The second page has also been completed, the arrival at Old Castle. Tomorrow, there's a new airport because that's closer to this hotel, a new *pick up*, a new destination, new pages. When organising the pages in chronological order and according to tasks, she has verified everything twice - *double check things*, the invitation advised - and even numbered the pages by hand, so she can see at a glance where she is at any point.

Her watch shows her eight minutes past six, this time is entirely unreliable.

'*You have to be very organized,*' Tom writes, that is Thomas, the American organiser and later friend, when all the details of the trip are finally put together, 'Oh, that's not a problem for me,' she replies, 'Well, it is for me,' Tom indicates. He teaches at a prestigious university, this is surprising, '*I thought that all Americans are organized.* How do we say organised in our mother tongue?' It's the opposite of being scattered, scattering, drifting. Drifting is the greatest danger, she reads in an article on the plane, making use of a dictionary. The article 'No Greater Danger than Drifting' was appealing primarily because of the unknown word in its title, but the term *drifting* isn't included in the dictionary, so its meaning has to be inferred from the context. She infers that the greatest danger is drifting, scattering about, and this appears to be a useful truth for the moment. At least regarding the first two decades of her personal drifting, the essence of which one cannot yet see on this flight and on the subsequent further flight to a university town, because during these twenty years it is essential to be always *very organized*. That is to say one has to organise time and keep it in hand, plan future trips, further prospective American visits, a presentation in Prague in a few months, a report on a theatre festival in the Baltics, one has to be *very organized* by way of letters to be answered on time and applications to be submitted, so all this can end up printed out and arranged in a navy blue folder made of fine-grain paper in the shape of flight tickets, details of destinations, invitations and *local currencies*, awaiting the fulfilment of clearly established goals. The navy-blue folder, bearing a university crest, hails from this first overseas trip and is a promising sight in its own right. It will be the place where the proof of potential grant applications and details of international contacts will be collected. The navy-blue folder is a serious promise of worlds one can get to know. It's only in the summer that time transforms into an expandable matter, the days don't even follow one another in the absence of names and numbers but simply blend into an interconnected and boundless unity without a vanishing point, and all this doesn't even look dangerous, on the contrary, it seems most desirable and the only thing that's possible. By this point, the greatest danger has no name or graspable form. Danger, in case it vaguely exists, and it can be surmised from the traffic cumulated by the navy-blue folder over the years that it does, cannot be cured, either with carefully structured diaries or so-called observations and organisational strategies, such as the meticulous demarcation of aims tied in with highly determined goal-orientation.

As for the Son, the Son to be, in fifteen years he will express a wish on the last evening of August, at a point when they have both lost their faith in sensible goals following endless arguments over bedtime, asking for the whole summer, including the holidays and uncountable time and sea, to start all over again. And he just looks at his parents, hopefully and desperately, as if they were magicians and would actually have it in their power to produce such incalculable time from thin air. After all, it is down to these two parents to conjure up, as of tomorrow, a fresh start for this expandable time. They are gods, no less.

What could possibly be the greatest danger?

That night, when the Son to be didn't want to go to bed and they had already got past asking nicely, then blackmailing and shouting, even exhausted desperation, dark clouds suddenly started to gather on the sky and the swallows took to chasing one another on the streets, squeaking and flying much lower than usual. The imminent storm released all of them from the clutch of time. This will in fact be the very duty of the Son: to release them from the clutch of time. At first, only a distant flash of lightning lit up the child's room, which made the Son run to the window, then the sky thundered with a majestic bang, as if those in heaven were slow at getting started. Silent raindrops landed on the roof, gradually getting stronger and denser, as if wanting to warn the world at first: go find a shelter! Next, the rain started to gush down, the storm continuing to flash with lightning, luminating the huge and dense black slabs of the sky. The Son announced that he'd be watching the storm, and this was exactly what they all did in front of the wide-open window. This heavenly orchestra carried on blasting for ages before it slowed down and the monotonous rhythm of the rain sent the child to sleep.

At this point, during this evening in Jamaica, the seemingly useful yet dubiously light truth, namely that the greatest danger is drifting and being scattered about, seems like a good guide and a suitable line to follow. The ultimate danger, should that exist, is most probably nameless, that is to say, it has no name and no cure.

What would constitute ultimate danger for mankind? Even if taking into account that our protagonist would be unable to embody 'Man' fully, at least according to her theatre studies, which posits that a woman has to always embody a woman on stage, and a man embody a Man, as if it were out of the question for either of them to embody the same thing, something slightly more (or less?) than themselves.

During these two decades, she can only surmise that in order to gain any peace of mind one has to cover something much greater, and lean forwards rather than backwards, akin to those who tackle the wind or storm head-on, she doesn't yet know that right ahead there lies the entrance to a personal story with as yet unknown outcomes, a story none other than human adventure in a tailored form.

In this adventure, it is hard to know when storms are likely to break out and bring solace, as in the case of Pilate who has such a terrible headache that he could not think of anything else. Or the case of desperate parents.

Once the adventure is over and one has an overview of sorts, one can lean back and relax. Perhaps that's when peace can be obtained or one becomes worthy of it, though one may not even be aware of this or at least not in the manner of the Jamaican evening.

'*A perfect Mayday for you! Welcome!*' Tom messaged her when the plane landed. At the promised land, NY LGA airport.

It would be great to go for a walk, on the eve of this '*perfect Mayday for you*'. The clouds are lying low, the sky is so close one can almost touch it: '*Close to heaven*' could be a response to Tom if she wasn't embarrassed by being sentimental, besides, it's not clear how close the gods really are. So she doesn't say anything, after all Tom was born here, in the heart of this city, and he'd struggle to imagine how Jamaica could be close to heaven for anyone. One should get over this as swiftly as possible, get over this business with boroughs in case these exist at all here. *Survive it*, because it's poor and black, *to put it simply*.

She had printed Tom's letters out, too, they are also resting in the folder, with some of the most important instructions highlighted, such as *don't walk alone in Jamaica*. Fine, how about walking up and down around the hotel then. From the window, one can see much lower houses, two floors at most with gardens, there is no one on the streets only large vehicles parked here and there. The late afternoon is mellow, a little humid, with the astonishingly loud rattle of the distant city of New York. Well, this is New York but different from the imagined city, of which nothing can be seen just yet. There's hardly any traffic on the wide roads, yet there's noise streaming from all directions, it's inarticulate, deep, without any striking notes, tones, melodies, it's whizzing from above, from the blanket of smog covering the city in the distance.

It's eighteen minutes past six.

Tom is struggling with insomnia. Whenever he's away from home, he switches on the *ambient day* or *ambient night New York traffic* on his device, this comes in one-, six-, nine- and twelve-hour noise bands and is used to help native New Yorkers fall asleep. The noise is similar at all points of the city, surrounding it like a cocoon, even here on the edges, like Jamaica. '*This is home for me*,' Tom explains why he can only fall asleep to this noise.

Low houses with small gardens. Enormous old cars parked along the streets and in the yards, with American number plates are just like in films. The houses seem to be built of wood. Smaller constructions, looking like garages or deposits, are prefabricated and built of corrugated sheets, without windows. *Greater Love Ministries Our Lord Jesus Christ*, it says on one of the garage-looking makeshift structures. The heavy metal shutters are still closed above the entrance. *Universal Calvary Church* appears on a small red brick house, on another *African Methodist Evangelical Church*, then *Redeemed Christians Church*, as well as *Muslims of Jamaica*. Semi-finished buildings, American flags, and *deli shops* at every other block. These are grocery stores, she realizes a few blocks later, she could probably buy some food here if prepared to take the risk. *Car repair, undertaker, Greater Rescue Church of Christ. Ten Commandments Church, Furniture Deposit, John the Baptist Church, Electrician, Deli, Mount of Olives Church, Deli, Sports Bar.* Self-service launderettes everywhere, clothes spinning behind large windows, motionless black women reading the paper while waiting. These launderettes are situated on either side of the street, in almost every other building. How many gods are to be found here, how many gods do these people need when they opened a church in every garage, deposit or half-finished building? How can they have so much laundry needing to be washed outside the home? She is no longer hungry, so won't go into the deli, by the entrance of which a group of elderly dark-skinned men are smoking and drinking, sitting on the chairs and benches laid out on the pavement. Black man with white hair, the world turned upside down.

Back to the hotel, the Old Castle. She paid great attention when heading out, always turning right when walking from street to street, so now it's time to turn left. *You have to be very organized*, as per the reminder, not only turning always right but also making a note of the various street names, before eventually heading back after a ninety-minute walk.

Lord of Mount Calvary, this is a surprise, this is new. There was a *Calvary Universal* earlier, but perhaps she wasn't paying enough attention. Losing her way would lead to certain death. *Launderette. Deli. Electric shop. Barber shop. Funeral Parlour.* She will get lost. Tyres. Cars and trucks. Live poultry. This is also new. Launderette and deli in one. *Pizza. Healthy Foods*, though they were taught about fifteen years ago that this noun doesn't have a plural. That's it, she has got lost.

Local time at destination is nine o'clock. There is no particular time within her body, even time has lost its way, it fell apart and got flattened, it's not endless only impossible to catch up with. At the corner, there is *John the Baptist Church of the Resurrection*. This means she has made it back. John the Baptist, hurray! Back at the hotel, having miraculously found the way back to this new red brick building, evocative of the past. By this point, it's not only time that is out of joint, but space, too, so is there another Jamaica in addition to the original Jamaica, and how did this new Jamaica come about, have the old Jamaicans left their homeland? Jamaica with its countless gods, churches and launderettes, where the existence of these launderettes and prayer halls and churches and chapels is most probably connected, these are all needed for human survival, however, these correlations, in case they exist, are invisible and incomprehensible for her. The eye is always focusing, observing and taking note, unable to relax even for a moment because that leads to instantly getting lost in space. The moment for space to finally loosen up as well, is far away, light years away.

She is heading up to the hotel room on the fire escape not having managed to locate the lift, feeling so exhausted that it wouldn't make a difference if she walked with eyes closed or wore the eye mask carefully purchased when compiling a list as a future *very well-organized person*:

1. tasks
2. stuff to buy
3. stuff to print out

and so on, all to ensure being well organised, but after this over two-hour-long steady though gradually slacking and increasingly heavy walk, during which the faint body has turned into jelly, the sights encountered aren't in any way rivalling what one could see of these – by then unrecognisable – streets ten or fifteen years later on Street View, this is and remains something inconceivably foreign, starting with the number of gods, launderettes and size of cars to the distant yet ceaseless noise that is so comforting to Tom. This noise is most foreign, as it is the smell and sound of cities that make them ultimately foreign.

The amazingly patient Tom, who suffers from insomnia (is there a connection between patience towards others and sleeplessness?), will soon explain the reason behind all these launderettes. '*It's simple*,' he begins, 'as most American things are *simple, we're all very simple*,' he adds modestly, as if he wasn't saying that we Americans are simple but rather easy-going and approachable. 'The explanation is that homes are so tiny and expensive that your entire life's work is needed to make it possible to live and rent in this city, there is simply no space for a washing machine.' In other words, it's not so much a matter of money but of space. In his case, however – Tom points proudly at his front-loading remote-controlled blood-red washing machine on the top floor – '*This is my temple*, the apogee of my career as an educator,' he adds laughing, he's now finally tenured, meaning he is on a permanent rather than temporary contract after fifteen, no eighteen years, '*the absolute pinnacle of my career*,' this blood-red, quiet washer-drier that could be squeezed into the flat, and Tom, akin to Professor Pnin, Nabokov's hero, regularly keeps staring at the clothes twirling about in the washing machine, with all this fitted into the Brooklyn flat, which is now his, theirs, albeit with a thirty-year mortgage. And what about all those Gods? Temples, chapels, prayer halls, convents, congregations, she would like to ask, because the reasoning for the launderettes was easy to follow, logical and practical, like most things in this inconceivably foreign country. Who are these myriad Gods? The world itself is an immense launderette in which everyone washes themselves clean. '*It's not about God, it's about community*,' Tom postulates.

Community?

Fortunately, this is the only night spent in Jamaica, with a body heavy as lead when going to bed and crackling like a freshly ironed shirt when getting up, the body can still conquer everything, every time zone and sleeplessness, the legs are strong, in fact they have just recently become strong. From NY LGA, the next destination is Northbound, having received a grant to present a graduate research paper at the first conference on Nabokov and immigration literature. Thankfully, the time spent among Jamaica's gods and launderettes is less than half a day, more like a quarter, in fact only a short evening. Because in the end, she might have second thoughts and put any previous life aside, together with the carefully prepared folder with future projects and meticulously coordinated travel destinations and stay here, where beauty is invisible, and there is hardly any past and magnificence, only a momentary place that has never appeared on the desire map/map of longing. Longing has never reached as far as Jamaica, since desire is yet unaware of it.

'And what's your story?'

Susan asks in a slightly bored voice from the back seat, looking down as if she were somewhere else but still wanting to start a conversation. The question is followed by an expectant silence, a possible opening between two people. She then looks up, between the two seats, focusing on the interminable journey. Like someone who really wants to know. She's Zsuzsi, known as Susan, Kincső's American daughter.

This is an easy, borderline casual question uttered with fascinating yet annoying American simplicity. *'I wish I knew my story,'* should be the answer, but this sentence is promising too much, a commitment to a longer autobiographical conversation, important stories full of dramatic turns, new beginnings and, ideally, a catharsis. Our protagonist is still getting to know this story, her own story, even on this journey home. The various potential answers to *'what's your story?'* would have the advantage of easing Susan's boredom on such a long trip, while also distracting our protagonist from the seemingly endless challenges of driving that are impossible to surmount, which is not only the opposite of boring but also dangerous for someone so irritated by not being able to be in control of space. Being engaged in a conversation, let alone in this all-concealing language, as well as paying attention to myriad things while driving makes one feel like a guinea pig whose brain has been connected to a capful of electrodes with the sole purpose of irritation.

A possible answer could be that this is exactly the reason for being here, on this road, on this actual tarmac: to get to know her story. Tarmac, concrete, asphalt, who knows the difference between them. *On this concrete*, what a beautiful name for this surface! *What a wonderful word. World, word*, these two terms always tend to blur into one when saying them out loud and require major effort in differentiation. The word is fabulous, not the world. So, our protagonist is on this very journey precisely to get to know her story, her adventure, this is her 'via negativa', a process of moving in reverse, heading homewards. I wish I would know my story, could be another way of putting it, how great it would be to get to know our story, by way of getting started, finding fulfilment and then rounding it off, just like Aristotle stipulated in his *Poetics*: beginning, middle and end.

Our protagonist promises to tell this story some other time because she enjoys telling stories, being a *storyteller* rather than an *author*.

'*I am an author*,' she replies to Susan's question, and the moment the word author is uttered, her gaze disperses on the road ahead, striving to encompass every important and dangerous event, yet losing focus and direction for a moment. The road, the concrete, is luckily empty, and grey. 'I am what I'd like to be.'

Would it be wise to even share all this at the very beginning, at the risk of causing disappointment and exposing herself to a young and peachy American girl, the adult daughter of a classmate, with whom she has nothing in common other than having gone to school with her mother and they having visited each other's countries. All they have in common so far is also shared with seven and a half billion other humans. Since they haven't met before, they have nothing to do with each other, they haven't stood together on the shores of a lake, haven't watched sunsets, got drunk or discussed a single book together, they haven't even found disappointment in each other. Why should Susan be the one, well, because at least she can't ask for accountability, only marvel at most, because she'll have to believe that yes, this story is simply about being *an author, a storyteller*. And about the fact that writing takes up so much space in life, not life as in time and space or not even as in body, but what exactly? It's impossible to pinpoint, but it is precisely this struggle for naming that occupies our protagonist's life. Writing – and this has just become obvious to her while waiting at the airport and visiting a stationery shop that sold overpriced notebooks – there, in that moment it has become more important than bliss.

'*Salvation. How do you call it?*'

Susan doesn't call bliss or salvation anything, she's just listening carefully with eyes wide open. Yes, she nods, there is such a word, *salvation*. She wouldn't use it but has heard it, she adds in a serious voice. Yet she's uncertain whether this is the same salvation as in her mother's native tongue, because *salvation* is more like saving someone from drowning, so far, so good, as she's drowning, too, but will stay on the surface of the water at least for a while, not for days though.

She has recently read a book about a Syrian refugee girl who managed to survive in the sea for four days. True story. And because it's true, it's unimaginable. Impossible to compute with a human mind. This is the mystery of the real, and of art too. But the girl did survive, and now lives in Sweden. Her name is Doa. When an acquaintance sent over the book's manuscript, it didn't yet have the author's name on the cover. It was obvious that the heroine was the author. But hero and author are not one and the same, our protagonist knows that for sure. Because the author can see their hero, but can the hero also glimpse at their creator? In any case, the girl made her escape from the sea, at the age of sixteen.

As for salvation, that's not just about saving someone. *Salvation* is more than that. Salvation has to be about more than simply sinking or staying on the surface. Salvation can't be a mere ambulance with siren and lights on. 'In Russian, this is called *спасение. I can't translate it any better*. In our language, saving means slightly less, and salutation more. Hail! God bless! Who else? *Welcome*. Still, the word Salvation may still retain something of the Latin *Salve!*, 'hail' as in 'be well', though nobody gets this, so how could they be interested in actual well-being.'

Adding: '*I don't believe in translation*. Words can never be transposed into one another, just like people or trees or sparrows can't either. How many words and how many other things have to come to pass between us, between two people, in order to understand each other?'

'Writing has become more important to me than the salvation of my soul. I can't explain this. They say that it's irrelevant whether you believe in it or not, because the offer isn't based on that. My personal story is unknown to the extent that everyone else's story is unknown to them, seeing that it hasn't yet been completed, I haven't yet made it to the end of my adventure, let alone to salvation, should such a thing exist. Ultimately, there are two options. One: I'm writing for the salvation of my soul, in which case writing itself is a turn of duty towards salvation, should it be possible to carry out such a service rather than being simply deserving. Have you read *The Master and Margarita*? They are offering something to writers there, too. Hell, decapitation, peace. But not light. I'm unsure whether salvation can be earned, as I'm entirely uneducated from a theological point of view, *completely ignorant.*'

There's nobody to ask, it's pointless to search for words to describe her story, why this particular story, it's stupid to even ask, asking in itself is a faux pas, a question implies the existence of an answer and suggests that this answer is something finite, therefore things have to be that way and that's that, we've reached the end of human adventure. There is no answer. Only events that take place. We can't foresee their end, and we certainly can't give an account of salvation.

'Around 1850, this word was much more common in written texts than it is today,' Susan points out, immersed in thought after having checked her phone. She did a quick search and found several entries about this topic. She has never used this word herself though. 'We tend not to use it these days. *Archaic, isn't it?*'

'So,' our protagonist begins, hoping to gain time as they are taking over a fully loaded van, and this 'so' and subsequent pauses will last until they safely finish overtaking and get back into their lane, but now they have to overtake again, never mind, there's nothing at stake in uttering what the listener already knows anyway, '*I am an author.*'

'*Wow.*' Susan displays an instant reaction, because in the culture she comes from it is important to present others with some answer: I'm a body-washer, 'interesting', I'm a postman, 'splendid', it's important to signal that you hear what they are saying and it has an impact on you, and that you have an opinion.

'*Mother's told nothing about you. Mother never says anything. You know, just the flying projects, media, home, old country stories, newcountry stories, yada yada yada. So you write books.*'

'*This is what I do,*' our protagonist concludes, 'generally yes, but not right now, not for some time, but this is irrelevant.'

Next to the driver's seat, there lies the freshly purchased over-priced notebook and new pen, a new land, the promised land. Just looking at them gives her butterflies, seeing that for quite some time she hasn't authored anything, except for this forthcoming speech.

'*You were in the same class as Kincső, correct?*'

Susan pronounces Kincső perfectly, there's no hint of foreign-ness in this name. One can sense the blood ties between speaker and name.

'*Yeah.*'

'*Great.*'

What's so *great* about this, our protagonist would like to ask, about the fact that the two of us ended up classmates, this is mere fate, in other words pure chance.

'*She says it was a great class.*'

In the end, therefore, our protagonist decided to attend the class reunion. Ágó is sleeping on the back seat with her mouth open yet still smiling. The plan is to pick Kincső up on the way too, after crossing the border, in a multi-ethnic mountain village where she's working on her project. Kincső's daughter, as she calls her, is Zsuzsi, also known as Susan, as the girl prefers to introduce herself, who also needs picking up because Kincső was unable to come to the airport on account of the bishop. She mentions this but then fails to elaborate on how exactly the bishop hinders her in picking her daughter up so they can come together to the meeting as planned, she only indicates that the bishop is also part of the project. In other words, Susan has to be picked up, the same Susan who would chatter throughout the entire journey had our protagonist not made it clear from the start that this is her very first cross-border drive, and that she can't handle two things at the same time. The notion of not being able to do two things at the same time triggers Susan to talk about men and women's selective attention, 'us women,' etc., but this is mainly white noise with the odd familiar word, just melodious language and no attention to content. For a proper conversation, it's imperative to stop, the new driver can't cope otherwise. Besides, when they get to the border, they will have to turn around to pick up Csaba, but no-one knows this yet, not even Csaba. Even though all this is initially annoying and disappointing – Ágó falling immediately asleep, having to pick Susan up – this language, this feather-light and eternally foreign language akin to a summer ice cream session, is more relaxing than talking to Ágó in the mother tongue of eternal depths, where words are razor sharp and have a tendency to bite.

Susan offers to take over the driving at any point if needed.

'*Here?*' – and correcting it, '*There?*' – asking with genuine surprise, doesn't Susan know about the state of the roads, the driving style and, in general, what it's like back there? Oh, no – it has to be me, she concludes, '*this is my first time, you know, it is my first trial*' – but the word *trial* makes our protagonist lose her grip, unsure whether the notions of test and trial are merged together, are they one and the same? And what would it mean if they were the same, with the same root and content, for her this is a public trial. I must walk this way, this is my way, test, counter-test, penalty, release. I have to go on a pilgrimage on my knees and not fly there on a cheap, instantly accessible flight.

'*Have you ever seen those kneeling*...oh, can't remember the word, well it's not used very often, for those who in their desire for spiritual and religious cleansing...'

'*Pilgrims?*' Susan tries to be helpful.

'That's it, pilgrims indeed.'

As they have to come to a halt due to a jam caused by a trailer loading a car wreck, the car's driver looks back in the mirror and gazes at Susan's pale pink, delicately freckled heart-shaped face as she leans forward on the back seat. She's lifting herself up from her seat as if she wanted to be present with her body in this conversation loaded with the promise of many long, cumbersome and confined hours. She doesn't resemble Kincső at all, who is dark-skinned and has a prominent jaw. Susan is a proper American girl. But how could our protagonist explain to Susan, even if they stopped for a break to immerse themselves in conversation, carefully selecting the most precise and yet still empty and distant foreign words, how could this ... inching forward be explained, this slow effortful march, more like shuffling, knee shuffling, yes, shuffling on one's knees because this image suddenly strikes with the power of realisation. What is taking place is an unspeakable knee-shuffling back there, about which she doesn't wish to talk to Susan because the whole thing is unintelligible even to her. What does this knee shuffling mean? Why not with the head held high, triumphantly, or at least by way of an amusing drive? How could Susan understand this knee-shuffling person? What gods are meant to be appeased by this? And what sins should be forgiven? There is no sin, no sin has been committed.

Right now, driving feels like crucifixion, our protagonist simplifies the idea, translating it to language and articulate words around which one can have a conversation. Susan keeps paying attention, though visibly struggling to understand since she got her licence at the age of sixteen.

'*I am afraid of killing something,*' our protagonist clarifies by way of an explanation.

'*Mama has the same fears,*' Susan replies without the slightest hesitation, having finally heard a familiar sentence.

'*Who?*' our protagonist has to ask, because her own sentence is still trembling and echoing within her, as if the predicament of the sentence had already been fulfilled: the fear of killing someone isn't just a matter of mere words but an actual occurrence. A sentence that has been uttered is like a shot arrow, irrevocable.

'Kincső.'

Kincső's fears are known to our protagonist, who replies: '*We share these*'. This is due to her familiarity with Kincső's project which is about killing. But right now, it's a relief not to have to elaborate on what it would feel like to live with the thought of having killed someone. One can only carry on living if one doesn't beat someone else to death.

This American girl with a healthy and serene complexion, who still smells fresh after a ten-hour flight, comes from a country where changing place, moving houses, endless separation and being on the move is part of everyone's existence. It's a huge country where everybody is always coming and going, relocating to hundreds and thousands of miles, storing their increasing quantity of belongings in increasingly more numerous specialist boxes in specialist depots and storage facilities. As for this girl, in whom the most attractive bit is not this accessible language but time, and the youth that shockingly reminds our protagonist of the passage of time in the eye of the beholder, it will be impossible to tell this girl anything, even in this easy-to-access language promising a straightforward and clear order of things, about this undertaking, this journey home which is none other than a reversal of the story, a 'via negativa', albeit for a single week. Yet they are born, driving licence in their pocket, as people who will definitely be in need of continuous and easy relocation. As early as in their mother's bellies, they are preparing for a compulsion to be on the go.

In the course of her short, barely two decade-long life, Susan has already lived in at least five places, with Kincső and without Kincső, and to the question where she'd most like to go, where she'd live or where she'd want to move after university, she replies in the familiar voice of sweet desire that '*Oh, I love LA.*' She then spells out the placename just to be clear in case her travel companion doesn't know, 'Los Angeles,' placing a strong accent on the 'e' as Brits do, then clarifies that the long 'e' at the end of the word is the sensual expression of desire as angels are ascending to heaven. By this point, looking ahead and engaged in a safe overtaking exercise on a straight segment of the motorway, our protagonist is hearing precisely what she doesn't and won't understand – because this is someone else's desire.

Susan, with her heart-shaped face, all-too-white skin and chattering Englishness doesn't cause confusion, but actually makes the journey to the truth that's currently happening to her easier:

'*I go home. I really miss it,*' our protagonist states curtly, navigating between cars to the best of her abilities, uttering the exact words that are present with her in the moment. 'Not *I miss it*, but it's missing, not even it's lacking or it's absent, but it's missing from me, or I from it. "I" is an active agent, missing is a state.'

'*I miss it*,' this sentence she is finally able to utter to Susan with so much ease and simplicity isn't her own, well, it is now but it hails from Sam, an elderly American man who had first said it softly and dreamily, in a way capable of making others happy.

This phrase dates back to one of the many overseas trips when this elderly Samuel, known as Sam, had invited the visitor as a thank you for having once also shown him around her city, her new city and second home. Sam said that after a few months of spending the winter far away he always misses his home, the place where he was born. '*I miss New York*,' he said plainly, with a full stop at the end of the sentence.

In Sam's Fifth Avenue home there was an Oscar on the shelf. '*Is it real?*' the visitor asked with awe, and Sam explained that this heavy and tall Oscar statuette used to belong to his father, the elder Warner Brother. The visitor secretly picks it up when the host returns to the kitchen for some ice, but Sam is too quick to get back to the spacious living room, so there comes a moment of looking at Sam with an apology, while still holding the heavy statuette. '*Don't worry*,' Sam hastens to reassure, 'everybody wants to pick it up, *we all want to know how much it weighs. We all want to touch the top of the world, don't we?*'

Sam lives in a seven-storey building that once used to be a hotel, now converted into huge flats by today's standards. Sam has two balconies above the roaring and deafeningly loud city, both kitted out with large plants, so they almost look like a jungle. Jungle in a jungle. Sam doesn't say more than that he was born here, and he loves the place. And this smooth-faced man, who looks sixty despite going on eighty thanks to *slow plastic surgery*, and on whose skin careful surgeons only manipulate with tiny rather than spectacular interventions, to tighten the facial muscles with a view to counteract the passage of time, softly adds with a longing about which Russian authors have written books, and without any showing off or attention-seeking, more as a clarification and explanation for this desire, that he was simply born here, for him these houses and especially this area, this *neighborhood*, which has become too trendy and expensive, is home. When he's away for weeks, because, as he says, '*I am a passionate traveler,*' he always misses it because, as he enthuses, he loves it. '*I miss New York,*' he adds while he places his right hand on his chest. He is showing the place of desire. He has long manicured nails and two, by now much too large, signet rings on his fingers. Only the skin on his hands gives away his real age.

As Susan channels the discussion back to LA aka Los Angeles, accentuating the long 'e' at the end, and zooms in on her plans and dreams related to LA in that swirling intuition located prior to or beneath language, which one would be stupid to chop into words, our protagonist is full of longing while making steady progress on the motorway, observing the speed limit. Meanwhile, Susan is staring ahead in her radiant youth, which an hour ago was still painstakingly reminding our protagonist of herself, Susan is still dreaming to move forward, in the exact same way as had happened to her, or to be precise, as this happening has become her own and now the Son's and Susan's. Our protagonist is also looking ahead at the promising journey, but this 'ahead' is also pointing backwards, to home. It may be possible that they are all dreaming the same dream, the dreams of desire, the dreams that transport everyone forward and then forward and back.

Ágó

They have both left home and now live thousands of miles away from each other. In the first twenty years they didn't even know about one another and nearly lost touch for good. Light, should that exist at all, doesn't shine across the ocean, Ágó's gold-green shine is not yet known on this side of the Pond. Initially, they were both lined up at the same starting post, being young and edgy, with the sharply drawn muscles of horses ready to go into battle, anxiously awaiting the beginning of the race. One could write an anatomical study about their muscular legs and stamping feet. There's nothing on the horizon apart from their intent and goal, they don't look around and they are all alone.

It will only emerge decades later, when the Son will take riding lessons, that horses are actually rather meek and coy animals, so shy that it's almost impossible for strangers to get close to them. Our protagonist will leaf through the sketch book titled *The Anatomy of the Horse* with disappointment because it only features bones and muscles, which are of no interest to someone looking for delicate bodies and a discussion of that large, coy, warm animal, that restlessly convulsive skin, that silky hair and those dreamy eyes. Gentle play on the spring field with the Son, looking at the riding hall at the edge of town from afar, is similarly of no interest. What is of interest is light, as it's gradually dwindling in the eyes of the aging, departing animal. That gentleness, that connection and the streamlines of responsibility towards one another.

At this point though they are barely twenty, standing at the gate, ready to attack, Ágó and the former classmate are still frisky horses, prepared to compete at any time and only waiting for the gates to open – in the shape of a soft-cover passport granting the right to travel. They had recently passed their Baccalaureate and are now students. They have wanderlust, ever so keen to go. The gate opens, blindingly bright lines in the distance. Gunshots.

'Go! Run!'

And so it began: Trembling with excitement and ready for battle, desperate to obtain their passports in the long queue outside the police building; passports which would no longer need to be returned or handed back, only to be renewed or accompanied a decade or so later by new passports issued by new lands. From this moment onwards, the world is as wide as one is prepared to widen it.

Ágó starts a little later, she'll first finish her studies, travelling between countries, applying for short-term grants and then preparing her departure, having gathered her strength, ready, steady, go, starting her second specialism up there in the North where the Scandinavians are generous with graduate scholarships. With a degree in Maths and Physics in her pocket, she enrols in a Masters programme in Astronomy, while our protagonist goes to Russia to study literature. They are nearly on the same latitude.

The grown-up, nearly fifty-year-old Ágó, like our protagonist, is beaming on her own website, next to the *Little Baby*. She is flanked by a congressman and a congresswoman, all three of them placing their hands on *Little Baby*'s enormous silver body. Ágó's hand gestures convey peace of mind, 'there you are, *I got you*!' The particle accelerator looks like a huge metal whale. Ágó's now at the height of her mission, as an ambassador for science lobbying Congress on behalf of science. *Little Baby* is about conquering time, she will explain later, *time reversed*, a reversal of creation and a glimpse into birth. Re-birth, re-naissance, with the accent on the second syllable.

On the photo, she's wearing a tight skirt that finishes above the knee. Her high heels draw attention to her calves and the muscles showing under the skirt betray a serious runner. She has trained her legs to this level over thirty years, travelling backwards to the legs of a twenty-year-old.

Her fondness for high heels has developed in parallel with her scientific career, which gradually moves beyond professional publications and the sphere of academia. She is fighting for science and its institutions, applies for money and sets up a research institute. Meanwhile, she's keeping her leg muscles on alert. The shoe collection is growing slowly but surely, and the muscles are at work both in the calves as well as the thighs. Her Soleus muscle, however, didn't get trained in high heels but at the various latitudes where Ágó had spent time on scholarships, studying for graduate degrees, and then, following a master stroke, started her doctoral studies overseas. As the Hungarian name of this muscle indicates, she had to wade into water, into the Pond, to get across, because only the Prophet can walk on water and that wouldn't require particularly strong muscles anyway. Ágó is determined to go to America and applies to four universities. It is for this stamp of the foot, for this *Little Baby* capable to re-enact the creation of the world, that she needs to train such strong calf muscles, so she can cross the Pond. One simply needs strong legs for walking, moving about and going away. Ours is a mighty leg.

But she only studies temporarily in America, then ends up at a German research institute. That said, transitions are none other than unrecognised final stations, the centre of gravity within stories is not visible. Centre of gravity? Point of rest? She's conducting research, first on a scholarship then as an assistant, she works and publishes, yet increasingly continues to think about America as a final destination and applies for a teaching post. At this stage, one needs steel-hard thigh muscles, which give stability to her professional position and keep on developing as a major proof of staying power. *Stamina.*

They agree to meet on our protagonist's fourth or fifth trip to New York, by which point the city appears tamer and solitary astonishment is no longer her driving force. They haven't seen each other in twenty-five years but they know about each other, light is becoming visible, has crossed the Pond and allowed stories to attract one another. Ágó is elected as an honorary member of the Academy back home, even though the laudation still calls her a young lady. Ágó will look back on this, amused, pointing out that one is still considered a young lady in science under the age of fifty. Here and everywhere. Here, it's a great privilege that I'm white. Otherwise, I wouldn't get anywhere. I'm white, which is a bonus. I'm a woman, which is a handicap.

During the trip when the meeting with Ágó takes place, our protagonist stays at a hotel by the river. The menacing Gothic city has softened. It's now possible to resist it and not be swallowed by it, although it's still not inviting her to stay longer. The best is to yield to it, allow oneself to be felled by it, wonder at it, get frightened by it, and recognise one's littleness among these endless spires, one can get used to them and find their strangeness almost homely. By this point, she doesn't want to be more than a visitor, as it is impossible to find a permanent home and to cope with more foreignness. In order to acquire and conquer it, to make it one's tiny home, she should have started much earlier, around the time when Ágó did: when the leg and heart muscles were still capable of such dazzling performances and when the metabolic rate was still racing. Our protagonist's knowledge on the life span of muscles is minimal – could it be that muscles have a secret time?

She heads to the river at dawn, as the hotel is only a block away from the enormous, slow and hazy body of water, on the other side of a busy and noisy road. It's a struggle to wake up in the cramped, overpriced room, and it's not yet obvious that the rate will be even higher than expected when booking, as *taxes* come on top. The heavy lava-like sound doesn't come to a standstill, not even at night, despite using earplugs that cover the entire outer ear (specialists claim that this country has the most famous earplugs in the world). A heavy grey substance-less humming has entered the heads of locals and turned into matter, becoming part and parcel of nerves, ligaments and synapses.

At this early morning hour, the flow of cars on the three-lane dual carriageway is not yet entirely compact, the traffic is still rolling, people are getting started, applying the breaks, moving forward, waiting, starting again. In barely two hours, cars will be tailing one another without the tiniest gap, stuck together as one, undivided body. In this city, this is the way to be – a sole body, moving and rushing forward as one.

Despite only being a block away, it takes a long time to get to the Hudson. The river originates in a lake called the *Tear of the Clouds*, and it embarks on a long earthly lamentation until making its way, as always, to the ocean. It would be possible to climb the world's tallest, inconceivably tall, towers to look down on the river, but our protagonist opts for the nearest viewing point. Those towers even taller than these buildings are no longer in existence: scratching the sky leads to the story of Babel and to collapse. The water is within reach, but not close enough for her hand to touch it. She doesn't climb towers because of a fear of heights, as dizziness triggers an urge to jump in order to compensate. As if all poetry absented itself to make way for sheer gravity, only being able to walk on the ground as a true resident of the flat plains.

The wide and massive river is seemingly slow and rather safe in this city where everyone is in a constant rush, going somewhere... following goals, targets and meticulously planned timetables. The clouds, being as they are many hundreds of storeys above us, must have plenty of reasons to cry here, too, and their tears fill up the proud river at the supposed centre of the world. 'Am I drinking from the Tears of the Clouds?' she has asked herself each time she is kindly offered a glass of water at each restaurant or café, in this city everyone's thirst is unquenchable.

'*Don't like the city*,' the Sikh taxi driver announces with a touch of loathing after being hailed.

Under his pointy turban, the man wears his hair long, as a sign of devotion to God, but this hair is not meant to be seen by others. He doesn't look back, drivers are separated from their passenger by plexiglass, with a palm-sized opening through which one can talk or hand cash over. He has been living here for thirty-five years, he replies idly to these annoying questions in a language hard to understand, avoiding adding anything to the answers that could move the conversation forward. He doesn't reveal where he was born, where he has come from and why, whether he has a family and if so, where.

'Just look out of the window,' he says in an almost rude voice, '*look out the window, traffic, million of cars, don't like*,' he snaps. 'How could anyone like this?'

The river is separated from pedestrian traffic by a waist-high barrier. This area is paved with occasionally unstable, badly fitted cobblestones, making a dodgy pavement for runners. There are no pedestrians as it is still early for dogwalkers and babysitters. Many of the runners are or appear to be young – they are fast, muscular, competitive, as if every day was a race day. Their gaze is forward-looking, they aren't looking around, aren't paying attention to their left or right, only to the next few metres in front of them, which they conquer one step at a time. They are wearing earplugs, which help with blocking the world out even more. This is the city of struggle, an invincible city where everyone could truly become nobody. Our protagonist's legs, though strong but not sturdy, just stable, couldn't cope with this pace. Having arrived too late, it's not possible to compete, only to be a good loser.

Right now, the visitor is very much looking forward to the meeting with Ágó, which is set to take place after the literary evening, in a restaurant a few blocks away. Finally, a city where one can't get lost, where the intersection of Fifth Avenue and 49th Street is obvious. Only East and West aren't clear at all. Only East and West. The American Writers' Trust, in collaboration with a few publishers from home, has organised a festival entitled *Writers on Wire*. The title isn't really clear but our protagonist is concerned that the invitation may not be valid for long, so accepts without too much hesitation. *Writers on Wire*, is this about swallows dressed in black sitting on high voltage electric wires or fragrant sheets put out to dry in the wind? The event is organised by true professionals, the large auditorium is full of highly determined agents and immigrants. Prior to the talk, all ten writers – for some reason, it's always ten – are invited to present their work in three minutes each. She jots down a few sentences, reads them out loud and times this, two minutes and fifty-eight seconds. The sentences are long and sinuous, and the intricate sentence structure of the mother tongue wraps itself around the foreign language. Affirmative sentences in three minutes about a book that took five years to write. A few sentences, during which the speaker, *the author*, is standing on a low rostrum sweating, having learned to sweat in secret, not on the forehead but along the spine.

After blowing up the photo taken at the event and zooming in on her ears, it emerges that veins look like a system of streams and rivers flowing into the sea and oceans. The delicate blood vessels glow under the surface of the skin, colouring the ears crimson red, the back-lit outer part looking as if ablaze. Our protagonist wrote her first book in such a glow, and can still feel the scorching: I come before you with flaming ears...people tend to look for peace while writers seek the flame, how could they ever end up side by side? Should one make a tiny incision in a pretty ear, the blood would spurt out in jets. This red ear of hers has nothing distinctive about it, and would be unrecognisable if found on the street, it would look alien...oh, whose ear could this possibly be? Who could have been so desperate, seeing as one cannot die as a result of a cut-off ear. One wouldn't die, even if one chopped off this body part, because there are no arteries in this area, which is otherwise well-connected with blood vessels. In other words, this is yet another thing one can't die of, for death needs more determination and much more desperation. She takes a proud look at the Darwin's tubercle in her massively blown-up ear: not everyone has such an atavistic feature, shared with our distant animal ancestors, and originally intended to aid with hearing distant sounds. These days, hearing distant sounds in a city would lead to losing one's mind.

An elderly couple comes up to her at the reception following the talk. Their skin is smooth and soft, and they are wearing bright clothes. They are light and beautiful, like a pair of fairy tale grandparents. They arrived in the wake of the 1956 Hungarian Revolution, having travelled through four countries, still young, with freshly-acquired degrees, holding each other's hand. They would like to talk about the distant world they had left behind and, in the books that have been presented, they are looking for traces of this threadbare homeland. At times, the man touches his wife's shoulder or hand, and they look into each other's eyes – their tenderness is a primordial covenant. They are disappointed to hear that writers are writing about their dreams though.

'Why are you writing about dreams? Why not about what's real?'

'Dreams are greater than the real. Once upon a time, people believed that dreams were sent by gods, as an encouragement, warning, exclamation or mirror. In which the light is so bright that one goes blind if attempting to look into it.'

The conversation would falter at each sentence if Éva and András, aka Eve and Andrew, were unable to lift it, with an enthusiasm for chatter acquired in their new country, over the awkward obstacles that separate them, akin to the endless and eternally steely bright ocean. They are standing there, looking back on their long, hard life since crossing the Pond, starting their sentences in their former mother tongue and finishing them in American English with a strong foreign accent, having been tottering, hand in hand, for sixty years between notions that are now impossible to name in their first language. They are standing there ready to reveal this triumphant life to someone, looking forward to the short time still ahead of them and looking back fondly on the many years left behind, charting the arc of their personal story. They have had their battle with time and space and have won.

The literary conversation comes quickly to an end. Instead, they talk about their extended family, their half-Australian, half-Chinese grandchildren and the successes of their children. With every sentence, they come closer to easing their visible foreignness, which is well-tolerated and considered natural around here, in this melting pot of three hundred million people surrounded by oceans. A *crucible*. Maybe one should call this fusion pot a crucible. What does the cross have to do with this though? Maybe a huge baptismal font then, where everyone can acquire a new name.

Our protagonist doesn't feel embarrassed about her accent while talking to the couple, this isn't a country where people fetishize language, everybody here talks the way they can, even though this is only seemingly sufficient for certain things: such an accent would be inadequate for climbing the heights of Yale or Harvard or Columbia, in which case this kind of linguistic fragmentation will never do, there, such foreignness is instantly visible and in this visible foreignness one has to perform twice as well as everyone else, and besides, as Ágó will later testify, one's battle also has to be fiery as well as heedless.

By this point, Éva and András are showing family pictures taken at *Thanksgiving*, Éva is holding the phone in her dark wrinkly hands and taps in the pin with her long, manicured nails. She's holding the device close to her eyes, scrolling through dozens of photos taken in a bright family home featuring two children in their mid-fifties and grown-up grandchildren. Their children married foreign men and women, our protagonist concludes in a flash, while looking at the beautiful young people of Asian and Hispanic origin. Viewed from here, the world is inconceivably wide and accessible.

'*A lot of slow plastic surgery,*' Mike, an old acquaintance who came along to this far from *deplorable* event, sums up.

'*Slow?*'

'This is when they only touch the skin a little bit, not radically or spectacularly, they only do a bit of sewing here and there, gently cancelling out time and slowing it down, stretching it like skin. *They stretch time.* In the end, they want to turn it back and conquer it. *Time reversed.*'

That evening is spent with Ágó. Upon entering the small family restaurant, our protagonist instantly recognises her, but not the grown-up, middle-aged face seen on photos, the face of the scientist and lobbyist, but that of the child in year four with the radiant gaze, whose shine is just as bright today. In her gaze, time has stood still.

Ágó has chosen a quiet spot, 'but *you know* about quiet around here,' she laughs. They haven't met face to face for twenty-six years. She is walking easily and comfortably in her stilettos, wearing the shoes without tights as Americans do, her upper body strong, muscular, almost sturdy. Her above-the-knee dress reveals strong leg muscles, as if on some sketch for a painting that could have only been based on male models because women's muscles are invisible in visual arts. Brits place the accent on the second syllable, *renaissance*, not on 're' but on 'naissance'. That said, in the competition between renaissance and naissance, the main event is seeing the light.

That evening Ágó sheepishly tells the story of her collection of high heels.

'I shall always wear them, my pedicurist confirms that my feet are suited for this. Suited? Am I correct, is there such a word? I won't have such a *hammer toe*. You know. Over-toe. The feet have to work extra hard when you wear such shoes. In my case, these feet worked really hard,' she laughs with that inimitably shy yet radiant laughter. She's looking at her legs and feet. 'They no longer have to work quite so hard, I've made it. *I am done.*'

She bought the first expensive piece of her collection on passing her PhD viva, and this reddish-brown Italian designer shoe when publishing her first single-authored article in *The Physicist*. Later, when already working at the university for some time, she found out that it's much better to be one of the authors in a larger authorial team; it's not *single author* publications that are worth the most but when several people are arguing the same thing, six, eight, up to twelve people! Twelve people, the same number as the disciples. At that point, she purchased these shoes, and shows the picture of some orange strappy sandals. Every shoe, every piece of footwear a landmark.

'Fair enough, I also bought a few out of boredom or desperation, let's not beat about the bush. *Despair, as we call it.* When you are overwhelmed with ... *I can't explain it.* When you're worried people might find out that you have scammed everyone.'

Ágó still laughs as she used to in year four. With awkwardness and bewilderment, a degree of shyness, as if it was accidental and surprising that we are talking about her, though she is the ultimate protagonist of this conversation, all this is her story, at this dinner table where they are serving red tuna. It's astonishing to be talking about her, the owner of these shoes who at each anniversary keeps acquiring yet another pair of footwear to propel her into newer, even more dazzling heights, she laughs at the coincidence, the lucky chance, that these articles – for which it isn't customary to receive payment as this would be ridiculous and humiliating, after all how could one underpin truth, scientific truth with money ... happen to be authored by her, one name among the twelve, or one very similar to hers in any case. The coincidence that she is the owner and brain behind this *Little Baby*, smiling on that photo while caressing the golden metal body of the baby, her invention, created to offer an insight and lesson into birth and creation. Perhaps she might not even be too surprised to find out that it isn't her, that it isn't her own story that she told, but that of an impostor, a cheat ... she has always felt this *impostor syndrome: 'This is what I have and what we share,'* she laughs, 'after all, apart from luck, what else could be behind all this? Strong legs?'

Yet Ágó is talking enthusiastically about the *Little Baby*. Light, her personal light is *aurum non vulgi*, not any old light, she didn't become an astronomer by chance, she is light itself, excitement, the excitement, passion and fire of creation. Her enthusiasm for publication, science, teaching and the recently introduced methodology is unbroken, as it is for high heels, in which she'd still like to cover many more kilometres.

To the class reunion, however, Ágó will come in snug sports shoes. She will only bring two average pieces of her shoe collection for these three weeks spent back home. This is not a place for high heels.

Right now, Ágó is telling the story of her shoes and of the last thirty years, while they are frugally drinking red wine from enormous glasses. A bottle of Californian red, two glasses each, this is their limit. Here, in this space, this is the limit. The light of the *filius macrocosmi*, that is to say the daughter of the cosmos, is retreating, and they are both incredibly tired. At the end of the evening, before saying goodbye and hugging each other very tight, they compare legs under the table. Two fairly similar legs, strong calf muscles, with the soleus running down the centre, sturdier at the top and more delicate further below, *musculus soleus*, perhaps named after solitude. Ágó doesn't have children. At the class reunion organised to mark twenty-five years from leaving school, mother-of-three Hilda charges at her in front of the whole group. 'And how about children? Or is it just about career?' Soleus. In Hungarian, also known as 'wader muscle'. Those who had come up with this name realised this connection and set out with a strong soleus because they were aware that, ultimately, each and every one of us has to forge our own path in the world.

The Teacher

A woman has awkwardly opened the book at the flyleaf, barely uttering her name and pushing it in front of our protagonist. She's not so much scared as excessively humble, someone who may expect others to pay attention to her and offer some encouragement or take note of her admiration. It's not customary to sign books on the flyleaf, our writer might point out, because the people in the queue make her tense and irate with their desire to chat, tell stories, express their appreciation, and this is bewildering, especially if readers greet her as if they knew each other even though they can at most remember her family. Awkward smile. Fifteen years ago, she was just as clueless about which page writers tend to use for signing their books. The ageless, badly dressed woman just keeps standing there, waiting.

'Apologies, who's this for?' she has to ask as she couldn't catch the name.

'No problem, shall I add a last name, too?' She asks again, keen to accommodate.

'Yes, please.' Looking deep into the writer's eyes, the woman utters a name, just as softly but having mustered some courage, as if she was revealing a big secret. The writer puts down the first name, adding the date, a brief note, place and her signature. She omits 'aunt', after all an unknown older woman isn't an aunt. Mentioning the place, however, is mandatory, town, area, event, street, anything that embeds the moment into a given space. Place is mandatory. Place and time, the rest is irrelevant.

The woman waits until everyone has finished, and then begins to stare at the writer, unwilling to let her go, inching closer and closer but without looking up. She wants to talk but doesn't know how to begin. It's not about the book, she would have raised that when asking for it to be signed. She steps in front of her prey when the space is finally vacant. She apologises, again in an annoyingly soft voice, and talks in roundabout ways. Then apologises again. In return, she gets an encouraging smile, tightly controlled from within.

'My mother would very much like to meet you. Would you be able to visit us today?'

This comeback may well have been a mistake, the writer surmises. To come back to this town with a book and organise a launch, even though it was her idea, in fact not only the idea but also the organisation, normally she doesn't have to do this because everything just seems to happen by itself, elsewhere the publisher is discreetly doing their job but here, the writer has to do everything from ordering copies to room hire. Foxes are setting up their own traps. Their fur is precious, but it can only be worn in secret, or perhaps in Russia. Their flesh is inedible.

'Tell me something about your mother.'

'I thought you guessed who she was from her name.'

The woman's face suddenly shows signs of disappointment, her voice turns serious and deep, shifting from entreating to reproachful. Finally, one can understand every word. Her plan collapses. The world deflates. Humility turns into a weapon. They stare at each other cluelessly.

Perhaps it was a mistake to come back here with this book like someone for whom the past, the very subject of the book, is an organising principle of existence. Pompously, like someone who managed to organise something. She has simply grabbed something triumphantly and is now offering it as a present, making a personal effort to be somehow present in this town to which her sole attachment is the heavy burden of cemetery plots. Only the press didn't need nudging, they came out of their own volition and wrote about the event. The articles focused on her amazing ability to remember, the fact that she must have kept a diary as a child, perhaps her ancestors too, and that she is a keen researcher of memory, revealing aspects of the collective past and shining a light on dark corners by way of works that open up connections and reasonings behind events.

And now, she's sitting here, exhausted after a talk that brought uncontested certainties to the fore, she showed what she could do, giving clear answers because, looking at the silent audience, it made sense to assume that they wanted reassurance, a kind of absolution before heading to bed. They may well have been suffering from the same insomnia, mind you. Shared insomnia is when we are preoccupied with who we are and why this happens to be our story. In fact, the only genuine and change-making revelation would be to stage one's own ignorance and restlessness, drawing the curtain aside and silently acknowledging that one doesn't know shit about any kind of why, all there is at hand is the story itself. This would be the actual truth: 'I don't know shit. I don't know shit about who we are and why this is our story.' She's lacking the courage to tell the truth.

As her Son tends to says: 'You don't know shit about this.' When he had first heard this expression at the age of eight, the Son was genuinely surprised, but then started to savour it and repeat it, test it out in sentences, enjoying the flavour of these bawdy words and, bending over and adopting a squatting position, had a go at releasing wind himself, which didn't seem to work at first but then it did, letting out a loud fart that he accompanied with glorious laughter. 'You don't know shit about anything,' he said, angrily, when he would have expected an answer to questions such as, 'What is the Sun made of, if it is really blazing, what kind of matter, if any, can that be since it doesn't seem to burn out, why does it have to blaze in the first place?' 'Don't know,' she replied, immersed in thought and with great interest, taking the Son's questions very seriously as the only opportunity to catch up with missed things, this new knowledge and potential for enthusiasm had an electrifying power that brings a genuine joy of understanding and amazement. After some research, there is time to share the findings, but the question about why the sun is blazing has still no answer. 'Nuclear fusion,' she utters these words slowly, articulately, but the words are just orbiting and hovering about, rewriting the moment of creation, the fusion of two nuclei. 'It's not creation then? Can't explain,' she concludes with the resignation of someone accepting defeat yet hopeful that all this could be perhaps clarified in a Physics lesson. Still, the oddness of the expression makes her wonder, why is it an issue if someone doesn't know shit about anything. What does this mean? For the latter, however, there was an answer, which could be delivered proudly and with precision: 'Shit is life itself, as the Prophet claims, whoever is full of shit and has breath in them, that is hot air, regardless of whether this passes through the upper or lower body, is alive, is a Live Body.' But the Son wasn't happy with this answer. 'You don't know shit about anything,' he snapped. 'You haven't heard about coatis, either, we learned about them today. You could get one for us, they sell them for five hundred,' he added petulantly, sounding like someone who has a clue about finances. He throws this last sentence in as if he was certain of the answer: let's release all anger because he's yet again the loser, yet again he hasn't received anything, he never ever gets anything he wants. And indeed, the answer is: 'There won't be any coatis, and that's that.'

After a conversation about the book, the past, shared responsibility and the role of victims and perpetrators, she's overcome with dry disappointment, like a collapsing tent, while this woman, who's not even a reader, is just staring expectantly at her. The woman's mother had taught the author for four years, yet her name went unrecognised even as a copy of the book was signed for her in the author's scrawling handwriting, due to the fact that she was made to switch from being left-handed to right-handed by the very mother of this woman. The woman can't possibly know that as soon as the writer makes a note of a name, she forgets it, seeing that writing is a form of instant forgetting.

'I don't know who your mother is. I am sorry, my memory is dreadful,' she replies despondently.

She sheathes the drawn-out sword. The fox doesn't carry rabies and won't cause any wounds. She could gladly continue the sentence, adding that although I should know who your mother is, because we must have obviously had something to do with each other or have previously met, I can only suspect that she might have been my mother's classmate or a neighbour, a famous actress, a former teacher, or what's worse, a character in one of my books. I don't know, please don't be angry with me for causing such disappointment.

In a muted voice, the woman repeats the name the writer had already written down earlier but then only paid attention to forming the letters, and to the fact that they should appear on the relevant page, to the orientation of characters in space, as well as to her own unruly and stiff right hand, which has never come to terms with the fact that the only acceptable hand to be used for writing must be the right one, the nice one, and by now this whole thing has been irreparably messed up. During their conversation, the writer kept gesturing with her left hand, at times lifting it as if she wanted to hide her face behind it, meanwhile, dangling the right hand along the body and, by the time she got to the book signing, the right fingers ended up swollen and stiff, so it was essential to focus on composing the winding letters, in addition to space and time and her own name which she continued to sign with a habitual sense of alienation.

'Indeed,' the writer finally breaks the silence in the empty room and tries to evoke the name from which the label 'aunt' was left out.

The existing emptiness acquires a pale blue hue. Just like the sky, as seen from the study window at noon, when the wind dispersed the clouds above the town, leaving only a large stretched-out, translucent cloud, beyond which there lies the deep promise of the sky. This realisation leads to her curving her lips but, at least from within, her face manages to stay soft, smooth and foreign – foxes don't bite, don't carry rabies, however, can be legally hunted.

This moment could potentially mark the end of their meeting. It's obvious that she doesn't remember the 'aunt', her face and story faded away and broken apart in personal memory, the unwritten events of childhood and youth worn away and written stories now foreign. In-between, there is nothing and no one. In-between, there is her, the author. The author is dead, the author is alive, but her personal past has burned itself out.

'Will you come to visit us then?' the woman inquires again, getting over her disappointment and sadness, like someone who's merely completing a task.

The writer asks for a phone number and makes a promise. The mistake is irredeemable, she feels it's her duty to go. There is something really naive in this woman's face, something blank, monotonous, unreadable. It's a decomposed face, without a focus. Could a painter find the centre of this face? The only escape from this face is thinking of writing about it.

'My mother, that is we, would like to ask you a favour.'

An address is given, and an appointment made. Tomorrow late morning.

Tomorrow late morning, promised, 11 am. She makes a note of the address and doesn't remember ever having been there.

'You have actually.'

The Teacher lives in a two-bedroom flat on the other side of town. In the larger room, there are embroidered cushions on the sofa, tapestries on the walls, a woollen blanket on the sofa, which must be really old and prickly, the writer concludes, she certainly isn't in the mood to sit on it in such flimsy trousers and can already feel the irritation of itchy raw wool. She opts for an armchair instead. Fish-shaped savoury biscuits, raspberry cordial with soda, salted peanuts. She asks for a glass of tap water. The woman brings it most willingly. A famous son of their town, a Chemistry professor now living overseas and mooted for the Nobel Prize, said in an interview that what he misses most from his homeland is the taste of tap water.

Whenever she drinks her hometown's strong and fresh tap water, she thinks of this professor who could describe the chemical composition of water, not by way of words and in detail, like a writer, so everyone could imagine their own tap water, their own desires, their own homesickness, but reality itself, the formula of the real. With precision and without nostalgia, the formula of this place's unmistakably unique tap water. Words are incapable of such uniqueness.

The woman introduces the guest to her mother as the writer from class IIIC, 'you know, you've been looking forward to seeing her, remember.' The timelines blur together, past and present overlap. With a set smile, the Teacher repeats what she has just heard, that she's been looking forward to seeing the writer, who is looking great.

'You look great,' she says dryly. In this, there's a glimpse of her former toughness, though they haven't met for thirty years.

The Teacher still has the same hair style, a huge bun created no doubt with the help of a bun maker, impossible to achieve such a thing from one's own hair. She's wearing tights and slippers and is struggling to walk on her stiff legs.

As for the writer, she's just sipping the water, trying to experience that flavour the professor has been talking about, but can only taste a lukewarm, almost hot water that doesn't quench the thirst.

The daughter takes a seat on the sofa. Her hands are shaking when handing the glass over, she's careful not to touch the guest. As she sits, she pulls her legs tightly under herself, withdrawing from the conversation like someone who has completed her task and waiting for things to take place without her intervention. Her gaze has no focus, settling at times on her mother, other times on the hard-to-invite guest who still found it easy enough to get here. She's expecting something from both.

'Will you tell us a bit about yourself? Mum would very much like that. And about the others,' she asks in a colourless voice, breaking the silence.

The writer is looking at the blank expression, searching for the eyes but they are always running away, looking at her temple while they talk. She can't remember the eyes of her former teacher with a burning gaze, either, the face has gone cold, too.

Who are these others, does she mean family or classmates? Perhaps she wants to hear about the class, the people who have become famous and are mentioned in the papers, or maybe the ones with lots of children, who got rich, who moved to the countryside. And the ones who went abroad. The writer knows barely anything about anyone, not having attended any reunions.

'We haven't yet read your writing,' the daughter hastens to fill the silent gap. 'Many people said that they enjoyed it. Very much in fact. You've put it together really well.'

'Tell us about the others. Tell us about yourself dear...' the mother takes over.

She pauses.

'How should I address you?'

'How does it feel to be back home?' the daughter asks, trying to be helpful.

Fine, the writer reassures them, though this tour is a little tiring. But it was fortunately possible to squeeze in a good walk along the river. She has never seen the river so dangerously high, it's on the verge of flooding the area under the bridge. It has become a really massive river that doesn't look like its former self.

'What river?' the Teacher asks after a long silence.

They never call it river in this town, only by its name. They articulate its uniqueness, that doesn't resemble anything else. Only strangers call it a river. The writer resists the temptation to utter the river's name. It's a childish resistance, intended to keep the distance.

'What tour?' the Teacher continues after her daughter has helped her out with names.

'Well, book tours... yes, books.' They all repeat these words with some hesitation, savouring them respectfully, weighing them up, as if something uncertain had to be corroborated. They ensure its existence by uttering these words.

The writer asks for another glass of water. Cold, if possible, thus throwing a stone into the silence, into this conversation going nowhere. The Teacher's nameless daughter obliges straightaway.

'There are many famous people in this class,' she shouts back from the kitchen while running the tap. Her mother is staring out of the window with an empty gaze and a frozen smile.

'There is for example ...' and she pauses.

'Ágó. Mum is thinking of Ágó,' the daughter helps her out, still from the kitchen. 'She became a Physicist or Mathematician in America. No, an astronomer. That's it.'

'Astronomer?' the Teacher asks, sounding clueless. She's the only one the guest is in touch with, as she reveals.

'I visited her at CUNY. Then she was working there. Now she teaches at Yale.'

Ágó is now tenured at Yale. Soft words feel really good. *Tenure*, Yale. She knows what they mean. The world.

'Tell us more, Mum would like you to tell us about this amazing class.'

The writer takes another sip of water and apologises, saying she'd like to use the bathroom. By the time she's back, the Teacher's daughter, whose name was left out of yesterday's book signing and today's visit, has already produced a large burgundy photo album and laid it out in front of them. In it, there is a group photo with every single class the Teacher had taught. The daughter most helpfully finds the picture of their class. The Teacher keeps leafing through the album in which reds and browns are the dominant colours.

'Large class.'

The Teacher is in a navy-blue skirt and jacket, wearing the same towering bun as today.

'Remember this outfit,' the daughter observes, somewhat vaguely.

'No,' the mother replies.

The way she utters this 'no' immediately brings back the harshness for which she was known at school. When she asked a student something and got the wrong answer. This 'no' has a high pitch, sets up expectations and is menacing.

'I've never had a navy-blue jacket and skirt combo,' she insists. The daughter hastens to find a picture of the visitor taken over forty years ago.

She points at it as if she had been preparing for this. She doesn't have to search at all, she knows exactly where it is. Even though the person in question isn't facing he camera, like the others. The teacher nods.

'Are you turning your head? What are you looking at there?'

The writer isn't looking at anything, she turns away in protest. She would have preferred not to be on the picture, as she didn't want to be photographed.

'Shame that you turned away,' the teacher observes, slowly.

'Nice picture. Shame that it's you who turned away, as in this class you were the most...'

'Talented? Successful?' her daughter is trying to help.

'So many of you.'

'Thirty,' her daughter specifies.

'Thirty-six.' the writer corrects the daughter, as she remembers this one detail.

'Thirty-six wonderful. Children,' the Teacher mumbles with a misty gaze.

Is she about to cry?

She's examining the photo, looking for something that's not on the picture. They won't be talking about books, slaps in the face, one can't bring up a slap delivered in front of the entire class in year four. On the picture, they are lined up in rows of six, in a square. In the middle, there's the Teacher in her navy-blue outfit. In the middle of the third row. Six and six had a bag of tricks; inside the bag was thirty-six. They used to come up with rhymes to memorise the multiplication table, as an exercise in mnemotechnics.

'Tell us about the others,' the Teacher summons the guest again, this time in a firmer, almost commanding tone.

Perhaps this would be a good time to admit that she doesn't know anything about the others, having left a quarter of a century ago. Three decades ago, in fact.

'I got a smack in the face one day in year four, when I was standing by the blackboard, in front of the whole class,' she replies eventually, because the water may not conjure up anything, but the bun does.

There, it's now out in the open, as if this was no longer a wound and there wasn't anything at stake. This could even lead to victory but that's not really necessary. Others have also been slapped in the face, by other teachers, too. The daughter pulls her legs even further in.

'I don't recall that,' the Teacher announces, in a dry voice.

'You must be thinking of another teacher. My mother has never...'

'No, I'm not,' the writer concludes the conversation, trying to smile. That smack is irrelevant now, just as it's irrelevant where one has come from. Wounds aren't personal, they have no name but place.

'Ágó is a good topic to talk about, she got her *tenure* at Yale. Ágó is now dishing out smacks at Yale,' the writer is trying to be funny but no one else is laughing at this joke.

You've become a *tenor*!, she laughed uproariously when meeting Ágó in New York. But Ágó didn't get it, in her case English words no longer had a connection with the mother tongue. She has taught herself out of language.

'Yesterday we saw István on TV,' the Teacher's daughter observes enthusiastically. 'He was dressed in traditional national costume. He has just been made a director. No, a minister.'

'István?' her mother reacts with surprise. 'Which István?'

'He was in the other class, not ours.'

The mother doesn't see the guest out, they say their goodbyes in the living room, agreeing that the writer would come again on her next visit. She knows already that this won't happen, this was it, she had paid her dues and made it up for forgetting the teacher. They are standing in the open door, the guest already past the threshold, looking with a calm, impersonal and well-practised anticipation at the woman who's more or less the same age as her, yet who appears much younger, as if worries and cares didn't leave their mark on her face and diffluent gaze. The hosts wanted to ask the guest something, that's why she came in the first place. There's nothing at stake in this, she'll decline no matter what they ask. It's most certain that she'll be abroad then, she's always abroad. She holds her hand out as a farewell. The Teacher's daughter seems at a loss at first, but then shakes this hand.

'Where's this thingy for the TV?' a familiar voice can be heard from the room. It's menacing and dangerous. The owner of the voice thinks that the door has already been shut behind the guest and she's alone with her daughter.

The writer's stomach is churning as she recognises this scream.

'Will you do this please?' the daughter asks with a set smile.

'What?'

'The class reunion. Write about it.'

'What reunion?' the writer asks, holding on to the familiar plastic handrail, almost a floor below. Meanwhile, the woman has caught up with her and is whispering.

'This would be a nice surprise for my mother, you know, next year she'll be,' and she looks at the door left open. 'Kati is the organiser, will you write about it please?'

There's no need to make any promises in the hallway because the Teacher starts shouting again. 'Fuck whoever has put the TV's thingy away.' The daughter has to dash back, looking concerned, but still waving gratefully.

By the time the writer gets home, the invitation has also arrived. To the class reunion that takes place next year, with the request to deliver a welcome speech to the class and to the Teacher. There'll also be a joint visit to the form tutor's grave, where they'll light candles. It's a shared celebration, as they said goodbye to school thirty years ago and the Teacher will turn eighty, Kati, the organiser writes. 'Give a speech. You are the best writer among us, you know everything about us and the place, seeing that you've put everything so well together in your books.'

'You'll come home, won't you?' Whatever happens, this must be declined. Perhaps it's best not to even respond, one needs the right words to decline something, and such words don't exist. Besides, that place cannot be found anywhere, it only exists in dreams. She has no desire to talk about dreams. Dreams are solitary, people laugh at those who talk about their dreams. Dreams are fire and flood, scorching God. Could one possibly carry on dreaming forever?

Staying at the Theological Institute

On this occasion, she's staying wherever it was possible to find accommodation: at the *Theological Institute*, or the *Divinity College* as the bilingual sign indicates. Since she no longer has a family home in this town, on her rare visits our protagonist tends to stay in consular guest rooms, university accommodations, or hotels, depending on the arrangements made by those who invite her. This time, an acquaintance recommended the Institute as cheap and centrally located. There are no friends, close friends, with whom she would prefer to stay. The town is jampacked due to some event, which escapes her attention at first and by the time she realizes this, she has already arrived. Guests have to pay for accommodation at the Institute. She has never paid for the privilege of sleeping in her hometown. This foreignness is shocking yet fascinating at the same time. And liberating. As if one was taking to the air on a trampoline without the pull of gravity.

She's registered as an anonymous foreign guest at the Theological Institute, seeing that this is an incognito visit. When handing over the key, the receptionist specifies that payment for the accommodation has to be given as a donation. It feels good to bear the cost of the room, though things get more muddled in this way and it's not quite a proper hotel.

She doesn't really feel like leaving the Spartan surroundings, enjoying the stay in this temporary foreign space. Concerned at first that the town will be hostile to someone who once left it, she ends up preparing for the journey as if it were an exciting encounter, for which one only starts out at the last minute, stalling for time and enjoying the anticipation. Anyway, the real reason for coming was to put the secret police files to the test. There are two items on her agenda: the book launch that turns out to be a misjudgement – it would have been best not to initiate it – and her father's documents.

'Why do you ask my name?', it says on a small sign by a door at the Institute, by each door a Biblical citation. Sporty-looking young boys are dashing abound the courtyard, greeting each other with a melodious 'Be-pe!'[3] but when they see a teacher or someone they don't know, they hasten to utter the full four syllables of the greeting: 'Blessings and peace!' When our protagonist is finally walking down the stairs, after a long cold shower, ready to explore the town, the same greeting is heard, which only leads to confusion as the visitor has no idea what's the correct way to respond.

The view from the fourth-floor guest room offers a new perspective, even though the institute is close to the inner core of this town without an actual centre. Looking out of the window above the rooftops, she loses her sense of orientation, which has hitherto always worked like a compass – here, and only here, she always used to be able to tell where East, West, North and South were in the past. In any other place the magnetic forces would be sending their secret messages in vain, the inner compass dial wouldn't budge, noticing only landscapes, directionless desolation and spaciousness.

It takes a while to get used to the fact that what used to 'belong to her' is now so 'foreign'. The sky, however, is extraordinary, always recognisable. The wind has swept the heavy clouds away from the town, then even chased away the remaining ruffled clouds, and the sky is now blue and spacious. The sun is determined to shine all day, so every nook and cranny can be taken possession of. The light is bright, the shadows compact, suggestive of the impending autumn. When our protagonist wanted to write a book about this town, she often visited, seeking out new perspectives, new vantage points, including the building work carried out beyond the old town, the meandering hills, the unknown quarters and new forms. It takes time to get used to and learn about foreignness. In that book, the town became an imaginary and insignificant place, barely recognisable. At a later stage of future alienation, she may well have another go at writing about this topic, by then making use of a novel gaze in wonder.

Right now, there's this unknown language with its confusing and consequently mandatory greeting: 'Be-pe!' What if one responded with a simple 'good afternoon'? Would this non-belonging be offensive? This outsider-ness? On the walls, rows of pictures featuring the alumni of the Institute, from the beginnings to the present: serious faces, very few women graduates and none among the teachers, God's male day-labourers, put to work. Our protagonist is ambling about the East and West wing, unable to find the finance department to pay in the required donation. How bizarre that this building has always been standing here with its unknown language and story, just a few streets from her home, yet sealed off from each other.

She has returned to the town and place where she had been collecting documents about her father, the town where she had grown up and where all her ancestors were laid to eternal rest, with a view to put the secret police files to the test in this once familiar place that now appears unfamiliar when viewed from the window of her accommodation. She's testing out a replay.

Yet, for now, the foreignness of the building confuses her and carries her away. She was under the impression that she knew everything about this town, yet here she is, in the middle of her hometown, in a foreign space that has existed for centuries. In a building in front of which she must have passed even as a foetus in her mother's belly, and then countless times as a child and teenager, during which time an unknown life was going on inside, 'Be-pe!' A caste, an island with its own language, a state within a state. One needs time to get used to this place, this view, as it takes one out of one's comfort zone. Our protagonist has no intention of engaging with the history herein, or even getting to know it, though it must be very complex and difficult to access. It's nonetheless compelling once one has stumbled upon it.

'Be-pe!' the boys keep shouting at one another, looking cheerful as they dash about the courtyard in their shorts and polo shirts, but as soon as they notice the unknown adult, they immediately splutter a proper greeting, to which the belated response of the visitor staring at them in bewilderment is 'Good afternoon'!

The initial plan has been to spend four days here, but this stretches to six, until this sense of the unknown eases off. The non-existent becomes existing.

She has brought along thirty pages of the secret police file, aiming to follow in the footsteps of the surveillance diary and get to know the story, at least in an embodied form. The story of her father.

'The main gate of the Theological Institute is locked at 11 pm,' the porter announces in a singing voice, greeting with the same Be-pe, thus letting the visitor know about the rules in operation in this space. When she returns, the main gate is still open and the porter is watching TV, his feet on the table. Noticing the returning visitor, he jumps up: 'May I have your autograph, madam?,' which makes her think that he wants a signature next to the passport details, madam's signature that is, but the porter quickly produces the new edition of her second book from a plastic bag and asks her to sign it. 'For the Tóth family,' he adds. That's it, the Tóth family. Signing books, even at night and at the porter's lodge of the Theological Institute, fills her heart with warmth. After the signing, she con-vivially changes the subject to the topic of hot water. One has to run the water for a long time, the porter shares the secret while accompanying the guest to the East wing, switching the light on, wishing her good night and asking for God's blessing. 'May God bless you too,' she replies, having found the appropriate words. Climbing the steep stairs, one can smell the scent of mint or lemongrass tea instead of the cabbage smell in the morning, the clothes drying in the stairwell earlier have been collected and, in their place, there are a few swimming trunks and towels. Discreet music and muted conversation can be heard from behind a couple of doors, the 'Be-pe boys' are having a quiet party. In the bathroom, she lets the water run for several minutes, and indeed, hot water eventually makes it to the fourth floor. It's so austere that they don't even have hot water, she writes home on the first day, now there is. She opens the window and finds that the terrible day-time traffic, noise and stench has gone, the town and the alienation is slowly calming down. The sound of the event previously coming from all directions is also fading, even though a humming background noise persists, which is strange and foreign. Entirely new and existing.

She checks the desk drawers but can't find a single Bible. Early next morning, one of the cleaners in the back yard – in the middle of feeding cats – shouts at another woman, 'Anyway, blessingsand-peace,' and they utter this 'nanyway' as if this was the actual start of their day, and an opening to a longer conversation or get-together. The scent of bread is lingering in the staircase, they aren't baking here, it's being brought up in large plastic baskets bearing the logo 'the bread of the year'.

The visitor is leaving through the back gate, which she has started to use lately. The modest, unassuming wooden gate opens to a quiet street. The main gate is heavy, dark, carved – the word *pompous* comes to mind – compared to which this is a quiet entrance only used by cleaners and the boys when they are going for a run. This age-long unapproachable building stayed unnoticed by her while living here, perhaps because it was so forbiddingly large. Once the smaller back gate comes to the fore, it's much easier to feel at home and come and go several times a day. New times, new entrances to new times.

At dawn, mist descends on the crest of the hills. One can only see an idly undulating line of new houses built on excessively priced plots of land on the hillside, all blurring into a grey-white mass. Traffic is cascading down the former dirt road carved into the hill, the awakening town is minding its business, heading to work and rumbling on. The sound of this new space is novel, reminiscent of foreign cities. The town has exploded, gained so much weight that it can be barely contained in its body, its skin struggling to stretch further, almost at choking-point. Only well-insulated, double-glazed windows can keep the noise out, and the windows of the Theological Institute do just that.

On the horizon, is that the edge of town? Or does it continue beyond, being an expanding, overflowing agglomeration that overgrows everything? The light is switched on in the odd house on the hillside. When her family used to have a house there, this area was considered outside town; just a hut made of fibreboard in an abandoned garden, even drinking water was in short supply. Now, large multi-storey houses, designed by award-winning architects, are being carved into the hillside.

The aim of coming to this town was to chart the routes on which the main character of the secret police files used to be followed in the early morning hours. Words don't give anything away, no matter how often they are read or examined. The words are aghast, staring blankly off the copies of copies, digital copies based on photocopies of typed documents. The person under surveillance leaves his workplace through the gate. Only his route can be known for sure, only space, only time, the passage of time – according to the report, two, two and a half hours pass while this person is being followed from one place to another. The aim is to chart this same route and identify street names and houses.

At six am – the man who's being followed stops in front of a printing house, today turned into a garden restaurant. This is where the route starts from. She stops, waits, following the script. Grocery store, stopping to buy some bread and cold cuts. Pub. Downing a quick shot. Tobacconist's. Buying some cigarettes. The pub is now a shoe shop, the tobacconists can't be found anywhere. Sitting on a bench. The bench is no longer there. Why would they make note of such mundane details? A man sat on a bench for eighteen minutes and smoked two cigarettes. He could have even slumbered for a while. Perhaps the April sun shone on his face and warmed up his chilled bones. By the time they follow him to his former rental basement flat, it's past 8 am. There's nothing there except for a walled-up cellar. The cellar is probably colder than the lukewarm spring sunshine on the bench, so the person following has a long wait ahead.

If the body walks along the path that words cannot disclose, it may get nearer to 'something' that definitely isn't written down. The space that has been travelled and the time that has passed are the only certainties in those documents. Fifty years to the day, her father has been followed on this journey by a secret police agent, and now she has retraced this route. Her father bumps into a friend, which comes in handy for the surveillant and a photograph is taken. He visits a relative, then goes to a concert but has to leave at the interval because he's on night shift. Or the concert was bad? It might be possible to find out what was on the programme. Is it worth bothering? Or it's more of a reassurance to know what concert it was? Well, if it leads to reassurance, then it's worth it.

They say their good-byes at the entrance to the printing house – now a garden restaurant. The protagonist of the secret police files goes to work, while she will have dinner here, at the very same garden restaurant. The restaurant is very spacious, with large wine coolers in the vault cellars where the toilets are also situated. The kitchen serves Mediterranean and local dishes, and the noise is almost unbearable. She is no longer ashamed of producing her pale pink wax earplugs. Sitting down feels great after all the waiting and standing, and her feet hurt despite wearing trainers. Her initial idea was to take notes along the way in case some lesson emerges or anything comes to mind, but following the route is tougher than expected: one has to study the map, which is a challenge because the town is only in her body and not on a map. One also has to pay attention to time, yet it's in the nature of time to defy being seized, like fine dust. The task is to find the houses where people who no longer exist were coming from and going to, in fact the houses don't really exist, either. There is nothing to make a note of, there are no words. She has completed the task she had set herself: '*this is what I do*'. There's nothing left to be done. In case there is such a thing as a lesson, it has to be somewhere else.

A murder of crows appears from behind the hill, they are pitch black rooks, in fact. They squawk and caw, their procession drowns out the humming sounds of the town. In the morning, they fly from East to West, and at dusk, in the opposite direction. They aren't making their move at dawn, but late in the morning. As if even the birds start their day later here. She can still hear the crows through ear plugs in the jampacked garden restaurant, the sky is clapping as the birds whizz above town in formations impossible to decipher. There was a time when former alumni of Divinity College, knowledgeable about gods from long ago, were able to tell the future based on the formation of birds in flight. She'd be happy if one was able to tell at least the past. Earplugs are really useful, best to be kept in for the night, too. The first literary shadow of earplugs appears when the sailor wanted to go home, and in order not to yield to temptation, he covered his ears with wax. If she listens carefully beyond the subdued and sizzling sounds, she can hear her own heartbeat.

Csaba, Sweden

Her phone rings a few kilometres before they reach the border, but she only responds to the insistent call when they stop at a petrol station. Her parking is rather clumsy, as if stopping in the midst of this continuous movement was really cumbersome. The call is from the self-appointed organiser of the class reunion. They have to go back to pick up Csaba, whose car has broken down. Do you remember Csaba? Csaba lives on a farm on the Great Plain.

'Csaba lives here?' – she asks, taken by surprise.

'What do you mean by here?' – Kati asks, laughing. Ever since she married a Dutchman, she started to introduce herself as Kathrin. She's straight to the point and jovial on the phone. When they met face to face a year ago, she simply stated: I read your book. I loved it. That was all she said about it.

No need to ask which book. Kati lowers her intonation at the end of the sentence and simply stops, considering the conversation about the book over.

Csaba and our protagonist had last met in Sweden over two decades ago, when, lured by distance and the curiosity about new continents and new gods, she managed to obtain an invitation to a festival up North. To be precise, the invite was for a professor, who recommended her in his place with the proviso that she should write about the event for some magazine.

The fee she received amounted to about a fifth of the expenses, seeing that travel wasn't included. Neither was accommodation, so she had very little money to spend. This was when Csaba came to her mind, as he had visited a few times while in transit. 'Would he possibly have a mattress for her?', she asked the voice recorder on which Csaba had left a greeting, solely in Swedish. There was no reply for ages, but just before it was time for her to depart, he called: 'When are you arriving and how? I'll come and pick you up.' Years ago, Csaba had given her a lift when she was still a student, and they spent two days on the shores of a lake with a larger group. They haven't been in touch since meeting in Sweden. Well, well, so now Csaba lives here. 'He bought a farm and is breeding goats', Kati sums up, stressing that they must turn around and bring him because Csaba simply won't take the train.

'I won't travel on a filthy train next to some unwashed people,' Csaba concludes a few hours later, when he's already sitting in the car. He's used to being in the driver seat and finds this slow and cautious driver rather odd.

She's anything but keen on turning back, she has never been. She seems to lack the lightness of those travellers who can easily juggle routes and directions. After nearly three decades, she seems just as tense about travelling and focusing on destinations as before. She just wants to go ahead. Only ahead. Home.

Fifteen years ago, Csaba had done everything he possibly could to make her feel welcome in his Swedish flat. This mandatory generosity is now annoying.

Csaba lives on the third floor of a brown Swedish block of flats. He got to live in this small flat on a cheap rent for social reasons, due to being an immigrant. The flat is bleak and lacks any touch of homeliness, the council furnished it with items everybody could find useful, irrespective of nationality, religion or cultural customs. The medium-size threadbare towel that Csaba has put out looks eerily familiar: just like the once orange set they used to have at home, now faded to a pastel colour and turned coarse with too much washing. A towel that has travelled more than fifteen hundred kilometres. How can Csaba's sizable body get dry using such a tiny towel? Why did he bring it with him? The pale pink striped bedding is another familiar item, her grandmother had such a thing once.

Csaba takes his own mattress to the kitchen, his large frame can just about fit in. The guest is invited to sleep on the extendable sofa. Csaba works as a taxi driver. In the cellar – where he rents two other spaces from the neighbours in addition to his own – he has seventy aquariums in which he breeds fish, to be sold on to Arab traders. 'Who then sell them on to these dumb Swedes', he adds, lowering his voice when he says dumb, 'people here don't have normal animals because they are expensive and the vet's bills cost a fortune'. Lowering his voice, he talks in his mother tongue about the stupid life of these Swedes, even though they are in a cellar, far from other ears that can't understand their language anyway. 'Anything can be sold to them, they love this shit, seeing that fish don't have to be taken for walks and barely need any food, they look good in the room, don't have to be seen by the vet, and if they die, one just throws them into the bin or flushes them down the toilet. They are mere decoration, like books. The Arab, who runs the pet shop, however, is shifty. Shifty and shady like all Arabs,' he concludes.

Whatever he can't sell in six months, he discards. The snag is that it's hard to tell what will be in demand. At times, people seem to be obsessed with anything that's in lots of colours, right now some Japanese shite is on trend, but it's a very delicate breed so he came off badly as half of the stock died on him. There's a punch bag hanging in the passageway between two cellars, this is where he comes to work out.

'I'll show you the ugliest fish I have' – he points triumphantly at a grey fish, with a hook nose and reticulated back. There are at least ten tanks filled with these, swimming swiftly in the hope of a better life.

'These are the best sellers right now. This is what people deserve. Bloody hideous they are.'

They never clarify whether the fish deserve their unfortunate looks or this rather introverted Northern nation, which, according to the host, is also unfriendly. Sturgeon, Csaba points out, while she adds that Russian literature talks a lot about eating sturgeon, could this be the same thing?

'Definitely not, this breed is too small for that sort of thing as they don't grow any bigger. In this city, Russians are the customers who keep taxis in business, they have the most money.'

Last Friday, for example, a Russian and his girlfriend threw up in his cab.

'They have money to get drunk in this country! You know what I did? I dragged them out of the car and wiped the seat with the man's coat. The chick was just squealing and guffawing.' Csaba peeled off her coat, used its lining for wiping the car, and then gave it back to her. It took some convincing to make her wear the coat again. You know, like this. And he shows his fist.

He has no permit for the fish business, he adds in a muted voice, these dumb Swedes want a permit for everything, this country is a jungle of red tape. In his pronunciation this sounds like red tap, as if he had to tap on something. Not to mention that he'd have to allow in some lesbian animal protection people or perhaps some greens to obtain the permit. A neighbour has reported him, but he sorted it out.

'How exactly did you sort it out?' – she asks innocently.

'As is our custom' – Csaba replies mysteriously.

Judged by his looks, Csaba could actually be from Sweden except for his name, these dumb Swedish people can't pronounce anything properly that's foreign. Still, they have stupid names, too. For example, his boss is called Agfast, he roars with laughter at his own innuendo that makes the name sound as if he meant pulling a fast one.

They take a taxi to do some sightseeing on a free morning, and when Csaba, who had made himself available for these six days, asks her to suggest a destination, the request is to see a proper Northern landscape. 'Fjord?,' she asks cautiously, having forgotten to check the map, so this is just a random utterance of a word, the foreignness of which is most promising nonetheless. There is no real experience behind the word, at school they had never learned about this in geography and her only image of these ripples of water is based on dreams. That said, the world is opening up, and it is this very thirst for a sense of space that had brought her to this brown block of flats, too.

Fjord, Csaba acknowledges her request dryly, I know. Before leaving town, they order some food from a drive-through fast food restaurant. Csaba is talking through the half-open window to someone who can only be seen from the shoulders up and who asks him to repeat every sentence. Possibly to clarify or verify details or because they can't understand his foreign accent. Csaba is uttering his melodious Swedish words firmly and slowly, with more and more articulation, while he mumbles a fuck you under his breath, he's on his third Swedish language course but these people aren't ever pleased with anything, fuck it, they will never accept you and will always let you know that you're nowhere near to speaking bloody Swedish when you are actually talking in this fucking language. He's so worked up that he continues to mutter in the car even after they place the order.

'It might be easier to use English in such situations,' she gently offers an alternative. 'What situations?' Csaba asks, startled. 'When they can't hear very well,' she replies, sounding more like a question. 'When you can't see each other, it's harder to hear.' Csaba defected right after their Baccalaureate. Perhaps he's trying too hard to speak this language, he's too tense, when languages shouldn't be tense but flutter on your shoulders like a butterfly.

Like a butterfly?

They wait for their food in silence.

The loudspeaker projects the voice of the sales assistant in this melodious language only known from films, going over the various items they ordered together with the price, and then suddenly switches to English: '*Card or cash*?,' and hands over their purchase in a brown bag. Csaba pays with cash. A shiny brown hand emerges from a rolled-up shirt sleeve. Struggling to lift his bottom off the car seat to put his wallet away, Csaba doesn't even look up and only holds his hand out, waiting for his packet. But then he starts shouting, disfigured with rage: 'fuck you', followed by the Swedish *jävlar hund*, and grabs the bag so vehemently that the paper handle rips off, then hits the gas pedal and turns the steering wheel so wildly that even the back tyres screech. 'I don't eat food prepared by black people. I don't want niggers to cook for me.'

They end up swallowing the crispy fried chicken and chips without any gusto, sitting on a bench by the fjord in the ice-cold wind. Csaba pushes the tiny jam jar away, 'they even have this with frankfurters,' he says with utter disgust, 'jam with frankfurters for fuck's sake.'

She has been dreaming about steep cliffs and wild Northern landscapes. Instead, the fjord is more like a river channelled into a concrete basin in the town's industrial zone, without any sense of space or crests or ripples that could be reminiscent of the sea. By the fjord the wind is so strong that they can't even talk to each other, she has to settle for walking a few hundred metres, head down, while Csaba is patiently waiting in the car. They have no map to show the exact location of the sea or how it had carved this bay out, so they'll never find out. Csaba isn't interested in fjords, he doesn't understand this almost guilty pleasure in the sea – 'why do they have to go every single day to visit yet another section of the coast?' It's not just the fjord, he also dislikes the acrid and salty smell of the sea – they simply can't agree on scents, so he just goes back to the car while she's nosing around.

She's looking at this thick oily water splashing about in a narrow concrete basin. The water is impenetrable and menacing, revealing nothing apart from the reflection of the grey sky. After a short while, it's time to slowly return to the car, like a frustrated sailor.

Csaba is keen to show the nearby military museum – he explains all he can about the Second World War bomber jet on display in a huge bare space, enthusiastically translating the information on offer. The wind is blowing furiously.

They are planning a farewell dinner. The last performance of the festival will end early, according to the English-language pro-gramme, because it features old people who are usually in bed by 8 pm. It's strange to see the spectators adjust to the performers and not the other way round. The performers are elderly women who live in a care home, from where they will be accompanied to the theatre to see the show, then to a shop to pick up some groceries and lastly, back home, that is to the *care home*. 'Get out of here, are they really coming from an old folks' home?' Csaba asks in total shock, using the term he had learnt back in the day for referring to a nursing home. In that language, the focus wasn't on care but on being old. 'How about folk?,' the writer muses, 'how did that get there, from what source?' Once home, she will visit the Library of Foreign Languages and Cultures where she often works, to check the dictionary, and on her first laptop will write the required article about the festival. The dictionary doesn't explain what she's looking for, but lists the term 'old woman's speech', which refers to a claim or statement that (untruthfully) exaggerates and embellishes facts. Well, in this case, literature is old woman's speech.

What's crucial though is that in this Northern country such places are the homes of care.

When the camera crew arrives at the care home, they are met at the bottom of the stairs by a cat with a little bell on its neck. A wheelchair ramp is lowered, and while they are waiting, the cat is reeling between their feet. Eight elderly women will appear on stage, wearing light summer clothing, their flabby arms and bare feet reminiscent of an aged Isadora Duncan. At first, they perform a silent Greek-style round dance, with flower wreaths on their heads, then it's the turn of the chorus who sings the *Carmina Burana* accompanied by an orchestra. In-between the various acts, the women come up to the mic, introduce themselves and say a few words about their present lives. In the group, there is a woman with early onset of dementia, someone who used to be homeless, a kleptomaniac who warns others to pay attention because they are about to go to a shop and will be filmed on camera. They are all spinning round the woman in the wheelchair, she has Parkinson's disease. By now, all of them are on their own, their husbands either died or they had never married. 'I didn't have much luck with men', one of the women says. 'Well, I'm actually in love', the woman who used to be homeless announces, sad that she can't live with her beloved in the care home.

The writer wanted to invite Csaba to this barely hour-long concert-performance, offering to buy him a ticket because she still has a lot of pocket money and her host has been chauffeuring her around to the various shows and talks in addition to feeding her. But Csaba, who used to transport patients, hates old people smelling of wee. This was his job before starting to work as a taxi driver, 'you can't say anything here, you can't comment on anyone, the patients are allowed everything, you nothing at all, this is the famous democracy we have here.' No way, he's going to stare at old sods in dirty nappies. He'd rather watch a film while waiting and borrows a war documentary from the local rental.

For dinner, he opens a bottle of Italian wine he had brought back from his travels, because these Swedes don't even have wine.

He prepares some sausages. 'Sausages are pretty shite here, they aren't made from real meat,' he growls and drowns the skinny sausages in pepper. 'The bread is inedible, imagine, this is called bread,' he points at a rectangle-shaped wedge he had bought especially for his guest so she can try this Swedish speciality. 'I love it,' she says, chomping on one. Csaba prefers to boil some potatoes. He puts on some music, the photocopied CD cover features a name she hadn't heard before, Nina Simone, in a white turban, holding a burning cigarette by its filter between two fingers. Her gaze is heavy, her eyelids droopy, her mouth unsmiling, her skin puffy. She looks like a battered warrior, ready to take on suffering.

Csaba is opening a second bottle of wine.

He talks about classmates, various events at school, mischiefs, parties and trips where a whole crate of vodka got finished and everybody went skinny dipping in the lake at night. Quite a few people fancied Csaba in their class. He had his own group of friends, five guys who'd always go everywhere together, they were good at fighting and kicking up a riot. Csaba was the first to own a car, he was smoking and drinking, not with a view to get drunk though, and went out with older girls. And now, in this pastel-coloured Swedish house, with seventy fish tanks in the cellar and a job as a taxi driver, he's dreaming about a life back home. He tends to go home for three weeks in the summer. 'When everything is as it used to be. We are all together. Everybody goes back home.'

Every so often, he visits the fish in the cellar. He buys beer, even though it's bloody expensive here. He usually has two at a time. He can't afford to get drunk, and neither can these show-off and penny-pinching Swedes in whose homes these fish will later live, they are drinking in moderation, a glass of wine at dinner, and then put the bottle away. He sits in the cellar, switches the light on and stares at the fish. He has a large camp bed forgotten by a neighbour when he let out the cellar, he lies down and puts his feet up. He positions the bed right under the lamp and the low red pendant light shines right on his shaven head, he even removes his T-shirt, as if he was sunbathing at the seaside, at an arm's length from these harmless fish. He's on holiday, daydreaming and watching the fish as they are slowly swimming towards the Swedish living rooms. Behind his closed eyelids, there's summer, he's lying on the grass, on the shores of a mountain lake, while the others are building a camp fire. The light is too strong and blazing hot. He covers his eyes with his T-shirt.

After this visit to Sweden, they won't contact each other for two decades.

Csaba would find it difficult to sit at the back with Ágó and Susan, so at the petrol station the latter moves to the front, also to get more involved with the driver's story. They slightly gather together the legs of a still sleeping Ágó, she wakes up, smiles at them, nods at Csaba, wondering whether they recognise each other, and then just pulls in her legs and falls back to sleep.

The driver lets Csaba know that she can't chat while driving and won't let him take over either, as it is essential for her to gain experience at present.

Csaba wants to talk about his goat cheese business to Susan, but she cuts him off:

'I'm vegan, you know.'

Still, she allows him to carry on. Csaba talks about non-violent cheesemaking, his English seems effortlessly fluent despite the slight Swedish accent. After he bought the farm, he did a course in France to study *non-violent techniques of cheese making*. Whoever pays thirty per kilo, because this is how much buyers have to pay, cares about the process, too. He goes up to the capital and sells his own produce. This way he can also ask more because buyers can meet the producer. Goat cheese made with traditional, violent methods cannot fetch such a price.

'*Sounds convincing*' – Susan nods at the end of the conversation.

'What happens to the goats who don't have milk, *what do you call a young male goat*? Finally, something where females are more valuable,' Susan giggles.

'Seriously, what are you doing with the male goats? Do you keep them?'

He has no permit to slaughter them, Csaba replies. Goat meat is healthy though.

'They're called *buckling and doeling*,' Susan lets them know the proper terms she has just found online, adding that she's never heard these being used by anyone. Csaba lets the gypsies have the meat at a low price. *The Gypsies eat everything.*

'This is where I picked you up twenty-five years ago' – Csaba suddenly switches from one language to another, and points out of the window.

That was the trip when she saw her grandmother for the very last time. At first, she used to go back every summer and for every family celebration, taking either the train or getting a lift from acquaintances, even hitchhiking at times. She was too close in time and space to break away, offer resistance or start a new life, besides, all her relatives live back home, too.

'I'll never see you again,' her grandmother said to her one hot August afternoon, as they hugged and waved goodbye in front of the house.

They'd spent a whole month together. She'd get up late, read well into the night, work from noon till evening, go swimming in the lake on Sundays, have dinner together, do grandmother's shopping and take the fresh laundry up in the attic to dry. Until she moved in, all this was routinely done by her mother, after ten to twelve-hour shifts at work.

On this last occasion, she was trying to transmit the solace and hope inherent in leave-taking. Stress that the trip had a point and purpose, being worthy of confidence, and that it will be well, all will be well, and she'll call her grandmother once she has returned, but right now, this departure is necessary and unavoidable. She could see the sorrow of those being left behind in her grandmother's scaly eyes, which used to be bright blue and now are grey, concealed by old-age cataracts. She even had to hold on to the wall as they stepped out of the light to the shade of the cold gateway, as forms and shapes suddenly ended up undiscernible.

Her grandmother died a month later, at her home. They managed to talk on the phone three more times, but never met again, just as the grandmother had predicted. This had also meant that our protagonist now had one reason less to keep going back home.

It would have been possible to stay two or three extra days, but she was rushing back in the hope of a job, for which a university professor had recommended her, as they were looking for ambitious young people following the appointment of a new head at a research institute. The time for 'I'll never see you again' was getting closer and closer. In her grandmother, the organs, as well as the world had started to disintegrate and fade away. Once upon a time, they used to be the same height but by the time of their last hug, there was a difference of a head between them so the grandchild refrained from a good squeeze, not to cause any harm. The grandmother had never been able to see the new home of her grandchild, who gets the job and will work with her former professor. To attend the funeral, she asks for a two-day leave, coming and going as fast as possible and, exceptionally, taking the train.

As long as somebody in her family is still alive, she simply has to go 'home', because she is expected 'back home', it's impossible not to celebrate festivals and events 'at home', even if all her efforts are about arriving at another place, into another house, a tiny flat on the fourth floor of an apartment block – still, she can't leave her mother all alone for the festivities.

As a student, she'll continue to go back home during the summer to earn some money. She even moves out of the rental room for the duration of the holidays, seeing that place, in the sense of a home away from home, has no importance and the only thing that matters is the cost. She'll find another one. In her first year at university, she cleans refurbished homes, offers language classes, data entry earns the most money and although she doesn't yet have official documents, nobody wants to see any. That summer, she's working in a convenience store where they sell everything from stockings to cognac, and from fake perfume to notebooks, vases and fur coats. She hitchhikes a lot and on one occasion, is being picked up by Csaba. When she returns in the autumn, she'll have a job, a much-desired research post, with a salary and bank account, and foreign trips will also start as her new role is to handle international relations on behalf of the institute. To go places, to be on the move.

Once, a small truck took her to the edge of the Great Hungarian Plain, having transported pigs to a farm at the nearby village. The famous photograph *Wandering Blind Musician*, featuring a barefoot child, was taken at the next village. The child, probably the musician's son, is leading the man on the now infinite road immortalised by the photo. There is a third protagonist on the photo, too, a child learning to walk, who doesn't seem to belong to anyone. The photo was taken by André Kertész, who had left Hungary to discover the wide world at the age of thirty, and who was still able to return to his homeland in old age. At this point, however, she has no idea about this photo, about time frozen into infinity, about the eternally mendicant and eternally vulnerable blind musician and his children, who are helplessly accompanying him barefoot in the borderless and blind world. The next village is far away, and she is simply waiting opposite the pig farm.

The wind is blowing from the South, so one can barely smell the heavy animal stench. The sky is vast and thick, multi-layered clouds are hovering above the Great Plain. The only signpost in this unknown landscape is offered by the sturdy round-shaped haystacks, these days built by machines. There isn't as much as the slightest whiff, no traffic whatsoever, as if the world had come to an end in the distant village.

The horizon is deep and welcoming, the beginning and end of time, at once past and present.

They are expecting her to arrive home in the evening but she may get there earlier. As a rule, they welcome her with her favourite dishes. She arrives, all sweaty and dusty, having walked through the summer city in addition to eight, nine, ten hours of travel on random means of transportation, chatting to people in at least three languages because foreigners are also offering lifts to hitchhikers and they don't even accept money in return. She arrives, the door of the house wide open, with a radio humming somewhere in the background to counter solitude. Suddenly, the squeaky old floorboards give way to the sound of joy:

'Finally, you're here!'

Thirty years later, she has no relatives left in town. 'Here, we have died out altogether,' she says at the class reunion, adding: 'but have resurrected and even multiplied elsewhere.'

At this point, however, she still has a pair of pyjamas and a tooth-brush here, the bare minimum for a home, and having dropped her off, the truck turns into the yard of the pig farm, and she returns to the main road. She props her rucksack against a row of acacia trees. The trees are young, huddled together and competing with one another in terms of which grow faster. There are no taller trees to offer some shade. Nobody is traveling by cart anymore.

Being in the truck made her sweaty, so she dries in the sun while waiting for the next lift.

The odd car drives past but they signal that they are either full or only going somewhere local, which is why they can't take her. One of the signals is pointing backwards, showing that people are already sitting at the back, or opening the arms sideways, appearing to be at a loss. Another gesture is pointing the thumb downwards: to say that one is only going locally, right here, to this very village. There is no ambivalence, no misunderstanding. Nothing to worry about. She has always managed to get home so far. There is no need to plan or to rush, as it's summer. Landscape and time are in a soft expansion. She slightly turns her back to the road and sits on a milepost, enjoying the warm sunshine. She misses a few cars. In a good twenty years, by then in full knowledge of the *Wandering Blind Musician* and the photo's far-travelled creator, she tries the same thing again – this time, out of necessity, because after a summer endurance hike, they miss the last bus from the village and there is no train, the sunset is far ahead, so they have a go at hitchhiking, not in the least out of nostalgia and spirit of adventure. They take waving at cars very seriously, even if it starts as a game, at first, they only allow twenty minutes for it, then half an hour, and by the end it will be three quarters of an hour. The drivers of mainly local vehicles look straight through them as if there wasn't anyone standing by the roadside. As if there weren't two adults with backpacks, herself and the Other, a man carrying a *Nordic walking* stick.

'People in Moscow have changed a lot,' she points out after an hour. Cars, some in better, others in worse condition, occupied by one driver go past.

'What's Moscow like?' the Other asks, not paying attention, picking acacia leaves... she loves me, she loves me not.

Finally, an old minibus stops when it's almost dusk. The driver looks surprised rather than helpful – what could these two people be doing here? He takes them to the nearest railway station. The landscape is the same. The straw rolled into squares, the sky scattered with tiny clouds, the light brushing through the imminent dusk.

When the sun starts to burn her face, she just turns around and, without even standing up, waves at an approaching Merc with a German number plate. She doesn't assess cars in the light of hope or hopelessness, she only waves at them impassively, knowing that she'll get home somehow anyway. The car drives past her, without the driver looking out of the window, it's someone who doesn't normally need to take hitchhikers. Then suddenly the car sways to the left, to the service road leading to the pig farm, and turns around before stopping, windows down, right in front of her.

'Good job I recognised you.'

She barely recognises him though.

'I never pick up hitchhikers,' he says after she's already sitting in the car.

They are pleased to see each other, displaying the sort of simple joy when two people's encounter hasn't been tainted by any hard feelings. There's no rivalry between them, either, Csaba has always been longing for engines and cars, while she for books and a student life.

'What are you doing here?' he asks with consternation, even though it's obvious: she was waiting to hitch a lift.

This 'here' refers to the moment. There's no perspective, no need to explain the past, why is she in this other country, what is she studying, where is she going and what is she dreaming about. Csaba defected to Sweden right after the Baccalaureate and she started her studies, so they vanished from each other's horizon. To continue the conversation, she explains that she tends to hitchhike because the train is always full and getting increasingly expensive. Driving doesn't even come up as an option – car, driving licence, there's no money for these things. Besides, she usually gets sick when travelling by minibus on these winding roads.

'I never travel on these filthy trains,' Csaba points out. He's overtaking, leaning on the window with his left elbow.

He invites his passenger for lunch on the other side of the border. At least, they can come up with some decent cooking, he observes, and explains that he is on a business trip. During his summer holidays, extended with the help of a medical note, he travels to Germany every four or five days and imports cars to sell on:

'One can sell any number of cars these days, people have shedloads of cash. The point is that cars should be large and black. Mercedes, Audi, BMW. No other makes. You can't sell French cars at all. Leather seats. No estate cars. Alloy wheels, yes. Automatic cars, no. People are this simple,' Csaba concludes.

While Csaba is studying the menu, she mentions that she's at university, a student of literature, she adds cautiously. And of languages, but she forgets that part, language is uninteresting compared to literature and it's not going that well, especially linguistics. Csaba appears to be immersed in thought but finally nods:

'Uhum.'

As if he understood that someone who hitchhikes, doesn't have a car and needs to rely on others, including filthy trains, should at least study. In the restaurant, he produces a pile of cash. They praise the thick soup and the aromatic roast meats together. Csaba finishes the meal with a beer:

'It's allowed here,' he states. 'You should see the situation in Sweden! Zilch.'

The alloy wheels of the black car glimmer in the afternoon sun, Csaba bends down to wipe some invisible scratch or dirt from the side of the car, looking utterly content. She can't help thinking that she'd be reading her book if she was on the train. When did the distance between them grow this much? Noticing her thick book in her rucksack once they are back in the car, Csaba asks:

'How can you read this much? I've never been able to do that. I can't concentrate. How many books do you have to read for an exam?'

'For the 19th century Russian literature, around three shelffuls, ideally in Russian. The critical edition of Tolstoy comprises ninety volumes that of Dostoyevsky thirty, but the actual books are thicker. Chekhov is also thirty, plus fifteen volumes of correspondence, though that's not required. Not everything is required. Then there is Turgenev. And Gogol.'

'I could read you an excerpt if the road wasn't so winding,' she offers.

'Do you know anything by heart?'

'By heart?'

'A book or something.'

'Shall I tell you the plot of a book?'

'Well, whatever's the best from the 19th century. I'm a little worried after lunch. Last time I fell asleep at the Polish border. Drove into a fence. They revoked my licence for three months.'

'What licence?' she asks, because she's already thinking about the book to talk about, this is why she isn't paying enough attention.

'Sure. Gladly.'

She opts for *War and Peace*, as Csaba would like the war aspect. The writer had fought in the war himself before becoming a writer, but something must have touched him in that pointless killing. In Csaba's view, war is never gratuitous.

'All right, go ahead,' he says yawning. She lists the main characters: 'Pierre Kirillovich, Count Bezukhov,' proudly placing the accent on the second syllable as they do in Russian.

'Is this now French or Russian? How can you remember these names anyway?'

She doesn't spend much time with the love scenes. Csaba is interested in the description of the palace. And in how they could have that much money, how they were so rich.

'They were aristocrats, with lots of land, estates, forests, and so on. The author was a member of the aristocracy, too, but then gave up his fortune. He gave everything away. He divided his wealth between the peasants and liberated the serfs.'

'Idiot,' Csaba declares. 'Total nutcase. Idiot!' he's almost shouting with anger, his ears turning redder and redder. 'How much money did he have?'

'It wasn't actual money, so it can't be quantified exactly. The aristocracy didn't have cash as such but assets, especially land and forests and this yielded a good income.'

'Land ain't worth shit,' Csaba snaps. 'Less than shit. Who wants land these days? Look at the state of it,' he points at the road.

They crossed the mountains and make it to the hills. As they are going past the edge of a village, they see a woman in a straw hat working the maize field, her chubby thighs showing under her skirt. Then there is a smaller potato patch and an older man, sat on a stool, is picking something from the stems and throwing it into the fire – perhaps potato beetles. In the distance, the grass has grown tall on the pastures, there is no sign of animals having grazed there for a long time. The land is uncultivated. To the left, there's an unkempt apple orchard, surrounded by a rusty broken fence. On the top of the hills, a herd of sheep in the shade of a large tree. Tall, slim-line haystacks.

'Nobody wants any land. They want a flat in some town and a car – trust me, this is what they want. This is what sells. Land is good for nothing. It's finished. Nobody wants to claim it back anymore.'

She has never seen land in this light before.

'Have you claimed it back by the way?'

She has no idea. They have no land to claim back.

'That's impossible,' Csaba states, 'everybody had something that they could receive compensation for.' He utters this word with the same expertise and satisfaction that he displayed when talking about alloy wheels.

'The writer has a story in which the count promises a peasant that he'd give him as much land as he can cover by walking as far as possible in the course of a single day. In short, he'd give him the land that can be marked off by way of walking for the day. You know what happens?'

'He'll get bloody rich?'

'Not at all. He dies.'

'Of all this wealth?'

'No, of greed. The peasant kept walking and running until he dropped dead.'

She goes on about the peasant as he's striving to break off the maximum amount of land, dashing around without eating or drinking from dawn to dawn, until he finally breaks down himself. Csaba keeps silent. Back then, she explains, people derived their livelihood from the land: 'This book had a huge impact on society. And it had on impact on the Revolution, too. The author experienced a conversion so to speak, became a prophet and lived like a peasant, wearing peasant clothes and leading a simple life in his castle. After his conversion, the church excommunicated him and never retracted this position.'

'Fuck the church. As far as I'm concerned. Fuck them all. I hate priests. But was he the instigator behind the communists? Is he a communist? Because if he is, stop talking about this at once. I hate communists.'

'He was on the side of the poor.'

Csaba wants to hear about the war, and she has to invent a battle as she barely remembers this part. Csaba is asking detailed questions about the battle, which confuses her, but then she lands on her feet: we can only see it from afar.

Just as they can only see the city from afar as they are descending from the mountains, their hearts pounding and details blurring into one another. She can talk about it nonetheless and about the two love stories in the book. The uglier girl ends up beautiful, though not in a situation when an insignificant girl grows up and transforms into an amazing woman, but when somebody is examining people, who are neither ugly nor beautiful, from a close-up.

'What do you know about the others?' Csaba asks as they are getting nearer.

This makes her think about Andrei Bolkonsky. It takes time until the word 'the others' rings a bell about a particular group and individual faces. Their former classmates.

'The others, well, I haven't seen anyone since I've moved abroad.'

'Me, neither. Except for the ones we are doing business with. They look down on you because you've left. Yeah. Come with us to the lake on Sunday, a few of the old gang will be there, too.'

A decade later, Csaba will move away from Sweden, though not back home. The old gang, his old gang, will reform itself.

Csaba and his business partner later discuss the next day's departure. A few others will also come with further vehicles. They go to an artificial lake, a water reservoir squeezed in-between steep slopes. Csaba and his business partner have something to attend to and will arrive later, but bring two crates of beer that they lower into the water and fix with a rope.

'We're going to set up an avalanche,' they laugh.

This business partner, already a German citizen, has imported an old car. They park it by the roadside and then roll huge rocks on top of the car. The narrow gorge is echoing with the rock-fall. In the evening, a police car arrives at the site and they take the details of the event on record.

'I bought it for two-fifty and will get at least two thousand for it back in Germany,' the business partner points out. 'But one has to be a citizen for this.'

The older policeman is shaking his head.

'The number of rockfalls around here is unbelievable.'

They take their time in preparing the report and then move on to discussing when to pick up a hard copy. Csaba starts haggling that it's too late, they have to go back abroad. He lowers his voice and bribes them with some German marks. They nod and leave without saying as much as good-bye.

'Filthy peasant,' Csaba hisses as they get into the black Mercedes he's planning to sell the next day in a nearby village. 'You couldn't bribe a German like this.'

Five cars have arrived on this trip and four will return, the broken one will be towed away the next day. They bring piles of marinated meat and several crates of beer. They set up court by the edge of the forest, in the semi-shade. The women spend time sunbathing and chatting in a low voice, while the men get louder and louder, laughing out loud. Her adult life, with exams, books and prospective conferences in Vienna don't mean anything here, no one is remotely interested in such things. This is a different way of living.

Somebody brought an inflatable boat, which is moored on the dark green surface of the water, utterly still without a single ripple in sight. She borrows the boat in the afternoon. Csaba invites her to visit him in Sweden, offering full board and lodging. 'I'll show you what proper water looks like,' he adds.

As she gets into the pale pink boat, it moves away from the shore and nearly capsizes but she manages to sit down and redress the balance. She pushes the boat away with the oars and, gaining distance from the shore, surrounded by the dark water, she feels butterflies in her stomach. She's sobering up, clearing her head after the lukewarm beer. Her mouth is dry and she drinks from the turquoise water, using her palm. It's sweet and has an unfamiliar taste but it quenches her thirst, so she keeps drinking. The racket made by the group on the shore is less audible from here. She lets go of the oars in the middle of the peaceful lake and slides down the boat, almost lying on her back and curling up, feet pulled in, to fill the available space. She's surrounded by the warm rubber, exposed to the sun. Her head and stomach are churning as she's rocking on the water before everything comes to complete stillness. She can hear a bird fly close by, huh-huh-huh, the wings of the large bird flapping slowly and steadily, unafraid of the crouched-up motionless human. This is the last full summer she spends there. A new life is about to begin.

The Pyramid Scheme

She has a new job the following summer in an employment agency: domestic helpers, cleaners, gardeners, as well as men and women able to cook are employed by this new company, in addition to carers for the elderly and the ill, and even dogwalkers. One of her classmates set up the company to deal precisely with these sorts of jobs. She handles tables and spreadsheets on a computer, places ads and sees new candidates. There aren't enough cleaners, they advertise everywhere, including the local TV station. There's plenty of cash in town, it just seems to be pouring in, people are buying homes, cars, furniture, while others are selling their assets to invest it in this scheme. Once she's finished work, she uses the office computer to write a commissioned dissertation over several evenings and weekends, immersing herself in the analysis of a favourite novel using the structuralist theory they studied, focusing on binary oppositions such as black-white, up-down, right-left, day-night, permitted-forbidden, God-Man, life-death. This dissertation will earn her enough money to pay for three months' rent; the cash will be handed over in a cardboard box: money, like all matters unable to withstand time, has lost its value, it's a light, transparent entity. She exchanges it at once into a more stable currency and stashes it away. The cash is paid out by the parents of the student about to graduate, he was a year above her at school but now doesn't want to finish his degree, 'there's no point,' he declares, since he doesn't want to be a teacher but a businessman and start a company. The parents buy the dissertation printed out in four copies and bound in fake black leather, it looks like a proper book, and she enjoys leafing through it before handing it over. The student reads it three times, and she even explains him the gist of the analysis: Smerdyakov dives down from above, into the cellar, into the depths of consciousness, from up to down below, *смерть* in Russian, death, life-death, parent-child, man-devil, woman-man, body-soul, дух, душа. In other words, body-soul-spirit, дух, душа, things are situated in contrast with each other, in opposition. Despite her efforts, the student just keeps asking about the plot. She starts summarising it, but the various threads get entangled, the important female line is left out and she spends too long on the devil's visit, so in the end advises him to just read the entry about *The Brothers Karamazov* in *A Hundred Famous Novels*.

The work with people and tables stretches over Saturdays, too. Those who have no movable or sellable assets are forced to sell themselves. On Sundays, she joins the lads, Csaba, Tomi and the others to go to the lake or to the mountains, for a barbeque. From the mountain, one can see the long compact queues of people, as they are standing in line day and night to deposit their money. The pyramid scheme has inspired freshly founded companies to bring cash from other parts of the country, with a view to take out eight times their deposit in three months. People are holding parasols above their heads in the blistering heat. They look as if they were in different weather conditions.

'People will never change. They still like queuing,' Csaba observes.

Csaba and his friends have stopped depositing any more money, they called it a day at the end of Spring because in their view, the end was nigh. It's impossible for all this to keep going with so many people. Still, their business is built on a game too, importing as many as three cars a week.

'One can sell anything at the moment,' Csaba states.

She tells them about the dissertation and that Dostoevsky can be sold as well. She hasn't earned money before, certainly not this amount and certainly not with Dostoevsky.

In May, she came to visit in the company of a journalist, it was hard, even risky, to play truant from university for five days, but she was paid a lot of money, fifty dollars a day. The Anthropology department recommended her as an interpreter, though she had never worked with an actual person through the medium of English, and the spoken language is jarring in her mouth. At the start of the journey, she feels that she has to respond immediately to everything at once, showing that she understands the question and retaining the illusion of being able to speak a foreign language. As they engage in conversation in the hired car, she realises that she can indeed speak but not converse, seeing that she barely understands the questions. Mark, the American journalist has lived in Hungary for a long time as a correspondent on the region. He talks a lot and is now interested in the pyramid scheme. He is hoping to sell this topic, though it's far from easy.

'*This region is a hard sell.*'

'This region is no longer of interest,' he explains, excusing himself as if he wasn't conveying his own opinion. 'The scheme, however, could prove to be of interest. The thing is that this region is simply getting on with it, there are no decisive turning points or threats, *you know, no dramatic events, no wars, just the slow transition. But we need stories, not slow processes, we need war, anger and rage.*'

'*Yeah, this region is a hard sell.*'

It takes time to get to grips with these words, initially they only mean something in isolation, on their own, but not put together. Right now, the topic is war, that's in focus. War is far away, she muses, but she doesn't utter this as if it wasn't appropriate to find any war faraway. War is always here, every war and anger are always here, with us, in our vicinity, after all this is what war is all about: anger, μῆνιν, *ménin*, this is the word with which the Iliad begins, she had even passed an exam on this topic in her first year. When it comes to war, there is no such thing as near and faraway, now and once upon a time, war is always in the present.

'*It is a hard sell,*' the journalist repeats, 'and we'll have to see whether we can obtain any useful material, whether we can gain access to the founder who has come up with this scheme, *this whole game.* Perhaps then we can sell this material,' Mark explains.

'What game?' she asks, somewhat unsure, asking for clarification in every other sentence.

'*Fuck you dog,*' Mark growls, as a dog crosses the road in front of them and they almost drive into it.

The conversation falters after they cross the border. There are carts on the road, and herds of cows returning from the pastures at dusk, one can barely move forward. Mark is unsure whether this is the main road.

'Is this really an international highway?'

'This is the way they usually tend to drive,' she replies. 'We always come this way,' she says.

Their goal is to take a closer look at a so-called game, a pyramid scheme that will end in impetuous, devastating rage. Things do begin or end with rage. She's just coming to terms with this. Rage is good. Rage is power. It gives you a push, propels you forward and calls you to account. '*Sing, Goddess, sing of the rage of Achilles, son of Peleus*'.[4] One should write a book about rage, seeing that plenty of books have already been written about the nature of rage. Heading towards Troy it's rage, on the way back to Ithaca it's tears. The endless tears of the returning Odysseus. He who is faraway is being lamented, he who is faraway laments. '*But the great-hearted Odysseus he found not within; for he sat weeping on the shore, as his wont had been, racking his soul with tears and groans and griefs, and he would look over the unresting sea, shedding tears.*'[5]

As for her, she's only coming home to visit, truanting from university. This is no proper homecoming.

They have four days to gain access to the big boss. It's impossible to call him on the phone to make an appointment, but it's surprisingly easy in person. At first, it's really challenging to fight their way into the office because of everyone queuing up to deposit their cash, but then Mark sends in his business card that introduces him as a correspondent. They gain instant access. A small bald man is smiling at them. She now has to interpret from two languages. Mark would like to find out how the pyramid scheme works. The man knows a little English.

'*Very simple. You go here with money, go back three months, I give you...*' at this point, he gets unsure and continues in his mother tongue, 'eight times as much ... Yes, eight times more. Eight times.'

'Trade secret,' he responds to the question how the pyramid scheme works from an economic point of view. 'You wouldn't ask big corporations in the States, would you, what their secret is and how come they are so successful?' He fixes his gaze at the much taller American man and sums it all up: 'every successful businessman has his own secret.'

Mark also asks the people in the queue what they know about this whole thing, and they reply that they don't care. They don't care as long as it works: 'See, it works. Someone's brother-in-law has just come out carrying a sports bag. Do you know what's inside? Loads of cash. One million six hundred thousand. This is enough to buy a flat. But he won't be that stupid, he'll re-join the queue, reinvest and then walk away with ten million. Get it?'

'Still, what's the secret of this business venture?' Mark insists, smiling at the founder.

'I'll tell you the secret, but you won't understand it because you can't understand our world from the other side of the ocean. The secret is that there is a man, a good man with a capital M, who wants to help the poor, our poor nation. Someone who finally helps people, not like these thieving billionaires and politicians. It's very simple: all is needed is a good man who loves his people. His country. Understand? This is the difference between the West and the East, get it?'

Mark thanks him for this, smiling. Then asks another question. This enrages the man who looks at the interpreter, asking why is he unable to understand all this when it's so clear:

'*Very good man,*' he can say this, too. '*Very good man. Simple man.* That's all. *Love country.* For us, it's not the love of money but the love of our country that matters,' he explains. 'This is the difference between an American businessman and myself. We aren't interested in money but in the happiness of all these poor people. Ask anyone, absolutely anyone who's leaving this place whether they are happy. Just ask them.'

Mark is wondering whether he can sell this story before the big collapse. '*If not, we come back to see the rage.*'

Mark is finding out about the dreams of those still queuing and those leaving with cash. The dreams include houses, city flats, new cars and kitchen furniture, trips abroad and expensive foreign treatments offering miraculous recoveries. Dreams and happy lives that will turn into reality in three, six, or nine months' time. These dreams are quite communicative, pouring out of everywhere. And soon enough they will be contagious, like rage and despair, because after the collapse of dreams and hopes, rage is the next mandatory stage. Dreams and cries hold together and accompany each other like good and evil, close and faraway, hope and hopelessness, the latter emerging in the former's wake.

In the autumn, she returns once again with Mark, by then payments have started to stall and people are increasingly concerned as they continue to queue. Eventually, this narrative, this *story* can be sold on. This time Mark brings a photographer, too. Csaba and his mates have stopped bringing in cars, everyone has got more cautious as there is less money. People are scared and keep waiting in the queue in silence. Dead calm. The antechamber of rage. There's no wind to set sail, so a girl has to be sacrificed. Iphigeneia dies, the wind arrives, and rage erupts. Battle.

She dashes back to university, which starts a whole month earlier in her new homeland. She has to find new rental accommodation. This is only the second time she's moving house. Good wind. Good year. In no time, she's even awarded a scholarship.

The course 'Russian Émigré Literature' was advertised as one of the available options in the hefty print copy of the syllabus. It was too early for her to enrol, due to linguistic, literary as well as emigration matters alike. At this stage, she's only coming to terms with deciphering the language of Protopope Avvakum, in the Paleolithic so to speak, and literature is to be found elsewhere, beyond her. And so is returning home. 'In this lesson we'll get to the bottom of it,' the exceedingly confident Professor announces, the hero of her new country, sporting a high bun. She has never met such a confident woman before, who insists on teaching students not only about departure and the three waves of forced, voluntary or desired emigration, but also the impossibility of return. According to the Professor, Russian emigre writer, Yuri Mamleev, stated that there is no such thing as a comeback. It's not clear where Mamleev said or wrote about this, because they only read a single work by him, a short story, and even this is utter torture; trying to figure out the untameable sea of Cyrillic letters, with all those drowning words and symbols, while holding on to the familiar terms on the stencilled pages, yet still relying on the information provided by the Professor about Mamleev's work and the impossible return. Mamleev turns out to be harder to read than any previous author, as if émigré writers, Nabokov included, had set up a linguistic botanical garden where they salvaged every single plant from their old country.

The Professor teaches her class with such enthusiasm, as if she had just escaped captivity and was finally in a position to speak openly on Russian émigré literature, without any constraints and opposition. Because she can now teach what she wants. Freedom has been ushered in. Everything is permitted, finally everything is allowed, just like in a misunderstood Dostoevsky novel. She teaches what she wants and what she can. As for the country from where these writers had left, fled or been sent away in three major waves, they are taught about the first wave of white emigration after the foundation of the new Soviet homeland, the second wave after the Great War, and finally the third wave in the final two decades of the empire, involving constraint and forced emigration.

What they aren't discussing in class – and what's not yet visible in the two-way street of time – is that the fourth wave is also on its way.

It is possible to leave but not to return. Because, Mamleev argues, or rather the passionate and over-excited Professor on his behalf, only those who have failed elsewhere are likely to return, those who have been a flop in their new country and new world. Those for whom the new world didn't work out, who couldn't fulfil their ambitions, *реализовать себя*, for whom things didn't go to plan. People who weren't accepted or who didn't accept anything from their new world, which isn't even worthy of the name 'second home' or 'new home' and is merely an empty space and a soulless transitory land. Mamleev argues, and so does the Professor, that those who come back are the ones who weren't any good and who have basically left in vain in the first place.

This statement by Mamleev, also reinforced by the confident Professor and acting as a triad of knowledge, faith and prophecy, is factual, precise and unquestionable. Like a heavy meteor, it smashes the floor of the literature department, on the fourth floor of the humanities building, during a 'Russian Émigré Literature' class. Meaning that only those who failed the exam come back, those who failed in the New World. 'There's no return,' Jurij Mamlejev states icily, voiced by the Professor.

Still, in what literary genre does he say all this? By means of which words? In a novel, interview, in a drunken conversation with friends? According to Mamleev's memoirs, even drunkenness has changed: what in the past used to be mysterious and euphoric about drinking lost its secrecy and turned into the mere material victory of alcohol over the body. 'There is no return, therefore, only failure can return,' a Russian writer claims on a dramatic tone devoid of nuances.

Failure returns home.

The sentence is a black hole, and pulls in everyone who dares to get close to it.

Despite the Professor's prediction, uttered in the shadow of the recently and triumphantly collapsed imperial walls, Yuri Vitalyevich Mamleev did actually return home. He waited for a while, so the heavy stones that used to support the walls could be removed and the wounded and castaway could climb out from under the ruins, and then went to visit Moscow to have a look around, getting re-acquainted with the new-old city he had left twenty years earlier and was now encountering amidst transformations within the new-found explosion of the material world. He did return home after this, and even penned his memoirs, nearly three decades after the collapse, memoirs end up being purchased by the one-time student, by this point past her own mid-life, venturing both into the jungle of emigration and literature, and shielded against other people's disastrous foreign sentences. Taking a deep breath, she delves into the five hundred pages of the book, even though her Russian has become too cumbersome for a pleasant read. She starts reading the book because there must be enough knowledge under the Russian linguistic rubble to find that sentence about the impossible return. In fact, what did Mamleev actually say about return?

Besides, there is also a contradiction to resolve: if returning is such an impossible task, how come that Yuri Vitalyevich chose it nonetheless?

Flicking through the book, she reads about the forest engineer of Mamleev's early years; the writer did return, therefore, he failed, as any writer who emigrates fails, because they commit linguistic suicide. 'Above all a Russian soul,' the Professor adds, layering one rock-hard sentence above another, 'a Russian émigré writer can only be a failure, as the case of Nabokov, the extremist Limonov, or the various Russian-speaking voices in Berlin, Paris, America and Switzerland illustrate. They all had to arrive into another language.'

As for her, she won't swap languages, only homes. Linguistic suicide for others doesn't amount to more than a cat's scratch.

A tom-cat is an important character in Mamleev's departure, too. The cat was left behind by a friend who had to leave very suddenly, and it was down to the emigrating writer to take the cat with him and deliver it to the friend. At the time of departure, however, the cat had vanished and Mamleev nearly missed the Moscow-Vienna train. At the very last minute though, the cat emerged from a wardrobe most officiously – *важно* – and finally made it to America.

Upon arrival in the USA, Mamleev headed to a university post, like so many other Russian writers and poets: teaching Russian language and literature at Cornell, despite his degree in forest engineering. In the days of the Professor's lectures, this sort of thing may not have seemed quite so shocking to her as later, when she was leafing through these memoirs with her own life experience and enough failures behind her to realize the unimaginable generosity of this appointment. These new arrivals are not being scrutinised on the back of their diplomas and qualities but feel welcome on the basis of their self-value: Brodsky didn't even have a university degree. Who else should know about Russian literature if not Russian writers?

Still, in ten years' time Mamleev leaves the US and moves to Paris, where he spends the 1980s.

He writes the following about this return: 'The West has always remained a mystery for us' and uses this expression to describe emigration: *оказаться без социума*.[6] We were left without a habitat, without *a sotsium*. What does language compress into this cold foreign word that it has never been able to engage with and assimilate? Habitat, spiritual as well as human environment.

We were left without a habitat.

Mamleev, who at the time of the Professor's classes hadn't yet returned to his homeland, but was possibly thinking about it without making use of the medium of language, not yet knowing the new words because underneath the new language and new notions there was something old billowing at the core, perhaps *русская тоска*,[7] the Russian longing for home, a longing to get away, perhaps melancholy or nostalgia? Could this be the ultimate failure that will eventually send him away and make him drift home?

During her university years, she doesn't relish coming to her journey's end, she favours being constantly on the move instead, avoiding arriving at destinations too soon. She finally makes it home over the summer, thanks to the respite offered by a generous holiday. Her faraway life does come up in the course of rare conversations back home, and she is expected to present this under the hallmark of success, keeping silent about the exams she didn't pass, the unsuccessful college applications, the scholarships and jobs she failed to obtain, the messy relationships. All along, Mamleev's phrase echoes within her, even if she's unable to verify its reliability. The writer returns home, and dedicates the last two, deeply religious, decades of his life to 'Russian thought' and the 'eternal Russia'.

She hastily enrols on an optional course, then keeps dithering and deferring the exam, which constitutes yet another minor flop. She just continues to defer and dip into these astonishing writers, the pornographic Limonov, the amusing Dovlatov and others, though she does manage to come up with a seminar presentation that is deemed interesting. That mysterious Mamleev sentence conveyed by the Professor, which she wasn't ever able to locate, even in his autobiography, will continue to haunt her for two decades. This is something she can neither refute nor confirm, however, she no longer needs an explanation for the claim about the loss of habitat. Mamleev argues that with a French or American one cannot establish the same emotional connection one naturally has with one's compatriots, with whom one can simply chat over a drink in one's mother tongue, sitting around and covering anything from parents to books to God and the nature of evil, well into the small hours.

She now comprehends that the old habitat has crumbled away, including the town itself, together with its people, the trees, the hills, the river, the classmates and fellow choir members, the youth, the firepits, the two sycamore trees by the entrance of the park, the neighbours, not to mention the shared hobbies and passions.

The excruciating imperative of the impossible return is hesitantly fading away. She has waded through the small print of

Mamleev's memoir, unable to find the sentence about the impossible return. Regardless of what Mamleev thought or wrote about this, he did return. Whether it was possible or not.

Mamleev departed from this maritime country from the very place where our protagonist eventually ended up thanks to a much-coveted scholarship.

The windows overlook an infinite whitish-grey square. Can one possibly see as far as the Spitzbergen or Greenland or the North Sea on a clear day? Shame that she's unfamiliar with the map, she'd then know what could be found on the other side if a strong wind were to sweep away the heavy smog smothering the city and reveal the horizon. She has absolutely no idea of the latitude, as she neglected to check it, despite her sincere desire to come here. For her, this Northern city is not a reality in latitudinal space, but a notion, the disembodied setting of books and desires. She doesn't want to travel the world on a map but in her own body. Now that she has arrived, it's rather late to find out where she really is, besides, she couldn't ask anyway because the word latitude is beyond her barely intermediate linguistic knowledge. She simply wanted to go to the city where that particular Gogolian nose can appear on a boulevard. Could it be that the edge of the world is already visible from here?

When she looks out of the window, she can only see something greyish-white, the square devoid of sunshine and shades of colour, cars driving along streets as wide as avenues, and slushy, salty snow being splattered along the pavement so passers-by have to keep close to the buildings.

The college is a hundred metres from the Gulf of Finland, and from the eighth floor one has a direct view of the gulf. One can't tell where the land ends and the sea begins. As far as the eye can see, the sea is covered by a white field of snow, leading towards the endless whiteness, the sun positioned fairly low on the sky, invisible. This snow has fallen before the students' arrival, then froze and turned grey, the first snow fell as early as October, the friendly *дежурная*[8] informs them, keeping an eye on order at the college from behind a small desk. This October snow was later followed by new layers, which quickly became sullied. The surface of the snow is crumbly, forming a thin crust as the group is about to leave the beaten path. Can they be above the sea level already? They wonder, because the water has no edge, no shore. The surface of the snow is getting cleaner and cleaner as they move forward and the greyness of the city is soon left behind. The path suddenly vanishes and the field of snow opens up in front of their eyes. A car appears from the right, leaving dark smoke in its wake. In this whiteness, this is an offensive sight. They are heading towards the sea and the college building is gradually shrinking in the distance behind them. They are approaching a fisherman, sat on a stool by his car. Next to him, on another stool, a woman wrapped in a large woollen scarf is knitting socks wearing mittens. It would be great to check what's in the plastic buckets. Or peek into the ice-hole. The woman has spotted them from afar, way before they make it to the buckets to peek in.

'*А можно посмотреть*?'[9] she asks awkwardly, as usual when speaking this language, hoping to seek permission to peek in.

There's no need to say hello, it's not customary when not initiating a longer conversation. They have already been here for weeks, a whole month into the six-month course. Every so often, they approach people because this is acceptable, this is a country where people are talkative and like to chat, complain and lecture one another. It does happen at times that somebody rudely ignores them, as if they didn't hear a word. Their group of visiting students retain the appearance of foreigners; always asking questions or needing clarification, trying to tame this foreignness they had been craving for so long. The bascule bridges that lift up towards the sky, the row of two-storey palaces along the waterfront and the canals, that typical Russian smell in tube stations and gateways, the place where theatre tickets can be obtained, known as *лавка*[10] and stubbornly called 'lavka' by their group even after being here for month: little shop, little booth, everything equipped with a diminutive.

'*Можно*,'[11] the woman replies confidently, perhaps proudly or even arrogantly, and just carries on knitting. She uses a tone they can't decipher for months. 'You may,' she says, 'you can take a look,' though the invitation 'to go ahead' is not extended, although it is indeed possible, after all this was the question. If anything, her tone conveys a hint of doubt. Their question, '*А можно посмотреть?*' instantly reveals their foreignness, perhaps the phrasing is awkward, somebody local wouldn't ask such a thing, they wouldn't ask anything at all, a true native of Saint Petersburg, who has grown up with people fishing out of ice holes in the Gulf of Finland, perhaps whose grandfather was also a fisherman, can instantly tell the difference between the various kinds of salmon.

In the meantime, they realised that the most interesting thing wasn't the content of these plastic buckets, the various kinds of fish, sea creatures or crabs emerging from under the icy water. It was the ice hole itself. What is such a hole like? A fishing hole. One should start a conversation about this, about the ice hole itself, if only they knew its name, she tries *дыра* meaning hole, or perhaps with a diminutive, applying it two-fold *дырка, дырочка*. A conversation about how deep, how thick or how one produces such a hole is entirely hopeless, language simply doesn't obey its speakers and they falter at the very first word.

They stare at the ice hole.

'*А вот это?*'[12] she tries to ask again, pointing at the hole.

The man doesn't even look up and just carries on fishing, dead still as before. They keep pointing downwards while asking questions, as if they had always talked like this, without nouns and verbs, as if this language had always been in their trouser pockets but they were too lazy to produce it, so they just keep pointing and hinting at things. They don't want to get entangled in these cumbersome sentences with endless consonant collisions that are impossible to pronounce, and with which neither their language, nor her tongue or their tongue, this stiff piece of tree-trunk-like flesh in their mouth, seems to be able to comply. When they do end up saying something, most people think they are Estonian.

To conceal this, the foreign speaker tries to sound as if she was talking with great ease, as if it was effortless for her to ask what that thing over there was:

'That there. That thing. What is it?'

'Что?'[13] the woman asks them to specify, in a bored voice.

As if she knew what the question meant but didn't want to help, let them ask properly, she instructs, teaches, educates, corrects: a Russian always teaches, every sentence must have a mission of its own, especially for the older generation. If you want to know something, you must ask properly, in the meantime, she waits for you to get your act together and behave like a proper foreigner, seeing that she can tell you are from abroad, so she asks the question on your behalf, this time phrased properly, because then it can be answered, so let's take a look at that properly put question. When it does happen, the dialogue inches forward, slowly but surely, at the pace different continents move closer and closer to one another.

'Вы про что?'[14] she asks.

So, what is it that they want to find out about, and they point at the black hole, the *дыра*, though it's probably not that, just a smaller version of it at the very best. A hole in the sea.

In response she utters the relevant word, as if she didn't want to withhold it from them, there, she displays it in front of them, after all, they own this word, rich country that this is, and they don't begrudge their visitors in this way. No, they don't withhold such information, they are always teaching and the relevant word has just been served up.

'Прорубь.'[15]

She articulates the word for ice hole really slowly, staring ahead, with an intonation that suggests action. They would have never come up with this, since they hadn't heard this word anywhere, in their reality there was no ice hole and no sea. What's the point of an ice hole if there is no sea anyway?

The surface of the sea is rock hard: cars, lorries, buses are driving on it, everybody is travelling on water in the Gulf of Finland. In conclusion to their conversation, they are asked where they come from. 'The Baltics? Are they Estonian?' 'No, not quite, but we are from the colonies,' Ari, one of the classmates replies, with a silly laugh. *'Колония?* What colonies do we have?', the woman objects indignantly. What are they doing here, they explain using the correct jargon – *стажировка*[16] – they are students of literature, to which the woman replies, 'literature is the classics, Pushkin, Tolstoy, Turgenyev.' The fisherman's wife is a literary expert, too, and when it comes to literature, she is talking classics. When they utter Nabokov's name, the woman casts a resentful glance, why bother with Nabokov when we have the likes of Pushkin, Tolstoy and Turgenyev. Dostoyevski isn't mentioned though.

'*Причем тут Набоков?*'[17] she asks, as if they had offended her culture.

Her question about why should we need Nabokov impossible to answer, because there are no persuasive words that come quick to mind and can be uttered correctly and convincingly to argue that he is a good and important writer. She doesn't even try to search for words, because there are no arguments, either, as to why Nabokov. Perhaps she should list his novels written in Russian. Whoever writes in Russian, is a Russian writer. Isn't that so? 'Brodsky,' Ari adds proudly. 'Бродский,' the woman onerously repeats the writer's name.

'*I haven't ready any Brodsky.*'

Genitivus negationis. Negation + living being = genitive case.

'*Эмигранты такие,*'[18] kind of emigrants.'

The woman doesn't seem to complete her sentence. Or perhaps this is a completed sentence, she muses. The woman may be un-impressed with these foreign students who are focusing on these émigrés who abandoned their country instead of studying the great nineteenth century writers.

'*Надо читать Пушкина,*'[19] she adds dryly, and starts reciting Pushkin: '*I write to you … when that is said / What more is left for me to say? / Now you are free (I know too well) / To heap contempt upon my head.*'[20] 'This is what I call a poet.'

They stare into the ice hole, filled with an inch and a half of water. *Prorubi*, she keeps repeating to herself, departing from the verb prorubity, perhaps there isn't such a verb at all, or perhaps there is, why shouldn't there be, there is rubity, meaning to break, to break through. They stare down the ice hole, it's a small dark hole filled with water, not looking dangerous in the least. Dark hole. A single step, and one could disappear in it, without the possibility of return. Perhaps there is just enough space for someone really skinny to slip through if one isn't wearing much. What happens to the hole once these people leave anyway?

The icecap is endless. One could even walk all the way to Helsinki.

The water in the ice hole looks still and of an oily black hue, like some thick resistant matter. One can't figure out the thickness of the ice layer because the ice hole is filled with water. So she can't tell how thick the ice is on which she stands, but she's too tired to ask further questions and doesn't want to learn any more new things. Where she comes from, there's never such a thick icecap on the water.

Next time, she'll check this word in the dictionary, in the copy of Fasmer's etymological dictionary that she purchased during this trip. This will be her main acquisition despite the high price for the four volumes. In it, the word ice hole (*прорубь*) comes right after prophet (*пророк*). What's the prophet got to do with the ice hole? Consulting the dictionary, she finds synonyms for 'ice hole': iordany, spelt *иордань*. It's a cross-shaped hole on the ice, used for baptism. It was perhaps named after the Jordan River. The scene of inexplorable customs and rituals.

This highly praised etymological dictionary was written by Max Julius Friedrich Fasmer, named on the cover as М. Фасмер, known as Максимилиан Романович Фасмер. A German-Russian man with a stern look, high forehead, attractive elongated face and fine Germanic features. He was born in this city capable of producing such thick icecaps that only start being dangerous to walk on towards the end of March. The famous Slavonic expert writes his masterpiece, the four-volume etymological dictionary, in exile, after leaving Russia in the first wave of emigration in 1921. His next monumental work is the dictionary of rivers and other so-called hydronyms, in five volumes. The Venice of the North gives birth to the author of the hydronym-dictionary, as if the place attached itself to the person who left it behind, or the person who left, took the place with himself, at least at the level of language.

The topic of her dissertation and the aim of her scholarship to Russia was to examine the work of a Russian writer, both in Russian and English.

At that point she was still unable to grasp that the two, Владимир Владимирович and Vladimir Vladimirovich, were not one but two very different writers, one Russian and the other American, with the Russian having barely written anything while living in Russia apart from a volume of poetry published independently. To use the Saint Petersburg accent characterised by the dz sound, Vladzimir Vladzimirovich is the protagonist of her future dissertation. As the visiting students find out as soon as they arrive, whoever doesn't pronounce this dz correctly is clearly not a native of Petersburg. At first, getting this Vladzimir right seemed dead easy for them, they have a dz sound, too, but that's entirely different, so much so that nobody who had heard them utter as much as a single word or a single iteration of Vladzimir would think for a moment that they were from Petersburg.

Instead, they were generally asked whether they were from the Baltics. Perhaps Estonians? In response to this, Ari would generally stick to the joke about the colonies, which would invariably lead to confusion, as it stated that their Russian was so good because they came from the colonies. This wasn't true in the least. They could barely speak any Russian. The joke, by the way, was wasted on the target audience, and even if they did get it, they wouldn't have appreciated it. They must be from the Baltics, people surmised, because it is the Estonians who tend to have such broad - rather childish - accents. Strangely enough, the possibility of hailing from *Zakarpatskaia* oblast had never come up, what's beyond the Carpathians is ungraspable, from up there in the North, those Carpathians in the South are invisible and utterly unknown. In the South, in the Ukraine, that is *на Украине*, why do they use preposition *на* and not *в* is hard to fathom, however, as their strict language teacher insisted, one's job isn't to solve a riddle but to memorise a phrase.

Pribaltika was easy to figure out, even over a beer, compared to which Zakarpatskaia oblast is really grim. Nobody was reluctant to ask from which corner of the empire they had arrived to this major city, depicted by the likes of Pushkin, Gogol, Dostoyevsky and Andrei Bely, even Akhmatova, there's no shame in asking where you're from. One doesn't have to pretend that coming from somewhere else is shameful or awkward, as it doesn't concern anyone, let alone a local, a native of Petersburg, a true Russian, who can rightly take pride in being so important that they get these random visitors from all corners of this endless empire.

Владимир Владимирович is not a foreigner in this city but a native, while the same person known as Vladimir Vladimirovich is an American from the shores of Lake Geneva in Switzerland. How can Vladimir Vladimirovich, a foreigner, an author working in a foreign language, not even a proper writer, be the topic of her dissertation? Владимир Владимирович, on the other hand, does visit her at night, wearing a silk dressing gown and soft leather slippers, and invites her for a walk along the river, which is not so much a river but a canal or an embankment. They may even walk past the area where little Владимир used to live with his parents as a child, they may stroll past the palace, but this isn't important, the past isn't important, the home that he left behind, that childhood paradise depicted so often over a long life isn't important, because much more important paradises have been lost than this small palace, this provincial mansion with white pillars, this is irrelevant, this is just a walk while being dressed in a silk dressing gown and soft slippers, in the silent and not yet white night. As for Владимир Владимирович, he is a writer not an author as the Americans tend to say, meaning he is a *писатель* (writer) and not a *автор* (author), a writer, poet, translator, teacher, lepidopterologist and entomologist, a proper butterfly expert, creator of chess puzzles, and lastly a scholar of literature, in other words he has license to create new words, albeit in the dreams of other people.

Взаимносведение, he encourages the shy student, who is writing her dissertation in this famous city, or rather not writing it while they are taking a walk along the embankment. Mutual notification, excuse, news report, mutual news or rumour, she tries to unpack the above word heard from Владимир, who notifies her of himself in this way in a dream, in his silk print dressing gown and soft slippers, even though they only overlap for a few years, Владимир dies in 1977 and this student of Russian literature visits Petersburg twenty years later. This city is apparently a place of dead souls and where the student travels to write a dissertation about one of Владимир's works, but in the meantime, she forgets about it or just doesn't write anything, she doesn't read or research or show any interest or inclination that would keep her focused on the task of writing. In this dream, however, it becomes clear that Владимир Владимирович is in need of this student's dissertation even though the latter's Russian is rather limited for a work of literary ambition. At first, she came up with a serious, well-focused and entirely researchable topic but then all got entangled and vague in the course of the fragmented time and missed classes, because she started to have doubts about a foreign student with a modest knowledge of Russian writing a dissertation on the poetics of naming in one of Владимир's Russian language masterpieces.

Even though Владимир Владимирович had publicly declared, promised and stated in his volume of interviews entitled *Strong Opinions* that he'd never return to Russia and this promise was indeed observed by his living body, he was still able to return in the dreams of others, seeing that this couldn't be forbidden by anyone.

He himself, in his increasingly heavier bodily manifestation, would keep his word and never return. In his dreams and literary works, however, he'd keep returning over and over again, in other words, it was only his body that didn't return, while the works did go back. He'd been carefully guarding and visiting his own paradise, which he was the gatekeeper of, along the embankment and Bolshaya Morskaya in Saint Petersburg there are the imprints of his childhood and youth, from butterfly catching to the French governess, the deep humming gardens and the family mansion on the large estate in Rozhdestveno. In Montreux, one can only find his grave and a statue depicting him in travel clothes, as if he was someone who saw life as an excursion, catching butterflies in the Alps. VV had lived his entire life in hotels, for sixty years or so he had never set up home, he didn't buy property or a house, because there's no such thing as home, home in his view being the one and only Russia.

On a mellow Saint Petersburg night, along the Naberezhnaya, Владимир Владимирович transmits his clear and kind-hearted message compressed into a single unknown word, perhaps coined by himself, this suggests that writers do have messages to transmit, he puts an arm around the student, as he's still much taller despite his old age and wearing only slippers, and urges her to finish that dissertation, in Russian no less, and if the foreignness of the Cyrillic letters is getting unbearable, she should just pop to the Publichka, the city library, where one can find books in any language, some in one's mother tongue. After all, she didn't come all the way here to pass out drunk on the shores of Lake Ladoga or play chess with Israeli students into the small hours.

Владимир Владимирович in the flesh is totally alive, soft and kind as he appears on the banks of the Fontanka River: '*For the last time, we met, / On the embankment, as ever*',[21] because the poet, this time Akhmatova, claims nothing less than that they'd always meet along the canals or places other than Saint Petersburg. *Взаимосведение*[22] – he compressed the aim of his visit into a single unknown word, perhaps coined by the dreamer and imagined into the mouth of the person being dreamt about, the second half of the scholarship period is on the horizon and the countdown has begun, time is running out and there's no trace of the dissertation yet, however, she has managed to get disgracefully drunk on the shores of Lake Ladoga, so it's now time to get her act together and get cracking at what she has come here to do. If it's about naming then it should be about naming and that's that, it's all the same to him after twenty years of being dead.

The writer compresses his message into a single word and states that it's all the same what the impact and reception of this short dissertation by a foreign student will be and how many people will read it. This is his sole advice and the gist of his message: never take such things into account. He knows that his 1966 work *Polyommatus icarus*, on the evolution of the common butterfly, hadn't been acknowledged by the scientific world up until his death in 1977, not even until this dream-based meeting at the time of the Saint Petersburg scholarship, nobody takes him seriously as an entomologist and it will take until 2011 for the *Proceedings of the Royal Society of London* to rectify this, when the heroes from the dream will be written about by their author. In 2011, ten co-authors publish a scientific work, imagine – ten authors, which also means that ten authors have to agree on a conclusion according to which his hypothesis from fifty years ago, namely that the blue common butterfly spread to the New World from Asia, was not a dream or fantasy but science. All this achieves the status of certainty at a time when he, Владимир has been dead for ages, whereas the student, should she be still alive, has long given up on Nabokov, the study of literature and the poetics of naming and is focusing solely on her own language.

The point is that time doesn't have a hold on us. One simply shouldn't be afraid to write a dissertation, only stop whining and drinking.

It's strange, even weird and totally unpredictable that there is a return. This seemingly firm and self-sufficient man, who according to biographies and carefully fact-checked interviews was trying to conceal his timidity, and who appears as a kind-hearted figure in slippers in the dream, utters the only thing that is in our power or is, rather, our only power: the validation of one another. The dissertation and the suggestion validate each other, why don't you go to the Publichka to borrow a book in your language if you miss it so much and can't handle the burden of foreignness with all these Cyrillics? One's mother tongue is always within reach. Always. But this wasn't the purpose of the present trip, was it?

'It looks as though you were fishing for triggers. Okay, I'll write at some point,' Ari replied hastily when she contacted her requesting a chat, because she agreed to give this talk and write this speech, but hasn't seen her classmates for thirty years. If she could get back in touch with Ari, she might just about be able to come up with something.

'Where are you exactly? Which country?' she asked at the end of the third line, because Ari's personal page indicated only an unidentifiable location in a geographically and linguistically fluid transcontinental context, albeit chosen for an enthusiasm for the quirkiness of the name itself. It didn't look like a real place. Just as the category social status was also described in inscrutable and confusing terms. Regarding status, they have both gone back on their promise: during a walk at dawn when they were still students, they vowed that they wouldn't start a family or have children. *Мы выше любви!*,[23] Ari cited Chekhov with an above-average Russian accent in the former Russian capital a good two decades earlier: 'We are above love!',[24] pausing after the *мы*. One could feel a gentle breeze and that complex, uplifting, forward-leaning and mysterious ы sound formed at the back of the mouth cavity. With the confidence of someone who perfectly understands and forms the sounds of togetherness. Like someone whose goal in life is to be able to acquire and pronounce every single sound spoken on this mud globe, from tongue-clicking to smacking, like someone who's preparing to travel the world and find oneself at home absolutely everywhere.

'I'm contacting you in my capacity as a future speech writer,' she began her letter addressed to Ari in a roundabout way, she might have even added some emojis had she been able to find some that were 'serious' enough but this wasn't possible, since 'serious' doesn't have a face. As it happens, with Ari there's no need for explanations. Over the last thirty years, they continued to be there for each other, at first quite regularly, then less often, and in the end, only exceptionally, always retaining a degree of spontaneous curiosity as if they were only at arm's length. Their student years, Kokkorevo and Piter, that is Petersburg, Saint Petersburg and eventually their kiss, led to an indissoluble contract between them.

'As though I was always fishing for triggers,' she kept repeating Ari's offensive response, perhaps she could even write it down and start her shockingly honest speech with this. She utters these two attributes in Ari's harshly mocking voice. 'I agreed to this speech because I'm always fishing for triggers,' she could start with this and their teacher and everyone else, except perhaps for Ágó, wouldn't understand, and instead of some elevated talk they'd only hear the foreignness because the word trigger in itself is proof of failure, alienation, elimination as well as an announcement of the end from the opening gambit onwards. Proof of the fact that language has ceased to exist in the mouth, using instead other people's borrowed language, which for them is at most a hired hut, a cheap bread and breakfast, a rental room but never a proper home. Triggers. Ari has perhaps wanted to suggest that this trigger is a means to hang on to the past. 'What are those triggers?' Ari has read her books but would always compliment some minor details, such as the light reflected on a character's black toe-caps or someone balancing some bags full of eggs. All the rest is nostalgia.

In the first ten years, she wanted to impress Ari with her books. She managed to hand over the first publication in person, then sent her the second one, albeit not as a print copy, but has given up on the rest.

Ari started two years later in the same literature department at university, but they both proceeded with equal hesitation and slowness towards graduation, deferring countless exams, failing at linguistics and with endless shared nights spent together under the pretext of study and deep dives leading to brisk walks at dawn. '*Let's take a deep dive*,' Ari would say, oozing confidence when learning about American linguistic connections. When they finally managed to graduate in one subject out of the four they had attended sporadically, they left with three hefty volumes of lecture notes each. On most pages, there was a note of the names of the subjects they had started to study but never actually finished.

Like most cynics, Ari was extremely attractive in their student days. It wasn't just her tiny bird face, sharp gaze and narrow eyes, but her always rough and dangerous sentences, her arrogant tone, worn-out shoes and borrowed coat. There was something provocative and generous in her, something devoid of sentimentality and ambition, the menace of unadulterated truth. Ari would write taut poems in the Russian acmeist manner or the Futurists' favourite zaum style, without any ambition for publication. 'We are above publication,' she insisted alluding at Chekhov, and it's hard to say whether she meant this and looked down on the 'local papers' and cliques, or was hinting at the impossibility of approaching a significant literary magazine coming from nowhere, as an unknown entity, a distant nobody, with the hope of being published. When it came to literature, she was most interested in inconsistencies and this infuriated many professors. In a lesson, she kept elaborating on how Pierre Bezuhhov is short and fat until he wins Natasha's hand, following which he turns into a tall and respectable man.

This is love, she would have said to her cautiously, if someone were in love with you, they wouldn't be concerned with your almond jackdaw eyes and sharp gaze but see themselves in your narrowed gaze as your chosen one. Ari would basically live at a different address each week, a different friend, acquaintance or lover. At her student hall base she only kept her modest belongings. She wasn't too bothered with tooth brushing, either, if suddenly finding herself in a new place in the morning. Ari had often spent the night at hers, too, in that hard-to-afford rental room in a distant borough. When one morning she bought her a toothbrush to accompany the morning croissant, she was taken by genuine surprise: 'You don't want to snog me, do you?'

Eventually, when Ari ends up on a tiny Scottish island with her IT specialist husband, who is able to live anywhere in the world, she declares that this attachment and clinging to places was something she had never understood, 'this is only in you', she writes in a letter, she doesn't call any place home, and was two when they had moved from village to town and then to another town, when her father was transferred to another job. But this isn't all there is to it. When our protagonist contacted her regarding the speech, Ari was waiting for her third citizenship and didn't specify whether she'd attend the class meeting, perhaps she'd have to stay permanently in the country now, following the exit. '*What?*' the originator of the message asked, because they had switched to a faster mode of communication, writing in tiny message boxes, 'What exit?' Oh, I see, she suddenly realised. Following a detour in Singapore, Ari was now living in the fifth country, 'we'll stay here until the end of Year 8', she said, sounding like a serious mother who makes responsible plans, 'I am doing counselling, mediating between the state and *people with very different backgrounds.*' For this, she's traveling from their Scottish island to a nearby town two or three times a week.

'I'm no longer writing', Ari pointed out in a longer, hard to read message box, it doesn't make any sense to write for three people. The question didn't in the least refer to writing. Looking at Ari's friends on social media, it would seem that about three people would understand if she were to write in her mother tongue. She barely has fifty friends, so perhaps she doesn't really use this platform which charts a world from Singapore to Dublin, impossible to grasp and get a sense of. Ari rarely posts, and if she does, then it's usually some drawings by her children or herself, most recently she posted a series of screams – five ageless and genderless faces screaming. Teeth, tongue, veil of the palate in the wind, long wrinkles on the faces, all drawn in biro. Onc of the drawings is on a thick restaurant napkin, from a Punjabi Restaurant. Other times, she posts photos or films, without any captions. Ari couldn't even manage to round up fifty readers, the linguistic space has fallen apart around her. 'I don't give a fuck about my mother tongue, I don't give a fuck about my mother, one has to transcend language,' she says. 'Language is prison, captivity. What's only available in one's mother tongue is nothing but failure.' Ari is no longer dreaming about books.

She wouldn't write for three readers, either, she replies curtly. Fifty readers – this was the benchmark in their student days. There's no need for more. The fifty people who bought that first collection of poetry. A group of attentive readers who could fill up a small space. One writes for those fifty readers, into whose gaze they stare to suss out their interest in literature, in funny-shaped poetry and fiction with a tar-like density presented in the shape of slimline paperbacks. Fifty genuine readers. The rest is failure, she thought. Slimline volumes, dense texture, no chaff, no narrative representation of the soul. Only the monograms of existence.

She sent the book to Ari by air mail, when the latter was stationed in the North with a *work and travel* programme. It was in Kokkorevo that they pledged to send each other their very first books. Yes to books, no to marriage! After university they both went their own separate ways and she had less and less faith in Ari, but still wanted to please her and gain her respect. Ari had predicted that she'd go far in life, 'far, based on your own definition of the term, and you won't give a fuck about anyone'. By the time she got to her third book, she no longer felt like sending it to Ari, this was the one with the betrayal, their mutual betrayal: including a narrative, psychology (and written for one's mother, which they had promised never to do). It was a long book with many readers, which for Ari was the epitome of failure itself. When she finally reaches out to Ari again, they barely know anything about each other. She's avoiding unnecessary digs.

They visited Kokkorevo, a village with a hundred and fifteen – as it turns out revenant – inhabitants on the shores of Lake Ladoga, without knowing what to expect. This was during that long scholarship in Russia, when Ari decided to minor in Russian on a whim, more out of spite and to annoy her family, not having any plans to use the language. It was a barely noticeable and impossible location from a touristic point of view, chosen straight off the map. It was April, and the stiff dirty snow was still covering everything in the dim grey light. They didn't have the courage to venture onto the lake itself, as no one else was doing that. The wind had iced the waves into dark crests, protruding menacingly above the surface of the water. They simply didn't dare to set foot on it.

'As far as I'm concerned, we can try. But I can't walk on water,' Ari warns. 'You want to be a prophet, the Light of the World.'

They stroll around the lake, in the endless, colourless space. She announces proudly that she'd choose an entirely different form of suicide, not drowning in icy water, in a *prorubi*, to make use of a newly acquired term. In the local shop reminiscent of the Soviet days, in the absence of vodka and not even having tried to ask for cognac, they buy some sticky sweet *портвейн* after chatting to two persuasive dead souls. It bears no resemblance to the real port wine they taste a decade later. 'Scent of Orchards' is strong and sickly sweet, and it's sold in half litre brown bottles like oil and vinegar used to be marketed in her childhood. The wind on the shores of Lake Ladoga is blowing in all directions and, while sitting on a bench, they drink the whole bottle of so-called port together with three hundred grams of *Doktorskaya kolbasa*, a Bologna-style sausage, and some dark bread. They gulp down the drink as if they were in a rush, despite being only halfway through the scholarship, in the middle of their third year. Three months have passed and another three are still ahead of them, but at this point, time seems to be frozen still and is passing at a deplorably slow pace, regardless of the Armenian cognac they easily manage to lay hands on day in, day out.

На Ладожское озеро, they are sitting by Lake Ladoga wearing jeans, because in June a proper summer suddenly announces itself. They have made it to the very city she has been preparing to visit for two years, but after three months these foreign letters that find it easier and easier to mould into sentences and words when reading or listening, right now, under the port's swift and suddenly intense impact that paralyses their feet, have now revealed their infinite foreignness and impossibility to grasp. They have revealed the failure because the Master's language, these soaring, Greek-looking letters, these soft unpredictable symbols that have once seemed so fascinating, such as Ж Щ Д Ф Ц Ъ Ь Э Я Ю Ы, will never be her letters of fire, *Buchstaben von Feuer*, as the Master puts it, they will always retain their foreignness.

These letters will never become her own. MAMA is the only example we say and write the same way, this is the sole common ground and shared word, here even the Persian students call their mothers *maman*, she tells Ari as they are going Dutch on the second bottle of port. Ari can hold her drink much better. Perhaps cynics can hold their drink better, because their cruel life is deployed in the light of telling the truth.

Oh, dear mama, *МАМОЧКА*, please can someone take me home, she's whining, head bent down and sliding under the bench. This port sheds light on everything, the unbearable alcohol-fuelled truth and above all, one's mother. This is the reason why her father was also a regular drinker, to gain this light and shine, to gain this unbearable sense of truth: but this much? And always? Because he liked this much to illuminate truth? Which truth, once seen, he had to die of?

Not to mention the Old Russian abbreviations on religious icons, such as свет, how could the words for world and holy be the same, perhaps they are derived from the same root – light – she elaborates on this celestial correlation to Ari, these three words, world, light and holiness, come from the same source, *свет свет свят*,[25] she'll double check this in the Fasmer dictionary because she has now finally understood. In Ari's view, the inner frame of words is utter bullshit, laughable, 'there are no inner frames,' she adds sternly yet almost soberly, while she keeps insisting that there is, people had gotten to the core of the matter once upon a time, when such a thing as essence did exist. Valaam Island, with the monastery of the same name, is also in the middle of this lake, this is the world and light and holiness all in one place, in a single vanishing point: 'Just look into the distance, isn't that light Valaam itself?' In Russian, the word *свет* is akin to book and hook, neither can exist without the other, there must be some sort of an inner frame, some dangerous gizmo at the bottom of things. Ideas? 'You're drunk,' Ari concludes. Earth, ice, lake, sky, greyness, all is made of the same mass.

This drunken state that overwhelmed her in a flash at Lake Ladoga was strange and novel, and it was also her last. Ari will change her dissertation topic and phrase it in terms of topography,

Topographical errors in Dostoevsky novels, for which she'll need to spend a lot more time there. As for her, heading towards the end of the dissertation and the scholarship, she doesn't know that she wants to go home straightaway, not home in the sense of the student hall on Povarskaya Street, the Korablestroiteley, or wherever they happen to be staying at the moment? And not even home in the capital, her rental place that she had already given up when going to Russia and left her three boxes of belongings in the cellar of a young tutor, and not even homehome where her grandmother's house is available to her. 'What's the time right now at home?' She asked glazing at Ari, 'which home?' And they stare at the Soviet wristwatch. At her grandmother's they are about to serve lunch while she is sliding off a bench by a frozen yet still uncrossable Lake Ladoga, sitting on the splintering grey snow, weighing up options that range from spending the night right there and freezing to death in April, or utilising some makeshift excuse, flying home that very night, on the wings of a lie, for instance that she has a life-threatening stomach ulcer that makes her stools black, she'll call the embassy and ask to be taken home, if only something could finally happen, she moans.

This is when the kiss happened.

Or as Ari told the story later, she just bent down and snogged her. After all, she said she wanted something to happen at last. The kiss isn't long but justified and comforting for the time being. It's not passionate, only sobering. It only gets awkward several years later, did they really snog under the influence of that port, or was it because of homesickness or what? After the kiss, she clambers back onto the bench. The port's swiftly descending and rising mist does reveal the truth, but it also conceals the visible world. Insuperable, directionless desire turns into a roar, and then it stalls.

She's carefully tearing a piece from the crumbs of this sour and black bread. She's staring at the lake, until now she failed to notice that the huge surface of water was obscured by the disappointment of arrival. In lieu of the much-anticipated magnificent lake, she came across an empty grey lowland drifting between edges and aggregate states, the carbon copy of the Russian steppe she had never set eyes on.

A few birds appear. A hawk is harking on a tilted pole, highly alert to the pigeons, crows and seagulls in the distance. The other tiny birds are unknown to her. Not far from the shore, a man in a boat is fishing straight out of an ice hole. He must be sitting in his boat so he can stay on the surface in case the ice breaks, seeing that it's of dubious consistency. It looks like it had been there for a long time and the water had gradually frozen around it. The fisherman pulls out the rod, a smallish fish is fighting for its life on its end. He removes it from the hook and examines it, lifting his chin and twinkling like a mole.

'Just go on living', he says loudly and throws the fish back into the ice hole.

After that night in Kokkorevo, Влагимир Влагимирович pays her a visit in her dream.

At first, up until the first half of their scholarship, they drink a lot in Saint Petersburg, much more than anywhere until then. They watch from Dvortsovaya Square as the bridge opens up, a road opens towards the sky, a 700 ml bottle of Armenian cognac that the two of them share is empty by dawn. The tram lines also protrude to the sky at night on the Dvortsovaya, Troickiy and Liteyny bridges. They never open a bottle before seven in the evening, and if they go to the theatre, then it's ten. During winter nights, they visit bridges, while during the day, they sleep till late and miss their university classes.

In order to learn this hard-to-acquire language, she goes to the theatre. Ari speaks much better Russian, her ear is more attuned to languages, as if her future fate was to swallow up any foreign language, together with its geographical location and adjacent citizenship like a whale. Her choice is to go to the theatre to learn languages. The productions at the Maly Drama Theatre don't bring her any closer to language, she fails to grasp the Arkhangelsk dialect in *Brothers and Sisters* even after several performances, but the stage astounds her. She had only encountered this much pain and happiness in books so far. Theatre is a place for strange works, in which light and shadow fight one another.

Their nights are dedicated to the city, where they roam like the solitary protagonists of fiction.

From spring to summer, as the diminishing darkness makes place for daylight, she can closely observe the tram lines protruding to the sky. And then, the white nights arrive. The sky is greyish white, murky and dim yet determined, as if it had conquered darkness. Light doesn't seem to have a source, it's invisible, the only certainty is its victory over darkness. The white nights at the end of June are unsettling, the city is alert and everyone charges onto the streets. She walks up and down along the bridges in the dusk-like light at dawn. Perhaps everyone who wants to see the triumphant victory of light over these two short weeks is foreign, hoping to dream under the pretence of white nights.

There's no need to get drunk, what she sees is drunkenness itself.

'*It was a wonderful night, such a night as is only possible when we are young, dear reader. The sky was so starry*',[26] Dostoevsky opens his early masterpiece *White Nights*, the hero of which is an agonising lone dreamer in the city.

Everything is as it used to be in this city almost a century and a half ago, everything is as before, including solitude. Only the stars cannot be seen from the city at night anymore. The Earth has grabbed the light and wants to glow, no longer trusting the sky. In the distance, the windows of the Winter Palace, a museum these days, are all lit as if there was a grand ball inside. Few buildings take siege at the sky in the city. The term skyscraper, *небоскреб* is still unknown at this point. But by the time the correspondence with Ari starts again and they organise the class meeting twenty years later, the continent's tallest building will be searing the sky by the coast. People in Moscow have changed a lot. In Saint Petersburg, too. And everywhere.

The bridges open at three o'clock in the morning, determined to allow the ships to make it to sea with their heavy cargo. The tram-rails on these bridges lead up to the sky. This direct path to the sky seems completely self-evident and as she's staring at the heavy perpendicular bridge segment on the Dvortsovaya, the metal tracks promisingly lead up to the firmament, as if they were a ladder where angels can make their way up and down.

After Saint Petersburg she'll struggle with alcohol, perhaps her body has had enough already. Or perhaps it's a warning to the crippled soul – 'do you want to live or die?' Or only the light has become intoxicating and wants to be victorious over darkness.

Eventually, Ari ends the conversation, they always end it for a while, like kindred spirits, her other, homeless and worldly soul who doesn't ever look back, doesn't look for triggers from the past, that she imagines for some reason, until she understands the term, as some hook that is waiting in the lower depths for some living being to latch on. Ari is expecting something from her third citizenship, not sure what, but after the exit it's probably worth obtaining it. As for the class meeting? She won't go. 'Not interested' – she writes back crudely. – 'Not interested in those people, with whom I happened to go to school with. I might go though. Have no idea at present.'

Perhaps she should tell Ari that they have something to do with one another, they had or could have again, why not, at least for that afternoon when the meeting is scheduled. She doesn't have any idea, either. She isn't going because she has an idea. And the class meeting won't be wrapped up in an afternoon, although she doesn't yet know this, but stretch across a whole weekend, two nights and three festive days. Where the nights and days will blur together just as much as in the North, and darkness will chase the light, or the other way round.

She has already discussed the issue of foreign tongues, or to put it differently, the issue of one's own foreign tongue in the mouth, with Dr Rostam.

The windows of the dental surgery decorated in green open onto a large, spacious garden. This is the garden of a newly built row of houses, one of which is a peaceful, two-story home for the elderly. There's never any commotion around this building, as if it wasn't yet open for business or all its residents had already passed away. Although the bright light above the dental chair has been left on after finishing with the previous patient, Dr Rostam hasn't yet invited her to take a seat in the comfortable grass-green chair. This creates the impression that it hasn't yet been decided whether the patient has come to open her mouth or try to get away with it by making an appointment for a later date. Dr Rostam is talking about property prices in the area, pointing out how shockingly high they are. He also flags up the latest football match, 'won by us greens', but only after extra time, despite playing on home turf. 'It was such a depressive match', he concludes with a sad face, without making it clear how playing on home ground can contribute to victory.

'How are you doing?' he asks at long last, still refraining from inviting his patient to take a seat and continuing this no-nonsense conversation. 'We've seen each other fairly recently, haven't we? How's your new bridge?'

'The new bridge is great, in its own way,' the patient adds swiftly, even though she much preferred her crumbling teeth despite them being pretty useless at chewing in the end, after all they had plenty of time to get used to each other over forty-odd years. Having said that, the new bridge is quite satisfactory, and she can now actually chew with the upper B6.

Could the dentist please take a look at the lower B7, or perhaps B6 on the other side, not sure which one, and perhaps round the edges off a little: 'It's really annoying. Especially when reading out loud. It feels like new,' and adopting Dr Rostam's style, she adds, 'even though we haven't touched these teeth at all.' Yet they feel as if somehow they weren't really her own.

'Do you often read out loud?' the dentist asks sympathetically, as if he was talking to a really special patient whose mouth and teeth were equipped to accomplish extraordinary tasks.

'No, not any more,' she replies, 'hardly ever. Mainly because of this problem.'

Dr Rostam spends ages examining the erosion patterns on the lower back teeth, takes three different impressions one after the other, smooths and rounds off the smaller premolar, and after the fifth attempt, the patient finally concludes that it's much better.

During the next appointment, this time for scaling, she cautiously asks whether it's actually possible for someone's tongue to grow in the mouth.

'What do you mean?' Dr Rostam asks in a serious voice, he always treats his patients as if they were his guests, weighing up and pondering their questions.

The circumference of her tongue simply keeps growing. This makes her feel as if there wasn't enough space in her mouth, she explains.

'This tends to occur in cancer patients, and when there is an inflammation elsewhere in the body or even in the mouth,' Dr Rostam replies in a colourless voice. He recommends taking a blood test.

Not aware of any tumour, the patient responds falteringly, though it does feel as if she had a foreign object in her mouth, she adds in an awkward yet confidential tone.

'I also have this feeling from time to time,' Dr Rostam muses, getting carried away with thoughts.

He looks out onto the peaceful garden, where a group of linden trees have joined together.

'I've been thinking that this may have to do with the fact that I only learned this language at the age of two, as until then we only spoke Farsi at home. You know, I've told you that I arrived in this country aged two. First, I've been talking through my nose somehow, just like my father. Like gypsies, you know. I'm not a linguist, so I don't know about such things, but perhaps this is the norm in Persian, or perhaps this was the way my father was able to speak for some reason. I only got to learn to form sounds in my mouth at a later stage.'

The dentist takes another impression.

'I'll work a bit more on the 6.'

As he's carrying on with the back tooth at a leisurely pace, he returns to his story. He actually visited a specialist back in the day when he was doing his practical training, a speech therapist, whose job was to teach elocution techniques to acting students.

'Imagine, the therapist said that my speech was perfect. Literally perfect,' also adding that he'd be thrilled if his lazy acting students were able to utter such perfect sounding vowels. 'He also praised my s.'

'Well, the s is a big problem for me. Especially the s. But other sounds, too,' the patient replies. It seems as if her tongue wouldn't fit in the mouth when trying to pronounce the s, when the back of the tongue, that muscular body of the tongue would have to reel up in the mouth.

'I see. I'll smooth it further then. By the way, the therapist was praising my breathing, too. I don't dare to shave down any more, as I don't want to end up under the enamel. But I take your point about foreignness. I can hear it, too. That of my own.'

Yet the sensation of foreignness in the mouth doesn't go away. It's most obvious when she has to read something out, at a steady pace, loudly and articulately in front of an audience. Her tongue, like a heavy inelastic block, is barely rolling, always smashing into either the B6 or the B7, or even the barely there yet still semi-protruding B8, the latter seemingly displaying sharp edges despite Dr Rostam's attempts at smoothing it at least six times with that slow but extremely loud drill. The text intended for reading out loud has become inaccessible in the course of the process, despite consisting of her own sentences, woven together slowly and metic-ulously. She can no longer relate to it and, what's more, the words pulverize like sawdust as soon as they are uttered and said out loud. Does that make sense? As if she wasn't talking, but something entirely different was going on. Some sort of a background noise. Something quite unusual.

She no longer takes on public readings. Spectators sitting in the dark auditorium while she's bathed in harsh reflector light, she can't even see those she's addressing except for the blurred faces in the first two or three rows, and there are these sawdust sentences and the agony with her own tongue – she can't cope with this anymore. She can't say any more on the topic but it's due to a physical impediment, she points out whenever they ask her to take on an assignment.

'Don't you think that we may be trying too hard at work?' Dr Rostam continues. 'I got to this conclusion when I was talking to the speech therapist. I was at the start of my career then, and it was very important for me to get everything right. With the therapist, we went as far as recording and measuring the sounds I uttered, since you work with languages, you must know that this is a form of science. We took these measurements and the speech therapist demonstrated that everything was sounding exactly as it should, it's exactly as long and deep and high as required, back then there were no monitors or computers, so the machine charted everything on a piece of paper, like an EEG. Everything was just perfect. Perhaps this is our problem,' the dentist lets out a laugh. In this summer heat he no longer looks foreign but suntanned, his skin and hair barely darker than that of anyone else. 'We're simply too good, don't you think?'

She would have had the opportunity to have her large, dark amalgam fillings replaced with pretty, white ones in two, maximum three appointments. '*Wisdom tooth, for, Hiding in the mouth, / The ruins of the Parthenon cleaner*'[27], as Joseph Brodsky writes, preoccupied, like all poets, with foreign matter in the mouth. These heavy amalgams could easily be replaced with some inconspicuous foreign matter, a filling or overlay in a carefully coordinated shade, in his case 2, as befits an ex-smoker. It wasn't the considerable time or financial investment that held her back, and not even the lack of self-concern. Even though Dr Rostam had enough on his plate already not to have to seek out additional commitments, he felt that it was his professional duty to inform his patient about these options early on.

'Some people have such old fillings replaced. We remove them, clean the area and take a look underneath,' the Persian dentist sums up the process, 'after completing the 'bridging' in four sessions, as promised. – Let me know if you'd be up for this.'

'Is this a necessity?'

'Well, it's a possibility,' he smiles emphatically.

After that, they've never really touched on this topic again. Still, this possibility has come to her mind every now and then, mainly as a way of killing time, to literally chase it away or fill it with sensible content, as if it were some empty bottle in which she could place an actual message to the past. 'I'm done with you, amalgam fillings.' In this time-gap, where, using her favourite Russian phrase, there was *от нечего делать*[28] and, as a result of having nothing to do, she was overwhelmed with inertia. She could have had them replaced indeed, even if not with sparkling white but with the recommended shade 2 composite filling, in lieu of the old grey metal mixture, of mercury and another metal, perhaps silver. Yet she was absolutely convinced that emptiness could not be filled up, not even with a matching colour. In that shared mouth and shared past, the Painter, a recent acquaintance from home, was also sporting amalgam fillings, who'd now simply ask, when finding her sitting on a stool by his hospital bed upon waking, whether she minded witnessing him put his teeth back in.

'Or to be precise, other people's teeth – because his own have long been lost somewhere.' In his new homeland. He adds that he wouldn't even mind not having them in, except when really necessary. But he can't speak without teeth, seeing that sounds cannot be formed in his mouth in the absence of teeth. The head is the only body part studied to some extent by all portrait artists, but the tongue is your domain, he makes a stand. Without his teeth, he speaks in a soft childish voice and his words blur together.

Dr Rostam, known as the Persian, was only two when he arrived in his new homeland, which he'd often describe as dearly loved and only rarely find faults with. His accent was perfect, much to his pride, resembling the speech pattern of newsreaders, achieved no doubt at the expense of intense facial muscle work. In short, he spoke the language to perfection. After all, those who arrive have the duty (or possibility?) to acquire perfection. It was precisely this confident perfection that gave his rarely and vaguely revealed foreignness away. At the age of two, he couldn't have brought any foreign fillings with him, but while pairing his excessively articulate sentences with a soft and sympathetic intonation, he senses that his patient's attachment to her fillings is rooted in an unnameable stubbornness. Like cement, this stubbornness doesn't let this foreign matter go, not to mention that it's also irrational and utterly pointless, as it is an attachment to its own striking foreignness. Dr Rostam is most sympathetic towards this human stubbornness, in relation to which he chooses not to take a stand, seeing that the oath he had taken only covered healing and not... At this point, he gets stuck and is looking for the right term, would this be a matter of beautification or perhaps modernization? As it happens, the patient comes to his aid in no time.

'We can replace these fillings when they fall out,' the owner of the teeth announces, with the confidence of someone who takes their own decisions in such matters.

The other teeth take up all the time, they need bridges and root treatment involving an awful lot of effort, but these amalgams are simply unwavering.

In her new homeland, she only got her first filling after she had found herself with less holiday time, so could no longer jump on the first train, like in her student days, every time she had a toothache or a cavity, or just lost a filling. She had never managed to get into brushing her teeth, she'd always brush without any conviction or passion, unlike the American boy she used to bump into in the college bathroom during her first visit. That boy would carry on brushing his teeth for minutes on end - during which time, she'd go to the toilet and take a shower – he'd just stand in front of the mirror with an otherworldly face, brush his teeth and stare at the ceiling as if he was admiring the frescoes in the Sistine Chapel.

She wouldn't make a proper American, for that she'd have to be in a much deeper and more loving relationship with her own teeth.

So instead she went to the local health centre with this freshly discovered cavity in her tooth. Looking into this unknown mouth opening wide in front of their eyes, the flabbergasted dentist, clearly committed to the profession of dentistry with all its history, couldn't refrain from asking with genuine curiosity for the unknown:

'So where do you come from?'

Having her mouth propped wide open and kitted out with a saliva extractor that painfully drilled into her soft lower palate, she couldn't respond. By the time these tools and tampons were finally removed, the dentist was no longer interested in this piece of personal history.

She had to reiterate several times that she and the Painter didn't know each other, that he was her fellow-countryman but they had never met before. They hail from the same town; how come they don't know each other?! So, at a gathering she responds to this by telling the famous Russian joke: 'look out for Ivan if you go to Moscow', but people don't get the gist. She explains the joke: someone has finally made it to Moscow to try their luck, possibly having travelled for days on foot or by cart... just making it there from their village would have been a miracle...when suddenly an acquaintance moots the idea that he had heard about a certain Ivan, known to an acquaintance of his neighbour's fellow villagers, and that the traveller should just find this man because he'd most certainly help him in case he lost his way in that great city... perhaps even spend the night or get a bite to eat at his place... She keeps explaining the nuances of the joke but nobody gets it, so by the time she finishes, she's lost the point, too.

Why couldn't someone find Ivan in Moscow after all?

She's invited to a panel discussion about émigré art, and they point out that the Painter will be present, too: They can get to know each other there.

'I'm not an émigré' - she states hastily, as if she were a fugitive fox.

She accentuates two words in this awkwardly uttered sentence, the first and the last, placing the stress on two syllables, as if she wasn't using her mother tongue. The word 'am' is unaccented though. Existence is unaccented. Her voice, as she's uttering these words, is high-pitched and strident, on the cusp of screeching, and is coming from the head and from the broken heart, like a cry. 'No, I don't want to be an émigré writer. I want to finally arrive. I belong here. I want to belong here, just like' -

Long silence, the veil of the unknown.

Still, the next sentence is about to begin on the other end of the line. Perhaps she should say something about who she is then. She agreed to this appearance for the Painter's sake, for the sake of their encounter.

She's waiting for her turn in a concert hall, among the other pan-ellists invited to take part in the event 'Émigré Art and Literature'; after all, everything has to have a title. On stage, there are Zoli and Virág, who arrived at their New Home as children, their original names being Dong, meaning East, and Chunhua, meaning Spring Flower. They were both given their new names in childhood, at a time when their parents were shopkeepers and their local staff kindly came up with these names to make it easier to address them in their Second and Final Home. Zoli is a documentary film maker and Virág a dancer and performer, and they form a couple. Chunhua aka Virág has become famous due to their collaboration entitled *Your Foreign Body*.

The fourth panellist is a man with a craggy face, for the sake of whom she agreed to come to this event: the elderly Painter, her well-known and most successful fellow-countryman with a repu-tation for being a cynic. He holds a long natural pause after the question 'When did you arrive?', keeping silent and staring straight ahead, as if he had fallen out of the situation. Eventually, he forces his mouth to move as if he was experimenting with forming words, which seems impossible, as his mouth is already in motion on the projection screen, where there is a close-up of the rugged, angular grey face but no sound. His lips are forming something devoid of sound, as if only warming up the muscles around his mouth in order to articulate a word. As if uttering a word would be painful. In the end, the answer will be too soft-spoken and he'll have to repeat it. His face looks crushed: 'I emigrated when I was forty-five.'

'As for me, it was straight after finishing school,' she replies, piggybacking on her countryman's sentence when she's asked the same question. She doesn't utter the words – I left, emigrated, moved away. This is the beginning of the story. My story. How much longer will this be my story. How much longer am I meant to be an immigrant. Virág was six and Zoli two when they came here. Their foreignness is visible, and two or three further generations will also bear the hallmarks of their non-native race. The language they speak is perfect, the moderator observes, whose exposed lower arm is tattooed with a cloud that partly conceals a sun and some raindrops. Zoli Dong and Virág Chunhua tell their story and share details about their work on the large screen. She'd much rather talk about the Russian émigré literature she studied, she'd have something to say about that, Nabokov, Brodsky, Mamleev, other people's stories have always been much clearer for her, while her own was blurred and impossible to grasp. The conversation is racing ahead in time, she has already emigrated, went to university, started a career and published books. Next, an actor is reading from a poetry volume of hers, about the town she was born in and from where she moved away. She and the Painter. The actor makes the reading interesting, adding a touch of curious excitement, as if visiting a foreign place. She looks at the Painter – would he recognise the town in the poem – but his expression looks blank and bored. It's his turn now, the Painter is the highlight of the event. Projection of portraits, naked bodies.

The Painter shrouds himself in a milky, silent cloud. In the shared silence there is an emptiness not yet conquered by words that can be misinterpreted. 'By now, we can indeed be categorised as émigré art and literature,' he says in the end, staring awkwardly ahead. 'We don't know who we are. An empty shell. A plastic bag, swept away by the wind.' The Painter talks about his paintings as if he was able to see them yet their origin and creation were alien to him. He's neither the creator, nor the expert of his work.

She's listening to the Painter, who's still staring about a metre or so ahead, chin pulled in, as in the Alexander technique, this is all one needs to see in order to move forward. This much is quite enough – to see the ground on which to step next. Whoever looks up and gazes further ahead will be overtaken by longing. The longing to go away. Longing, nostalgia, in Russian *тоска*. Except in the case of cynics, after all the Painter is known to be one.

Cynics don't have a country, a home, they are roaming the world. But the Painter's latest exhibition – ten years ago – did focus on nostalgia. Back then, he couldn't possibly be a cynic. Or nostalgic. These two beasts would tear each other apart.

She's listening to the Painter and is looking into the audience sat in semi-darkness, familiar and unfamiliar faces are waiting for something, strangers who have purchased a ticket, at a price that would have been enough for an expensive theatre show, to attend 'Émigré Art and Literature', and panellists who haven't even been consulted about whether they'd like to be a commodity and sit on the well-lit stage in exchange for some cash. Expressing a view for money is a sin. Truth cannot be told for money, therefore, truth will be silent this evening. One has to utter some words, because this is what the audience has paid for. They will ask for their money back if the words aren't adequate. The Painter talks the least, every single word that leaves his mouth after some effort is the equivalent of a kilo of apples. The entire ticket sales divided by five, by the five panellists that is, means that each participant utters an average of twelve hundred words.

In the course of the 'Émigré Art and Literature' event, they talk about comings and goings, art works and books. Truth was utterly silent that evening, the Painter pointed out when they met up at a later date.

She looks into the darkness, where the expressions seem expectant, curious, bored, blank or full of longing and enthusiasm. It would be great to make contact with them, with those who are unreachable, who in the total darkness of the last rows are also waiting for this impossible connection. 'I'd like to be one of you.' There is foreignness that is visible and foreignness that is not. Perhaps it's easier for those whose foreignness is striking.

She made foreignness so visible that she appeared to be a chronicler of distant lands and fell into her own trap, thinking that this distant place can also be everyone's and it will be familiar, as it isn't any different from you. Instead, she's sitting here in the full glory of her foreignness and would much rather hide, conceal or annihilate what she has created. It would be best to jump into the midst of the audience. Vanish from the stage. May the world explode. Do a cartwheel and make tracks at once.

She can still do cartwheels and has taught the Son, too. 'Why are cartwheels called gypsy wheels in their mother tongue?' he asks somewhat surprised, frowning as if this was a dirty word. He's ten. The Son looks into the deep well of words. The deep well with clear water, poisoned water, dried-out well with stale water (he insists it's stale). Looking into the well is an ancient command, even if one can't see its bottom. Gypsies didn't have wheels, she explains. 'They didn't have all four wheels,' the Son snaps, without missing a beat.

They may not have had carts and the wheels to go with them, perhaps this was their only wheel to use as a means of transportation, she explains. Their very own wheel. This is how they moved in space. This is how they conquered space, by turning into a rotating body, just like the Earth. Or on the contrary, because they were always on the go, they had a wheel under themselves, a cartwheel that was always in motion, hence the name.

'So they did or didn't have a wheel then?'

'Not sure,' she replies, 'I don't know what wheel they had but they were on the road a lot. Who doesn't move is stationary, caught in a trap, so to speak.'

'Why aren't we on the road a lot? Are we caught in a trap, too?'

In a trap, and the only way to escape is by cartwheel.

Once upon a time, on an abandoned farm, they found a fox at the bottom of a dried-out well. They were going down a hill, along ancient apricot trees, abandoned vineyards and old farms. The fox was still alive at the bottom of the pit, trying to move, turn around and jump. From above, it was a terrifying sight though. The Son insisted on saving the fox and started to cry, throwing tantrums while sitting on the edge of the well and threatening that he'd jump into the well, too. On the farm, they came across a cellar with a rotting door, which they managed to push in with a bit of force. They found a ladder in the cellar, lowered it into the well and it was just the right length. The fox was still circling at the bottom, dead scared. Somebody had to go down, but they couldn't possibly allow the Son to do it. She had to go, because she was the only one with long trousers and a raincoat, like a person always holding herself ready that she was. She put all her clothes on, raincoat, waterproof trousers and the leather work gloves they found in the cellar, covered her face with a scarf, put on some sunglasses and fastened her hood around her face, in case the fox were to attack her. Before going down the well, she threw a fishing net over the fox. The animal froze underneath. The others were holding the ladder from above. When she got down, the well was so narrow that she couldn't bend down, only squat. She could feel a tiny animal under the net, but it didn't make as much as a move when she touched it. Perhaps it perished. She grabbed it under her arm, still holding the net, and climbed up using her other arm. Up there, she placed the fox on the ground, and after waiting a little, carefully removed the net. The fox cub was light and dead still, only its eyes were moving. It continued to lie paralysed for long minutes, but then slowly started to rise and crawl. In the end, it was standing high on its feet and ran into the bushes.

In the early summer heat, she found herself soaking wet under all these clothes and raingear. After she dried herself in the sun, they had a good look around the cellar. They found a shovel and a pickaxe, plenty of useless items, glassware, plastic buckets, bottles, several sacks full of rags, collected perhaps with a view to use them for heating. They decided to close up the well. They started by making use of the discarded grapevine found on the adjacent abandoned plot. The well was filling up fast and they also threw in some rags among the vine. The Son kept jumping for ages on the top of the pile, to ensure that all this matter compacted. He was triumphantly propelling himself upwards. They even watered the closed-up hole with liquid from a rain collection tub, to compact the filling even further. In time, it will shrink and a new pit will be created which may hold other living beings captive.

The Son went down the hill throwing cartwheels, speeding up so much that he was almost flying by the end. These carts are always on the go.

The edge of the town where they lived was far away, so heading home they tried to hitchhike but nobody wanted to take three people, in the end they caught a bus and then a train. She felt totally exhausted by all this excitement and trouble. She could barely drag herself home. She would have paid for a taxi just to avoid making another move.

'Why aren't we ever going anywhere?' the Son asked impatiently when they finally took a bus.

'The cartwheel also means that everybody is one's own wheel. You'll be your own wheel,' she said. 'Everybody is their own wheel and no two wheels are alike.'

The Painter has indeed come from the same place as her, but much earlier. That evening, they don't exchange a single word with each other though.

Turkish Coffee

There's an age gap of three decades between them. They could be parent and child. They've met once before but have never spoken to each other. Not even at the event on 'Émigré Art and Literature'. The Painter was still unknown when he had first arrived from their shared, distant homeland. In the press, they say that his talent developed slowly and inconspicuously during his years in exile. His personality isn't really suited to the limelight.

According to critical reception, the Painter is a major innovator in both landscape painting and portraiture. His signature act is to paint the human face as a landscape. He has stopped painting rural landscapes since mankind alienated itself from the natural world, has given it up, so to speak, handing it over to cameras. As it stands, mankind has no immediate connection with the environment, having propelled it towards ultimate decay.

The form he uses is age-old and simple. In his third exhibition to date – this is the number of times he has exhibited in his new homeland over the span of three and a half decades – the Painter depicts the industrial estate that was once at the edge of the town but now has become the new centre: focusing on the vegetation sprouting in between the buildings, on nature that restrains the exhausted and seemingly-futile human activities. The exhibition is entitled *Nostalgia Forward* and is typical of the Painter's heavily charged style, that balances between the boundaries of different worlds, a sort of homeless landscape.

She has been thinking about the Painter for some time. She'd quite like to meet him. She keeps seeking his work out, reads exhibition reviews, and has just managed to see one of his portraits and an industrial landscape at a gallery shortly before an auction. She finds that in these abstract analyses, his work is comparable to that of artists who are famous, even if their names are unknown to her. She purchases his art catalogue, *Extraterritorial*, published by Orchard, an Indian publisher with headquarters in New York and London. She also watches a documentary about him, which confuses her – will they be able to sustain a conversation if they ever meet?

During the event 'Émigré Art and Literature', no opportunity for meeting up was offered, however. In the end, it was through the generous mediation of a mutual critic that the Painter received news that she'd like to meet him. As the critic pointed out, their respective homes have a lot in common; he had interviewed them each at their own place:

'One can tell you come from the same place,' he adds. 'Write to him. He'll be delighted,' and he gives her the Painter's address.

She writes him a letter, suggesting they meet up in order for her to ask a few questions. The Painter replies on the same day that he'd be delighted. Could she please give him some time to read her book. He's a slow reader, he adds. He's not a great friend of letters. Can she also please send him any questions she might have, so he can think them through.

She redrafts the questions three times. At first, she writes about their onetime shared space, but she's unable to ask any questions at the end – such as, what does that city, his former home or homeland, mean to him? Is it possible that some people have nothing to do with the place where they come from? The second draft is about homelessness – she'd like to know (she deletes this), she would like to talk about whether he had found a home in the end, and whether his foreignness had actually eased off (she deletes this, too). In the third letter – the one she sends – she only writes that she'd be delighted if they met up and talked someday. She's unable to formulate a question. She's no longer a friend of letters, either. She hesitates around the word 'conversation'. Is it even possible to have a conversation with someone who finds constructing and uttering words so difficult? She deletes this section and only writes that she'd be delighted to meet him one day.

Many months go by.

Eventually, the Painter invites her to a restaurant in the vicinity of his home, where, as he writes, they still come up with decent cooking. The conversation is much more animated than she had initially expected, though at first the Painter talks just as slowly and fragmentedly as he did at the theatre event where they had both appeared. As if he were in pain or had to move some rocky mountain on his face in order to make conversation. Or as if a statue was forcing itself to speak. He's read one of her books and has plenty of questions, he begins enthusiastically. He has questions about her parents, her family history, about how she wrote the book, where and how it has been received, here and there, what's the difference between the two, what did 'those critics' have to say, were there any translations... The Painter's face becomes animated, betraying signs of restlessness as if he is awaiting the revelation of great secrets. Gone is that aging and stiff panellist she had met at that theatre. His bluish dead-looking eyes are radiating excitement and temptation. Her book was a tough read, he had to battle with it, many times he felt that he needed a dictionary as he no longer remembered those words, but was glad to have read it, he concludes in a matter-of-fact way. They are already having coffee and dessert by the time he grows silent and asks why she wanted to meet him.

'Not bad,' he comments on the curd dumplings. 'Though there's no need for so much powdered sugar.'

Powdered sugar. Language has given itself away, she muses. This is called icing sugar in their new home.

'Yet they are useless at making tarragon soup.' He had experimented with tarragon ragout. 'The tarragon from back home is not known around here,' he adds sternly.

She'd be happy to get him some tarragon from her garden, she offers modestly, she has a huge tarragon plant that couldn't be killed if one tried.

'Really?' the Painter asks suspiciously, almost harshly.

'You mean whether it's proper tarragon?'

'Yes, the real thing. Is it?'

'Sure, it is,' she replies, before starting to doubt herself. Is it indeed the real thing?

The Painter says that he hadn't had decent tarragon lamb chops for forty years because one couldn't lay hands on proper tarragon in this country.

'How about back home?' she asks cautiously.

'I don't have anybody left there. I don't go over there anymore,' the Painter replies in a matter-of-fact voice. 'You can't order tarragon lamb in restaurants.'

We're getting somewhere, she thinks, but is unable to move the conversation forward. It feels as if with each sentence she is delving into some exam situation, where new details are needed, new nuances and bits of knowledge are required, but hers is somehow inadequate, too general, too rough-and-ready; take the case of tarragon for example. Or that of other dishes, seeing that she has learned about the Painter that, in addition to his exquisite taste, he is also a great cook.

'I don't go over there anymore,' is the way the Painter expresses it, bearing in mind that those from around here go over there. As if he had deleted the name of the city from his vocabulary. Perhaps he doesn't feel comfortable enough to say 'home'.

She doesn't want to continue the conversation about tarragon, to make sure that they steer clear of her mother's usual complaints about the undrinkable tap water, the factory-made sour cream that doesn't dissolve in hot soup, the dry and tasteless cheeses, and the watery squash that cannot be baked but just cooks for a while and then falls apart. Nothing is good enough here. Not even hospital provision? That certainly isn't, her mother snaps, because back home she used to have her own doctors, she had two doctor neighbours, nothing can compensate for that. As if this palpable breakdown in material conditions could be an obvious proof of some other impossibility – of the failure that they are now all, or to be precise, they are now both here –

To live, for good.

Towards the end of the meal, she decides to mention his latest exhibition, *Nostalgia Forward*. She has already seen it, and it had a major impact on her, she's about to begin.

'Which exhibition?' the Painter asks, absent-mindedly.

'*Nostalgia Forward*,' she says, far too softly, because she utters the word nostalgia in a Russian manner, accentuating the 'i', even though she has heard this word pronounced differently before. She's struggling with the English pronunciation, as if this word didn't exist for her in English, not having established a connection between this word and the English language despite the latter's international presence that has also propelled her career world-wide. English is the language of counter-nostalgia that has propelled her across worlds, akin to the legendary gryphon with its huge claws. It seems to her that she has already heard this sentence before, in her own voice: *I have a certain nostalgia. A certain.* She was fascinated by this title, the title of the exhibition. No, she rectifies, the correct term in fact is 'swept off my feet'.

Ностальгия, she watched this famous film again after the Painter's exhibition. She'd quite like to talk about this. In Russian, the accent is placed on the letter 'i' (nostalgía), but she has also heard the accent placed on the 'a' (nostálgia), as if this had been an entirely foreign and freshly adopted word, not a Russian one. As a matter of fact, he wondered whether it was included in the good old Fasmer dictionary. Most probably. They retained its foreignness, as if it didn't mean anything in its adoptive language, it didn't gain a meaning of its own but remained foreign, a foreign sensation, belonging to others. This foreign word with its fluctuating intonation cannot get a proper hold, it merely hovers in the Russian language. Why the famous director gave this title to his film is beyond comprehension. Perhaps he did this because he was shooting it abroad, far away and badly longing for his homeland, as his diaries revealed. Yet he had written the script back home, if journal entries can be trusted, as if the word, the longing – to be away and to return – was navigating between two countries and two worlds. One is at home yet longs to be away. But where? A foreign Russian film. Tarkovsky emigrated in the early 1980s, but his arrival and his never-to-return took a while. And then he was dead by 1986. Did he bring his cancerous cells with him? Or did they develop in him there? Cells are silent, they don't tell their story. In any event, they didn't have time to renew themselves this time.

So they are related, the Painter and the Russian film director.

The Painter signals with an indignant wave of his hand that he hadn't come up with the title of any of his exhibitions, he would never ever come up with such a stupid title.

'Yet it was this title that has brought them together,' she says softly, slightly ashamed, aware of the risks of admitting this. Perhaps this will be the end of their conversation, before it could have really taken off.

'This wasn't what I meant,' the Painter replies, slowly and immersed in his thoughts, as if sensing that the battles he'll have to fight aren't going to be against the person sitting on the other side of the table covered in crumbs. 'It's not such a bad title. Not so bad at all. I agreed with it in the end.'

His face has suddenly turned wrinkled, tired and old.

'We'll take it then that in your view nostalgia isn't a sin,' he observes, without looking at her.

He looks calm, as if he had been forgiven.

The waiter recommends some coffee, but she'd rather not have any, and the Painter gestures that he's no longer allowed. Once the waiter leaves, she tries to steer the conversation away from the constraint of nostalgia. Glancing at the distant and buttoned-up Painter, she points out that the only coffee she likes is her own Turkish coffee that she makes at the crack of dawn. She only drinks one cup, as befits her age.

'Turkish coffee?' the Painter asks, measuring his words, slowly turning his head. His grey face is radiating with a metallic glow, like rocks after a rain.

'Yes,' she shyly replies.

She'd like to add that this kind of coffee is the easiest to prepare at dawn, it makes the least noise, and even though the Son is now fairly grown-up, she has gotten into the habit of moving about silently in the house. She looks awkwardly at the Painter, eager to avoid some dreadful conversation about different kinds of coffee beans and coffee makers, fashionable capsules and great pressure, or baffling bars and temperatures.

'Do you add sugar before bringing the water to the boil?' the Painter asks with sudden excitement. He adores it that way, too; this is the word he uses, emphatically and articulately, he adores it, and his craggy face radiates like the Half Dome in Yosemite Park when the rocks sparkle with a glowing sheen.

'Yes.'

'Do you let it come to a boil twice?'

'Always twice.'

And she tells him about the Son stepping on a stool when he was a little child, to witness the complicated manoeuvre of the rising coffee. 'It's bulging!' – he shouted with fear and excitement, about to spill over, as it indeed appeared to do. In such situations, one either had to turn the flame down or gently remove the metal pot, in Turkish the *ibrik* (using Turkish for something Turkish), she explained to the Son, and then put it back and wait for the second and final time for the water to rise as it comes to a boil, at which point the Son shouted again: 'It spilled over!' But it didn't, though he could see what was about to happen if no one intervened. The final touch was a gentle blow on the bulging coffee, in order to restrain it and keep it in the pot, making sure not to blow too hard and thus splatter it over the top.

'Do you skim off the foam?'

'No,' she replies, but she doesn't want to disappoint, she likes the richly soft flavour of these precious tiny rainbow bubbles, 'I let it settle, and then pour the drink very slowly, without straining. The foam slips into the cup intact.' These rainbow bubbles have never been of any interest to anyone else.

Rainbow on a soft brown coffee foam – one should really paint that! But she lacks the courage to talk about painting with the Painter, to try to give him ideas like some amateur. The Painter isn't simply interested in her novel or in fiction, either, but in the person writing the autobiography, whose relatives, schools, and favourite streets he also knows himself. Or used to know. The shared space. And to some extent, the language, these strange ancient words. As if fiction and imagination were gateways to one another, so they could articulate their most personal questions: do you skim off the foam?

Having discussed Turkish coffee they just sit there, exhausted. So that the sentences they have exchanged with each other, at first cautiously and then dauntlessly, can find some peace and recharge them. Contented silence settles in. As if they had arrived at their destination and agreed on an important matter: before pouring and very gently, one has to transfer this rainbow foam into the cup. Or wait until the coffee grounds settle, and carefully pour it together with the hot black liquid. There is no other method to preserve these tiny, glittering brownish bubbles. The rainbow bubbles are the tastiest.

The Painter offers to pay for their lunch, waves his hand and doesn't take no for an answer. He can finally spend money on something. Something worthwhile.

She wants to talk about this, too, not just about time. – 'What has time done to you? And what has money?'

'Next time, it will be your turn to pay.'

She only finds out much later and by mere chance that there are indeed two different kinds of tarragon, a more flavoursome French and a somewhat sour and bland yet exuberant Russian variety. She has no idea whether the Painter is aware of this botanical difference, but she wants to discuss it nonetheless. His tongue and his tastebuds, those eighty-year-old warts, which are none other than his memories, do know that tarragon is French back home and Russian over here.

They didn't exchange phone numbers, relying on correspondence instead. When a few months later she suggests having lunch together, the Painter's curt reply is that he moved house. His new address is the Saint Benedict Hospital. No, he didn't become a monk, more like a future corpse.

She knows the hospital psychiatrist whose private practice is opposite the hospital. She calls him to ask about the Painter. 'Let's go over together,' the Psychiatrist offers and announces the visitor in a loud voice, while laughing as they make it to the ward.

'Someone is here to visit you,' he jovially informs the Painter, who is lying on his side, his long and gaunt body nearly vanishing in the huge bed.

The visitor is waiting in the small antechamber next to the ward.

'Everybody wants to visit me. Everybody is curious about death,' the Painter notes impassively. 'Me, too.'

'Listen, leave death alone,' the Psychiatrist responds in the cheerful voice reserved for his patients.

'I brought someone with me, an intelligent person. A writer. Much better than antidepressants. Don't keep the poor thing waiting, okay?'

'A poor thing and a writer?'

The Psychiatrist takes her arm to lead her in. The Painter turns around unwillingly, squinting as if he didn't recognise the visitor. His face only softens when the Psychiatrist leaves.

'I never take the medication he prescribes,' he nods after the Psychiatrist has dashed away carrying his large bags. The Painter invites his visitor to take a seat on the edge of his bed.

'Tell me, does literature pay anything at all? Are you really that poor?' he asks, and his long, rugged and unshaven face lights up, not even waiting for an answer and hastily adding, of course, poor her, he has read that she returned some award with all the prize money involved because 'she didn't like the look of the bloke' who offered it.

'You did the wrong thing. One should take all the money that's being offered.'

The Painter laughs with such an elemental force after the word bloke, as if he wanted to proclaim their complicity to one and all, despite only the two of them being in the room. He pulls himself up, holding on to the plastic handles on either side of the bed, designed precisely so patients can pull themselves up, turn around and hold on without assistance. He doesn't accept help, dismissing it with his strong arms. He doesn't use the remote control, either, with which he could tilt the bed. Same goes for the infusion or the catheter sticking out from under the duvet, he simply ignores them.

'My arms are fine. I haven't died yet!' he shouts after pulling himself up, he's still animated by that furious fire that keeps him alive. 'I'll tell you something about this bloke. Not this one, another.

About fifteen, maybe twenty years ago, they contacted me from one of the ministries, saying that a secretary of state or perhaps a minister, must have been a minister because it was some sly representative of the latter, so the minister in question is turning fifty or sixty and they'd like to present him with a portrait. They thought of me. Even though I have never painted on command or done rush jobs. This isn't what I committed myself to. I told them I can't commit to the task just yet. They shouldn't say anything to the man but ensure that we meet somehow in the same space, so I can take a look at his face. They offered a huge sum to the gallery, because by then I had an agent to deal with such matters on my behalf. I can't remember whether it was six or eight. Million! Adding that they know how long I tend to work on a painting. All I asked was for them to arrange a meeting, without him knowing that I'd be there, so I could observe him. It emerged that he'd attend some official opening ceremony at a theatre on the national day, followed by a reception and seated dinner. I was sat almost opposite him and could indeed observe him throughout the whole dinner. I realised straightaway that I was unable to paint him. Even though I did think for ages about that pile of cash. It frequently came to my mind even during the dinner. In those days, I gambled a lot more, never mind, all this belongs to the past. To cut a long story short, I was grateful for every single penny. At one point I went to take a piss before the soup, the starter was rubbish, all plastic, fake aspic, you know, made from a sachet, soulless factory food, I knew it wouldn't work. Unless I reimagined him, to paint that figure instead of him. It so happens that he also went to the loo at the same time. Perhaps a nude would have been more interesting! He had a huge, ball-shaped belly and a tiny – forgive me, but I did see it – roundish ball-shaped member that he produced from his pants. As to his face, however, I was unsure what to do. It seemed like the face of someone who was always elsewhere, without a presence. He had a face put together from random parts. He had taken each section from a different place. He himself, was nowhere. Besides, I would have had to stare at such a face for a hundred and fifty to two hundred hours while working. It was totally blank. Someone who doesn't show anything from their self, who isn't here, can't be painted. I sent a message via the gallery that I couldn't paint him. I'd be happy to paint him as a nude, as he's lying on a bed, sleeping or looking at his phone, showing his belly and tiny ball-shaped willy. But the gallerist didn't want to negotiate such a deal. The whole thing ended up with a major grudge. Not wanted for his face, only for his penis. They were in government for three terms, during which time I didn't receive any state-sponsored recognition. A little while ago I spotted the man at a public bath, on a men-only day. Do you know how I recognised him?'

He's showing the other man's measurements with his left thumb and index finger.

He's speaking with such rage and passion as if he wasn't talking from that gaunt and fragile body. He adds that the nude would have been able to show the fate of this timid man. His thin and wobbly legs supporting his puffed-up body, his sad virility, his naked, smooth and hollow chest, even his child-like face that's always adjusting to others, always dancing to someone else's tune... A man who has never wanted anything, only others wanted things from him. And when nobody wants anything, he's like an empty sack left in a corner.

'What can it be like to come across such a tiny, roundish penis at a date?' he asks, accentuating the 'a' and staring at the ceiling, laughing crookedly. He's panting due to the passion he put into the storytelling. He's now tired but continues regardless in a bland voice.

'See, it was a mistake not to paint that minister. This is why I'm telling you about it. There is the odd piece of crap in everyone's body of work. Yours included. And there will be some more. That said, there aren't many crap works worth eight million in many people's accomplishments. I was too opinionated, too full of myself. This wasn't a political matter; it was a matter of blandness. If you get commissioned on a decent pay, you should just write that piece. No need to shit your pants. Which is your shittiest book?' he asks, laughing. 'Forgive me. You probably don't have such a thing. You are a serious writer, preoccupied with death, God, time. I've read your work. You are preoccupied with death. This is why you came here, right? You wrote about this,' he's putting together the words so impatiently and erratically as if the visitor would have only popped in for a short moment, ready to leave with the sentences swiftly cobbled together.

Yes, she's preoccupied with death, but this isn't why she came. She came because they agreed to meet again.

The Painter only knows about the prize she turned down. He doesn't know about that meagre allowance she receives as a creative artist. It was established by an independent foundation, about which the usual stuff emerged in due course. Besides, it was set up by a fellow-countryman of theirs. The Painter continues by asking her whether snobs are still in the habit of buying her book. Because they used to be, at least in the past. They do buy his paintings. Readers, however, can easily hand a book down from one to another, can't they? One can't make a living in this way, he adds.

'Since people are now bidding on my final works, their price has gone up. I thought I'd offer you a painting, in case that helps. What do you think? Does literature pay at all?'

'Sadly, it does,' she responds, with some of the Painter's joy in telling the story about the minister having rubbed off on her. She's also thinking slightly too much about money, she adds on a serious tone, but only because she now has some. 'You know, writers are dying for the number of copies sold. It would be great to start again. With the first fifty readers. At that point, there were no print runs to worry about, only love. That would be great,' she says, blushing. 'Hot love and ice-cold fear, what if it doesn't work out.'

The Painter mentions that he had read an old interview with her, dating back to the first decade of her career. At that stage, she was complaining that there was no connection between literature and money. Now she's complaining that there is one?

This is no longer the issue. The issue is that all this is too safe.

'What we write is safe, lacking in danger. Everything is too cold, words no longer move mountains.'

The Painter closes his eyes, lying on his back. 'Please carry on talking,' he whispers. 'Start from Homer, okay?' The Painter is absolutely still. Perhaps he's about to fall asleep.

Her sentence begins softly but surely: once upon a time, poets...

Once upon a time, poets were able to move mountains, wild animals and trees with their songs. Poetry was able to save one from death. She's thinking of the story of Orpheus, who later divulged the secrets of gods, for which he was punished. In other words, he knew these secrets! He didn't only spill the beans on these secrets but he might have imagined himself as one of the gods, too. This is the only thing we carry on with all honesty. But perhaps the gods were angry with him because they were jealous of the power of poetry. Zeus struck him down with lightning, and the Bacchae tore him apart and threw his head into the sea.

Yet his head continued to sing. The poet couldn't be silenced.

This is the only hope. The poet's death is not the end or beginning of silence. This song was capable of raising the dead. Nothing moves upon our words, yet we still think of ourselves as gods.

But she'll try, she can promise that much, even if she'll fail dreadfully, she'll try to raise at least one person from the dead.

She has got to the point of talking about the death-defying power of poetry. She has witnessed such a thing, has seen someone wanting to raise people with the power of poetry. She'll talk about a theatre performance.

The Doctor dashes in, not wearing her white coat, loudly opening the door and clicking her heels.

The visitor has just started discussing the production: the poet, a famous Italian director has attempted to raise from the dead a patient suffering from *locked-in syndrome* (LIS). She looks at the Doctor, who shakes her head in disapproval, indicating that this isn't the best choice of topic for them right now. This is an attempt at resurrection with the means of the art, she replies. The Doctor consults her watch, then carefully lifts the duvet and takes a seat on the bed. She's also interested in resurrection, she says, though she isn't really able to practice it.

The patients suffering from this condition, from locked-in syndrome, are basically buried alive: they can only move their eyes and blink, but unable to move any other muscle. They can't even talk. The Doctor nods, fortunately she hasn't yet encountered such patients but has read about them. Complete stillness in a transitory space, one is neither alive nor dead. Yet already dwelling in the realm of Hades. On the empty stage, the opera Orpheus and Eurydice begins. Using short sentences, they project the story of a person onto the back wall. Birth, childhood, love, marriage, children. And then ooops, one day she suddenly collapses. We can't see the person during the first half of the show, we only get to know the story. Then we learn about the syndrome and can finally see her, projected onto the screen, lying in bed wearing headphones. In a hospital bed like this one. They are transmitting the opera live to the young woman suffering from LIS, and she's listening to it in her hospital bed through her headphones. There is a recording crew on stage. The woman is called Els, though this isn't her real name, the subtitles inform us. This production is the perfect encounter between reality and theatre.

The Painter mumbles very softly yet clearly, without interrupting the storytelling: 'What reality?'

'The two spiritual realities,' she replies.

'We see the woman's face projected on the screen for the first time when Orpheus addresses his lover. The woman is listening to music lying down, with her eyes open, occasionally blinking. She's listening to the supplication of Orpheus, who is standing with his back to the screen, facing the audience. Orpheus is addressing his words to her, and he'll lead her, Els, out of the underworld, of confinement, in other words, he'll resurrect her. Because a poet's task is to resurrect the dead. For this, it is essential to immerse oneself in the underworld. Orpheus has tried this, and so did the Italian director. By the way, the Italian's name is Romeo, Romeo Castellucci. When Orpheus turns around, Els vanishes forever. The experiment has failed. Women cannot be led out of confinement, of Hades'.

'So did the Italian director actually raise this woman from the dead in reality?' the Painter asks in a soft voice, with his eyes still closed.

'What reality?' they laugh in unison, and the Painter opens his eyes.

'I don't think so' she replies with some hesitation.

'But at least, he tried. Would you like to hear the aria when he addresses her?'

The Painter nods. – Should a woman sing the part of Orpheus or a man? – The female Orpheus is holding her lover in her arms. She's singing. The three of them are leaning in towards the old recording. Grabbing the handles by the side of his bed, the Painter sits up. The Doctor is also watching the screen. A magnificent sound fills up the dimly lit room.

'Is life this easy?' the Painter looks at the Doctor, who has also listened to the story. Her looks betray her disapproval of the story-teller chattering about LIS at someone's sick bed.

The ginger doctor lets out a stern disapproving sound and adds that one should aim not to die on this day. She then steps closer to the bed and runs her hand along the Painter's unshaven and suddenly elongated face, revealing a lot of suffering. As if she was caressing and hence conveying an act of love but also analysing something, perhaps the temperature of the skin.

'There. How are these strong legs doing?' she lifts the duvet.

She presses her index finger into the flesh right above the knee on either side, and then removes it. The white trace of her finger keeps showing for a long time on the leg, it takes ages for the skin to regain its original colour and smoothness. The Doctor shakes her head and makes a note on some scrap paper she finds in her pocket.

'We'll give you some more blood platelets tonight. Maestro,' she looks sternly at the Painter, having changed her tone of voice. 'You must stand up and walk,' she adds scoldingly.

'Walk. Walk. This is what Jesus also commanded.'

'Maestro, you have work to do. You'll need your legs. Stand up!' the Doctor orders in a slowly articulated voice.

The Painter looks out of the window in defiance and keeps silent. He doesn't make a single move. After the doctor leaves, he contends:

'You're lucky. You don't need legs to carry out your work. Instead,' he continues after a brief pause, 'you need an arse, I imagine,' and he laughs at his own realisation. He displays a row of yellow teeth in his lower jaw. The teeth elongated as the gums have receded over time. His face looks like that of an old and agitated horse.

Long pause and stillness. The only sounds are the trickling of infusion from above and the dripping of brownish urine, through a plastic tube, into the bag attached to the side of the bed, leaving the body unconsciously, without the hindrance of constrictor muscles. The curtains are drawn, and the Painter is looking into the corner, towards the darkest point of the room. Like someone accustomed to working in blacked-out studios, in the light conditions adjusted to the requirements of the work in progress until it's finished.

Her plan was precisely to ask him about light, as early as their first meeting. To ask him about his thoughts on the origin of light in painting. About light and foreignness, and now, also about everything going black. All these visitors the Painter is complaining about come to this quiet hospital ward with a high ceiling because they want a sneaky peek into this very same thing. Not so much the man on his way out but death that's grabbing him away. As if death wasn't in him but was coming from outside.

'Would you be so kind to ask the Doctor to come back? She's in her office at the end of the corridor. Tell her it's urgent.'

In the Doctor's office, there are only two chairs, one behind the desk laden with piles of paper and folders, and an armchair on the opposite end, reserved for patients, guests and visitors. All over the place along the top of the cupboards and on the floor, there are gifts received from patients, impossible to take home or regift to others, in smaller and larger gift bags, still in their original packaging.

The Doctor takes her time to comply, she carries on typing into her computer the various diagnostic observations she had scribbled earlier on bits of paper, but in the end announces with a triumphant click on her keyboard: 'All done, let's go!'

'Tell me, why is the Maestro always so angry and edgy? He's always tense and irritated as if he had to go into battle. His heart is very weak, his blood pressure like a rollercoster, he can't sleep and even though he's given sleeping pills he refuses to take them. Due to not sleeping well, his entire body is under great strain. Now he says he can't even stand on his feet. We have no idea why. There are no physical causes. But if he just keeps lying in bed, there will indeed be problems. Do you understand?'

They discuss the fact that she doesn't know him all that well. Not in that way. Perhaps, she's trying to carefully search for words, also mindful that the doctor, being so rushed for time, may not want to wait for the slowly evolving thought, in her opinion the Painter has given all his patience and peace of mind, and yes, all his love and attention to his paintings. Nothing has been left for life itself.

'We can't cope with him here. He doesn't quite mistreat the nurses but he's incredibly edgy. He refuses to take sedatives. He quickly dispatches his visitors and then keeps calling the nurses and argues with them all day. We should send him home but he doesn't want to go. He claims he has no home. He told us he has a studio but not a home. Do you understand what he means?' the Doctor asks again and adds, immersed in thought: 'What's this business about not having a home? Is this some artsy thing we can't understand? All these patients should be sent home but the problem with most of them is that they don't want to go, even if they had a home to go to. They don't want to go home anymore. As for the Painter, why doesn't he want to go home? What does he mean by not having a home?'

She understands some of this, she replies. Perhaps he should join the world of his paintings seeing that his art practice has come to an end.

'I've lost the use of my legs,' the Painter informs the doctor when the latter is standing by his bed and is holding both of his hands. 'I can't stand up. Do something, you are a fantastic healer.' He acts as if he wasn't entirely serious.

'I can't help you if you don't keep trying. Please make an attempt.'

'You are my last hope,' the Painter replies, holding the doctor's hands, his fingers turning all white as he's clutching them. His face and voice may be putting on an act but his hands give him away.

'I give you everything I can, but we do know what you refuse to take. Please make an effort. Just get up and walk.' The Doctor urges him in a stern voice. 'Don't you think that Lazarus also had to want to walk?'

The Doctor suddenly transfers her gaze from the Painter to the visitor, as if she was expecting some sort of endorsement.

'Apparently, resurrection isn't picky. It's not a matter of wanting,' the visitor adds awkwardly.

'My legs were my main working tool,' the Painter points out. 'It's over now. Lazarus could no longer want anything, dear Doctor, because by then he had been dead for three or four days. He must have even started to stink, no? It's understandable that whoever does such a thing as resurrect a three-day-old corpse, will end up crucified.'

Even as recently as half a year ago, he'd be still standing upright for seven to eight hours a day, he explains. He was looking after his legs all his life. He'd stand still, studying faces. A painting, even a smaller one, takes a year, more like a year and a half to complete. He had been standing on his strong legs an awful lot in his time. Observing. The landscape emerging on a face. And in the end, the thirty-something muscles of a face.

'How many facial muscles are there? The Doctor must surely know,' he asks enthusiastically.

'No idea, though I had to pass an exam on this topic,' the Doctor replies. She'd definitely know if she were a plastic surgeon. She continues: 'I've spoken to the physiotherapist, the rheumatologist and the neurologist. Not yet with the psychiatrist. They all say that everything is fine with your leg from a physical point of view. It's time to finally stand on your feet,' she utters the command again, this time louder, pursing her lips, pulling in her chin and tilting her head while looking expectantly at the patient almost vanishing in the twilight.

The Doctor takes the long, greyish-blue fingers and narrow hands in her own two hands.

'Promise me that you'll try to stand up. I shall leave the room and you'll have a go, okay?' she looks at the visitor: 'Will you help him? Let him lean on you.'

The careworn face shrinks, as if it was trying to imagine this superhumanly impossible undertaking. The Doctor strokes the patient's face with the usual professional care and leaves the room.

The visitor is trying to encourage the Painter with her smile after the Doctor's departure, they were given a joint task and her job is to help him. But the Painter is staring at the folds of the duvet. He has no intention of standing up whatsoever.

'Where would you like to die?' he asks after a while, looking at her with a previously unrevealed kind gaze seemingly reserved for their shared concerns. 'You must have thought about this.

You had written about your own death, I read your poem about disappearing.'

His family would like him to be buried here, the Painter says. And he doesn't want to be taken back home for his final resting place if that comes with a triumphant march and a funeral train, accompanied by a state delegation on public demand.

'It may not be a moment of peace,' he adds.

'And may not be the final moment, either,' she laughs.

The Painter is shaking his head: 'are you starting this again?' He doesn't need comforting.

'This isn't about comfort but about clarification: we have no idea about the end.'

The Painter explains that he feels uneasy about these reburials, these symbolic homecomings.

'You mean in the sense of being taken back to the beloved ground of your homeland?' the visitor cites a famous author.

The Painter looks questioningly at her. He's concerned about his body being transported back to his former homeland for ceremonial burial. Besides, he's also concerned about final peace, he adds laughing, 'but I wouldn't like to end up like your colleague, that writer.'

'Who do you mean?'

'You must be familiar with the calvary of Transylvanian writer Áron Tamási's burial. It has been well documented. The body started on its way to its birthplace but only arrived there three days later. As it happens, there are two villages by the same name in that country, one on this side of the mountains, and one on the other. They sent the train to the latter by mistake, to the south. You can imagine, as it got there. They didn't document what really happened there. They removed the carriage from the train and turned it back by taking it to the nearest station, but in the meantime various permits needed to be obtained. Once at the right station, they placed the coffin onto an open-top vehicle and headed towards the village. But this is still not the end of the body's calvary. In that village custom dictated that the dead returning from afar were meant to be met with the tolling of bells. I imagine, this custom must symbolise homecoming. Though the procession arrives at the hillside from where one can already see the village, they overlook the car and fail to ring the bells. The second car accompanying the funeral vehicle has to drive ahead and alert them. The journey home can be this complicated.'

'I'd rather stay here. I can get a state funeral, the ministry will mourn me as one their own, as will the Academy of Arts, and the kids won't have to worry about a thing. They can organise a mass entertainment there, too, and I can be mourned as someone else's personal loss. You are so clever, do tell me what to do.'

'Stand up,' she says encouragingly, because the Doctor placed this burden upon her. 'Leave the rest to hell. Fuck the funeral.'

Over the next few days, she visits the Painter daily. She doesn't seek permission to visit but before leaving she asks whether he needs anything.

'Bring me some boiled egg for breakfast. Do you know how to boil an egg?'

'Everybody can boil an egg. Even I, though I can't cook,' she laughs.

'You may think that but I have eaten plenty of badly boiled eggs in my time. People overboil them and they end up like ping pong balls. Or they are badly peeled. Or the inside is still runny. Yuck! Boiling an egg is serious business. And so is making proper jam. In which there is no thingie. You know. Gum.'

'What time is breakfast?'

'Seven. Is that okay or too early?'

'Great. Boiled egg and jam. Anything else? Butter? Fresh bread-rolls?'

She makes him promise that, in exchange, he'd try to stand up the next day.

Mornings are the trickiest time of the day for her, but she doesn't reveal this. More fragile than death. Silent mornings, if possible spent still, without any words, only waiting for words and dreaming of the book. Without words spoken out loud. She's working at a narrow, earth-coloured desk. She had only broken this rule when the Son was little. Back then, it was for the sake of the Son, now it's for the sake of the Father.

He's the only one she'd like to resurrect in a book.

The miracle could still happen, couldn't it?

These days the road winds around the mountains, but once upon a time it used to cut straight through them.

The mountains look like dark blue and turquoise waves in the early afternoon sun. The ones further afield are becoming lighter, almost washed out to blend in with the colours of the sky on the horizon. After lunch, Ágó resumes lying on the back seat and soothes her longing for the buzzing embrace of the big city by listening to the white noise of home plugged straight into her ears. Meanwhile, Csaba got swallowed up by the cheese shop in the parking lot. 'Yes, I have a certain nostalgia,' she replies to Susan while they are waiting, faced with the mountains. Susan nods, like someone who recognizes the words she's hearing. She recognizes them and adjusts them to her own image, substituting the ones she does know with something else. '*Mama said that, too. For those mountains,*' and she points at the formation running parallel with the road. Kincső has spoken to her about the mountains. 'When they lived in New England, she used to call that landscape and deciduous forests *homy. That feels a little like home for her.* Though she also said that everything was entirely different over there.'

Not the mountains, she points out to the girl. They have never lived among mountains, she was brought up on the plain she utters, and these two words blur together again: *plain, plane.* The mountains have always been a site for excursions, something one has to battle with and admire. As if they had closed in the space within the mountains. Perhaps because she hasn't yet been on the top of the mountain, from where the world could have opened up to reveal its greatness and completeness.

She used to know somebody who has chosen the mountain as a home.

One winter when the Son was still quite little, they rambled around here. They would often come to this area after he was born, as if she felt it her duty to show him where she was from. To the right of the narrow and winding dirt road, there is a precipice, to the left, a row of young mountains. They drove up to the top and then got out of the car. While they were still sitting in the car, she felt as if she'd be tilting off the road, as if something was pulling her into the abyss to the right, so she was leaning towards the left to redress the balance. Space wanting to rip the body apart. Once they get to the top, they hold hands, the Son is there with her, huge shepherd dogs ran towards them and she held on to the Son's hand so hard that it hurt. The kid isn't afraid.

'I'm not afraid of dogs, only of people,' the man says before the birth of the Son, the future father of the future son.

Despite this, she picks up a few stones and is about to swing her arm as they get closer. Her fear of the mountains blends in with the wild dogs, but then a man appears in the distance and as soon as he blows his whistle, the beasts obediently turn around and follow the command to regroup behind him. He's wearing rubber boots and worn-out modest clothing, and has a rugged, dark brown face and pungent smell. He hasn't said a word to anyone other than animals for a fortnight. He's guarding the Canadian wooden huts at the top of the mountain, seeing that their wealthy owners only live in them between May to September.

The sky is lying low and near, it's about to fall on top of them. The man is offering some spruce tea. He's separated and has been living here for twenty-five years. He could no longer live in a city. He hates the city, it's filthy and cruel. The city is a prison. His children don't come up here. He doesn't go down there. Too many things have happened down there, he concludes the conversation. The city is cruel. What's cruel, has fallen out of God's grace. The man makes the sign of the cross three times. He doesn't tell his story. He uses a strange word for cruelty, in which one can recognise the word for dog.

'How about when you are old?' she cautiously asks the man, who says he's only sixty despite his fragile wrinkly neck and slow speech.

'In your opinion one can only die in the city?' he asks and winks. When he reaches the point that he can't get any work, he'll go up the mountains and sit down. He has already decided what to do. That's when the story will end.

Space always leaves a visible mark on you, Ágó explains. She researches the universe on the other side of the world, wanting to unravel the creation of space and the beginning of the story. It will always be visible where I'm from. No matter how high up I'd get. You're coming from another space, being born under a different sky, she muses while walking among the New Haven buildings modelled on medieval English universities. Everything and everybody wants to look like something already existing, for example these little red brick buildings with their large green lawns. But if you come closer, you can see that this isn't medieval brick, these buildings were built by slaves a bare century and a half ago. Or the donations of plantation owners were carved into the walls. But space will always be visible in her, too. Whenever Ágó opens her mouth at an academic conference, everybody can tell that she wasn't born here, she didn't attend these expensive schools, and this is an intangible and invisible handicap to her scientific career. This in addition to being a woman, though she couldn't really say whether her origin or her gender was a bigger hindrance, which she had overcome somewhat in time. As opposed to the priceless advantage that she's white – Ágó declares almost triumphantly, searching for the right word, 'is it *irretrievable, how do you translate irretrievable*?' She was born white. Which, to be honest, 'is just another merit of space, isn't it?'

'*How do you say isn't it in English*? That's everything by the way. Skin colour. Isn't it. Who wouldn't have wanted to jump out or shoot oneself out from this spatial captivity?'

Ágó might have signed up precisely for this. For conquering space. Once and for all, and all of it. But it may well be, she adds still immersed in thought, that you'd find this easier because you were the best at English in our class.

'Me?' she asks, taken by surprise.

She has never been able to clarify the meaning and usage of tenses, and she pronounces similar words the same way. Bear and beer. I go down the pub and ask for a bear.

'What sort of nostalgia, then, if not for the mountains?' Susan quizzes her.

'Neither space nor time, but the two together,' she explains to Susan. *'Maybe nostalgia is not the right word. Lust? Maybe lust. Longing?* Yearning? *Lust. I am tired of my own lust, you know.'* As soon as she utters the term, the natural accent of her mother tongue intervenes so lust and lost merge into a single word. 'Aren't they related?' Damn it! Something she had never known, only imagined at most. How can one lust for such a thing? So she clarifies straightaway, *'not the things I have lost,'* she doesn't merely understand the difference between the two words but has them on the tip of her tongue, except that she's unable to pronounce them correctly.

This place, this establishment where traffic is now rolling on four parallel lanes has no significance. She read about the fact that once in this small town, by now only a village, theatre companies used to appear and perform the odd show at the local hotel on their way back from the capital. Famous actors from the capital city, major tragic actresses as well as romantic heroes would turn up back then. Today, it's a characterless small town with identical buildings, with an agglomeration of swiftly erected cheap glass and metal surfaces, this greedy capitalism is just as dull as its concrete forerunners that nobody will ever demolish except for decay itself, or maybe an earthquake, in short, it can only get swallowed up by time and space one day. This place no longer carries any significance, it has lost what it had once had. By now, this is simply nowhere, nothing, Sheol. A place that has fallen from grace. Sheol is the Hebrew name for hell. A space that has been emptied, a place of transit, where she hasn't had a stopover either in the last thirty years. Hell isn't a place of fire but of emptiness and meaninglessness. Of homelessness. As the man who got offended by the world and went up to the mountain said: the place that has fallen from God's grace. What she is nostalgic about is the place of grace.

She had never stopped here to hand over her body to this place, her body and heart, which is one and the same. As she's listening to her own wavering words arguing that beauty and strength can only exist in the past, while this place here is a meaningless and empty space, a place reserved for transition and waiting, with a view to moving on, she realizes that this isn't what she actually wants to articulate. Rather that we want to invest everything with meaning, and this is maddening and tiring.

'That we can't, I can't exist in meaningless places, in places devoid of significance. We can't bear this emptiness, this nowhere.'

She is of course aware that this town is home to many people who have been born here and moved away from here, who are thinking of their home with the same silent longing in case their fate has assigned faraway landscapes and foreign lands to them. This Sheol is someone's Ithaca, where they want to return. For some, this is what home is.

Susan is listening to this monologue in silence, looking out of the window, without interrupting this fragmented, alien and tiring voice. She has been given too many tasks with which she'd have to connect in order to understand the past, the present, foreign places, local conditions, too much to be aware of and think about that's not hers, only her mother's at most, but definitely not hers. She backs out and closes her eyes. This isn't her world. These are not her empty spaces devoid of meaning. Not her nostalgia. 'It's Kincső's business.' This is her mother's business.

'*This lust is killing,*' she concludes, thinking that Susan is still listening with her eyes closed, this endless longing is killing her. 'Longing for home, which leads you into a narrow alley, where you can neither come out from nor delve further in, and you just stay captive therein. These *disgraceful places*, these cruel places fallen from grace, as the man on the mountain put it, they have fallen from God's hand like dust. But don't we all want to climb back to the same place, do we?'

She's not really on top of her words, this is why she keeps chattering, in the hope that the person listening to her is able to put some order into them in some way, seeing that she isn't. Basically, it's all a matter of craving, that's the gist of her words.

Edina

After graduation, she had only met up with Edina from among her classmates, after the latter came to one of her literary evenings. They exchanged a few more messages thereafter and discussed going on a trip together, now that Edina had a dog. In their correspondence, they call this a walk, implying a lesser commitment than a trip, which would be too much of an undertaking for a catch-up taking place after twenty years. Edina's heavy black SUV is waiting for her at the end of the road, near her hotel, and it suddenly reminds her of Moscow with its distant wealth. They are going to the edge of town, and the car rolls onto a dirt road leading into the forest before coming to a halt on a meadow dotted with places used for barbequing. Edina leaves her soft leather gloves in the glove compartment. They are instantly struck by the heat as soon as they step out of the car, which is equipped with a seat cooling system. The Shetland shepherd is waiting in a cage in the boot.

On the edge of the forest, the pungent sweet smell of unburied corpses emanates from an area along the approach road. It's trying to warn the living about something. Along the edge of the gravel road there are burn marks and tufts of hair and bones of unidentifiable colour and origin; a dog or lamb, perhaps a fox. The remains are barely visible above ground level as the frequently passing cars and carts have already rammed them into the dry cracked soil. Dust to dust. Unfamiliar fate. Only the sharp stench of decomposition is reminiscent of the animal's former existence. What has become one with the soil is no longer an animal or a body, it has returned to its maker and found its rest.

The dog would like to pull in the direction of the smell but the leash is holding it back. It would be able to recognise the story with its snout. They live nearby and often come this way especially since they have a dog, much wanted by the kids, Edina explains as she's confidently heading towards the forest. They were watching the dog's birth on camera, across country borders, and the kids were even following what the mum ate before giving birth. They would have no doubt scrutinised the moment of conception, too, had they not missed it. They have been longing for precisely this breed and dreaming about this dog, first seen in a TV series. Except that they are not taking it for walks.

The edge of the forest is tidier than expected, they note.

Edina is making her way confidently, without looking at the remains of the corpse. The fallen leaves are rustling under their feet, the dirt road has cracked and it's hard to make any progress among the cart-tracks frozen into the onetime mud. Despite the drought, the forest is brimming with mushrooms protruding from under the fallen leaves. Perhaps nobody is harvesting them anymore, not even the locals, and they aren't sold at the market, either.

Edina's family bought a house on the other side of the forest. It's a large house with a view onto the hills behind the town, with a security system, strong walls, good sense of space, round-shaped living room with floor to ceiling windows. After the walk, she's invited in. She falls captive to the good life and a good word, and only returns to her hotel late at night.

'Where would you rush to?' Edina asks her to stay. 'To a hotel?' For someone staying at a hotel, there is no reason to rush or to lead a private life.

Edina contacted her when she read about her literary evening and invited her on a walk. She even offered to pick her up, so the writer gave her the address of her hotel. Edina can barely conceal her shock and asks whether she lives there. In this town, the writer has no living relatives left, only dead ones, she replies.

Edina would like to initiate a conversation about the house, the home they sold. 'It must be hard,' she begins cautiously, as if she wanted to discuss some deadly illness. 'I don't remember,' she replies, they have nothing left here since her mother also moved away a few years ago. Only the two times two metre burial plot in the cemetery, the lease of which they are still paying. But they won't want to get buried there themselves.

She's not so much attracted by the prospective story, which is Edina's story, but by the forest at the edge of town, the dry mushrooms, the middle-aged woman who's the same quiet and shy girl she went to school with, the unfamiliar life. She didn't come for the story lying behind but for the events still lying ahead, which could bring about some good news. She couldn't possibly know that she'd be getting a piece of good news on this very walk. So she gladly agrees to this walk. 'Gladly,' she says, but the heart is silent, only the body goes, it's here in this town, drifting along, ready for something to happen. Right now, Edina would also like to tell a story.

She's being offered up so many stories. People begin to tell their story, their densely dramatic story that subverts their whole life, a story that just bursts out of them, as if it was unwanted by anyone, including the protagonist. It's cascading down like a waterfall, impossible to narrate or listen to. Both the story and the storyteller would like to belong to someone at long last. The story is dashing through the forest like the black dog that runs past them with its unknown past and goals. At times, people just come up to her saying:

'I used to know your father.'

'I didn't. I have no idea who he was and what happened to him', she could respond.

In the familiar forest where she hadn't set foot for at least three decades, the confident and well-built middle-aged woman suggests: 'You have written our story.' Now she wants to tell the story of her family. That of her parents and grandparents. Of the religious sect.

The reason why Edina couldn't come to pick her up from the hotel and from the street where the hotel was situated because that in itself is the story. The gist of the story. The small chapel also used to be on this street but has since moved away, the church has grown in size, having received a major subsidy from the centre, and the building where the congregation would meet back in the day was demolished. Since then, she is unable to go to that street, not even by car. She simply doesn't set foot there.

'Something beautiful...' Edina begins on a wavering note and her steps lose their pace, softening and slowing down, like waves crashing onto a rock. 'Something beautiful went down the drain. Our world has collapsed.'

She has only written about this sect in one book, but from an entirely different angle, meaning that she avoided any critical note regarding them, the church and its members, this was even picked up by some critics who wrote about the bigots, the blinded, without having a clue, instead of writing about the people she was talking about who saved their souls, because their salvation was more important than their everyday bread. They gave the book to a film institute for a famous elderly director to turn it into a film, but the tiny female director concluded that there was no proper storyline in the book, except for a few small images that had the potential to be used perhaps, there was no story as such, so 'it will be difficult', she added, as if she was grading a student paper after mulling it over for a while with disappointment. If there is no story, there is no good news. Every true story is a piece of good news.

Edina is telling her story in her short vowels, she finds this so irritating about her mother tongue at other times but now it adds a touch of familiarity, they have already made it back home and the husband joins in, so they either switch languages or use a mixture of the two. They got to know each other through the congregation, which was above language and origin, 'back then', Edina adds bitterly. Later, the congregation split up along ethnic lines. Thousands of details in the story are budding, meandering, breaking up and rustling under their feet.

After the walk, they finish off a second bottle of wine over dinner while sitting at the heavy teakwood table, in the distance, the dark blue outline of the forest with the pungent smell of the animal corpse flattened on the road, and opposite the low-rise Finnish-style villas on the hillside, far away from the buzz and lights of the town. 'What would be our story', she'd ask, swiftly surpassing the boundaries of sobriety, she's drinking fast, like her father, with 1.66 per ml of alcohol in her blood, this is much more than her father used to have, about half a century ago he would start his day with 200 g cognac, which is 1,28 per ml. She won't be able to find out whether this was his entire daily intake because they only made a note of his morning routine, the rest of the story was left in the dark. After all, nobody could hold his hand 24/7, not even a snitch, even though he could have done so because only that would constitute a complete story. The story itself will only be sought out, if at all, by distant descendants. 1.66 per ml is characterised by euphoria and excitement, from which it could result that she'd instantly find out, interrupting Edina, 'what would be our story? And what would be such a good news in it?'

Edina is talking about the schism and ethnic conflict in which they live, the miserable ways in which people are turning against each other. A few hours ago, they were discussing that 'at this age' a person is either an alcoholic or only drinks a glass of wine at most, but in the end, they follow Edina's hard-working and late-returning husband to the wine cellar and undermine every alcohol-related theory from the past as well as present. 'We have a free evening on our hands, the kids are at camp,' Edina explains.

It takes eight hours for toxins to leave the body, a good sleep, which is never good enough because it's restless, dry, superficial and swirling. In contrast, the heart is unable to get rid of its many questions at this rate, because theories have nothing to say about the fact that at 1.66 per ml, one's dreams, like some highly determined and enraged waves, are ready to drift away everything, even the largest and best-controlled vessels.

'This story of ours, namely that you stayed behind while we left, had to happen exactly in this way, even though it could have taken place the other way round, too. I didn't want to go anywhere,' Edina concludes.

'Perhaps you could be the good news,' she looks at them, 'you are two beautiful people who have overcome division.'

Edina's childhood face can no longer be seen as she's sitting next to her husband, holding hands, and in the husband's gaze one can no longer see the little boy, either, only the middle-aged man. The good news is the gospel, which means story. This is their story, two languages, a large house with floor to ceiling windows, a small divided congregation, something beautiful that has been lost and something that has stayed with them. Their love is a shared glow and warmth, she feels like lying down on the floor next to the Shetland dog. Her paternal inheritance, the commandment of her father's fate, is that she is forbidden to drink. This is something she thoroughly breaks this evening. When she drinks, she turns into two people, she and someone else, a bit like in Chekhov, but in her case, the double has a twisted story. Dreams become menacing, as if it was possible to reverse, rewrite and hence re-live her own fate, as if she wasn't trying to get back to a hotel room that night but could return to another homeland, another life, next to the Shetland dog on the wooden floor. Her paternal inheritance when she drinks is that she wants to emigrate or immigrate, migrate again and return again, never to come back, just go somewhere, to the end of the world, beyond the icebergs where the final homes await. Iceberg, melting iceberg, Greenland, final countdown with everything even though she has only lived one half, the half of those who left. It could have panned out in such a way that she was the one to live here, on this hill by the forest with three children and a dog whose very conception could be traced back if need be. She leads another life. She shouldn't drink anymore, she concludes again the next day.

Edina, in any case, thinks so, and she leans back and with a remote control she elevates the footrest of her armchair, the body has done its work: it was able to tell its own story.

Diligent and docile Edina graduated in three languages, the state language, a Western and an Eastern language; this was the most they were allowed to study at the time when they obtained their Baccalaureate. With the opening of the borders, however, the number of language programmes has gone up, and by now a myriad of languages are on offer everywhere. Edina, by then the mother of three children, has started a business together with her husband and opened a language school. They started in a centrally located flat, in only two rooms, while these days they are renting two adjacent buildings where they teach twelve languages plus any additional ones on request. Meanwhile, she has barely left town, instead of her making her way towards these languages they came to her.

'You won't guess which is the most popular course,' she asks cheerfully, while they accompany her husband to the balcony for a smoke.

She's pouring a large glass of cold soda from the fridge, they have ice cubes and ice slush as well, which one would the guest prefer. 'Lots of ice', she replies. Entire icebergs. They have a sobering effect.

'Really,' she states with pride. 'Our mother tongue. It isn't taught anywhere as a foreign language. It can't be chosen at school, even though it would be so much easier to learn as a child. We are the gap in the market. *The market gap.* Do you have any idea how hard it is to find a teacher who can teach your mother tongue as a foreign language? Do you know what salary I have to give them? We are the gap in the market, *the unmet need of the customer.* We'll end up truly valuable by the time we die out. We'll even have a museum of our own,' she adds and laughs with a wide smile she hasn't yet displayed before, tilting her head back to reveal a dark amalgam of fillings in her upper teeth, meaning that she hasn't yet had them replaced with white ones. Her husband hugs her and plants a kiss on her cheek. They laugh together. Towards the end of the evening Edina mentions the class meeting planned for the next year. 'It will last for three days,' she shakes her head. 'Not possible not to go.' The words are being formed very slowly, as if a group of clueless soldiers were looking around and then rolling in all directions in search of meaning. She knows, she has visited the Teacher who has also invited her.

As they are waiting for a cab at the top of the hill in the warm night (Edina couldn't persuade her to spend the night because she has been holding on to this hotel room like some safe point of reference), a small black dog with matted curly fur dashes past them.

'It has business to attend to,' Edina states.

The animal charges forward, looking straight ahead, ignoring everything in its way, like someone following their goal. Perhaps it has to find its way home. Perhaps it's heading towards Nothing, towards nowhere, towards Sheol. Perhaps it has fallen out of its home, it has wandered off, was thrown out, wasn't looked after, or simply the house was sold on. It simply turns up and then vanishes, its story staying unknown for good.

Edina wants to know how long she's staying in town. She's busy, so she must already go back tomorrow. Edina offers to drive her on Friday.

'Fine, I'll go with you,' she responds swiftly, surrendering herself. She has well and truly yielded.

It all ended with a sunset.

Edina reached up and opened the car's double sunroof: the sky was basically looking over their heads as they were heading West. The sun was plunging lower and lower until its glare ended up being unbearable to the naked eye. Despite wearing a pair of snug fitting sunglasses, Edina was still bothered by the sinking red sun. To avoid crossing the border in a location where they would have had to wait for several hours, she left the motorway and chose a less busy but longer route. This is how they crossed the border.

'Isn't it strange that the borders are again.'

The sentence couldn't be finished because after a short bend the bright light suddenly slashed through the inside of the car. Edina reached up and pulled down the sunshield.

'They've sorted everything out in this car, except for the sunset and sunrise. Though I get to see the latter a lot less.'

They were driving along a quiet dual carriageway, in-between a scattering of hills.

'What's longer is actually shorter these days,' Edina explains.

The road is winding gently between the hills, barely traversing any villages. The setting sun is playing hide and seek with the hills. Perhaps it wanted to say that borders are impassable again. The number of motorways has gone up, but the waiting time is longer and controls are more severe.

'These days it's impossible to describe a sunset, isn't it?' she asked cautiously, before slowing down as a fawn was cutting across the road in the distance. Edina's electric car is really silent. 'Too silent,' she says, 'because neither people nor animals can hear it coming. So she has to be even more vigilant.'

'Besides, it's harder to charge these cars in our country than in yours,' she explains 'it really wasn't a good purchase. It's too silent and too fiddly.'

While Edina is talking, her passenger is keeping her gaze fixed to the roadside, as if it was mandatory for her to keep tally of the fallen. Edina stops talking, perhaps she's reminiscing about her own story of road accidents. She then states, as if she was able to read the passenger's thoughts: 'I have never run over a living being.'

She makes the sign of the cross. Yet her previous congregation was part of a Neo-Protestant church. She no longer goes to church but has had her children baptised. Now she's heading to the christening of her brother's child. Her brother left the country twenty-five years ago, and has now had a child at the age of nearly sixty, by his second wife. They rarely see each other and their relationship is rather cold. They are arguing even over their meagre inheritance, Edina says in a sad voice.

As they drive past a bush, several dozen sparrows shoot up to the sky.

Their plan was to discuss everything that was missing from the story during the long drive. But then these stories fail to merge into a billowing flow, as if the two women were unable to find their important life events or the connection between them. They pick up the odd shard from the past, but they drop it and move on to the next, unable to fit the parts together. There is no story. There are children, buried parents, a new dog, books and an enterprise. The children like to climb walls. The Son likes that, too, she interjects, and so does Edina's eldest, a girl. The writer remembers a recent rock-climbing accident but doesn't mention it. 'Son? What Son?', Edina asks, taken by surprise, as this is the first time she hears about this.

'I thought you don't have children.'

They both think that they are separated by visible worlds and stories heading in opposite directions. The envy of those who left with regard to those who stayed. The envy of those who stayed with regard to those who left. Edina's large family and their modestly displayed yet increasingly visible wealth that needs ever more attention. One of them stayed, the other left and filled the last few decades with books. And she didn't even talk about the Son, making him invisible. Some sort of an abyss emerged, measured in miles and lifestyles.

It could have happened the other way round, too. This time, it is Edina solemnly holding the steering wheel with her soft leather gloves and she is sitting next to her in the passenger seat. They could swap places though. Edina could be the one being driven, and she the driver, Edina, the one who left, and she the one who stayed behind, and then this other life could be hers, and her life could be anyone else's who took the decisions she has taken. These lives could be interchangeable, and there is no all-enlightening reason why that would need to be deciphered or researched to find out the reason behind the fact that this had to be their life and no other. This is simply what happened. This departure and this staying behind simply happened to them.

Edina didn't actually show off her children, she didn't boast about their successes, their skiing holidays in Salzburg (she says ski), the seasides, the kids' riding and music lessons, their weekly massage sessions, the super silent kitchen gadgets and household help, the endless work and gradually growing language school where their mother tongue is the most sought-after offering. Instead, she's concealing their wealth, the smooth surface of the visible world. She only shows something from it when they make a stopover on the other side of the border and she studies the menu in a restaurant, having meticulously wiped her reading glasses with a disposable towel, as if she was getting ready for library research, and holding the glasses with both hands, places them on her nose, immersing herself into a read-through of the dishes on offer. She displays such a stern attitude when talking to the waiter as if he were some medical student on his final exam, prior to gaining the right to decide over the lives of patients. The waiter is new and clueless, he has no idea what these eggs baked in black crust could possibly be, as they understand the name of the dish from the menu. Could this be a mistranslation? Or this is something actually baked in a black and crunchy crust? What the hell could it be? Edina calls for the head waiter.

Later they are staring ahead again in the pleasantly cool car, making their way in the infinite landscape, trembling in the scorching heat. The extended sunset, broken up by the hills, is the one and only most important event surrounding them at present.

'I was talking to my daughter about the past. Our shared past. She read your volume of short stories and said that in the book everything was clear. Perhaps you could even describe a sunset, couldn't you?'

Once upon a time, she tells Edina, she wanted to finish a book with a sunset, and the protagonist was wondering whether the sun would actually rise again. In other words, whether there is a tomorrow. The protagonist articulates a genuinely deep concern: is there such a thing as tomorrow. As if a book were to finish on Good Friday with an empty grave. The crucifixion has taken place, the body is lying still, there's no sign of breathing through the nose, the Light of the World has descended to hell and it's time for the burial. A believer might ask whether the story can continue at all. Whether there is anything else thereafter. In the end, she discarded this plotline. This is her answer regarding the sunset.

'Which book was this?'

Edina is trying to guess. 'I've read them all,' she boasts. She can thank these books, no matter how they might end and whatever they might be worth in the light of eternity that she was taken on this journey. In Edina's refreshingly cool car, space is light and endless. Like two shepherds playing their flutes, staring at the sky strewn with cirrus clouds. They have things in common – their language, books, the random fact that they went to the same class at school, the town where they once used to live – all this brings them on this journey and makes them sit in this car for a nine-hour-long journey because Edina is a fast and safe driver. 'You are mine', she thinks about Edina, 'you are my protagonist'.

'It doesn't matter which book it was,' Edina casts a glance at her passenger. 'You are still ours.'

Suddenly they look at each other. Until now, they were both staring ahead, the passenger as well as the driver. Until now, she was looking at the road, the hard shoulder and the now sparse traffic coming from the opposite direction. She didn't want to gain any particular advantage; she didn't want to look in the face of someone who can't reciprocate. Yet nonetheless now they are looking at each other, as if they wanted to see the sentence and not each other, to catch a glimpse of the spoken word: to belong to someone.

Every so often, one can see sentences in the glowing light of the summer dusk.

She remembers the case of two alpinists climbing up holding on to the two ends of a rope using the so-called simul-rappelling technique, then one of them slips out and plummets for at least fifty or eighty metres, whilst there are another two hundred or so metres below. They are climbing along the Path of Light, the Sendero Luminoso. The next thing is plummeting devastation. Or a miracle. Things then take a different turn, the climber grabs hold of a salient, and his mate on the opposite end of the rope can hold him because there is a knot at the end of the rope, not like in the finished story in which for some unknown reason there wasn't a knot that could have held up the two young people and one of them died. In this present story there is a knot that catches the nosediving person, there is somebody there to hold him, there is a salient that he can grab while falling and then hold onto – all this at the same time. This is life survived.

Every single question arising from their mutual anger or jealousy – 'Why did you leave? Why did you stay? Whose choice was good? Whose choice was bad?' – gets a complete answer in this barely one-second-long glance. The only question left is 'how do you live these days?'

'What's your life like?' 'You are the other person on the end of the rope.'

They are looking at each other.

'You saved me', she thinks of Edina.

'You saved me', Edina thinks of the writer, too.

Tired, square-shaped face, greyish skin, languid, burned-out fire. Every time she looked at her face, she was wondering what beautiful was. This time – due to the sunset or some other invisible thread – the face is glowing. And this sunset doesn't indicate that something is draining away but that something is about to grow.

The strange thing about sunsets is that they don't really differ from sunrises when represented in paintings, she explains to Edina at the end. In the case of famous artworks, especially if imagined by the Painter as fictional locations that one cannot identify in terms of actual spaces, one often has to guess what the artist might have wanted to express. Sunsets and sunrises are interchangeable and don't differ from each other except in direction. She wanted to ask Edina already at the beginning of their trip, she wanted to ask the impossible, to ask all those questions that if one listened carefully while looking into each other's eyes or while just sitting side by side, when differences are dissolved within a flowing conversation conducted as a result of investing carefully protected time and attention, perhaps they would have even volunteered to tell each other whether all these events, including their own story, has an actual reason or it's simply just happening.

Nice Words, Depleted World

This is her last evening in town, tomorrow she's heading home with Edina. On the extra day she has thus been gifted, she visits the Professor. A very long time has passed since she visited and who knows when she'll come again. As they are saying their goodbyes, the tiny and frail volatile body lets out a stern sound:

'Come again. Come every time. I can no longer travel to your world. My world has now become depleted.' By this she means that people have either left or passed away. The words she utters still have a strength to them.

In the beginning, back in the depth of time and the start of their shared time together, when she started to pay visits to the already elderly-looking Professor preoccupied with poetry, literature and aesthetics, the latter's life and home was full to the brim. With people, books, objects, various creative genres from Platonic dialogues to French essays, a myriad ideas and observations, conversations, world views and words. In this jungle inhabited by the Professor, a young author brandishing a manuscript had to fight for attention and the right to be present in her home, and whenever the door was open the visitor would not only gain access but also advice as well as books and new, unknown words in one's mother tongue and various useful languages in which one's *raison d'être* could be expressed. Viewed from this smoke-filled room, the world opened up like a huge wind-swept ocean, looking dangerous, boundless and desirable. A two-bedroom flat in the town centre, where everybody smoked and drank tea. They didn't drink any alcohol; the words and books were intoxicating enough.

Disciples, friends, acquaintances of acquaintances, young poets, emerging talents, quiet musicians and glum philosophers, colleagues as well as men and women without any particular agenda would keep coming and going, and just spend time at her place, sitting in silence. The Professor, who wasn't affiliated to any educational establishment, would talk, read, comment on manuscripts, correct, edit, recommend readings and say unexpected and surprising things about the essence of poesis, in a manner that wasn't taught at school. Most of the time though, she urged people to just listen to words.

Mothers in their private homes were jealous of this awkwardly dressed unkempt woman, after whose words the youth writing poetry in secret were continuously yearning. She was someone uninterested in cooking, good food, festive and family dinners, who considered driving a waste of time as it hindered thinking, and who never went on excursions because she solely lived among her books. In essence, she didn't do anything with her hands except for typing. Regarding childbirth, she declared that this was most suited to others, those women who were able to find fathers for their children, but she was unable to choose the right father out of several options and divorced all three candidates, and by now was thankfully past the age when she'd have to take such decisions: 'My name may well be Eve, but that doesn't mean that I have to give birth. After all, I'm not the first woman, we won't die out without my contribution.' She'd much rather ply other people's children with words, and as soon as they have taken a stance regarding light versus dark, good versus bad and have read their first Tolstoy, her door was open to them.

She did send the Professor her first book and then the second, but they hadn't met for ten years. She left and for a long time didn't look back. Now she's hesitantly preparing for the visit, somewhat scared of having to return to the past, to something that is behind her but not in her. As if she had fallen out of this past, by way of a window. She seized something and with that, she went out into the world. Now she feels guilty.

Edina told her that the Professor had read her book and would welcome a visit. Back in the day when she was still writing, Edina was also among the regular visitors, these days she tends to come for practical reasons and they don't talk much about books, as Edina helps with obtaining medication and other essentials.

Now it feels as if she was coming again to see the Professor with her manuscript and treat her like a judge, as in the olden days when the magnetic power of words was just beginning to dawn on her. This may well be the moment when it's decided what she deserves or what she has deserved: light or quiet, darkness or restlessness.

The Professor can't be contacted by phone, she learns from Edina, she can't answer the phone because she can no longer hear. She suffered two heart attacks.

When they meet the Professor hugs her, almost needing to grab hold of her in order to reach up to her, she has become so tiny as if they swapped places, or heads rather – now she is a head taller.

'Your father had the same smile,' the Professor observes when the unexpected guest arrives. The Professor used to know her father well, but they don't talk about him, after all her father had also fallen out of the world without saying a word.

The church worker delivers the Professor's lunch just as she's standing at the door, welcoming her guest.

Their short meeting barely lasts for two hours, and time is passing swiftly. Back then, there was unlimited time, but by now everything has its limits. They are not talking about the other limit where the Professor is preparing to go. She isn't interested in death, she concludes, she has survived it already, her own death twice, and that of others, many others, those who left, who died, who invited their own deaths, and who simply decided to fall out of the world without saying a word. There is nothing there, no need to be afraid. We belong to ourselves, that's all we have. The rest, is none of our business.

Her home is just like before but more neglected. Books, old manuscripts, newspapers, notebooks from decades ago, heaps of old diaries, she might even find her own manuscript at the bottom of some pile of paper. A defiance of everything that claims that things should and can be organised.

As she's sat there immersed in the armchair, they are struggling to converse because the Professor can no longer hear sounds and her hearing aid doesn't help in conveying other people's faraway and alien words.

'I'm deaf,' she puts it quite frankly. 'I've been deprived of the human word'.

She cannot tell her that when she used to come to this messy and seemingly dusty flat, the words that the Professor was uttering were akin to when a person about to drown lifts their head out of the water and then immerses again and continues with the drowning, as if this was the very nature of existence. These words that she cannot evoke at the moment have always shone a light on her path and she now knows that they definitely haven't been lost.

During the two hours she is sat in the armchair, they talk about everything, things she has heard many times but the Professor's conversation has become a one-way street, like old age itself. She talks about fleeing as a child, denunciations, home searches, snitches, she mentions book titles and authors, husbands and former friends, people who are deceased, committed suicide or emigrated, as well as people who vanished from her life without a trace, without as much as waving goodbye.

'You, too,' she adds dryly.

There is no time for ornate, elaborate stories, time is fragmented, nothing can be weaved into a coherent plotline, seeing that the exchange of words has also faltered. She has shared out her own story among those who used to visit her. Her secret police file that she received a few years ago is stacked away behind her bed, its pages jammed into a large bag, catching dust. She is complaining about the missing years, twelve years are missing before it continues again. She wasn't disappointed with anyone, she adds as she's leafing it through.

'What a pig he was and yet I even went to bed with him!' she cries out and closes the folder.

Never mind. Every sentence is a new turn in the jumble of life, but the Professor has already had an insight into every single bend. 'I shall be given a religious funeral,' she laughs, adding: 'I.'

Behind all this, there is still a person standing among the shards of her own life's events, of which the lucky ones continue to cherish a small piece in their pockets.

'Did I mention the chestnut trees?' she asks, sounding unsure.

They are standing on the balcony and the tiny and frail person is determined to light a cigarette. The strong and branchy chestnut tree reaches up to the windows and balconies and peeks into the world of the mortals. They look at the tree in silence, like people in need of acknowledging something more powerful than themselves.

She made a vow a decade ago when they started to chop down the trees on her street, the large and shady chestnut trees stretching all the way to her third floor flat and even beyond, that when they get to the last one, she'll follow suit and go, too. For good, from this world, she'll leave this town. By now, there is only a single tree left from the original eight.

'I have been around for eighty years and haven't had a quiet moment,' she observes, almost annoyed while triumphantly pointing at the empty sky. She is living with a pressure in her chest, as if her ribcage had lost its elasticity and was unable to expand with the air that is being breathed in, as if something was compressing it. 'There is a cat sitting on my chest. They simply don't want to let me be,' she continues and mentions that she telephones the town hall every single day despite making phone calls being so hellish! The device is whistling like hell and she can't understand a word from what they say, she can't hear it. When they chop down the last chestnut tree, she'll be on her way, too. The end. Which road? Which world?

Even though this disorderly flat, with lunch delivered every day on behalf of the congregation and with a prospective religious funeral, is her final home. She has never thought of leaving anywhere.

'Where should I go with this many books?' she asked, and with this concluded the discussion on leaving.

She'd always welcome bunches of visitors and laugh at the dilettantes who were compensating for their lack of talent with diligence and pay-offs, later starting fervent business enterprises and making lots of money. The young, the students, the adults as well as the middle-aged would continue to visit her for decades, until they started to visibly dwindle in numbers, getting married, giving birth, travelling and holidaying with their families, participating in foreign conferences, moving out of the increasingly suffocating town, emigrating, attending foreign universities, discovering new worlds with the help of scholarships and never coming back, or at most once a year, by which point visitors would no longer bump into each other unless in their writings, books and fulminant articles.

It was at least a decade and a half ago when her students' children had also started to travel the world, with scholarships and complicated funding bids, that was when she got an inkling of the imminent void, she opened her arms in her room, in the midst of several thousand books, and stated:

'My world has become depleted.'

Gradually, the number of visitors goes down to one a week, there are fewer people left to come round. Two friends committed suicide over the last few years, others died or went away, the frail Professor observes on a matter-of-fact tone while standing in the doorway. My world has become depleted. Ours, however, has become full, the visitor replies. Full with you. Scattered around the wide world in a thousand urns.

'I'll come again,' she whispers in the ears of the Professor, whose hearing aid is up for replacement, provided there is a stronger model on the market, because even the sounds have run out of her world. And as she steps out of the door, she'd like nothing more than to keep this promise. Not like those words written in books that aren't really true.

The Professor follows her with her gaze, there isn't and has never been any reproach in her ways, she's expecting her, she can come anytime, her door is always open. She's mellow like the home that forgives everything.

When the historian she contacted in relation to her father told her in confidence that 'there are some materials', he omitted to specify what the gist of these materials was. As if materials had a gist, like Polonius at supper in Hamlet (Act IV. Scene 3), 'not where he eats but where he is eaten', and she didn't yet know whether a certain delegation of government maggots would lay into her father, or her father would be wolfing down others in the presence of government maggots. Neither did she ask for clarification regarding the gist of these 'materials', they only agreed on what to do next, namely to hand in a request and prove entitlement *to these materials*.

The eventual encounter with the case file didn't quite take place in a cellar as she had imagined, among narrow, labyrinth-like corridors and heavy metal shelves, but in a small room with a low ceiling, lit by halogen lamps, where everything was simply too confined to the present. Even the dreary and irrelevant files seemed awkwardly in the present and dead. At long last, their death had become definitive.

In short, the said historian failed to mention the latter's gist, not considering this issue of importance since for him all these were only piles of documents, materials without any particular gist or indicative signs. The gist may well be indicated by the file's registration number, but these numbers were only intelligible to researchers familiar with this labyrinth: Those who lead their lives away from this material know nothing of their complex meanings.

She approached the materials with the curiosity of a writer, even though she had to get through two years and several thousand kilometres in order to obtain them: 'You won't be writing a book about state security reports featuring such case files, in which people are brandishing denunciatory reports, blackmailing and pointing the finger at each other while the broken victims are gasping for air, will you? And those in power are dark and evil? You won't, will you?', an acquaintance asked, almost beseechingly.

However her literary interest in the materials, in case it ever existed, evaporated quickly, since literary interests are generally prone to evaporation as long as the material is distant and cold. But as she's getting closer, even if not yet in time and space, she understands that although anything can happen and the materials can have any gist or even a combination of several options, there must be at least one certainty even when everything is pointing in a thousand directions in a tangle of truths and realities that are tearing the material apart. The only certainty is that I love you, ever more... she is whispering in her sleep the sentence dedicated to him in the absence of literature, because some certainty is simply needed. My beloved father.

'Your dad didn't do anything substantial. You can relax,' the kindly historian concluded at the end of their conversation, as if he had already taken a peek into these materials, still unwittingly brandishing the sense of direction.

It would indeed be great to relax.

'We shall go to pick up this package,' she informed the Son, recently turned eighteen, who could not have been known to the subject of the 'package' and who couldn't have known this extraordinary figure, 'We shall build a bonfire from it, okay? The past will burn. We shall burn out the past, like some wound.'

Didn't a French-Romanian historian of religions write that one can be connected to the past by way of two relationships or connections? Acceptance or purging? As for the file, they won't let her take the original. She would have to make it explode or build a bonfire on the spot, ideally the former. No big deal to bring in some explosives around the waist, but building a fire is tricky, a pile of four hundred pages – this is the size of the materials she'll be given – will be hard to set aflame, she had set fire to manuscripts before, so she knows. By the time the guards charge into the room alerted by the smoke detector, at most the edge of the documents will get scorched a little, and she'll only return home, if found worthy and extradited at all, after a major diplomatic kerfuffle, with criminal proceedings potentially lasting for years.

She no longer believed that she'd find some major truth, but she was shocked that four hundred pages only contained 200 grammes of truth. Four hundred pages. She was familiar with this length through her own handwriting and sweat, having written several books of this size. In the bundle, however, she was only met with 200 grammes of truth. Everything else was fiction, stupid servile literature from which definitely no masterpiece could emerge. Nothing is reminiscent of the past in the library where she eventually receives the file, the gist of which she cannot yet know, everything is in the present tense, one could just as well be in an interrogation or waiting room in some American state; large tables with smooth surfaces, chrome chairs and small halogen lamps on the tables. Everything is too new compared to this past, and one doesn't even have to wait long before they bring the documents on a shiny metal trolley. As far as one can tell, the staff working here are all cute and young, wear soft-soled shoes, are eager to help and silent. A young man in jeans suddenly appears and brings volumes bound in soft grey covers, slightly tattered around the margins, there is no hard back or spine in sight, there is nothing in them reminiscent of nails or barbed wire. The volumes blend into her lap, as she grabs them and holds them tight in her arms.

She's sitting there with her eyes closed, hugging, so you are here, my darling, my beloved father. Two volumes, held together with a string. Like a freshly sacrificed lamb, with legs tied together to make the murder easier. Zurbarán's lamb, waiting with legs tied together on a table or altar, in a black space devoid of depth. We know what happens next. There is nobody at its side, not a single human being except for the spectator, who should step into the picture to comfort it in its solitude. One has to step into the picture if one wants anything at all, otherwise eternal sorrow and inertia will stay with us, together with the lamb's endless solitude in front of the dark background. The lamb cannot be saved, at most, one can stand in solidarity. But why does the Painter present this animal in such an all-engulfing blackness? As if death was about to swallow everything up, with just a ray of light, – where could it come from? – capable of restraining it a bit, but the blackness, none other than the world itself, is menacing everything all the same.

She is holding the two hefty volumes close to herself. A soft, sleeping being, still and dead, nothing will ever keep us apart from now on, we have come home. The child is holding the parent in her arms, the parent's dead yet still warm body that had been waiting to be held by someone all this time. Only a hug can bring death to completion.

She hadn't yet read a single line from the actual content of the volumes. Was he a snitch? A person under surveillance? Both?

'Now that I'm holding your body at rest in my lap. Now that you've entrusted yourself to me forever. You are safe. You are soft. You are just heavy enough for me to bear. You weigh as little as a feather. There is no more struggle, it feels as if I was holding your drooping head and supporting your strong thigh with my hand. I'm hugging you, so we aren't alone. Now I know that this is ultimate peace. No one can see us.'

First the embrace, then language. In the beginning was the event, but there may not be a suitable language to address it.

Then there is the burial. I'll soon turn fifty. You return home and I have to go on my way. The soul, however, will linger a little longer with us.

Daddy, therefore, did nothing. Let's look at that nothing.

It all happened the way she had planned it: they took a plane together with the Son because he is also concerned with this story, she would have even considered the long overnight train, but the Son was in a rush. 'You have to know who your grandfather was,' she told him, but for the Son there is nothing behind the word grandfather, apart from some elderly man suffering from ailments, who is grumpy and doesn't smell very good, not the kind of person who'd take him to gather walnuts or paint the walls of the house, someone who has a warm and familiar scent under his sweater, the scent of home. They are staying at a hotel which is part of a reasonable international chain, this will be a proper excursion, she's explaining to the Son, in which we will invest time and money for hearty meals and long walks, 'we'll take a look together at all the good stuff,' but the Son doesn't really want to spend much time there, he is in a rush.

The day after their arrival, at the agreed time of 9 am, she receives him in the reading room of the far too modern library equipped with functional furniture that brashly ignores the past. She can hold him and place him on her lap for as long as permitted, 'Until when? *What time do you close*?' because for her this is the shared and comfortable language here, 'At *six*, but there is also a lunch break.' 'Fine, I'll come back then.'

In the end, out of consideration for the Son, they only spend a few hours there, before they have to give back the soft bundle in exchange for which the data will be transferred onto a CD, provided she brought one with her. 'A CD?,' she asks, baffled, 'Who still uses CDs these days?' she adds offhandedly, because one has to be offhanded in a capital city, or else people sweep you off the table like a fly. In preparation for her visit to this library, she practiced self-assurance phrases and familiarised herself with the regulations in order to obtain what she had been corresponding about for over a year; the reports with an unknown gist, be they about her father or written by him, or even a complex combination of the two. She arrived in the capital with a stern soul, knowing that it's a place where you simply have to be in charge, where you must be the one dictating how things should be, not someone else, so you'd better know what you are after, in a capital city you have to be a winner at all times, otherwise you're lost, you are a nobody, a loser, nought, zilch, otherwise they sweep you aside like a fly and you can go back home with a flea in your ear because you'll get absolutely nothing. Not even what you are entitled to, such as laying your hands on dead words. Isn't a pen drive, a data stick, a memory drive, a USB any good? she asks still offhandedly and incredulously, in response to which the youth in jeans just shrugs, fine, they can do that, too, it's all the same to him, '*I don't mind*'. In this capital city, the best thing is this lightness, this imperturbability, this volatility, when somebody in an office announces that things have to be done in a certain way but it's also fine to do them differently, where sheer force wins, her own force with which she has come to win, because she had once been a winner in another capital, too. She obtained the stuff and will take it home, *the whole stuff,* but perhaps this isn't a matter of the capital as such but of a certain so-called culture, the culture of negligence and improvisation. Fine, let's go for a USB stick, a pen drive, some sort of memory device. Not a huggable file with a soft grey cover, dead child, dead cat, only a tiny stick, a pen drive, a memory device, a USB in the pocket. The only certainty is that the file is about 'TOMA', seeing that the file she was given is the 'TOMA' file, solely preoccupied with a person named 'Toma', except for page 127, where it says 'Tóma'. This means that his code name was 'Toma', this was the name given to him – are code names only given to those who tail and monitor others, not also to those being monitored? Who could those astounding linguistic geniuses and jugglers possibly be, those creators of language who come up with such poetic yet referential names in their imagination? 'Toma' always appears in inverted commas, as if born out of fiction, after all, reality doesn't exist in these most secret, once dangerous and by now mainly soul-littering documents. This 'Toma', according to entries on pages 14, 82, 114, 117, 122 and three further documents generated on many different days in multiple forms by at least two dozen authors, among whom there are secret police workers, former colleagues, employers, and family acquaintances, was born at least seven times within the span of two months, on seven different days, he was given birth seven times by his mother. So much for precision.

'Toma' is not her father. This is the first certainty. 'Toma' is a fantasy, an avatar, born on seven different days.

'Toma' is not a certainty, of which so little can be experienced in the world anyway, even though some certainties are required in order to stay alive.

One finds out about 'Toma' that he worked at night and drank in the day, unlike everyone else, decent people would get drunk in the evening, after work. On his way back to his modest home from work, at dawn, he was capable of draining 200 grammes of cognac in one gulp, spending not more than three minutes at the bar, and this included coming in and paying, after this, he went to bed in a basement flat, a hellhole without a toilet; he lived in such terrible circumstances that even his snitches felt sorry for him. He repeats this six times a week. 200 grammes, *двести грамм* in Russia, because large numbers are reassuring and most certainly deliver the expected impact. 200 grammes is like being shot in the head. What sort of sorrow makes someone knock themselves out in such a well-targeted and precise way?

Black square. Pages and pages of black squares. They don't represent anything, they are redacting certain words, obscuring language as it were, provided there is any language there, one can't be sure. These could well be 'Toma's' sins, which only researchers can take a look at, with special permission. 'Toma' fornicated while drunk, he outraged public decency by sleeping with several people at once. She could perhaps ask the historian, who seems to have access to everything, to cast a glance and photograph the language behind the black squares, 'Toma's sins that have been covered up. 'Which 'Toma',' the historian asks. "'Toma', who is not my father.' Could he photograph for her 'Toma's' state secrets, 'Toma's' sexual adventures carefully covered up and duly concealed from us by the coy state, after having him under surveillance for thirteen years, having him watched, collecting reports on him, talking to him, inviting him for a beer or a cognac, photographing him, and in the end meticulously preserving all this evidence. 'But no, I shall not lift this black square off 'Toma's' groins, I don't wish to see him with his lover [black square], his woman, his girlfriend [black square], perhaps already with her mother, my mother [black square],' not her mother, she remembers, that woman doesn't even have a name, there is no name for her in the eyes of the state, she hasn't yet earned the right to a name, 'Toma's 'girlfriend' isn't my mother [black square], as 'Toma' isn't my father either.' Language is dead, black squares are triumphant.

The child might want to see what parents are doing in their bedroom. The child might. She does not. She'll soon turn fifty. She isn't 'Toma's' child. She doesn't want to know what's under the black squares.

'Toma's' wounded body – 'Toma' is not my father,' not her father – into which he'd drain 200 grammes of cognac in one gulp in order to burn through his throat and stomach and send a layer of mist over his mind because he had seen something unbearable. 'Toma's' wounded body in that awful, humid basement flat, as well as that unknown activity covered by black squares, is resting restlessly, although one can't rest while being restless and he certainly wasn't granted any rest or peace. Wounded body, 'this daddy didn't do anything special, you can relax' now that your body is exposed to the gaze, everyone's gaze, be it the gaze of researchers with special permits or writers, who might be interested in ordinary people, little people, with a view to write a book about them. He is resting restlessly under those black squares, under all-engulfing death. They can't stand language in state security. 'You can't stand it,' covered it with a black square, provided there was any language underneath at all, and not just some threat or a piece of hell. The black square is a mere burn scar, a scar of death, to ensure that restlessness stays with us.

We can't stand language either. We won't write any books about security files irrespective of their gist, relax, we only want to cauterize the past, that black square is our burn scar, too, language is dead, but this is irrelevant now, as you are the one who died above all, my beloved father.

This won't beget any fiction because this is already fiction. What she finds in that file, instead of the file, is dried-up meaningless hell. She has enough of hell as it is, she won't give it any more space. 'So, I'm done. *I am done with that.*' All she's interested in from now on is the sky and the clouds.

When the Son asks her to read him something from the file, she translates a few irrelevant passages because she can still read but is already struggling to speak this language. On these pages, the nothing feels as if it were a living person. Living, working, loving, drinking, having opinions about the regime, talking while drunk, displaying threatening behaviour and wanting to emigrate.

'Did he really want to go to Israel? And the GDR?'

The son wonders.

'Don't think so, he never mentioned anything like that,' she replies, somewhat unsure, because the real 'Toma', in case he existed, never wanted to leave.

'Shame.' the Son contends. 'Then I'd be German. Or Jewish.'

The dead, thousands, tens of thousands of lone bodies, including theirs, are lying on the cold metal shelves, separated by narrow corridors, the files are tied together with string and piled on top of each of each other because they are too soft to stand on their own feet, they are too fragile and shattered, they are lying like dead bodies, unburied, on top of one another, entangled in a huge pointless system, resting restlessly while waiting for eternal rest. Not light but at least peace.

'Toma's' wounded body is among them, with black squares on pages 50, 122 and 331. 'As you are lying on the cold shelf, blacked up, you are drinking your usual 200 grammes of cognac in full view of everyone, every morning after work, on your way home from the printing house. They say that you chose night shifts, and now I also know that the night shift was your choice, 'Toma's' double.'

Wounded body on the cold self. 'I shall take you back with me. We are heading home.'

'We had to make this diversion, this detour, this stopover, not a final stop but an in-between one, to safely deposit on the cloud the content of the file, which isn't actually a file but a pen drive featuring four hundred pages with photos and a few black squares. My father is already in the cloud, or to be precise 'Toma' is, the guy who isn't my father, the cloud is high up on the sky, thick in its consistency – what matter are you made of? – a cumulus cloud, so large and white that one can sense the depth of the sky. 'Toma' is in the cloud, this woeful 'Toma' with a wounded body, whose solitude, drunkenness and black squares, with very death devouring him, is right here in front of everyone's eyes, up in the cloud and registered under Inv. nr. 25–84.'

'Fortunately, he never emigrated' – she explains to the Son. He had a weak constitution and would have died of homesickness. On page 204, there is a claim that he would like to emigrate. To Israel. Or to the West. While she's saying this, she relies on facts interpreted by three other people:

'Toma' states at a gathering, after having insulted the system spattering rude words and making an 'inflammatory nationalist and irredentist speech', then somebody, who is in attendance at said gathering, memorises these details and informs a third person, who makes a note of all this and puts their signature confirming that these were the words that had been uttered. The fourth person, who was also present, added a sort of 'moodboard', a kind of cheerful account of who was there and what they said. By this point, 'Toma' is past several doses of 200 grammes, so his intentions explode in a momentary alcohol-fuelled bluff or rather a liberating deep-felt desire for truth, like some inscrutable yet flooded river with crested waves. We shall never know. Maybe he really wanted to leave. Had we been born in Israel or Germany, he would have spoken German to the grandchildren. Would he have lived to see the birth of his grandchildren, this is seriously in doubt because he wouldn't have coped, homesickness would have prevented him from awaiting the birth of his grandchildren, 'our birth'.

In hindsight, she'd definitely try to talk this 'Toma' out of his plan to leave, because homesickness is a really suffocating thing, especially for such a sentimental person, it's a powerful and painful struggle, a yearning, longing, nostalgia, she even knows the relevant Russian word for it: *тоска*, so that at times, when this terrible homesickness overwhelms her and she'd have to just drink, and drink a lot to somehow numb and diminish the terrible pounding of this longing, to silence the cry of the homeland that's gradually moving away and will soon exist solely in her dreams, and in order to become a little less sensitive she'd have to drink an awful lot, even in emigration. As far as she knew him, this homesickness, this terrible thing especially for sensitive individuals with weak nerves, his alcoholism and this agonising longing would eventually lead to suicide. Pretty much the way it did in the end, except that homesickness didn't actually play such a large role. Some sort of longing, however, had to exist, perhaps it was also for a homeland, a longing for another home, something more home-like, for a place that had not yet fallen out of God's grace. But this isn't written in these four hundred pages, those who wrote the material for these pages didn't notice anything of essence, they were unable to observe or detect anything, and in case they did look, it was from a middle view, because had they looked carefully and thoroughly and for a long time at what they wanted to see, had they leaned closer to observe the sorrow of the drunken man crying out loud, they would have had to use completely different words, provided they would have found these in their vocabulary. These pages failed to lift the veil from any of the secrets belonging to this man, because the barren language they used cannot touch anything, but can only cause wounds, hide stuff with black squares and bring about death. Those who wrote it have no idea about grace and mercy because all they know is cruelty.

They write about him that he was a traitor.

He is cussing and defaming his country, instigating people against it, besmirching it and being ashamed of it, damaging it with thoughts, words, actions and neglect. Those who put together four hundred pages in so many forms and with so many authors, because these are works of multiple authors indeed. 'Toma' is cussing his country at a gathering of friends, in a close family circle but, above all, while propping up the bar counter during those few minutes during which the 200 grammes race down his throat on a fiery chariot. 'This is unbearable, I had enough, I can't cope any longer, you always keep silent, I'm off!' He's hitting the table, instigating or confronting others for keeping silent, he is threatening to leave the country. The person he was talking to just about got away when he grabbed him by the throat and challenged him on his reasons for keeping silent. 'You can't possibly be a ...?' he asked and the individual cast in this role nearly blew cover.

Yet the inner home stays concealed, that painful homesickness that cannot be stifled and is so sharp that it turns desperation into a lion's roar. They conclude that 'Toma' is unpleasant company, a cynic who doesn't believe in anything, he's always political, they write about him, his acquaintances avoid him, though at his workplace – where he isn't political – they are afraid of him. What threatening actions might he attempt? Perhaps banging on the tin countertop of the bar, the words whispered in a low voice to burn others, those stern and bushy eyebrows frowning and that sharp gaze when the index finger is pointing at the first or second page of the paper, well, well! He did say, he said it already that it was the tyrant! That careerist, nationalist tyrant who got where he is by clambering on the shoulders of others! There you go, he is now triumphant, being welcome in foreign lands and you now believe that there will be help coming from abroad! They will never help, you should have learned this much, all we get is the embrace of the serpent, but you'll have to put up with this because I won't be here much longer, I'm on my way! And with this, his tongue that was struggling to roll suddenly finds its way, his thoughts become crystal clear and this fiction takes the shape of neatly rounded sentences and full theatrical monologues.

Which kind of emigration is he opting for? A real foreign landscape, as he promises on page 204, or does he want to leave this unbearable world in a single determined leap? Had he really wanted to leave, would they have let him go?

The traitor's inner sea is in such turmoil that those who voyage on its waves suffer a shipwreck. The sky above turns black, and flashing lightning draws attention to menacing sliding rocks.

According to page 276, in 'Toma's' fictional mouth the tongue finds it hard to roll, it has always found it hard, perhaps even from the very beginning, because 'Toma' had never really believed in language, while he is displaying threatening behaviour, he points out that one can also use language in order to lie and he had always been surrounded by such lies and this messy language that only serves the speaker, language that operates in the moment and basically hijacks truth. He triumphantly holds up the paper. He has had enough of this country, the landscape is whizzing in his body, storms are uprooting trees, he hates all of this, everything is hopeless and doomed and you are silent, as for him, he will leave, yes, he'll make tracks and get out of here, he'll get the fuck out of here, anywhere, to Israel or Germany, he's threatening with his fictional mouth and faltering tongue. The shower of his poisonous arrows is dangerous and irrevocable. One cannot retract a word that has been uttered, be it with the aim of healing others, causing wounds or getting trees chopped down.

A word that has been uttered has simply come about and no longer belongs to the person who said it. This is the only realisation that she owes to 'Toma'.

If 'Toma' leaves the country, perhaps he can escape from the storm that overwhelms him. He may die of homesickness in the end. 'Toma', however, stayed put. He started a family and had children.

'Toma's' conversation partner, the person who conveys all the information to be noted down, has the obligation to drink with him, he declares in his oral statement, which is then turned into a written protocol that he has to sign, he had to drink as it would have been conspicuous if he didn't, but there are no clear records of his consumption, it could have been anything between 50, 100, 200 or 300 grammes when 'Toma' was already at 400 and still going strong, as he often did until 600. This person is most cavalier with the words that refer to himself, like someone who wants to be precise only regarding others but leaves his own person in obscurity. In order to ensure that the reliability of his words is not questioned in this context where they are so many authors in so many forms, perhaps it is enough to highlight that he was playing his role well and accomplished it in a theatrical sense by drinking with his companion.

This conversation partner, that is the person with whom the traitor is engaged in conversation, isn't really concerned with posterity. Should he have considered, even for a moment, his potential future readers, who'd get to him on the distant waves of time, he would have had to take himself into account, too, as well as the amount of alcohol he consumed as part of his work duties and his own badly performed role. After all, a writer cannot extract himself from the world he is observing.

As it happens, the embodied reader gradually emerging from the mist of time would much rather snap at this drunken bullshitting bloke, this 'Toma', telling him to shut up, 'can't you see that you are drinking with your informant, who is just as fictional as you, his name and his role reduce him to that level. Stop it, both of you have already sunk into fiction!' Yet if words, like the words of Orpheus, were capable of bending trees and the wild animals came out to listen to the minstrel, then they, the drunken conversationalists from the past would stay in silent awe in front of the poet. And the past would burn out.

Two drunken blokes, fragile and frozen into time, there is nothing to keep them on the cold shelf. What do you think, dear 'Toma', whose drunkenly exaggerated, blown-up or, on the contrary, edited, subdued, tamed and harmless words are these? 'Toma', however, will not let himself be written up.

'Daddy hasn't done anything, don't worry,' the well-meaning historian reassures her before they get started.

As for the Son, he listens with interest to the story and asks her to translate the conversation from the tavern word by word once more.

'Let's write them a thank you letter,' he then says in earnest. 'I'll write it. It's brilliant that they kept all this. I'm really proud, as I would have never imagined my grandfather to be such a dangerous man.'

Because the Son is fascinated by the current of words, the roaring inner sea, the vortex of craving for truth into which many people succumb, but that's irrelevant, death is uninteresting, he isn't interested in that, he concludes. Longing, however, that's another matter, longing is fire.

For the Son, the interest is in fire, for her, in the burial. And peace.

There is a dried-out cat carcass along the two-lane road, separated from the pavement by a muddy metal railing. It must have fallen on the battlefield of cats back in the winter, and was even covered by some benevolent snow for a while. There has been no snow for some time now, and the desiccated remains are out there to be seen. This is Kincső's area.

Something should be done, but it's hard to tell what exactly. To look into its eyes, as with any animal fallen by the roadside. To soothe pain with pain. *Kill pain with pain.*

The animal dispatched in this way, known as *roadkill*, is the ultimate loser among animals. They are no longer the gods that coexist with us humans or the bodies that cohabit with us while servicing us, nor the sources of food and clothing, with which we work and lead a parallel life. Their bodies have become alien to us and their death invisible, their feet no longer touch the ground and their flesh comes to us in unrecognizable forms. Turned into a spectacle, about to be extinct, some sort of bored zoo specimens in a comfortable existence they will eventually die of. Meanwhile, lenses and cameras are observing and recording them and the thousand secrets of their complex existence, bringing to us what we shall never see, what has never been visible, and is now only to be seen due to the mediation of some device, by way of shockingly odd images, depths and heights. They themselves turned into a series of images, into fiction. We can already see and know everything, everything is distant and dazzling, alien and exotic, but nothing stays with us anymore. Only these annoying and stupid flies and mosquitoes, the existence of which one cannot really understand. In the so-called real world, we are surrounded by docile domestic animals deprived of a sexual life, longing for love in their solitude without descendants and violence. The soft and chosen are holding out in their confinement, hoping to share their loneliness with someone. In case they try to escape, they end up like this cat. Furballs by the roadside, blood-soaked tangles, roadkill, corpses, and one has no choice except to look into their eyes in case there are still any eyes left.

'Why aren't you looking after it?' the Son used to ask when he was little, as if every carrion was their fault, that of his parents. Perhaps this is exactly what he thinks of 'Toma', too, but he is now too old to ask such explosive questions.

To look at the blood-soaked tangle by the roadside, to look into 'Toma's' lonely and fictional eyes, sorrow to sorrow, pain to pain, to remember his miserable fate that could have had a very different and much more favourable turn. This final accompanying gaze is like a burial, like the repayment of some debt. On an amphora, Persephone is already holding her hand out, guiding the dead along their difficult passage to the underworld.

What she had been holding in her hand that morning in the library, that case file with the soft cover, isn't more than the debris of the past. Past debris. Something that is bygone, outdated, expired, invalid, a surplus of no use to anyone, and besides, daddy hasn't actually done anything, and yet it's there, reachable, accessible, on display. A surplus that one should clear out of the way, sealing its fate and saying something about it to mark its ultimate death, provided there is anything to be said at all. Something that is more than mere pollution, chopped-down trees and decaying nature.

She has to confront the miserable fate of this cat, run over and pushed to the roadside: others might try to avert their gaze from it but she owes it to someone, not the cat, which wasn't hers, but she owes it, not sure to whom, but she owes at least a glance, which is more than a sting and less than a deadly bite, because she sadly won't die of this, it won't be her who dies of this. As she passes by, she forces herself to cast a final glance, turning her head towards it, sharpening her eyes to see the colour of the fur and perhaps ascertain the animal's age, at least in case it's still young, to check whether it belonged to anyone and had regular meals, or whether it had a collar once placed on its neck by a careless owner. Perhaps it did belong to someone, perhaps it did rub up against someone's leg in some kitchen, provided there was a kitchen and they let it come in instead of chasing it away. Perhaps someone was enjoying its company for a long time, or they were just kicking it around in disgust, without granting it as much as a gentle stroke. The gaze acknowledges the end, there, it has come to an end, time to relax. There is no burial, the pained expression is in lieu of the burial, the corpse may well end up under the ground or on a rubbish heap, eaten by nocturnal animals. Persephone, however, is offering her hand and guiding it across.

Are animals, corpses, dead cats, those that passed away and are no longer, the have-beens, are they entitled to being accompanied on this journey?

The gaze pays off some of the debt.

Oh, Lord, let them come to you, keep them by your side, console them even if cats aren't supposed to ascend to heaven. Perhaps heaven may not receive them, either. May you belong to someone, may you all belong to someone, discarded waste that you are for some, but you are also sweet furry bodies, my plummeting father, you are all falling into a black square.

Not to worry, there will be no book based on the secret police files, she snaps at the friend-cum-reader, because nothing irritates her more than being berated on what to write or not write about, or how often. She'll agree to what she's asked in terms of 'not to write yet another book on secret police files' because this past-waste is good for nothing, it is a waste that cannot be discarded and reused, an urn for the deceased, where does it belong, where should I put it? She has no business with it after having looked into its eyes, sorrow to sorrow, pain to pain.

It is absolutely astonishing that there isn't any kind of so-called truth that one could actually write about among these hefty files, carefully signed documents, forms and reports, in this vast array of pointless pieces of writing housed along these narrow corridors, cellars, low-ceilinged rooms and fully loaded shelves. Not even about 'Toma', 'who didn't do anything', and is lying orphaned on the metal shelves, with his pointless words and by now waning life, unburied, in his final solitude, like those cats by the roadside. Could this have been the greatness of fathers, once upon a time? Triumphant heroes, Odysseus coming home. There is nothing left to be done. Except to love.

They chose a sleepy winter day for their journey, but are met with an early spring upon arrival. In the grey evening, smog descends upon the town and the lack of air is suffocating, but the next dawn, a swift breeze, always hailing from the sea in the South, races along and washes everything clean. Strong, southern colours appear in the landscape, and the sun clambers up the sky from among the hillocks at an astonishing pace, now it's no longer concealed by anything. The tiny light clouds offer the promise of a clear and calm day.

On their last evening they go to the riverbank, reachable only with some difficulty by crossing several busy roads. As if those who planned the road system had been put off by the river being within easy reach, as if this was some sort of primitive relationship between people and the river. With a thick pen, the planner drew a two-lane road along the river, thus confining it into a concrete basin. Following in the footsteps of some fishermen, they step over the low wrought iron railing and sit by the edge of the shallow water. No benches, no grass, just the cold stone.

A small group appears on the other side of the river. Three of them, the two grandparents and the father, look more or less the same age, so they are all of a similar age, those who watch and those who are being watched, only the Son is strikingly different. They had been immortalised at this very age by those despicable photographs from which their gaze is missing, seeing that they weren't aware of being secretly photographed on that early summer morning, the exact hour and minute of which was recorded by those who knew nothing about the world apart from the position of the hour hands. They are looking at one another lifting their chins a little, so they can see each other's gaze. They nod, as if they were all in agreement regarding the scope of coming to this place. They are staring at the Son. All their relatives are resting in the ground of this country. The dead cross borders easily. She will be the first among them whose ashes won't be returned home. And the Son will be the first to refuse to pay the mandatory grave lease for these unfamiliar dead relatives. 'We won't be coming back here anyway,' he explains, all this is an unnecessary waste. Somebody has to finally spell out that coming back will never happen.

The Son is looking down, already plotting a holiday for after their return, studying a map, charting new paths and a new adventure of his own. 'I shall hitchhike all the way to the sea,' he states with confidence, sounding like someone who is in need of new experiences and independent decisions. He doesn't pay attention to her. They don't pay attention to each other.

As for her, she snaps, as if she had become aware of an ultimate, irrevocable event, as if a second death was slashing her heart:

'Fuck it, he could still live. He barely got to live for fifty springs,' she points out, rubbing her eyes and nose with the back of her hand, she never carries a handkerchief, not expecting to shed tears.

The Son seems surprised, astonished by the intricate jumble of words, considering that they are not in the habit of swearing. She looks back at the Son, as if she was asking for forgiveness. The Son replies pensively yet cheerfully: well, fifty springs aren't actually few. He thought his grandfather was younger when he died.

She can't decide whether those fifty springs aren't that few or far too many. The double of the Son's life, or even more, viewed from there it's not that little, but these fifty springs are almost a carbon copy of her own life. And yet she still doesn't know where this amount of time is situated on the spectrum between a lot and a little. At the end of the day, one cannot know anything about time. Only crooks and cheats know about time, as they keep confidently glancing at their watches imagining that they have seized it. In her, several ages coexist at once, she often scrutinizes her mirror image with some consternation because she feels so much younger within, as if she was glowing like a child, if not a little girl. This is what she sees. Not the mature face, never, the fine yet clearly visible wrinkles, the creases and treacherous spots appearing on the skin. Countless ages coexist within her side by side, a multitude of figures are sitting on the barge of the past, trying to make peace with one another and the world, it seems as if the fifty springs, summers, hard-working autumns and increasingly faster-thawing winters had gathered together a proper crowd. Yet many more have sunk without a trace, people she would find it hard to remember. Fifty springs is an awful lot. Still, she is tormented by thirst, the thirst for being here. Or is it just gravitation towards an existence from which it is so hard escape? Which is so difficult to leave behind because bodies are gravitating together, towards one another. 'Me towards you.'

The setting sun is surrounded by tall, dark clouds, and the redness shines through them. The clouds seem to be floating towards one another, to form an alliance against the light. The birth of darkness is also a struggle. For some, it will be light, for others, dark.

She should explain to the Son, so he understands, that in the grand scheme of things the dead person they came to visit could have lived, the fifty springs are few considering how little time they had spent together. She should tell the Son that she is feeling the same thirst towards him, she sees him too little, 'you aren't enough for me, either, there is simply too little of you.'

'Come on, mum,' the Son snarls at her and keeps staring at the map, already underway in his imagination. Thirst, human thirst.

She receives a request from a foreign national gallery to write the introduction to the catalogue accompanying the Painter's exhibition. In their invitation they don't refer to anything that could offer a response to the increasingly burning question she has borrowed from the Son:

'Why me?'

The Son has been asking this question ever since he was little, frowning his thick black eyebrows and lowering his head, without meeting the gaze of the person who had tasked him with something or formulated some expectation towards him. On such occasions, the muscles above his eyebrows would protrude slightly on his smooth forehead and a slight cleft would form between the two black arcs. The kid had learned to use his facial muscles, of which there are over thirty according to the Painter.

'Why me and not someone else? *Why me?*'

This sounds as if one was trying to shake off the task at hand. It is also a question echoed by the Prophets when their Creator gives them a task. So, they simply run away. This question is becoming increasingly urgent for her, too. Why is this happening precisely to her?

She replies cautiously to the gallery, wanting to ask how it has come about that the curator has thought of her, but is unable to finish the sentence. She wanted to write that she isn't 'on such good terms with paintings', meaning that she doesn't know very much about them. But she changes her mind and crosses it out, she finds this a far too personal revelation considering that it is addressed to a large unknown institution. In the end, she still asks her question, albeit accompanied by a tentative yes.

In their response, the gallery staff don't emphasize the Painter's recommendation, though they do mention that they had *consulted* him, instead they list their arguments in bullet points, highlighting:

1. Their shared roots and emigration,
2. Their interest in autobiography and
3. Their openness towards psychology.

PM is the title of the exhibition comprising fifty years' worth of self-portraits, the curator points out, though they haven't got a poster yet.

She promises to be quick but asks to see the paintings displayed on a wall first, not piled up in some warehouse or as replicas, in other words, she offers to travel to see them for real. She ends her letter by stating '*I am an ISBO – I Still Believe in the Original*'. This observation triggers a response from the curator himself, who points out that this is particularly funny in the light of the fact that the exhibition interrogates the very issue of the original. It's a *CHQO – Challenges the Question of the Original.*

The flight awaiting her is an hour long, but she doesn't have to go to the opening. She can take a look at the temporary exhibition on mobile walls erected for her benefit in the gallery's warehouse. The exhibition proper will only open in a few months, displaying the Painter's autobiographical body of work. Kiran, the curator responsible for international work, is of Indian or Pakistani origin. His native accent indicates that he was born and educated here, most probably at a good school and university. Otherwise, he couldn't really work at a national gallery. They agree on a quick guided tour of the future exhibition's improvised display and then she's left alone with the works.

The first portraits, done on bits of paper torn out of notebooks, go back to times immemorial, a good half a century, and were executed in pen or ink or, sometimes along the margins of a hand-written letter. They feature full body portraits, depicting a young naked man. The original drawings on display were also photographed and these images will be glued to the floor, in order to mark a path to an inner, dark and narrow room. As the curator explains, visitors can make their way to the dark space named *AM/PM* while treading on young, strong male bodies. If visitors don't step on these images, they simply can't get to the tunnel-shaped small room above the entrance of which one can read the caption, just like in mines or caves.

Stepping on the blown-up images will be unavoidable along the narrow corridor, Kiran continues and illustrates this by walking ahead and throwing the A3-size sheets on the floor. Walking on bodies creates discomfort, an unpleasant sensation, and the visitor will try to avoid stepping on heads, penises, soft bellies or sensitive areas. She opts for strong shoulders and muscular thighs – walking on these as if these body parts would cope better with her weight. These naked bodies placed so closely together remind her of traditional representations of Hell, such as the naked figures on Michelangelo's *Last Judgement*. The unrepresentable *Sheol*, to which one doesn't have to look up but down in this case.

How did the paintings survive? Who looked after them, seeing that the Painter couldn't return to the place where he had fled from for nearly fifteen years. Kiran doesn't know the answer but promises to clarify. He forgot to ask the artist about this when they had met. Didn't seem relevant, he muses. Not so important.

In the dark room labelled *AM/PM*, there will be a series of dimly lit photographs that show the Painter as a young adult on various points of their formerly shared town. Sometimes alone, other times in the company of others, on the street, in parks, talking or standing idly, and on some photos, legs are cut out or people are sliced in two. The full body photos have been taken from a distance of about ten metres. Faces tend to be blurred on the tiny originals, and the subject is unaware of being photographed, and so are the other people surrounding him. The photograph only commemorates the fact that the subject has been at a particular place, alone or in the company of acquaintances. All expressions are blank, lifeless, without any purpose, reflecting absolutely Nothing. Only the person who took the photograph had an actual intent.

These pictures mean something. These pictures are without meaning.

The Painter drew himself, naked, on the original grey photos, using black ink. This was his much later self, aged sixty or seventy.

From the unconscious photographed body, there emerged a self-conscious, almost menacing nudity and an aged face staring back at the viewer. The perceptive gaze drawn onto the photo is now staring straight into the eyes of the viewer. Perhaps it wants to look back at the person who had once photographed him in his youth. *I'm watching you, IAWY*, will be the caption on display. The exhibition organisers also decided to blow up a few smaller images and the artist drew on these, too, with the aim of destroying the original pictures. And to reveal his own twofold nakedness.

The man in these photographs is in the AM phase of his life, prior to reaching his prime. On the nude drawings, he is in a PM phase. AM – the old home, PM – the new home.

Stolen pictures, the visitor will be able to read on the wall, complemented with a detailed description of the institution of surveillance and Eastern-European state security services.

'How did the artist obtain these original photographs?' This will be the visitors' most burning question provided they can decode what they see. What they see, is sin. Both in terms of surveillance itself and obtaining the pictures. *We might have legal issues*, the curator observes, after all we are dealing with photographs stolen from a state security library. But they want to take it on board, *this is the real challenge of this performance.* The income generated by the exhibition may even cover the ensuing legal costs. Will they reveal how the pictures got stolen?

'No,' Kiran replies, '*We don't want to provoke. Not with the process. Only with the work of art.*'

On their last meeting, when the Painter was still a restless patient at Saint Benedict Hospital, he tells her how he had stolen the original photos. As she looks into the mouth of the talking man sitting next to her, his yellow teeth remind her of her father and the brownish edge on the lower teeth of smokers. There is something animalesque, something horse-like in these teeth. The teeth are very similar, and so is their exposure.

'How could he steal them indeed? Did they give him the originals?' she marvels, considering that she was only given a copy of her father's file. He asked for the original file and they handed it over to him in the reading room, the Painter explains. The small reading room is naturally supervised by video cameras, as he quickly observed. Yet while leafing through the file, he still managed to cut out the page with the glued-in photographs, you must know this trick with half a razor blade mounted on a finger, whereby a snapped blade is fastened onto the index finger and only the elastic band shows because the blade is pointing towards the palm. A little later, when turning the page to that section again, he folded the paper in two. In the end – and this is an essential part of the performance – he accidentally dropped the entire file on the floor, so he pretended to rock his chair and got down on all fours under the table until he finally picked up the packet from the floor, after all an elderly man can get away with an awful lot. But by then the photos were no longer in the file, those eight to ten pages folded in two had already been slipped into his trousers, between his belly and his prick. When the Painter laughs, his lower horse teeth show their roots and his upper dentures move forward, nearly falling out. He has to use his tongue to adjust them.

There were about eight to ten pages of photographs in the file, with about ten tiny photos glued on each page. While browsing through the file, he had also made various incisions on the paper with his blade, adding patterns onto the statements and reports, for example a star-shaped one in several places, it wasn't a big deal because they had used bad quality, soft typing paper. The patterns executed with his half blade included stars, spirals, long slashes. The whole file will fall apart in the hands of the next reader. It will turn into a lantern.

The Painter observes that *PM*, that is *Post mortem*, is a most fitting title. The paintings will fetch a great price. Shame that the income will no longer be his. He wouldn't go to the opening even if he could – his presence would only lower the price of the artwork.

Up to this point she was convinced that the large-scale paintings of the last thirty years were created in the artist's PM, that is post meridiem, phase.

'The second room,' Kiran explains, 'will bear the caption *PM: Post meridiem*.'

On the painting on display the body is naked, awkward, the round belly looking soft and the legs slim and muscular. The hands are implausibly large, hanging heavily and inertly by the side as if they had no function. The back is slightly bent, as if bearing a burden. The limp penis carries the memory of onetime virility. The heavily distorted feet and hammertoes are a striking sight at the edge of the painting.

The hair is thin and sticking up. The body and the worn-out floor are of a similar shade, almost blurring together. Closer to broken and long-suffering than life-affirming and determined, as on the photograph. The elderly figure looks as if it was an effort to stand in front of viewers, which is why his gaze and nakedness are menacing. As if he had been taken aback and scared away by alien glances.

The two eyes – and here the Painter uses an old portraiture trick – are looking in two different directions, one behind the viewer and the other even further, to a more distant and diffuse point, as if they were trying to cover the entire space in front with their gaze. Present, past and future. The old man is anxious and reserved, aware that he is standing in front of his viewers without any clothes. But he still feels better on the painting than in reality.

The last and central part of the exhibition is a life-size painting, flanked by two smaller portraits, one of a sleeping man and another of a figure looking out of the painting. The sleeping figure could just as well be dead, and the one looking out appears not to be present. The latter portrait is executed in a *non finito* style: half of the painting is dominated by a blank canvas. He who has stepped out of the painting can no longer represent his own retreat (death?). The painting is unfinished and cannot be finished.

The large, full-size painting will be positioned higher than the others and under stronger light. The Painter spontaneously steps forward with his left foot, perhaps he wants to step out of the painting but can barely hold his balance – his left boot can no longer be squeezed onto the canvas. The movement evokes classical iconography, as in when the painting questions its own reality.

Christ and the saints step into the life-giving river, and in this same way the Painter wants to signal with the painted foot that he isn't simply painting a work of art but reality itself, because reality, akin to divinity, is impossible to represent. Divinity cannot be painted. The artist isn't a metaphor for divinity, only hinting at a visual tradition. The artist retreats and steps back into the artwork, the only space he can organise.

The weight is on the right foot, and for this reason, the body tilts to the right. The painting is indicating uncertainty and the beginning of the fall. The legs are crooked, barely able to bear weight, yet this existence within the painting is still safer. He is about to step down but not quite. The only certainty is the reality of the painting.

The two weary and hard-working old hands are dangling helplessly without a task or job lined up for them, their purple-black veins protruding. *Consummatum est* – something has come to an end. Viewed from a close-up, the brush strokes reveal an abstract painting. The old flaccid body has been painted with heavy and aggressive traits – from a close-up, it looks as if the object of representation was about to fall apart.

The creative energies would be able to continue flowing but the body can no longer carry on. The face seems to marvel, the thinning yet still tangled eyebrows pointing towards the forehead in an angular fashion. The eyes are being fixed upon the viewer, almost chasing them, no matter what position they are looking from, and forcing them to behold what they had never seen before. The same old trick is used again – the eyes are looking in two different directions, thus covering all bases. Perhaps it is a God-metaphor after all. Viewers may find themselves anywhere in the space and yet the beholder is still looking at them, keeping them company.

It feels as if she was looking at her own naked father. At something forbidden by Law. It may well be that only the drunken Father, the drunken Noah wasn't meant to be seen by his sons Shem, Ham and Japheth. This is because Noah planted grapes and made wine, and when he got drunk, he was naked in his tent, perhaps even in his sleep. She has never seen the drunken father naked. Yet the Painter is able to restore the Father's dignity. The Father can be observed old, naked, and broken, just before the moment of leaving the stage. In order to cover their father's nakedness, Noah's sons enter the tent with their backs to the bed. Visitors will also leave the exhibition rooms by turning their backs. The painting, flanked by two other portraits, will form a triptych at the rear of the room. These two smaller works won't look the viewer in the eye but depict departing faces.

It feels as if the Painter wasn't able to contemplate himself. He has to offer his own nakedness to the viewers. The gallery will block the exit behind the paintings, so people can walk past these works but will be unable to turn around or look behind them.

Szerelmes apám. My father in love, this is the title she would have given to this painting, she tells Kiran at the farewell dinner. This is when the curator reveals the actual title of the last artwork: *PM – Perennial mourning*. Incessant mourning. Eternal mourning. Endless mourning. The title suggests that not the painting is eternal, it's not *perennius, aere perennius*, the work thus created isn't longer lasting than metal ore, mourning is. The viewer is only presented with a retreat into the painting. There is no representation of death, dying or illness, not even a round-up of the iconography associated with ephemerality, such as skulls or fruit, or the props of music, arts and science, such as globes and compasses. It simply seems to be the end of everything, with a refuge into the painting.

At their last meeting, the Painter confides in her that he had never had the courage to give a title he really wanted to his exhibitions.

'It's not a matter of knowing the right words. But who dares to name... you know. The truth.'

'Not me,' she replies confidently. 'This is precisely why I became...' But she refrains from finishing her sentence. She thinks that she's a storyteller in order to avoid naming things.

According to the Painter, the last room was initially meant to be named *Departing Landscape*. But he was told that this is impossible to translate.

'How come? Rubbish!' the Painter snaps. 'Then I'll come up with something one certainly can't translate. So it ended up being called *Incessant*.'

'You are telling stories. You don't have to name anything.'

They share a laugh together. This is the last time they are revealing their faces to each other. It's impossible to know what the Painter sees in someone's face. The rocks on his face are shifting for the final time, they stretch, loosen up and then regroup. The Painter looks again towards the dark corner, he's tired and crashes into the hospital bed. He asks her to tell him a story. About what?

'It would be most fitting to talk about resurrection. I'd like to get to the end of it.'

The end of what? How does he know that this is the end? What's imminent, has to be the end? Sadly, she can't tell a story about resurrection. Or rather she could, but that wasn't written by her. Is ascension of interest?

'That will do, too,' the Painter replies.

As a storyteller, as a wordsmith, she should tell him about something. For him, there aren't any more paintings in store.

'For me, there are no more paintings in store,' he states, turning towards the cold white wall. 'What is actually there, on the other side? Do you believe in heaven?'

No, she replies at long last and unsure of herself, sounding like someone who hasn't prepared for this conversation and can at most share a story. It would be perhaps too much to believe but she has seen it with her own eyes. Strange, she adds, we tend not to believe in what we see. The Painter is waiting with his eyes just about open, with his gaze fixed on the boundary between the wall and the window.

She tells him the story of András. She has recently put it in writing, for him, the Painter. She tends to write up her presentations. They are of course much more boring in this way, but also safer. She no longer takes risks. She can't tell stories by way of live speech except if she writes them down.

'In that case can you tell some stories by way of dead speech?' the Painter asks, his eyes closed.

'I'll read it for you, okay? It's called 'András'. This isn't just the title but also the name of the protagonist.'

The conversation with András was left unfinished, because at that lunch, which was their last meeting, they had spent too much time on food besides choosing and rating a suitable place. They had little or next to no time for the main issue she wanted to discuss with András. The latter was also keen to meet and talk about her latest book, but all he said when they agreed on their meeting was that it was interesting and they should definitely discuss it. In the end, she could barely formulate her initial query, except in haste, towards the end of the meal, a query about the uncertain relationship between faith and psychology, that is between faith and healing, and she kept polishing and simplifying it in her mind until it turned into an actual question:

'András, what is the contribution of God to healing, and to your healing process in particular?' 'Not God', she clarified almost straightaway, because as they had already established earlier, András didn't believe in God's existence and was not concerned with him whatsoever.

'I am concerned with souls, but I'm not a believer,' he explained. 'We have indeed organised ourselves around the synagogue, those of us who had stayed put here or who had returned from elsewhere, but only as a connection to the organising principle of life.'

'In this case, this isn't an issue of God's contribution, because he can't really comment on that, but of the patients' personal belief in God, provided there is such a thing.'

'You mean, their religion?', András replied, 'because we have simply remained in a state of eternal waiting, it's a great relief not to have to believe in the Saviour, isn't it enough to just wait for him?'

He then swiftly added that he didn't understand very much of this.

'In such a case what does non-God contribute to all this?'

As it happens, András was uninterested in the Saviour, for him this proposition simply didn't exist.

'We are concerned with the only reality, the reality of the soul. This doesn't mean that I have nothing to wait for,' he said laughing with a touch of sadness. 'The point isn't that He hasn't yet come, but – you understand. The question itself is non-existent, not his coming as such.'

On the occasion of that lunch she failed to ask the question in the right way, because they got held up by the first Existing obstacle, the business of God, the Saviour, so she rephrased her long-formulated question in simpler terms. 'Does someone who has faith heal better?' András would have preferred to expand on the issue of 'what one believes in', and made a promise to think about it and discuss this topic during their next meeting at a mutually agreed future date. 'Besides, we should also talk about your book. It was interesting.' This means that András did believe that they would meet again. This also means that he was a believer nonetheless, and didn't simply organise his life around the synagogue, as he claimed.

András, however, suffered a sudden death, despite any logic, so they didn't even get as far as setting a date for their next conversation. The question didn't appear urgent, there was no crisis on the horizon, only the usual glimpse into the jungle, into the only reality, as András would put it: into the reality of the soul. They had no reasons to assume that the time set aside for András was running out. After his death, it has also suddenly become obvious that by searching for the exact words to drill into the essence of things, and by seeking endless explanations and clarifications, they delayed the very conversation about what they could have or would have wanted to talk instead of dishes and restaurants: the Saviour, waiting and faith, the role of life in a provincial synagogue after the Second World War, and perhaps about the book in which she writes about that sect. Choosing a restaurant and the menu involved more words and more serious negotiation than the Saviour, or the question of what would be more healing for the human soul: the belief in his coming or in the fact that this has already taken place. What does a great healer like András have to say about this? The challenging thread of the conversation, akin to veins on a leaf, just kept dispersing into different directions, departing from the question whether believers, provided András had ever met such people and recognised such faith, were actually able to make better progress in terms of spiritual healing. To put it bluntly, she would have been interested in finding out whether conversion, or at least waiting for the Saviour, was worth it from the point of view of healing. This might have been a very cynical supposition though, but the question had never come to the fore from the jungle anyway.

Khaddish was announced for the Saturday following András' death, in a smaller temple in the capital, which was difficult to access and invisible from the outside, protected by strict security. She decided to attend, or rather that it would be proper to attend, perhaps in order to bring closure to their unfinished conversation. She prepared for some sort of mourning, a mourning ceremony in any case, so she wore dark clothes, not exactly in black but in darker shades. This could be both an act of mourning and something else, too.

For quite some time, however, there was no so-called liturgical event, a few colleagues and students of András did take a seat in the back pews, staring at others and looking confused, while the others, the so-called believers, kept coming and going, heading to the Ark of the Covenant, singing a bit, talking, even laughing, as if something was happening at all times without actually having a clear beginning. Instead of a series of ritual events there were simple human activities.

After about an hour, she began to observe the others, the so-called civilians, the colleagues of András, psychologists dressed in unique and tasteful clothes, wearing bold-coloured frames and sporting striking haircuts, uncommunicative therapists and stand-offish psychoanalysts, she started to watch them for some indication of when it would be appropriate to leave without being noticed, like someone who has some important business elsewhere, after all, she had already achieved what she had proposed to carry out in this space, she did her part, honoured the dead and bid farewell. The conversation didn't come to an end, it has barely started. The so-called believers just kept coming and going, chattering, reading, talking, laughing, sophisticating, to use the perfect word to sum it all up, but there was absolutely no sight of a lofty ritual, or in case there was, she didn't spot it. Every so often, there were people bowing, talking to themselves, praying, in a simple way and not for very long, not in groups or in a loud voice, more like everybody to themselves, as if the Father Eternal was walking amongst them as their friend, and not as the menacing and punishing Father who'd put everything in balance with a view to the final judgement. As the Judge in front of whom everyone should bare themselves.

In the end, after about an hour and a half, by which time she was worn out by the wait, hoping for something sublime to happen the chattering and seemingly disorganised movement calmed down and the believers, as if they had already completed some sort of initial warm-up and negotiation with their God, calmed down and took their places in the pews. At this point, the singer broke the silence, addressing the Father Eternal and establishing contact.

After this, selflessly offering his own self, that is voice, he started to pray for András and uttered his name and surname, articulately to be understood by all and anchored in the depths of Hebrew words and melodies. Hearing this voice, lifted increasingly higher and more passionate while addressing the Creator, each person in attendance had felt the gaze oriented at them, and barely dared to make a move. The strong voice, the commendatory prayer to the dead, seemed to sever the singer, singing on its own, bodiless under the azure blue sky strewn with gold stars. During this prayer, the singer uttered the full name of András one more time, clearly and softly, in the same manner he sang the song, as if this time it was the Father Eternal calling the deceased by the name. This was a warning to the Dead, to be ready to depart. The singer's job was to lend his voice to the Father Eternal, so that human ears could understand the message, and after this, continue the prayer.

But by this time everything was all set. Heaven opened its gates to welcome András.

This is what happened.

Invasive Species

If she didn't know them, they'd appear outright menacing, standing on the opposite bank of the dead arm of the river like a stack of timber trees. Three immobile and unsmiling people, past the zenith of their lives: father, grandmother and grandfather. They look different from how she remembered them. One can see the impact of resurrection on them. The everlasting, late warm spring. Their skin is smooth, translucent, shadowless. They are fifty years old, with a halo above their heads.

The wide river bifurcates into a dead arm. The small group is standing on a small island, where the vegetation only includes a few dozen slender acacia trees. They couldn't see each other if they were on the other side of the water, as the river is several hundred metres wide here. One can only access the island by boat.

She is sitting on her heels on this side of the river, where it splits into two branches. The dead arm is known as The Great Stink by the local fishermen. She has never found it stinky. The dead arm is peaceful and still, surrounded by willow trees with broken branches, rotten sycamores and tall reeds. A grey heron takes flight, slowly, relying on only a few wingbeats yet still making great progress. It's a huge yet timid bird. The wild ducks tend to swim further as they had got accustomed to human presence. Grey herons avoid people, they are too fragile. She ended up with a tan from this exposure to the sun, spots appearing on her forehead and cheekbones, and her lips got really dry. Her arms are dark brown, the mature skin covered in spots. She is exactly the same age as her father, grandmother, grandfather on the other side. The passage of earthly life is showing on her.

The dead arm barely differs from a lake. The edge is muddy but it gets deep very fast. She is in a shoelace pose on the shore, waiting for the fish to spring up. No matter how hard she concentrates, she can only hear the splash. The water is dark and impenetrable. This is because of the rotting branches and the mud at the bottom.

A few fishermen are waiting in tense stillness. Sitting in silence far from one another, continuously engaged in some activity.

She recalls when the Son initially thought that the dead arm was a place for the dead. And this is why it was called The Great Stink, the dead getting smelly while rotting. As they rotted, was the way the Son understood this word.

He used to get excited at the sight of fishermen when he was little. He would often peg down next to them and scrutinise their activity. After a while, he'd initiate a conversation, and if he got a response, he'd start off an avalanche of questions.

'How big was the biggest fish you've ever caught? How many metres? Did you eat it? How many kilos did its head weigh? Have you ever caught a person?'

A fisherman told the Son that he had once caught a catfish that weighed sixty kilos in the dead arm. 'In this water? Sixty kilos? Catfish?' The fisherman offered ample details on the great catch, the highlight of his fishing career, starting from the first jerk of the string to the actual lifting of the fish out of the water. He was even able to show him a photograph, on which he was crouching next to the huge fish. The Son wanted to hear what had happened with the fish, what he used to kill it. He kept holding the killer weapon, a smooth and flat piece of wood, in his hand, slowly rotating it. While talking, the fisherman kept adjusting his three rods, throwing them in, pulling them out, but then he suddenly stopped talking and started to carefully wind the spinning reel. While doing this, the tension in his body suddenly eased off: he could sense from the weight of the string that the catch was too light. In the end, he lifted a tiny fish out of the water.

'Will you throw it back?,' the Son asked, already aware that one should throw small fish back into the water.

'No,' the fisherman replied, and threw the ten-centimetre-long fish right behind him.

'Why did you do that?'

'It's an invasive species.'

The Son went to check out the wriggling fish in silence. He then inquisitively looked at the fisherman and his mother: 'Will it die?'

'Regulations state that we shouldn't throw such species back,' the fisherman explained. 'Invasive. This means that they are harmful. Harmful in this water, meaning that they eat the eggs of the indigenous fish. This is why we don't throw them back. The fishing manual warns us about them,' and he produced a little book with drawings to illustrate his point.

'Amur goby. They come up here from Turkey.'

She took a good look at the fish and the drawing but was struggling to picture the map. How can a fish make it all the way from Turkey to this dead arm? On what ways?

'We'll take it home with us,' the Son announced, and fetched some water in a discarded plastic bag to save it.

At first, the fish didn't stir. Did it die already? But then it came back to life. She couldn't persuade him not to take the goby home. Bogy, the Son kept repeating at home. Amur goby, she tried to correct him. Yes. Bogy. Amur bogy.

Next, the Son asked why there were only drawings and no photographs in that small book. The fisherman explained that photos could only represent an actual individual but not the entire species, for which drawings are better suited. The Son mumbles under his breath: rubbish.

The goby lives for a week in a green basin, in the company of a floating plastic ray, under which it finds refuge every time somebody gets closer. The two animals form an unusual pair. The ray looks more realistic, while the goby, with its unusually wide head and triangular shape resembles a plastic bait. She buys some fly larvae for the goby from a pet shop but it refuses to eat it. After a week, she decides to either return the fish or throw it out. The Son continues to campaign for the life of the fish, but he doesn't want to return it or throw it out.

'It will perish under our very eyes,' she explains to him. 'We should take it back to the river if you want to save it.'

In the end, they take it back in a jar.

'Bye, bogy,' the Son bids it farewell.

'Goby,' she corrects him again.

'Yes, bogy,' he replies. They lower the fish into a shallow water, with pebbles at the bottom, at first, the fish freezes for a while but then starts to rummage among the pebbles and suddenly vanishes into the depths.

'What's it going to do now?' the Son wonders.

'Being happy,' she replies.

'Will it go back home?'

'Yes. It's home already.'

'Isn't its home back in Turkey?' the Son muses.

'He'll definitely not go back there. His father and mother may have already been born here,' she explains.

The Son wants to know whether they had committed a crime by throwing this invasive species back. He utters the word in earnest, yet also with a hint of excitement at the prospect of committing a crime. She explains to him that they aren't fishermen, the latter have to know such things but they don't. Fishermen throw them to the shore and they throw them back into the water.

'But we do know that they are harmful,' the Son continues.

'We do, but won't throw them into the bin. This isn't our job.'

'What is our job then?' he asks, hands on hips, hauling his mother up.

The Son wants to find out what's down below. He knows that the dark waters of the dead arm are populated with all sorts of giant fish.

Looking at the group of three it occurs to her that she should cross over to their side. She can do that by committing suicide. She doesn't reject this idea outright. She doesn't reject anything in principle, as this is the very nature of literature, to be without principles, she said to the Son's father when they had first met, when they were talking about her father and about the secret police files and the fact that she had no intention of getting cured of this. Of thinking about suicide that is. She is thinking about thoughts, she explains, not action.

'I don't want to get cured of this.'

She has become accustomed with this symbiosis with her thoughts, she is accustomed with thinking about the Father who fled from the remainder of his life. He didn't get given his own death. Death is being dealt out, right? And it's mandatory to accept it. The Father didn't wait for his own. She's thinking about suicide, about the thought of it to be precise. This thought doesn't trigger any action, more like a contemplation of a distant acquaintance provided they appear. At times, she talks to them. She cannot reconcile with the idea that this is the only platform, this overcast evening sky at the meeting point between the living and dead arm, with summer rainclouds on the horizon as she is sitting in a shoelace pose along the shore. Meanwhile, the others are still standing there, paying attention, perhaps in a protective or perhaps just observing fashion, they are present and want to let her know that there is another side, she can get there eventually, relax, even the blind can see that there is another side, she can cross over, either at some future point or even right now. After all, those who committed suicide could make it there. That evening, she's thinking about suicide while squatting and looking at the approaching anvil-shaped cloud. She's thinking about the death of others. The death of another. As she's watching them, waiting for the fish to spring up, her face is almost as smooth as the faces of those who had already crossed over.

This type of cloud is known as *Evening Glory*. It tends to bring a lot of rain. Everything has a name. Everything?

By the time she stands up and stretches her leaden legs with some difficulty, it has started to rain. The initially just drizzling but then gradually heavier heavenly waters flow together, the living and dead arms merge into one, and the island vanishes from sight.

On the other side, someone who has been dead for thirty years looks back with a clear gaze from which any earthly meaning has been rubbed off. One cannot describe but only recognise it.

'I'd give ten years of my life in exchange for three evenings with you,' she sends a message to the face while saying goodbye.

'The first evening, we'd talk, the second we'd have a drink, although we shouldn't really do that, we shouldn't drink together, so I'd rather show you this dead arm at the edge of town. I'm not yet sure what to do on the third evening, perhaps I could read you a passage from one of my books. I'd cook a really nice dinner, a hot Indian dish that I could never prepare for you because you didn't even wait for me to learn to cook at all, and I didn't really learn it anyway. I'd give ten years of my life, and not the last ten years of illness and old age, a time of sour misery and bitterness, but of the current stage which is still good. It's still too good, and you aren't a part of it. It's still relatively good though I have to attend yearly health screenings already. I'd give my salvation for it.'

'You're here, on the other side, with you, that is my family. It's odd that you aren't with your own parents but my maternal grandparents, who loved you like their own child, and we are now all the same age in this angelic state of inebriation. A state of eternal sobriety in your case.'

While squatting by the dead arm, she's planning the evening with the unknown old man. He used to be old in her imagination, always aging a bit because she tried to imagine him as someone exposed to the passage of time. Yet on the other side, she sees a mature man in his prime. She should offer him the best of all visible worlds. What should she serve for dinner? What did this old man like to eat while he was alive? What music? Russian composers perhaps? Tchaikovsky? Prokofiev? The 7th symphony by Shostakovich? What shores, rivers, clouds? A journey perhaps?

And salvation.

No, she can't give that. She doesn't know what it actually is but one cannot gift the unknown. She cannot give it up. In case there is something there solely reserved for her.

On that tiny 6 × 7 photograph taken with a hidden camera, which was photocopied, scanned and then printed out, everybody appears to be of the same age, they are standing together on an unrecognisable street and, indeed, there are only about twelve-fifteen years between them, they look at one another, though out of focus and hard to identify, and they are still at a time in their life that is healthy and perhaps hopeful. That photograph, their group photo, now belongs to everyone for good, anyone can get access to it even though it means nothing to them. The photograph on the other side, on that tiny island by the dead arm, however, is hers and hers alone. And the Son's. He can look after it one day if he wants. Or throw it back.

In the wake of her father's death, she'd often spot him on the streets. He'd suddenly appear at some corner, on the other side of the street, impossible to catch up with, as he'd jump on a trolleybus or show up among the cemetery trees and then immediately vanish. Yet he'd still look back for an instant, seeking her out with his gaze, nodding and then moving on. Sometimes he'd wear his furry hat, other times his brown herringbone jacket and tan-coloured woollen trousers, accessorising these with sandals or a trench coat, depending on the weather. He'd usually be at some distance away, out of her reach to address him but still easily noticeable. Once he came to a halt in the middle of their street, barefoot and in his trousers, so the autumn sun behind him nearly blinded anyone who looked at him. Cars and a leisurely trotting horse-driven cart managed to bypass him by slowing down, not to disturb this unusual human apparition. As if they knew that one should be gentle with the dead.

Initially, she had this idea that her father had gone into hiding or fled and started a new life because he had enough of what went on before, when he was put to shame, left helpless and shattered. All this would work out better in this new life, she used to tell herself. But as her father just stood there in this light traffic, barefoot in the rays of the setting sun, he conveyed the message that she had nothing to worry about, there was no mystery, he didn't swap his life for another, he didn't flee, just passed away and now he's looking at the living standing still and with a watchful eye, like she tends to look at the dead, and from now on he'll be in need of gentle treatment.

Yet he'll never show himself to her again after she moves away from her hometown.

Her first proper job after graduation is at a research institute, and her role is taking care of international relations, which will send her all over the world. At a Christmas party, her colleagues, with whom she doesn't really manage to develop a close bond, come up with the idea of playing a game whereby everybody brings in a childhood photo that will be projected on a screen and then they'll all try to guess who it represents. She is averse to this, as she is to any society game, but can't back out. In a brown envelope she finds a photo of herself as a young teenager, at puberty, with neatly combed hair, dressed in a brown check skirt and a red jumper, stockings and strappy shoes, holding a white puppy in her lap. In their family, only her father used to take pictures, but after his death they also had a few professional photographs taken. All photos of her are far away, in a quiet house in another country where her mother still lives. She didn't bring any photographs of herself with her, only documents, diplomas, statements, certified copies of registry entries and her birth certificate, necessary for starting life in a new world and essential for obtaining residency, work permits and subsequent citizenship. This photograph with the puppy must have accidentally ended up among the important documents obtained after exhausting legwork, and needing translation and certification. Objects, photographs, souvenirs don't travel in the first decade. The past stays behind, undisturbed, together with the dead. As if it wasn't yet needed, outgrown, without a practical use. The father never crops up on the streets of her new home, as if the deceased were sinking together with the old hometown and with childhood.

She drops this sole photograph she could find of herself in the collection box at the institute.

At the Christmas party they project the photos one by one and try to guess, amidst giggles, who is that laughing baby sat on a potty, who is that ill-tempered newborn, about to start crying, wondering which naked baby or toddler turned into which grown-up among those present. They get it wrong a lot, spending ages trying to guess who is who because the gender of babies is far from obvious, only their toys and pink or blue clothing indicate their future gender. She is the only one who is recognisable in an instant. In her indifference towards the game, she even wears her hair in the same backcomb back style. Among all these newborns, babies and toddlers, there is a single teenager displaying recognisable features: herself, whose childhood has vanished without a trace or photographic evidence. The photo appearing on the screen doesn't conceal any secrets, so it cynically ruins the game, there is nothing left to guess, and she's instantly the odd one out. Her nakedness makes her vulnerable, standing with nothing on in front of the others as an adult.

As the photo appears on the screen, a colleague sat next to her takes a glimpse at her and observes: 'You didn't have a childhood.'

Tamás says this, a proper cynic, holding the whip of God in his hands. The sentence starts as a question but turns into a matter-of-fact description.

The grown-up who graduated from university and speaks several languages fails at this game, despite all her knowledge, and is spectacularly worsted in an invisible competition. The grown-up nobody, the non-existing child. The others whose birth, childhood, kindergarten years spent in a nearby street, don't look at her with compassion, nodding that of course, her past is elsewhere, in another country, far away, she can't participate in a game from here, she didn't bring her childhood, the child about whom one cannot tell aged five whether it's a boy or a girl, not even on a photo, all this remained elsewhere, in a table drawer in a decaying house, in an album falling apart, from which all the photos keep spilling out. Meanwhile the adult is moving forward with a furrowed look, there is nothing to see behind, that's over, closed off. The child doesn't exist, it rolled down a hill, she overstrode it, while struggling to climb up a mountain. She not only didn't bring her childhood with her with its modest material evidence, but for a long time transcended it almost flawlessly and perfectly, that is to say, she nearly forgot it, as if there was no need for it in her new life.

This awkward childhood with its shapeless jump suits and eternal dependencies and lack of independence looked like a state that needed to be outgrown, some kind of illness one had to recover from, babies and toddlers with the appearance of helpless suckling lambs, a bunch of annoying and speechless beings viewed from the heights she had been inhabiting at the time as a young graduate, able to speak four languages and in charge of international relations.

And yet her nakedness and foreignness had become visible again. At the very time when she thought she had made it. Her colleagues showed no consideration for her absent childhood and foreignness. She got excluded from the game straightaway, while the other toddlers or children in arms remained the object of an extended guessing game.

She shakes off this numb state, colleagues wish one another merry Christmas – this is the first time she's not going back home for the festivities – and swiftly makes her escape through the loudly banging gate into the suffocatingly airless city, the smell of which had overwhelmed her upon her first visit: the scent of a big city. She hasn't yet reached any decisions, there is already a turning point, known as *peripeteia*, but no recognition, that is no *anagnorisis*, as she learned from the *Poetics*, in other words, the protagonist hasn't yet recognised her fate until the bus takes her home from the institute, via the river and up the mountain, into her first independently rented home.

She calls her mother and asks her to send her at least twenty photographs, straightaway. She gives her detailed instructions regarding where to go and what to ask for in order to achieve this goal as fast as possible. And by the time she'll be back next – 'when will that be?' – her mother interjects with caution, 'in two weeks', she announces on the same harsh tone she used when she announced that she can't go right now, she can't, she has no time even though she hasn't visited her mother for over six months –, she should put together an entire album for her, for her and her alone, to include everyone. Both the living and the dead.

If she ever wanted to pull out alive from *Sheol*, she must find out that little, inconsequential, hard to obtain and hard to understand information that can be known about the past, all that went on before, everything that has no visible cause or explanation only a story at most, seeing that the essence, the point, can barely be grasped in the sense in which the Son will later want to display it in a single sentence. She will also ask for her father's secret police file, provided it exists, she informs her mother when it occurs to her that she could look into it. Why does she think that her father might have had such a file, her mother muses when they eventually meet, taken by surprise. He didn't do anything. 'Your father didn't do anything.' She doesn't think or assume this, it has simply occurred to her that in case there were any traces of her father, other than waving at her in town as he used to, because the dead have every reason to be jovial, unlike the living, in case there were any earthly traces of her father, any unburied remains that are waiting to be put to rest, then she'd like to take a look at them. All she wants is to verify, just in case, that there aren't any leftover bits and pieces concerning her father that should be swept up, somebody has to rake these shards together, no matter what rubbish they might be, so he can receive his final rest. As it happens, it will emerge that even such a person who didn't actually do anything, anything at all that could deserve the attention of those in power, even such an insignificant life is noteworthy.

The dead don't devour the living but draw attention to themselves.

The Son learns about the reports concerning his grandfather twenty years later, twenty years is nothing in the eyes of the Creator. He doesn't understand the language in which these reports about his grandfather were written, as he was already born over here. He isn't interested in details – what, where, in which street, what time of the day, meeting whom or treasuring whom on the photographs – he is demanding the essence, 'the point'. In his view, it's stupid to retrace the actual itineraries.

'Tell me the point,' he demands dryly, when she tries to tell him the story of his grandfather. Hard to tell the essence of countless bits of handwritten notes in a so-called administrative style, compiled into a file. So she tells him about a random event, to be found on page 200, fifth line from the top:

'And then he popped into the already open taproom, betraying tiredness at dawn despite his swift steps.'

'Taproom?' the Son asks impatiently and defiantly, as if the story had to get stranded at the first detail, a decorative element that could have easily been removed by a careful directorial hand, to ensure that the staging of the essence is not disrupted. 'Why are you always telling stories as if ... ' and he doesn't finish his sentence, though he packs plenty of reproaches. 'As if you were writing some elaborate book, as if you were courting literary merit instead of ....' and he turns his head and interrupts his sentence again 'finally getting to the point.'

'I'm getting to the point,' she replies patiently. 'It's very important that the taproom is open at such an early hour, when he is heading home from the night shift, heading back to his lodgings, which couldn't really be called a home, even the person observing him, who might have been a woman, notes on page 18 that he lives in miserable conditions, in a basement, a half-cellar, without a toilet and with drinking water only available from an old tap in the wall.'

'I'm not interested in the tap in the wall, get to the point.'

'This is the point. That he's miserable and homeless. Your grandfather. My father. A miserable man is being followed on the street. This is the point. He isn't miserable because he's being followed.'

'But why then?'

'We don't know.'

In her latest spoken autobiography that she recounts at Susan's request on that excruciatingly long journey during which she just keeps driving with determination, she doesn't answer the question *And what is your story?* by wishing she knew what her story was, but by stating, even though this doesn't have much traction in the summer, or as the Son would say, doesn't help with getting to the point, but suddenly seems important: '*I am the first generation with a bathroom and a toilet which has heating. So you don't freeze there*', she explains this as if she was about to tell the story of that miserable basement flat with the tap in the wall, despite starting her story from the end, the present, the thoroughly heated bright bathroom, on the floor of which the Son used to enjoy lying down in his pyjamas as a kid, and this can be witnessed on several photos providing ample evidence. As if he wanted to feel the heat with his whole body. This is where she's at - a heated loo. Astonishing social progress, isn't it?

Yet the Son is demanding the essence about his grandfather, why had they written all those things about him, the taproom, the dawn, the basement, the tap in the wall, how much his grandfather used to drink and at what pace.

'Someone who drinks this much, there, in such a short space of time, in a single shot, is...'

'Alcohol dependent,' the Son proudly utters the correct term. He had been familiar with this word at a young age, this is what he calls the still sober alcoholics lurching along while waiting at dawn in front of the shops.

'That's right. And something must be very painful for him. When he gulps down those two hundred grammes, which for our standards are four halves, is like an electric shock in my view. So he can obliterate a huge pain with an even bigger one.'

'What is so painful for him?'

'We don't know.'

'Will we find out?'

'I don't know. Unlikely from this book,' she closes the file. 'But perhaps if we read this book, which isn't really a book, very carefully, we might find out a few things.'

She ends the conversation with the Son on the usual note: 'can we actually reach peace and tranquillity.'

'But it doesn't hurt him anymore, right?' he asks.

He used to ask the same when he was little and was eating hot dogs: were the pigs squealing while being slaughtered. And does it still hurt. Now. Does it still hurt, in this very moment.

'These are only the first seven years'; she could have exclaimed to her former self. She's standing in front of the office, like the progeny of a Kafka hero and an Amazonian. She can't yet see the passage of time or that of her own decades, only the pressures of time. Time is pressing, suffocating – this is the date until which you can stay, the Lord of Time, the Immigration Office states. This is still the beginning.

'Seven years, that's nothing!'

Things, the really important things will only get settled there-after, and they must get settled: should one go or should one stay, should one turn back and endure, hanging in there. Seven years are no proof for anything. Cells renew themselves in seven years, but what does that actually mean? Does the soul stay the same?

She arrived only recently. Entrance exam, the first four-five months, quick love affair, protracted disappointment. Excessive enthusiasm gives way to an adjustment to a practical way of living.

The first seven years are a period of survival, of struggle, trying to ensure that the swimmer stays on the surface and can get some air. Studying, living, earning money, staying here, surviving, endur-ing. Caring for the matter, for the Body. Sleeping, eating, studying. Holding the Body together and frittering it away at the same time. A new love every year or every six months. Body-dispersal under the moniker of love. She is very careful with her heart; the heart doesn't belong to anyone. There are other things more important than love: obtaining the necessary documents and rowing from the shadows towards legitimate light. The university welcomes foreign students but expects them to pay a considerable amount of hard currency for their studies, or to return to their homeland after graduation, in which case they can study for free. Home, to the beloved land of one's fathers. She signs the document in front of her without hesitation, it will stay valid indefinitely. She either pays or signs.

The latter then. The first seven years are a material risk: one has to make serious promises. It's still rather dim in her mind, but she knows already deep down, in the confined cells of her brain that this is a contract she'll break. The frontal lobe isn't involved yet, where decisions are made, but after surviving the seven-year itch there will be decisions, too. Slow decisions, the body is fast but the soul is slow. At this point, the intent to stay is only milling about, getting ready to emerge in the central part of the brain, where behaviour patterns are being formed.

But who could have an insight into the inner workings of the brain, into the depth of depths, into this one-litre gelatinous lump, covered by hair, skin and skull and carefully protected during creation. It's much easier to get to know the world from Greenland to Jamaica and the icy Lake Ladoga than this greasy something. The reality of the soul? She hasn't yet prepared for this journey.

The seven years rumble on. She develops militant techniques of endurance. Such as tacitly breaking the contract, because as she surmises, they won't deport her – though she did take care not to mention this at the university's administration department, it's not customary to deport students who speak the country's official language as their mother tongue, except in cases of criminal behaviour. That said, one has to set boundaries with regard to life here. Seven years, during which there is constant coming and going between home and the new life, she goes back three-four times a year, hitch-hiking, by train, even by coach at times. On the way back, one has to show proof of funds at the border or a valid residence permit, a student card isn't enough. So she starts setting the parameters of this new life. The period of waiting in various offices and obtaining documents begins. *Immigration Office, residence permit*, magical words. These keep hovering in front of her eyes.

Citizenship is still at an unpredictable distance, depending on unreachable conditions, she doesn't even think about that. Besides, that would actually be a decision, the work of the front lobe.

Residence permit – the clear and material goal of the first seven years.

She's a regular at the Immigration Office, every half a year, or in the best case, every year. Together with people from Asia, occasionally Africa, and the various multilingual nations of Eastern Europe. In-between the walls of the office she slowly develops the performance of survival.

She is sitting in the hall of the sanctuary, at the Immigration Office, and there are about eight people in front of her. Eight is not so many, she figures. Eight is a minimum of two hours, more like three, she has had to wait longer, seeing that everybody brings in a considerable pile of paperwork, the more papers, the more comfortable the Customer feels. The Applicant. People have official documents in every possible language, in the language of their country of origin, translations, certified documents, papers already obtained here. The Official in Charge thoroughly examines them, checking which ones aren't suitable, which have expired or don't contain the required information, and then the Applicant starts haggling, complaining, shouting, begging, provided they can utter a word at all – complicated moods, extremes ranging from desperation to violence, from humble silence to practical negotiation. The mood of the Official is just as much of a roller-coaster. Those waiting, the customers, the Applicants, who have left one river to dip their bare feet into another, immigrants, people on temporary residence permits, others with settled status, people on work permits, students, a whole range of unelucidated lives. Some get preferential treatment because an acquaintance or official or some agent brings their documentation in for them. For everyone else, there is a wait of two, but more like three to four hours, which feels like an eternity. Continuous discouragement. She looks around, trying to spot somebody who will be called in soon, with a view to approach them. She is testing the ground in one language, then another, English, Russian. She has studied some Czech, too, but that doesn't seem to be of much use here, also some French that can be helpful with some people from Africa. She is trying to suss out whether the person waiting to be called in can actually communicate in some language with the Official in charge. She is happy to help, she offers. When the door opens for the next customer, she accompanies them.

She offers her interpreting services to the Official. Those from Asia have priority – she quickly familiarizes herself with their accents, whereas the Official appears to refuse to understand them deliberately. As if they weren't so keen on them.

Bring your own interpreter, a notice advises people in the waiting room, but a lot of guest workers, students and various others can't afford this. She would never take money for her interpreting services, though nobody has offered any, either. There is no money in this miserable togetherness.

The Official keeps airing the interpreter, avoiding eye contact but listening to what she says.

Still, they may have given her air and looked through her, but she managed to get in. She is interpreting, helping, while remaining invisible. She's in there, in the office. She gladly helps sorting papers for others, tells them what else the Applicant has to bring in next, from where, what it should contain, such as details about *work, house, salary. Money*, she explains using the universally understood rubbing of the thumb and the index finger. As if she was trying to get Friday to understand the rules of a new world. Friday stays silent though has a pile of documents already.

They never grant any permits straightaway.

'Good job that you don't immediately want a res-perm for five years. Wouldn't you also like citizenship, as of today?' the Official mumbles in their mother tongue, the interpreter who's just got aired understands but that's irrelevant. 'Come back and bring something else. Meanwhile, we must be aware of you. You'll get a temporary permit anyway. There are no permanent things around here. This is a place for momentary things. You can stay. Up to a finite point.'

Indeed, this is place where they are truly familiar with the Finite.

'Is this clear?' The customer, the Applicant understood what they have to bring in, work-work, is being repeated to them on a loop. *Work contract*, the interpreter thus aired scribbles this word on a piece of paper and slips it between their documents. The

Vietnamese woman doesn't speak any other language, so interpreting for her is pure illusion. The woman packs up her stuff and leaves. Like a tree that has grown feet.

She stays behind in the office, and this is the really difficult part. For a short while, she has to continue with her original role: getting aired. And then slowly, sensing the right moment when the Official is ready to receive a new customer, she has to transform from being aired into an actual Applicant, and make herself noticed in a single instant. 'Can I come next?' Or better still: 'I only brought in a document', and already politely handing it over. Only a document, like someone whose case is simple and clear, like crystal. Above all, she has to be a very likeable Applicant, because in the new world one has to be likeable, a genuine jackpot in the eyes of the new homeland. An invaluable young person, a talented student, the hope of the nation.

'I only brought in this document.' A health certificate. Which is a complex compilation of actual tests (HIV-negative result, blood tests), together with a leprosy certificate, issued in the absence of sight, in fact without granting any attention to the sight of the Body. The doctor, bored out of his mind, scribbled a note and certified it with his signature: No leprosy. Also in Latin: *Sine morbo leproso*.

The Body continued its race, and in a mere seven years, it arrived at the destination.

She developed this technique after she started coming to the office on her own. There was no friend or lover who'd be able to put up with several hours of idle sitting around. Once she came with Ari, they even went in to see the Official together, after making sure that it was okay. They have similar documents, the same university course, two birds with one stone. This is the last time they mention their specialism: the Official doesn't ask any questions but frowns when hearing about Russian. It makes sense to know the language of the colonisers, Ari states. But colonisation is over, Russian has become suspect, and there isn't more of a lost cause for the Applicant than being suspect.

The Official leafs through both files in silence, then removes the respective statements issued by the university, turns them over and then crosses them out, no good, they need another document which would clearly indicate the length of their course and how long the country should expect to be honoured by their presence. In other words, when will they finish their studies. Ari lets out a harsh laugh and informs the official that every university course is five years long, so if they are quasi – and Ari accentuates the term quasi – second year students, then we are looking most probably at another three years. So they are requesting a permit for another three years. The Official looks up slowly and menacingly and announces that they can get a permit for three months. Ari explains that the university cannot know exactly when they finish, they may defer or go somewhere abroad on a scholarship, the Admin Department definitely won't issue a document stating that x and y will graduate at such and such a time, and that's that. By this point the Official has already got immersed into another case, and chose to ignore them. Their permit was issued for three months. After this, she has never attended with Ari. She decided to use her own technique instead, transforming from the one who gets air to an actual body.

After the person she has interpreted for leaves the room (she learned not to switch on hope – I'm going to be next, now that I'm here – because it's much better if hope switches itself on when justified), the Official takes her documents as if it was really her turn, not remembering how the Customer had actually entered the room, it doesn't matter, let them go next. Hope isn't the best equipment; she knows this by now. People tend to give away their hopefulness, and this can lead to a merciless shattering of hope. Bring in such and such a document about your earnings, accommodation, health, work status, after all, she no longer lives in a student hall but rents a room, how can she pay for it from a scholarship of a mere three thousand if she doesn't have a work permit? 'I receive financial help from home,' she says confidently, as one doesn't have to offer proof of that. One has to learn to stand there, completely blank and open, and not to experience pain if sent away or refused a permit. The Body can grow an armour, and this will work. Asians are great with armour, too. Those who have come from far enough know how to stand here, because the Body has to remain standing.

While interpreting, the person who gets air and not yet materialised into Body, is mindful not to be present as an Applicant, restraining herself, being helpful but not intrusive, not trying to act as an expert, not adding unnecessary details with which to draw attention to herself, she's just a touch more than the person she is interpreting for, but incomparably less than the Official, she is a mere invisible link. Thereafter, however, she materialises into Body, a healthy, likeable body that wouldn't jeopardise her new homeland with any infections. Following the leprosy document, obtained in a mere three minutes, she receives a permit for three years, which is utter fulfilment. From there, only Eternity can be the next step. She ends up on the winning side after the first seven years. A decade after her arrival, she swears an oath to her new country. She didn't have to do the same for the old one, because that home didn't request or inquire about anything.

The Body is ready for arrival. Seven years have passed.

As If a Foreigner

The elderly editor, the best literary stylist in the editorial team, points out about her very first article submitted for publication (not directly to her, but to a younger and less experienced colleague, who will ensure that this kind comment reaches the ears of the emerging author): 'this piece of writing reads as if it had been written by a foreigner.' She adds that it's good, meaning that the article is good, the review, the essay in aesthetics is so-called literary criticism, seeing that it still belongs to the 'so-called' category. But 'good' is only a basic and very brief word, not too memorable because memory doesn't extend to goodness, praise and recognition. The sentence returning to the addressee, sent to the young author with the aim to enthuse hard work and with an intention of good will, or rather with an intention, without any premonition, is met with open ears. There is no wax in the ears to prevent the fatal temptation of writing. The ear is wide open, ready to be deterred.

As if written by a foreigner.

Ari, her colleague and a professional cynic, the only person she showed the edits with comments scribbled all over the article in three different colours, dismisses this with a wave of her hand, calling them mundane stylists. Mundane. As if there were celestial ones, too. The mundane is always moving with the sentence, slowly snaking ahead, examining the text word by word, and line by line. The celestial ones, however, aren't concerned with spelling mistakes, word order, or the eternal grammatical agreement of subject and predicate. They are solely engaged with ideas and ideals, thoughts and feelings, as well as poetic heights, making their way above the clouds where the miserable repetition of words and commas cannot reach.

Linguistic fascists, Ari concludes disdainfully, at a time when they both live at a hall for foreign students at the edge of the city. Perhaps you could reply via registered post: 'Fuck you!'

They are studying the work of Brodsky at university. So-called poems, this is what Iosif Brodsky is told at court before being sentenced for five years for skulking for social parasitism, and he is deported to Norinskaya, in the Arkhangelsk area. This village is at a similar distance from Moscow as Saint Petersburg, the sentence could have been much worse, for instance the beautiful and most welcoming Siberia, but for the soul, such distance is much longer than these few hundred manageable kilometres. The expression 'so-called' poems is uttered four times during the trial by judge Savelieva. The poet asks – and this question is yet another proof of his parasitic behaviour –, why does the prosecution talk about 'so-called' poems. The court's response, that is judge Savelieva's response, is that this is their opinion of them. The witness, by the name of Romasova, called in to give evidence regarding Brodsky's so-called parasitic activities doesn't actually know him personally but knows his so-called activity.

At Brodsky's trial, journalist, writer and human rights activist Frida Vigdorova compiled a selection of notes, and this record has become her best-known work. Vigdorova and Brodsky departed in the same year in different directions – the journalist died and Brodsky left his country. According to these records, the judge asked Brodsky who had ranked him among the poets. The poet replied, no one. And added: who ranked me among the human race? The judge asked whether he attended some university where people were trained to be poets. The poet replied that in his view this wasn't a matter of education. The judge then asked how someone could become a poet. The poet replied that this came from God. The judge asked countless times why he didn't work, being instead a social parasite, a shirk. The poet replied countless times that he did work, he wrote poems. The word poem was uttered a total of sixty-seven times according to the minutes of the trial.[29]

According to Aeschylus, the science of numbers was also handed down to humans by Prometheus, so they could use it as they saw fit, because letters, fire, sacrifice and hope should be used by people as they see fit, this freedom is granted to them by the gods, together with fire and letters. Fire, letters, numbers and hope are the gifts of the same divine hand.

After Brodsky's exile, Norinskaya became deserted, fifty years later there was only a single officially registered resident. The most famous resident who had ever set foot there is Iosif Brodsky. From Norinskaya's point of view, the fact that Brodsky wrote so-called poems, for which he was sentenced and exiled there, is an undisputed advantage. Today, there is even a memorial house dedicated to the poet by the name of Joseph Brodsky, who had settled in America and won the Nobel Prize.

Half a century on a human scale is less than a blink of an eye for the gods. Brodsky won. Language and poetry are in any case above the state, the system, power, judge Savelieva and witness Romasova. And they can outlive them, too.

According to historical accounts, however, neither letters, nor numbers can conquer death. The gods will never forgive Prometheus, who had committed the impudence to not only give letters and numbers in addition to the gift of fire, but also hope to these mortals, so despicable to Zeus that he allows them to die. Hope is the ultimate impertinence. Because Prometheus didn't only teach them sacrifice and how to use numbers, but also gave them hope to go with their mortality. It is for these teachings that he has to atone, chained to a rock, and then plummet into the abyss and perish. Zeus, the Tyrant Father wanted to create a new species in lieu of these miserable and mortal humans but Prometheus felt sorry for them and didn't allow their destruction. He was the first Son who made good with his gifts: hope, fire, letters, numbers, sacrifice. So many celestial gifts, all dissolved in the stolen fire. *Buchstaben von Feuer.*

When she brings in the manuscript that reads as if it had been written by a foreigner to the editorial office of the reputable publication that dates back half a century, and where she ended up on the recommendation of a university professor based on a seminar presentation, it is also mentioned that speaking and studying foreign languages, in short, too many foreign languages and too much foreign environment, is harmful and in fact dangerous for one's own first language, because it heightens foreignness. This foreignness is already accentuated in her, a visible foreignness is blazing in her. She has no idea as yet that this will be her work equipment. For now, there will be a first edit, then another, followed by the copy editor's final version. Weeding out this much foreignness is akin to breaking up a virgin territory, taking charge of it, removing the large stones, roots and howitzer, as well as the weed itself. Howitzer and the other weed are creeping and crawling at such a speed that they have to weed it out with a huge effort, because it's able to generate a complicated underground and overground network of roots. One day, in the very distant future, due to bountiful rain and manure resulting from the joint efforts of human and divine intervention, this soil can become fertile. 'You have to learn to write,' the elderly editor concludes after reading the first page of her typescript. 'The edits will be posted to you. What's your address?' Temporary place, foreignness: 'student hall'.

The entire editorial team is leaning over her manuscript, following which they hand the typed text, the so-called manuscript she has personally brought in, to one another, in order to correct it using three different colours, red, blue and charcoal, and in the end, have the foreignness of her sentences, the homelessness of her word order be tidied up and typed up by an editorial secretary, so that the undissolved obscurity of her thoughts can come to light and dissolve.

The lords and guardians of language include the editor-in-chief with a sharp eye who's using her claws to rip manuscripts apart, and the others, all elderly, slowly spoken, stern men. She hears them on the voice of the judge and witnesses in the case that sentenced Brodsky for his so-called poems: every single one of them self-assured, owning language as if it was some property, a home, a house, a snug nest, a final refuge. Language is in their hands. Language is theirs.

The multicolour edits are the last judgement upon a school test. She hears every voice connected to the guardianship of language on the voice of judge Savelieva's deep twang.

Judge Savelieva's neat and economical handwriting and firm marks in red, blue and charcoal pencil that don't give away gender end up at the bottom of the drawer of shame.

She ignores the letter accompanying her article that is sent to her address at the hall for foreign students. It contains the clean copy, accompanied by the mountain of edits and a note that informs her to send in her corrections, in the end, the article will appear as it was in these final edits she submitted for publication. The editors congratulate her on the article. She can get a new commission; would she like to come to the editorial office. She withdraws the manuscript, at least she thinks that's what she does. But the manuscript doesn't burn. She'll never go to the editorial office and won't send anything back. The clean copy is neat and foreign, the thoughts are glowing with a heavy weight. The thoughts of others. As if a foreigner has written them. The piece appears in three months and they send her a print copy. Her professor conveys his congratulations.

Letters and hope. She has to reconquer language in order to feel at home in it. The only liveable space is language, if she loses it, she dies. She turns to books, over which there are no guardians, letters that were stolen by gods for humans to give them hope. Now they are everyone's letters. Their linguistic guardians, in case they ever existed, are invisible. Only letters, God's strange gifts, are blazing in her, akin to the gifts of Prometheus, *Buchstaben von Feuer*, letters without authors and editors, without the hollow trees and menacing rocks of power. She reads a lot, she's always reading. In the suffocating armour of language, she writes articles, attends university and is savouring the gifts of gods.

Poems are pouring from the sky, the land, the linguistic motherland, the land of the home is waiting for exploration. A year later, she returns to the editorial office with her articles. The verses are free, secretive, foreign, and language is twirling in them as it sees fit. As for her, she's waiting for land and sky to conjoin, even though she has no idea of this expectation.

She does come into possession of language in the end. They obtain and create their shared language with the Other.

They live together on the plateau, by the sea. Steep roads are leading up to it from two sides, the climate is arid, with hardly any vegetation. The landscape is not far from a desert. The heat is already unbearable at half past eight in the morning. Low fir trees are scattered around the coast in the deep sand, transported from nearby Africa, just opposite. There are two newly built holiday villages on the plateau, consisting of identical white and terracotta houses. The pebble road connecting the two villages is a place where at dusk one can see rabbits blending into the colours of the landscape.

Driving on the motorway by the sea, a sign draws attention to the fact that one can catch a glimpse of the coast of Africa at the next viewpoint. 'Let's stop,' they say almost in unison. Every weekend they explore the Southern coast. The air is humid and the distant coast is barely visible. They are staring ahead, searching for something extraordinary and unseen before. They look ahead. Other shores. Nabokov translated his own autobiography *Speak, Memory* into Russian and gave it a new title: *Other Shores. Другие берега.* Another language, another life, another shore. Nabokov was given access to two languages. As for her, she got given the first, far away from any previous homeland.

Africa is hiding itself. After the fake promise of the viewpoint, they carry on driving and leave the coastal road behind. They turn their backs to Africa, this giant vanishing into the mist. They are drinking in, sucking up, gobbling down this foreign world. Small Spanish settlements, towns reminiscent of a Moorish past, a magical flamenco under a huge tarpaulin, where a corpulent middle-aged woman is dancing with a fire and sorrow they haven't seen before. She can't take her eyes off the dancer. The fire is burning, yet she'd throw herself into it. Perhaps she should write about this dancer. And her elderly mother sat among the audience and whom she greets after the show, bowing only for her. About this woman, the fire, the Moorish fortresses, the half-desert. About this whole foreignness. She is sucking it in but she has no history and language for this. They are visiting countless fortresses, and eating fresh fish in small restaurants. They take in everything apart from bull fights – no killing, they insist, though they always peek into the ornate round-shaped buildings, the *corrida de torros*.

They are slowly moving away from the coast densely populated with apartment blocks. They left behind the resort of Benidorm, too, which brings up childhood memories. They both grew up in blocks of flats, in two different countries. Now they are comparing these memories. They've known each other for half a year, the two pasts reveal themselves to become one present. They've even found Benidorm in the publication entitled 'The Most Beautiful Resorts in the World', carefully left on the coffee table by their landlord. They are staring at the photo in silence: does this mean that the housing estate on which they had grown up is nice, too?

They head somewhere new nearly every weekend. Benidorm? the shared vocabulary is slowly shaping up, they are shaping their new language. 'Are you homesick?' they ask each other fondly. Blocks of flats? A touch of Benidorm? The modern tower blocks in Benidorm are eloquent proof of a greedy world, with a keen obsession with property development, which doesn't resemble the grey ten and five storey blocks of their childhood, but they are homely.

When the man invited her to visit – he was working in the South of Spain – he immediately warned her that this seaside place was just as hideous as his hometown. 'And yours, judged by the photographs I've seen. Multistorey buildings competing with one another, tall structures, concrete. You'll feel at home. And you can write if you like.' Perhaps he's just trying to tame foreignness. Yes indeed, it would be great to write.

When the Other invites her, they are still distant from each other. They correspond. They approach each other by way of words, not the body. First the word, then the body. She has given the body away so many times that it can no longer be reclaimed. Now she wants to take a higher risk, she wants it all – to give as well as to receive, *corazón* included. She wants the heart, she's not that protective anymore but still quite cautious. 'Want it?' They negotiate.

'What are you doing there?'

'Taking decisions.'

'How?'

'By way of words.'

She sends him her words, her decisions, poems, short stories. Her most important decision to date hasn't been taken by way of words but by the body. She doesn't really call it a decision but an occurrence. This is what occurred to her: she arrived ten years ago. He has never been around there, the Other points out, they should visit together. Together? They've been corresponding for ten days when the idea of together comes up. It slips into the words, as a first experiment. Now she lives here. 'Which borough?', they compare notes: who, where, what.

'What are you doing tonight?' the Other asks.

'I'm setting.'

'Hens?'

'Yes. Both hens and cockerels. There are more hens though.'

'Female poultry are more useful. And cattle, too.'

'Then I'm useful, too. I'm being milked enough.'

She works at a theatre, as a steward and cloakroom attendant during the summer festival, it pays well and she can see the shows for free, it's an okay summer job. It isn't official, but she has such a job elsewhere. Isn't she a citizen yet? Yes, but elsewhere. If we marry, can you get it? I can get it without that, too. She has already started the process. Regarding marriage? Citizenship. There is a lengthy procedure, involving lots of evidencing. What do you have to prove? That she's entitled. And that she comes from good stock. I'm glad that you come from good stock, my mother has also been telling me that an adequate stock is essential. It will be adequate. But they are not welcoming me here with open arms. I am. What are your plans? To write, and she shall write. Right now, she's also working in an office, this and that, pay, papers, in short: a life that is legit. She

257

speaks several languages, and one can always make a living on the back of that. Shame that she doesn't have a language of her own. She's rarely travelling back home these days.

They are coordinating their diaries using landlines and mobiles. She sends him the poem written for him:

I tried to call you.
You wrote that you forgot your mobile at home this morning,
and you didn't pick up the landline.
I had something superimportant to say,
that couldn't wait:
There will be a full moon today,
the sun is fading,
autumn has obviously arrived.
And that I bought some Kaiser bacon
on my way home, for two fifty.
And apparently there's a revolution –
(badly smelling men on the underground
they must be training in preparation for the night).
And that I'm getting used to the new home,
Gogol street
and your absence.
And there's another thing.
Yeah, would you wear an embroidered linen shirt? Shall I get
    a size M?
I'm slowly making my way to work
like the good prolley that I am
(four hours of theatre).
Just remembered: the 80 trolley is off schedule,
don't rely on it if you're coming this way.

At the end of the day, I only invited you
to offer up my transience.

Because
as of today, I'm no longer immortal,
the doctor said,
when I showed him the test results.

You may be back already.
I'll try again.
Let's stick with this life on earth
and a landline.

Except that this rhyme with the 'prolley-trolley' is awful. 'Fine, I'll change it,' but he still puts the poems down.

Even the poem written for him is only out there so he can change the rhyme. He's looking for the story. 'What happened? By the way, what sort of doctor is the one mentioned in the poem? What did he say?'

'This reaction is killing me. This is referential reading', she replies. Meaning that literary works are about the real word. She doesn't have anything to add about the doctor, it's too soon. They have been corresponding for eleven days.

'Come here, there's plenty of sun.' Nothing is too soon for him.

The time is nearly ripe for measuring up their bodies. The skin, the scent, the taste. To love so much that it can take one through decay. They sleep very little when they meet. And once they've met, they'll never sleep apart again.

To be the first human couple again, from beginning to end. On their Spanish journeys – in the course of the Spanish year as they will later call it – they hoard treasures, so much treasure to last for good, and which cannot be sold off, akin to the crown treasures, the Koh-i-Noor, the gates of Isis, the mummy of priestess Hortesnakht. They are laying the foundations of their own national museum. As later the Son, who was conceived here like a sudden celestial phenomenon, will keep asking tirelessly: how much did the Parliament's fine building cost? Nothing, because it cannot be sold. Yet the Son insists on knowing the cost. In the course of the Spanish year, they aren't saving up cash in the bank, as only the Other has a job, during which time her work is to round up meandering sentences.

Benidorm is part of the crown jewels. And replacement car parts, too. They visit Granada again and this is when it happens – the car jolts at regular intervals on the motorway. They even observe that the motorways have been pretty good so far and although there are no signs of any flaws, this is suddenly a bad one. After a few kilometres, this thud is becoming more and more regular, so they get off at the first available opportunity. The problem doesn't come from the road but from the old car. They are trying to find a mechanic in a nearby village, on a Saturday morning. After an hour, a young Spanish guy signals that they are in luck, indicating *finito*. *Una hora* – in another hour, they would have gone to pot. The man pinches three fingers together and passionately explains what they escaped from. They also learn a new word: *semieje* (pronounced: semiehe). Semiaxis. They can't make it to Granada, so instead spend the night in the village of Cabezo de Torres and take a walk to nearby Murcia, in the end the bill amounts to three hundred, almost as mush as they paid for the old car.

'We'll hold the wedding at Benidorm, okay?' they discuss a few months later when they are regularly driving past the tower block resort about to build its own legend. Or: 'There's a three-day public holiday coming up, we should visit some historical sites. Benidorm?' Apart from consistent sunshine, Benidorm is the epitome of botched human intentions, a synonym for the annihilation of nature. Yet on a late autumn day they do make a stopover in Benidorm – purely out of solidarity, a solidarity with places fallen out of grace. The resort is nearly abandoned, they can barely find an open restaurant. And when they finally come across one on a wide alley flanked by tall palm trees, they reluctantly turn around in the doorway.

They negotiate sleeping patterns. It's like a diplomatic consultation, between a late and an early riser, between two people where one is late and another is early to bed. They are sharing dreams.

'I've been to a wonderful place in my dream – one of them begins.'

'Benidorm?'

'Doesn't this mean good sleeper?'

They learn to sleep together. The cold house helps with clinging on to each other. They will never be as cold again in their shared life as in this early stage on the Spanish coast. There is no heating in homes except for a badly working, more like decorative fireplace. They make use of small electric radiators which they have to hide when the landlord comes round to check why the bills are so high and to insist that they don't use top energy consuming appliances because the network wouldn't cope. This is a holiday resort. *Centro de vacaciones*.

Life is more animated here in autumn and winter than in the major resorts. The identical apartment blocks are inhabited by Swedish and British pensioners, who have moved here from the North to spend their winters along the coast in temperatures around ten degrees and only go back home during the summer for a couple of weeks. Their loosely planned journey, without a particular destination, takes them to the mountains. They are climbing up to the arid red mountains from the direction of the sea, following a narrow white road. Hardly any vegetation and rocks in this semi-desert. Abandoned farms everywhere. Stone houses in ruins, remnants of stone fences, palm trees fighting for survival, huge agave bushes spreading out like a Medusa head, cacti covered in dust. No trace of life or water on these farms, the drought has killed everything.

Hot dry summer. Viewed from afar, the villages appear like flashing dots among the bare mountains. As the road ascends into the mountains, however, the white villages begin to come to life. An old communal laundry in the village centre. Rows and rows of stone basins are lined up in the building open to the elements from all sides, and water is piped in from a spring and is let out via the ground. The basins have ribbed edges, like a stone maul for scouring clothes. Carpets are drying on washing lines in the stone building. They take off their sweaty shirts and blouses, let some cold water into a basin and have a wash as there is no air conditioning in the old car. The Other is half naked, she is in her swimsuit top. They are washing their clothes side by side, but soon they stick their arms under the running water so it squirts, and before long, they start splashing each other, first on the face, head, upper body and then legs, sandals, everywhere. They even come up with rules: everything goes. The water is seething, their clothes on top of the stone basin, swimming like humpy corpses and clogging up the drain. They are soaking wet, as if they had just emerged from the sea, finally feeling cold.

In the villages they visit, they buy the odd item. Carpets, and claypots in which they are unable to cook or bake. The objects of their future life, the Spanish foundation.

The Other has been living here for over a year when she arrives at his invitation, he has been sent out as a local representative by his company. 'You'll get a Spanish scholarship' – he writes. – 'Literary scholarship.' Two languages at once? Of love and of the future book.

He isn't offering a pig in a poke, the Other informs her, he's earning 0.625 per second. 'I am earning a lot more, 15.625 here', meaning her work at the institute dealing with increasingly murky international affairs. They roam around the coast, the towns built on the rocks, the magnificent Ronda and in the end, the hideous Benidorm, too. They found each other via an international dating site. They've kept narrowing their search until the other was the only option.

By the end of September, the coast is basically deserted as the tourists leave the area. Only locals and pensioners, arriving from the North in larger and larger numbers, live here. Everything is peaceful, bright and azure blue. Uniformity makes the autumn monotonous. One doesn't need to wear long sleeves, not even in November. It hardly ever rains. The colour of the landscape, as they are standing with their backs to Africa and the sea, is a shimmery grey, a greyish-brownish faded green. Bare mountains, half desert. White roads and villages among the mountains.

She easily fulfils the conditions of the Spanish scholarship. She has already written a hundred pages by November, so this will be her first book if it's meant to be. She reads her short stories out loud. She writes the first one three days after her arrival, in the first days of April. In the morning, as the Other is heading off to work, he puts his coffee cup down in the doorway and says by way of goodbye:

'Write a story today.'

A story? She did want to write actually, but she doesn't have a story to tell. So she starts looking for her own story, by way of snaking and meandering sentences. The snakes make the stories jump, like joggers tend to make rabbits jump on the plateau.

There is a performance of a mystery play in the church at Elche, a mystery is taking place, they say, and one has to book at dawn to be able to partake in the experience. But they only make it to the end of the ceremony, as the morning has kept them very close to each other. They have missed the mystery, they note when they get to the motorway leading to it. Sweet scents on the motorway. Washing the streets with scented washing liquid is an excess of prosperity. The road leads to a plain from behind the hills: endless meadows of evenly planted blossoming orange trees. This strong and spicy scent is absolutely mindboggling. Their honeymoon is sweeter than they could have possibly hoped for. By the time they get there and park the car, the crowds are already pouring out of the church, the mystery is over, so they ask a woman who is smiling at them.

'*Final?*'

'*Si. Ma*,' a participant dressed in festive garments starts to explain, '*no se puede...*'

They are trying to make sense of the sentence they've just heard – 'what did she say?' There was a *corazón* in it. Heart. *Corazón* is present in every single Spanish song. There are no songs without *corazón*. One cannot miss the mystery. Mysteries take place in the heart. Perhaps this is what the woman wanted to say.

At the beginning of November, they have to decide whether they want to stay on. The contract is coming to an end, but the office would like to extend it. They are cautiously creeping towards a decision, from two directions. Everybody has a right to veto. They are spending the weekend on another trip. One can no longer swim in the infinity pool behind the block, its water is too cold but they still leave it there for the winter. They are staring at the pool, the manicured garden with oleanders still in bloom in winter, agaves and large palm trees. Behind the office is an American school – this is where the children of colleagues go. Some people only spend one or two years here, many others stay for five-ten years. Then they either go back home or to international offices in other countries.

This is winter. It's cold again in the flat, and one can't bathe in the sea. They go again to visit the town built on the rock, Cuenca, and the ancient temple at Alarcón, where a contemporary artist had painted a floor to ceiling work, the heart's dark and disturbing visions of heaven and hell, or as he called it: the ninth day of creation. The artist's name is Jesús Mateo. 'Is this a pseudonym? One shouldn't put it past him that this is his real name.'

The artwork that is surrounding and almost engulfing the viewer has taken seven years to create.

Every human creation is the ninth day. A work that cannot be sold off.

On their way, they drive past a huge fortress that has been turned into a hotel. Old forts transformed into luxury accommodation. They could hold the wedding here instead of Benidorm and check out the prices. Double room. 'Any kids?'

'Yes, one.'

After some research, she concludes: not too bad. Isn't it nicer in Benidorm? Three nights with a kid off season is just a bit more expensive than what she's getting for her first book.

The sun is setting earlier now, and they are slowly inching home in the old car, towards the next day. They have a week until the final decision.

'I miss the rain. And the mud.'

'Let's go.'

'Let's go home.'

The flat is cold, they can't use the ornamental fireplace as it is still too warm outside for the smoke to make it through the narrow chimney, so it just gets stuck inside and then they have to air till late at night.

Two years weren't enough for them to get used to this endless sunshine. They covered thousands of kilometres, climbed the Puig Campana, roamed around the Costa del Sol and the Costa Blanca, the Southern mountains, the white villages, visited Granada three times, went to the palm park at Elche, where there are five hundred species of palm trees, even made it to the absurd Gibraltar. They gathered so much treasure that they can barely carry.

This was their first time.

Copper Flowers

The body departs, but hasn't got enough time to actually arrive. This fast-paced and highly demanding time simply runs out while matter tries to bargain with matter, and the body with the visible world. This body can no longer arrive anywhere despite being the subject of wide-scale admiration: her mother made it to a new homeland at the age of sixty-seven. She came on the insistence of her daughter who had helped her, though it wasn't possible to also help with all the packing and with liquidating her old life. Her mother had started packing ten months before they finally loaded those carefully chosen few pieces of furniture, the boxes of books and kitchen utensils onto a van, and on a sunny February day sat her in the car and arranged for her to arrive at a newly decorated one and a half room flat in a random block on a random estate. From one set of orderly circumstances to another. What's more, this new flat even came with its own cellar.

'Copper flowers. They call these copper flowers around here,' the daughter points out when she visits her mother in the new flat and brings her a bunch of zinnias.

'Copper flowers,' the mother replies in the affirmative, without a hint of interrogation, yet with the indignation of someone caught uttering something absurd or plain stupid, perhaps because of misapprehension.

'How can people possibly call zinnias copper flowers?' This is more of a theatrical outcry, a pretend shock. This is her new voice adapted for the here and now: the voice of surprise and rejection.

She could of course continue riffing on this business with the copper flowers, the zinnias that are also known as Turkish buns in the Eastern counties. With this minor theatrical indignation, the mother sends the unequivocal message that despite having arrived here for good, she'll refuse to call zinnias copper flowers. Besides, the water is undrinkable here. 'Un-drin-ka-ble', she firmly stresses the syllables.

At the class reunion, the Szabó family use the same theatrical syllabication for undrinkable. It's shocking that city folk just gulf this stuff down, they are their own worst enemies, seeing that they have no idea what proper drinking water tastes like. This water here is dead and undrinkable.

Their parents have been classmates by the way, aunt Szabó and her mother.

The Szabós use spring water for everything, even for making soup, and they take a trip to the Holy Spirit spring with their jugs once a week. 'Now, this is water, proper water,' they keep stressing, and always use it for making lamb soup. 'You must visit us at some point, you'll see that this way the soup tastes just like at home, provided you manage to lay hands on some decent meat and vegetables. None of these are to be taken for granted, as people aren't familiar with milk-fed lamb and parsnip around here. Believe it or not, you have to buy such stuff in a halal shop!' She pronounces it 'hálál'. 'In our neighbourhood, there's a halal shop on most streets. When did they get so numerous?' What's most bizarre, the Szabó family tell us at the class reunion, tarragon tastes completely different here and they've just recently realised this. As it turns out, there are two kinds, one of which is completely useless, it has no tarragon flavour whatsoever, you can stick as many as five stems in the soup and it still ends up tasting of nothing, Mária explains, come visit us, then you can sign your books for us and we'll prepare some proper homemade lamb soup for you.

The Szabós arrived a decade later than her and, as they labour the point, their child was born back home.

The visible world has itself been carried along by the traveller, like thistle. Take me with you, the water cries out. So does the fresh air from home. And the winters from home. Take me with you, the sour cream, the cottage cheese and the zinnia join in. Take me with you and don't lend me to anyone else, ever. Don't get to know anything else. There's no other world.

So her mother moves into this new one and a half room apartment. 'One and a half rooms?' she inquired in her new-found voice, 'half-a-room?', she asked indignantly when they bought the flat. During her long and hard life of sixty-seven years to date, she's never heard of half rooms. She has of course heard of basement rooms, family rooms, box rooms, guest rooms, loft rooms, rental rooms, but no half rooms. The mother wobbles over to this half-a-room, holding the vase with the copper flowers in her hand, and shouts back at the top of her voice, as if she was trying to draw the attention of the occupants in the block opposite to the fact that her flat was engulfed in flames and she had to flee, what did you say the name of these zinnias was. She hasn't yet seen any of these flowers at the market by the way, even though she's had a good look around at all the markets in the borough, they have nothing on sale that she hasn't seen before. Battle cries in a new hostile world.

'Copper flowers,' she says in a colourless voice. Copper flowers, in other words zinnias or Turkish buns, as they are known in the Eastern countries because of their pom-pom shaped forms. Elsewhere, they call them youth-and-age. They are magnificent flowers, known by a thousand names, just like any other creation for that matter.

Perhaps it was a mistake to buy these flowers, something old and common that her mother would recognize and hence be reminded of the world she'd left behind. It's been nearly seven years since her mother had moved away from home.

Bodies move away. And cells get replaced in this amount of time. Her own body has already replaced its cells many times in this new homeland. Perhaps she has already changed altogether. She has adapted. Perhaps she's no longer the same person who has once left. Could she be different at the level of her cells, too? How much time would her mother's cells need before this could happen to her? And how about the soul? How much time would the soul require?

The body, of Andrei Tarkovsky is resting in Sainte-Geneviève-des-Bois, near Paris. It will never return home.

The body will not return home. Only the films.

The body departs. The body doesn't return back home. As if matter was able to speak more clearly. The journey of the soul is less comprehensible. It leaves and comes back in a flash. In a single extended dream. When will her mother dream about the world around here? The new world that she'll never ever call her home. Her mother rings her in desperation whenever she has a bad dream involving her. Things like getting into trouble or something terrible that just happened.

'No', she tries to comfort her, 'I'm fine, but please don't call me in the morning because I'm writing then. The dream is about you.' But her mother doesn't reveal any further dreams. The new world is dangerous and unpredictable for her.

'I can never get used to this,' her mother concludes on an unusually subdued voice, really softly, yet also glumly and clearly. Like a dry November day. She's surrounded by the best of all visible worlds that they could offer her.

'I can never get used to this, to being here,' she makes it clear. She could perhaps put it differently and say that I don't want to, I'm not able to or there is no time, as the cells have only one or two rounds left to replace themselves. It no longer makes sense; I simply don't have to get used to this. Fair enough, this isn't something typical for them. It would be wrong to comfort her mother, she thinks, it would be wrong to deprive her of recognition, of clinging to things, these are still the first seven years for her mother, that's nothing, despite all her cells having renewed themselves, these seven years are only the introductory period, the exposition, it's about organising the material world, half-a-room, the water, the sour cream, the tarragon, the white cheese, the tomatoes, the muscat, the Vienna sausages, the water, the dead water, these seven years are only about the struggles of the visible world. It would be wrong to make her mother move away from her sadness. We need your sadness, your old age, your immovable interior, she thinks. We need your nostalgia, your zinnias, your memory.

'Where shall I put it?' she asks, still holding the vase her mother has given her and forgotten about it, she's been holding this heavy crystal vase from home all along, a vase her mother received as a retirement gift, with her maiden name engraved into its base.

Where should she put these rigid purple, yellow, orange and pink flowers with regular petals that are nameless yet also beyond naming. Her mother takes the vase and as she does so, some of the water spills out, she doesn't notice, as she either can't see or sense it, or it simply makes no difference to her. She takes the vase to the main room, which is barely bigger than the so-called half-a-room, but it's known as a whole room. The half-room clings to her like a tight glove, everything is suddenly too cramped for her around here. This whole world is too cramped for her.

Lech Lechá

She's leaving just as the fox grape has finally clambered up the fire-wall of the nearby five-storey apartment block. The autumn days are warm, and the dense foliage has turned red for the first time this season. She's leaving just as a sunny and airy site has been found in the garden, perfect for drying the washing. She's leaving just as the dangerously decaying acacia tree, the one that used to generate so much rubbish, has been chopped down, thus freeing up a sun-soaked spot in its place, where one can airdry clothes during the day by moving the rack in the wake of the sun. When things have finally found their peace and place. Her mother is sixty-seven when she emigrates.

'*Lech lechá*', the Father Eternal said to Abraham. 'Go forth', and Abraham did go. He was seventy-five. And he didn't end up with a bad deal: he became famous, had a child, got rich and what's most important, he became a prophet. At the age of seventy-five. *Lech lechá* is one of the ten tests of the Patriarch. Exodus. Emigration.

So *lech lechá* then. Her mother is sixty-seven. In some way or other, both Abraham and her mother emigrated for the sake of their children.

They sold the old family home at a bad price, at the worst pos-sible price in fact. The land on which it was built was worth a lot, but the house itself was worth nothing due to its condition, as for the whole unit together, it could be worth just about anything in-between, depending on demand. The land was too narrow for a plot on which to build a larger apartment block. They've been trying to sell it for years as soon as property prices started to rocket in the suddenly enlarged town, undergoing a spectacular growth, which people both left and moved to all the time. Her mother wanted to sell the house herself, without involving an estate agent, so she placed ads in the local papers and even put up a neatly handwrit-ten notice in the street-facing window to let people know that the house was up for sale. Later, she changed this to a handwritten English-language notice, which was dictated by her grandson letter by letter over the phone – in the hope that the buyer might be from abroad. The buyer, however, only emerged four, almost five years later and paid within a month, leaving three months for the handover of the house in which the mother had spent nearly seven decades. As part of the deal, they weren't obliged to empty the cellar and the attic, and were allowed to leave behind as much furniture as they wanted, meaning as much as they didn't need, since the buyer would have everything removed. She has to sell the house and leave. Her child told her to do so. To emigrate. She shouldn't drag on time. She should just go. Her family, her grandchild is far away. She should sell the house and go. So she's going. She's going now.

'Live animals can't be left behind,' the buyer, a woman around forty, states on the second viewing when she's already paying a deposit.

A little boy, the son of the future owners, dressed in navy trousers and a jumper with a school logo, is stroking the large short-haired grey cat.

Her mother doesn't want any help with the packing, she's doing it all by herself. She's collecting boxes from the corner shop, emptying wardrobes, packing her belongings. She pulls most of the furniture – old armchairs and sofas, chairs and worn-out carpets to the middle of the room. Wardrobe, dining table, dressing table – only a few items are needed in the new life. There are hardly any old neighbours on this street that used to be at the edge of town and is now considered central: they passed away or moved into homes for the elderly, having rolled away from the street in the direction of their children or death. A restaurant, an alternative theatre venue, offices of service providing companies, and even an American chapel opened instead. For many years, lorries and vans were also driving through the street until they were banned, the house would literally shake in the wake of the clanging noise, with bricks and window panes dislodging from their position. Still, heavy traffic persisted on this street linking two main roads. The quiet cobblestoned street as it used to be fifty years ago now became a dangerous space, and the crossing of which turned into a proper performance in the morning rush hour. Despite this, her mother was only concerned about the wandering cat, always following it around. The traffic would barely calm down at night, so much so that her visiting daughter struggled to fall sleep even with ear plugs.

'Just like New York,' she observed.

New York, however, was more of a continuous, muffled hum, an all-concealing blanket of noise, a mist just above ground, under which the city is fast sleep. This street is the random assault of roaring and fading noise waves. Either of these are impossible to adjust to for foreigners. For the onetime child, this is already foreign, for the grandchild, and adventurous experience abroad.

The removal van is booked to leave on Friday, and the car transporting her mother, herself and the grey cat, within an hour, as soon as packing is completed. Both are handled by the same company, they are specialised in this sort of thing, as the dark angels of those who are moving away, helping them cross the wide waters.

On Thursday evening they have dinner in the restaurant that opened in their vicinity. The place is packed and loud, full of cheerful young people who can barely hear each other. The last supper.

Her mother starts talking, her complaints are built up of drops, vapours, fountains, and once they begin, they keep growing and then take a swing, swelling and rising like a flooded river, unstoppable and able to drag along even their silent listener. She's complaining about the public utilities, the authorities where she has to sort out details regarding the sale of the house and the move, she's complaining about her friends she couldn't say goodbye to because she didn't have time, besides, they'll see each other again, she'll be back, nothing is finite after all, 'I'm not going to die,' she concludes. She's complaining about the neighbours, who were asking too many questions and dishing out too much advice, or they died, or are in homes for the elderly, staring ahead with an empty gaze like meek plants, she's complaining about the silent removal men, dressed in black, who did the packing and asked for an exorbitant fee, the new buyers who looked down on everything, even the eaves repaired only last year, the low quality boxes she had to pay money for, her lower back, her legs, the pedicurist doing her job in a rush, her old life, her present life, her new life and any future life to come. The unstoppable words turn into an ocean, swelling, flooding and sweeping away the dinner and the cognac they order, Camus, Remy Martin, Martell, Hardy are the options listed by the waiter. 'I don't know any of these, you pick,' her mother mutters, 'there weren't so many kinds back in the day, you asked for a glass of cognac and they brought you one.' That was at a time when the world was still familiar and predictable. After dinner, her mother also orders a glass of wine, she wanted dessert wine but the waiter informed her that, with regret, they don't have any sweet wine on the menu. She continues to complain while drinking her wine, but this flood is slowly over, the rocks and trunks of wood are flushed away, the waters and stones get exhausted, only disrupting faraway lands and, somewhere in the distance, building a dam to hold all the water back. Pain has returned to a slow and quietly panting course.

While her mother was pouring out her pain, she tested three small local beers in a row, then they ordered another pizza, this time to share.

'All will be well. We can't leave you here. Alone. In this house. You can't stay here. We can't travel a thousand kilometres. Your grandson included. Just to see you.'

At the end, they had another glass, the final quenching, as your father used to say, a last glass, at the end. At the end of what. Or the beginning of what. Back in the house, there's only time to go to sleep in the all too short sleeping bag she used to have as a child, this will also be left behind. The scorching lava of speech is smouldering.

'Clenching or quenching, mum?'

At first, all this alcohol goes to her legs and then spreads through her entire body, which softens and blurs, muffled by her mother's plaintive voice that she could barely hear in the noisy restaurant. The very last dying complaint was about the cat's mandatory immunisations and travel passport and the carrier padded with old towels. The flooding waters dry up and turn back into misty and low clouds.

That night she's tempted yet again by Satan, who wins, and she goes to bed without brushing her teeth like someone with a dim future, unable to sense the purpose of things. She doesn't even bother with pyjamas and just slips stark naked into the old sleeping bag.

By noon, everything gets clear again, beaming after being glued together from the shards of the broken sky, her lips dry from all the pizza and alcohol with next to no water, her head numb, but the body must be put to work, it simply cannot collapse. Her mother has already made some coffee the night before, so it only needs heating up on the cooker, they sit around the large table, but are taking four chairs with them in the hope that they can be repaired over there, and this is a hope long entertained by the chairs themselves, too. The door is shut to ensure that the cat can't get away right now, it will only be put into the carrier at the last minute when the removal men arrive.

Nothing is irreversible anymore. In case the cat vanishes, they'll just wait until it turns up. By tomorrow it will appear and then they can leave.

Nothing is fatal anymore. Times have changed.

Just before eight o'clock they are sitting in silence on the chairs lined up to come with them. Those who are about to leave have to appease the guardian spirit of the house, so it doesn't get offended and look at their wake in anger, besides, those who leave the house, should do this considerately, not in haste or slamming the door but like someone who actually obeys the Great Plan. *Посидеть на дорожку*, sit down before starting off on a journey, as the Russians tend to say, they even have an expression for this, the prefix *на* seems to transform the road into a space, an actual place, as if one was to sit on the road itself or on the carpet. The flying carpet. The road is carrying its traveller.

The others, all those who have ever inhabited this house, both living and dead, are standing or sitting in the other room, there aren't enough chairs for so many of them. They are well-kempt, energetic and encouraging. Her grandmother, grandfather, great-grandmother, and at the back, her great-grandfather, whom she only knows from a photograph that is already packed up and ready to go. Her father and mother – a young, almost unfamiliar woman. By her side, a baby with big round eyes – her mother's deceased sibling.

They are all ready for the journey.

Out of the corner of her eye she can see that her grandmother waves her hand as if she was saying goodbye. Perhaps she should tell her mother that they are here. That she is here, forty years earlier, still with a slim waist. The cat, left unfed to counter vomiting on the journey, sashays through the middle room and rubs itself against the group, meowing. It's hungry. Moving between people's feet, endearing itself to them. The group stands around for a while before vanishing into thin air.

Her mother packs her dirty laundry away, nightie, underwear, toothbrush, toothbrushing glass, moisturiser.

At two minutes to eight, the bell rings. Her mother opens the window and lets the removal men know that she's on her way to open the gate. She gently grabs the heavy cat and places it into the carrier from above, securing the four sides. She opens both portals of the gate for the three removal men dressed in black, as there is a three-ton small van parked in front of the house.

A sort of new life.

Carcass Tags

In the end, they will not pick up Kincső, Susan's mother, in the mountain village because her work schedule calls her elsewhere – as she's announcing people by sending urgent messages on several channels, insisting that the addressee responds as soon as they open them. It turns out that the local Romanian priest will be able to see her that very day, but she'll be at the class meeting the next morning. The earlier plan was that our protagonist would pick Kincső up in her car after a slight detour from the main international road, despite having made a promise not to take any passengers. As it happens, she'll drive Susan but not Kincső.

Kincső found her about six months ago in the social media group set up by Kati to organise the class meeting. Kincső explained in her first letter that she wanted her to 'write carcass tags', because she is working on a project dealing with *roadkill*, meaning that she's engaged in an animal protection, contemporary art and community development project regarding animals fallen, that is killed by the roadside, and ha-ha, she's also writing a divinity project, despite continuous interruptions:

'And this is where you come in, I need names. I'm sorry I haven't yet read any of your books, but I heard a recording of you speaking in public where you said something I consider important about animals. You spoke about the animal within you.'

In a video she mentioned that she can see the primitive creature in herself. She'd like to transcend the human-animal dichotomy. The opposition, the separation. She'd like to transcend separation in everything yet still retain uniqueness. But instead of a philosophical discussion, someone in the audience asked whether she could see the crocodile within herself? Yes, the crocodile indeed, and all the ugly, repugnant and repulsive animals. Crocodiles rather than cats.

'Now I'd like to ask you to write for us', Kincső continued. She'd only need a sentence here and there. To go underneath the respective roadkill as if they were captions:

'I can send you the images, if you like. It's hard to explain this by way of words, nobody understands, she adds at the end of her letter, but it will be clear if I show you. The death of contemporary art is rooted in text, you know. So we aren't talking about something discursive.'

'Carcasses' is the working title, while the official version is *Roadkill Furs*. Or perhaps *Roadkill Fashion*, she still has to ponder on how attractive fur can be these days. A project on contemporary art, involving young artists, a project developing environmental awareness, activating local residents, 'a resurrection project', Kincső sums it up, with the cooperation of Catholic and Orthodox priests and deans. Giant roadside posters featuring 'the carcasses', who – and she insists on this who – have become rarer since she embarked on this work. Rare but still existing.

'Perhaps we don't even have to finish the project because it will come to an end by itself,' Kincső hopes. 'This is an anarchist and vegan animal protection project, but we are using a different label for everyone.'

She has seen enough of these during her travels over the last thirty years. No need for pictures, she hastens to respond. What do you mean by community though?

'Well, one of the goats is run over in a village and everybody knows that it belongs to say the Dunka family. So we are relying on the fact that everybody knows that this isn't simply their misfortune and loss but something that could be anyone else's. The goat, or rather the corpse is part of the *fur* project, we take photos and prepare the body, the Dunkas are part of the community project, as they give an account of the animal's history that we record and document. We get to know the life and habits of the Dunkas and their relationship with animals.'

At first, she finds it offensive to have her art of writing reduced to mere captions. How could she possibly write these if she hadn't seen the images?

'Wouldn't you like me to show you some images after all?' Kincső asks in response, adding loud emojis to her message.

As it happens, she also wanted to write about carcasses in the past. But she gave up and now could compensate for that plan, at least by way of a few sentences. Or captions. They could have a debate with Kincső about animal resurrection in Christian theology, seeing that she's on such insider terms with local religious leaders. Kincső claims that she is even 'chatting' to the bishop. But she is responding in two-liners, mixes in English words and sends emojis and funny pictures. One cannot peel off the truth from such stuff. She can't make any sense of *Roadkill furs*, let alone resurrection. That said, truth may well fit into two lines and in-between emojis.

As for corpses, she conjures up, imagines and creates her own images. She only asks for Kincső's photos afterwards. There are three kinds of animals:

1. At rest – animals that got hit by cars and had their spine broken, without penetration into the flesh (Are they sleeping? – the Son used to ask when he was little, whenever they saw cats by the roadside. Cats don't sleep by the roadside, his mother would reply dourly, thus concluding the conversation.)
2. Squashed – animals that are still recognisable, a bundle of fur, flesh and blood that can be identified as a cat, dog, fox, lamb, owl.
3. Traceable – animals crushed beyond recognition, in the best case, their species is identifiable by their size

She writes these carcass tags in order not to disappoint Kincső, the project, the local as well as the wider community. In order not to disappoint anyone. Except herself. But she's used to this disappointment, she has hardened up since starting to write with a fountain pen, because she has always imagined writers with fountain pens in their hand: there is even a callus on the inner side of her middle finger. Callus, as on one's foot soles. At first, she was applying some ointment but later excised it with a specially purchased scalpel.

So the carcass tags got written.

Hug an animal that's growing cold. Hug it and embrace it as if it was a baby. Pietà. The cooling body is leaning on you. Flowing into you. Back to the maternal womb. There is no resistance, will or struggle. It clings to you like a light scarf or a soft woollen blanket. And then it slowly lets go of you, sleeping child, inert body, unconscious death. Return. Brought to an end. Helped across.

On one of her very first journeys as a new driver, she ran over a grey long-haired cat in an outer suburb. She was unable to press the break. The person sitting next to her, who had had a driving license for two and a half decades, claimed that nobody would have been able to avoid this. The cat jumped out too suddenly. Her first thought was to just carry on driving. The second thought: stop and save. The delicate body gave up its ghost in her arms, amidst brief and soft panting. It could no longer breathe through its nose. As the Prophet has stated: you are too fragile for this world. We can't look after you.

But who would like to hug a blood-soaked hairy bundle?

Driving has brought her a step closer to destruction.

Now, she's looking at Kincső's photos. She asks for them in a higher resolution, to see them larger because she can't figure out anything from the thumbnails, she can't write if she doesn't torture herself enough. Two dozen cases of *roadkill*. Next to them, as if on a crime scene investigation, measuring tapes.

Killer road. Busy narrow road, crossing entire villages. Wild and domestic animals run over near motorways.

These photos won't be on display, they are only part of the documentation and the methodological foundation for the project plan. The photos are taken for our benefit. Memos, Kincső points out. They remind us of the starting point, that in the beginning there was – death, she explains.

A constant stream of cars is battling from capital to capital on these roads slicing through villages. Vans, migrant workers, commuters, people on excursions, people heading to and away from towns are crushing down and running over the frightened, lonely, stray, runaway, fleeing and freed animals, pets and birds. Now it's her turn to get past, for the first time, this death row that she has seen so many times over the last thirty years. She's holding onto the steering wheel and praying that no live animal comes out in her way.

I'm not going to send you the documentation for perpetrators, Kincső writes, we are the perpetrators, she adds, she has learnt it, too. The task is to clean and save the fur, many times also to darn it. This fur will be sold on later, one will be able to bid on it.

She has to write about the embrace of the body as it's going cold. Catharsis, generating fear and compassion – there are five possible theories on Aristotle's understanding of catharsis, this was on the syllabus at university and she passed an exam on the topic. The young body lets out a soft sound and the last breath leaves its nostrils. If something needs five theories it means that we basically know nothing about it.

Yet the spotty German shorthaired pointer didn't actually perish on this killer road she has to drive on now. That dog was following them from a holiday resort at the end of an outing, in the first months of her moving over here. They patted it a few times and the young animal came with them, and when they got into the car, it kept following them. Then it suddenly took flight, because a car coming in the opposite direction bumped it into the ditch. And then all one could see were the delicate legs drooping, the limbs under perfect control as if they belonged to a dancer. As in Pina Bausch's *Café Müller*, where the bodies drip down the wall, as she found out in a theatre class.

Her arrival started with this death. She should have learned there and then that one mustn't stroke unfamiliar dogs. We are only stroking unknown and ownerless dogs if we are able to stand by them with our whole being for the rest of our lives, putting everything at risk – to take them home or to the dog's shelter, in short to take care of them. Or else, there is nothing except for the shield of indifference. Go on your way.

You either join with your whole life, or there's the shield. There's nothing in-between. Near or far away. Hot or cold.

The prophet has told us that we are too fragile. Her art doesn't even stretch itself to captions.

In the backwater, turtles are enjoying the sun, advancing slowly and silently before gaining some speed on the slope to the river and then quickly descending and gently sliding into the water. Disappearing without a trace. Later, they return just as unexpectedly and scale back up to their place. Their wet and shiny armour dries quickly in the sun. After drying, they are the same colour as wet mud, so they are indistinguishable. Even the ducks and fish are louder than the pair of turtles. They immerse themselves every half an hour, like kids on a slide. Then they crawl to the shore, making use of their strong legs. They keep repeating this as long as the summer sun is shining. Whenever they hear some noise on the other side, such as a person with a dog or a child running up and down, they interrupt their rhythm and immerse themselves in the water at once. For the winter, they dig themselves deep into the mud.

She's watching this slow and measured rhythm of eternity from the other side of the backwater. She has observed them many times, with their slow immersion and wriggling to the shore, up until they disappear altogether into the autumn. Their movement could perhaps lift the veil of eternity. Death is now an easy way of disappearing. They no longer emerge from the water. They no longer appear from under the mud in the spring.

Disappearing in the water. Then coming to the surface. Lastly, vanishing for all eternity. Finding one's own death.

In a conversation she mentioned the turtles and that she'd regularly go to watch them at the backwater. She won't write about them as landscape writing has been long out of fashion. Kincső may well have thought about the turtles when she contacted her. She can't recall any crocodiles though.

While she's examining Kincső's high resolution blood-obsessed photos on her desk, she's also heading out to observe the living at the backwater. Akin to a shuttle, in the morning there's the dead, in the late afternoon, dusk and the suddenly setting darkness, there are the living, who vanish from sight together with the fading light.

In the end Kincső makes her promise – squeezing in rows of ha-ha-ha comments and random emojis, as if nothing had changed since they graduated from secondary school and Kincső, stuck in a childish phase, simply stayed another year at school – that she'll write the introduction to the *Roadkill furs* project, and this will be its key text. It's unclear, in fact everything is unclear from the content of the project to this very task, what sort of text, how long or in what language. The process of the project is equally unclear – Kincső's plan is to make it 'discursive and linear and factual and reflexive' only after the subsequent documentation, by which point texts will have appeared about the project, because texts can smooth everything out, they take away the edge of tragedy, and the possibility of shocking and awakening. She only wants to rouse and confuse. No, they certainly don't want to exhibit the photos, the whole thing is much more complex and multidisciplinary.

'*Roadkill furs* is a brand name we are about to introduce to the market,' Kincső writes. 'We are going to commercialise products made from the fur of run-over animals, such as vests, fur coats, capes, hats, as well as accessories to jumpers and ponchos. On giant posters we shall demonstrate the manner of manufacturing these items, from sourcing the materials to setting up the web shop. We shall drive in a van along the road where the animals are collected, setting up the production department right there, inside the van. We shall document and multiply this process.'

The process, therefore, the artistic 'material' starts with laying hands on the fallen bodies and ends with utilising and selling the fur. 'Needless to say, we shall manipulate time, there are no linear masterpieces, we shall concentrate the information and edit it. *No real time*, you understand,' she adds, 'people manipulate everything,' Kincső adds.

This is what she concluded. They go along the road and gather the corpses.

'Are you burying the animals? What's your theological principle?' she asks with unease.

'This is burial and theology in one,' Kincső replies.

'And what do priests say about animal resurrection?'

'Each has a different view. There is no definite knowledge. *Nobody knows shit.*'

Burning questions were raging in her: 'How will local farmers and peasants understand from all this that there is a need for a different kind of animal husbandry? Who's all this intended for? How will the world change? How will there be fewer victims?'

But she knew the answer already: it's not only the job of local farmers to change, not only their job. It concerns us. Everybody. Buyers. Car drivers. Carnivores. Killers. She abhorred the project. Yet she still had to write the text because she was afraid of rejection.

The carcasses are with us, she began. Then crossed it out. We are the carcasses.

She has nothing more to say.

Would she have the guts to send so few words back?

We are such carcasses ourselves; we are stretched out on the road. We have killed, are killing, will kill. Others, ourselves, people, animals, in-between worlds, homes and realms. Give them their own death. And to us, too.

'Maximum two pages,' Kincső insists, 'the introduction shouldn't be any longer. They won't read anything beyond that.'

She can't explain to the Son when, driving along the edge of the city, he looks out of the window and observes with an upturned nose:

'Disgusting. The innards of a cat. Yuck.'

'How do you know it was a cat?' she deliberately avoids looking at the Son, focusing instead on the middle of the road.

'I could see its tail and legs.'

'It's not disgusting. We don't say this word.'

'But it was disgusting.'

'Still, we don't say that.'

'What do we say instead?' the Son asks irately; it's not in his character to leave questions hanging.

The Son is sitting at the back, to the right, while she is in the driver seat. She can only see the grey cube-shaped buildings on an industrial site and the orange signs on top. She's careful not to look at the edge of the road, where she might spot something. Yet she does know that she has to see and look at it, and with a final glance accompany the thing that is indeed disgusting.

'We don't say anything,' she concludes. 'We are sorry. But we don't say anything. The corpse isn't disgusting. The body is never disgusting.'

'I think it is. A carcass is disgusting. Dead body,' the Son repeats assertively, like someone who is entitled to their own words. He purses his lips in defiance, pulls in his chin, as if he was about to stab. He looks out of the window. 'If you like them so much, why don't you look after them? You never look after anything that matters.'

So that was that.

She wrote the introduction, out of fear. About the turtles. Kincső's response was curt: 'Thx.' The text was about praying for one's own death.

The Painter's Death

In the Doctor's opinion, the Painter died of lung embolism five days after their last meeting. According to the nurses, after he attempted to stand up on his feet one night.

During this final meeting, the Painter lets the Doctor examine him, eyes pulled together and looking sharply into a corner. He takes a sharp breath when coming into contact with the cold stethoscope, he's fussing and fretting as his blood pressure is taken, and is visibly frowning when the Doctor presses her thumb deep into his flesh above the knee.

'Couldn't we finish this a little faster?' he asks impatiently.

The Doctor looks into his eyes, but the Painter turns his gaze away.

'Seeing that you can't cure me and make me stand on my feet, couldn't we at least get this done faster?'

'What would you like to get done faster?' the Doctor asks coldly.

The Painter doesn't reply, only looks into the corner again, so the Doctor wearily says goodbye.

Meanwhile, she is still sitting in silence, like an intruding witness. She's thinking how she could vanish without being noticed. Perhaps she should wait until the Painter falls asleep. She shouldn't have come here. But she promised.

Something stirs in the semi-darkness. A heavy hand is raised, sawing the air right above the head, looking for something. It finds the light switch, then presses it awkwardly until managing to put on the spotlight with a soft purple light, the reading lamp brought from home.

'I can see you better now,' she says softly, as if in the voice of someone else. 'You are so wise, you are a great writer,' he begins courteously. 'I read it. I know. Tell me, would you help me?'

She's smiling most encouragingly, nodding and opening her mouth for a smile so wide that her facial muscles could start hurting any minute, she's delighted that she can finally do something for the Painter beyond providing boiled eggs and homemade jam. The Painter informs her on the same courteous tone that he can't rely on anyone. His children, well, – he dismisses that with a wave of his hand – one in London, the other. All the same. They have no idea. I talked to them only yesterday. They don't understand. They aren't sitting here, witnessing this. They have no idea of suffering. At least the son did turn up. The other will only make it for the funeral. So would you do it? He doesn't actually utter his wish, only looks at her with a sharp yet painful and supplicant, even playful gaze, half in earnest and half flippantly – his gaze expresses as many states as his years and paintings have piled up in him, and all this is now displayed on his face with the weight of a heavy burden. Mutually concurring feelings and thoughts, the thirty-something muscles are moving in unison but in different directions. Sardonic supplication, enticing mourning.

'Would you?'

She's slowly starting to come up with excuses. The spotlight is directed at her, not quite extorting a confession, but illuminating her face. As if the Painter wanted to paint her portrait, and the face happened to be right here in front of him. They have both prepared for the long period of time, the endless hours during which the Painter stares into the face of the model, who is about to open up to him. After all, everything will be visible now, nakedness included.

But the painting will not come into being.

Paintings are done and dusted. She's stammering that she's afraid of death, she's frightened of the death of others which are also hers. She's afraid and lives with this fear, and now she wouldn't even want to give up on it. Yet she'd have to get to know it. But this isn't the reason why she can't do it. She's not talking about her conscience – she's excluding moral matters from the conversation – but about her mother. She can't do what the Painter is asking from her because she has already killed someone and knows what follows. She killed her mother. They brought her over here fairly recently, only four or five, no, six years ago. The mother succumbed to it even though she's still alive.

Suicide? Shouldn't he opt for that? But she can't ask or recommend such a thing. And why the connotation to murder, something that is usually 'committed' like a crime. In other languages, the notion of 'destruction' is at the root of the word. Death by self, would be a much better term. Chosen death. Or more precisely: invited death. Stone guest. As if he was able to read her thoughts, the Painter observes.

'There's still suicide,' his words sounding garbled as he chuckles and flashes his yellow lower teeth, living proof of decay and the passage of time.

'I'll keep this option open. Always open,' he replies confidently after a short pause, almost happily, and the sentence fills him with such lightness and outpouring joy as if he had always been searching for an opportunity to finally say it out loud. 'I'll always keep this option open.'

'You, too?' the Painter asks, shocked.

His startled eyes are searching for those of the other in the subdued light, but he can only sense their direction. This is when his hands start making their way towards her. Involuntarily but still afraid that they may not reach each other, she also holds out her hand. For a moment, the two hands striving for each other are held up in the air, her left and the Painter's shaky right hand. In the end, as if limbs were able to decide that they wanted to follow such a risky road, they reach each other. The weak man's strong hand slowly lands in the warm palm held out for him. The Painter's hand reaches its destination, offering a heavy, purplish and dry right limb which has the weight of a human head. The awkwardness between two people is blown away by touch. Once more, death can be pushed away – it's barely visible from here.

The Painter craves some cold buttermilk. As soon as he utters this word, he can already see a thick granite cup with a gold-blue rim in front of his eyes – his grandmother used to curdle milk overnight on top of the kitchen cupboard in this way. If there is buttermilk, then there is yet another day.

'Imagine, even the psychotherapist, I mean, you know the Psychiatrist who's visiting us here, said that I shouldn't disregard this opportunity. It's legit.'

She had made friends with the Psychiatrist before beginning her therapy, as they later recalled, they fell out of therapy, that is they started fraternising in lieu of the therapy she hadn't even started. Perhaps there wouldn't have been enough 'material' for a proper therapy lasting for years anyway, because she wasn't too keen on entrusting others with her material, much rather guarding it jealously, so she'd just slip the odd sentence into their chats, sentences she barely managed to stammer, as if she was in court, despite having formulated it for ages. As it happens, the court tamed down, and turned into a soft and accommodating blotter that soaks up human tears. They became friends. So, she told the Psychiatrist, in a manner as if she was about to take it back at once, even though this is impossible because as soon as words leave the body, they no longer belong to the speaker and there is no way back. She uttered this sentence formulated with great difficulty that felt like a stone in the mouth with her head held down, she has to start the verbal staging of his sadness and irreparable loss with her head lying low, even though she was actually quite defiant and proud of this insignificant sentence, seeing that she had finally understood something. Namely that ever since the Son had arrived in her life, she had to give up on her favourite – this is her chosen term: favourite – activity and consolation, her pet idea, after all she can't possibly leave this to the Son: the thought of suicide she had been carrying along with her, to have it to hand just in case.

To this, the Psychiatrist replied in a well-considered manner, despite dismissing this comment with a wave of the hand, as if the conversation was about the soda water not being cold enough:

'Of course, you don't have to disregard this option. Leave it right there. In case it helps.'

He was wearing brand new sea-green frames with delicate veins, his unnaturally bright cobalt blue eyes behind them – her father must have had such blue eyes until the light vanished from them. His gaze would encouragingly enfold the tottering child and her words, like a soft arm. She would have liked to ask how he meant this, does he really mean what he says, since they've already discussed that this was the greatest sin – without using the word sin, which didn't exist in the Psychiatrist's vocabulary as a professional or as a human being – instead, they used the word burden, stating that the greatest burden a parent can place on their child is their own suicide. The Psychiatrist gently shrouded her in the gaze of his azure blue eyes in which there was always some wanton spring spark, as there usually is in the eyes of children and simpletons. That said, in his gaze this azure blue light was more of a solace, accessible to everyone, even though this time he was reprehending her, correcting her sentence:

'But you, my dear, are a writer,' he added, with a touch of laughter not to offend. 'Can't you see the contradiction in your words?' And she could.

'His death is his decision,' the Psychiatrist continued, slowly. 'And yours will be yours. One day. He can't burden someone else with his own death. Do you get me?'

He added this 'one day' as an auxiliary note, already thinking of something else and making his way out of the room furnished with antique pieces and a comfortable sofa.

'You don't have to exclude any options.'

He's still wondering though, the Psychiatrist mumbled under his breath while gathering his belongings from his office, why aren't more elderly people committing suicide.

'Perhaps because we are all still clinging on. It's not so easy to give up on this thing, this misery.'

According to the Doctor's official opinion, therefore, the Painter died of lung embolism.

'We aren't going to make a note of the truth,' he declares dryly and removes his thin-rimmed spectacles to clean them. Under his eyes, the dark skin is puffy, having lost its elasticity, his gaze is blank and tired. 'You writers know more about this. Our records are just like literature in this sense. Fiction.'

He didn't take his medication, the Doctor explains. Even though the nurses would dish out the pills that he'd then put in his mouth and flush down with some liquid, and the nurses would always wait for the end of this process. Yet when they undressed him, they found the medication mixed with saliva and food remains in a sealable bag under his shirt – he continued wearing white shirts even in hospital, as he did previously at work. He must have spat it all out after the nurse left the ward.

The Painter was meant to be given a state funeral but his heirs living abroad didn't want to accept, just as his remains weren't transported to his former home, either, where another burial plan was in place. Perhaps he decided about all this himself and his children respected his wishes.

They did organise a memorial service at the Academy of Arts though, but the funeral itself wasn't open to the public. The exhibition *PM – Perennial Mourning* will travel to his homeland next year.

Hard to tell whether the heavens opened to receive him, or whether anyone prayed to the Father Eternal to urge him to welcome his creation.

According to the route planner, they are going to make their way along the new ring road of the town that has long outgrown its body, and arrive early evening at the inn where the class meeting will take place. She will only make it to the town itself after the meeting. She has to drop Csaba off at a petrol station before reaching the ring road, he has some business to attend to and will share a taxi with Tomi to join the group later that night.

Tomi calls Csaba and gives him instructions as to where to stop, and then wants to talk to the tired driver who considers herself a successful motorist and takes the call on speakerphone. Ágó tilts her head to the back, dreamily looking out of the window while slowly awakening.

Tomi has a singing voice, almost chirping at first, then his words getting deeper and richer, sounding garbled, growling, coughing and charting an entire range from arias to falling silent. He starts with an elongated 'Hiya,' without introducing himself, he thinks he doesn't need to, he'll never ever need to introduce himself anywhere, as the whole world is his mate and he hugs everyone to his chest.

'For me, you are the exact same person you used to be,' his voice fills the car, almost screaming with enthusiasm. 'You must come once to a proper party, not a class meeting but a proper big party, we'll have one at the end of the summer. Everyone in the old gang will be there. Huge party. The whole gang. Everybody. It will be on a truly picturesque farm, so it will feel just like home. Listen up. Do you remember Gogo? He has a guesthouse and we'll have it to ourselves for the party.'

'All of it. You'll have your own room, there's also a Jacuzzi and a sauna. Such parties only take place once a year. Everybody will be there, all the old friends. This isn't going to be the kind of party where we get drunk within an hour, not at all,' Tomi explains. 'We have serious conversations. There are huge conversations as a rule. Mind you, the odd drink gets consumed, too. Come on, do join us. We'll have a massive catch-up about the good old times when the gang was still together,' he promises.

In her student days, when she used to come home for the summer like everyone else, she did indeed party with them often. This shared past is still a strong connector for the gang, from which she has long fallen out. Tomi is listing the names, all sorts of nicknames from another time and place. People coming include Fatty, Gogo, Sami, Gypsy, Flappy, Grungy, the women will be there, too, not the children though, this isn't that kind of party, who else? Pupa, of course. Classmates and people from the parallel class, the old gang from home.

'I'm the organiser, and we'll make sure to loosen you up a bit.'

Double lives, parallel worlds that never meet. Gogo lives in a house with a garden in an expensive area of town on the hill, Csaba explains. He built a wine cellar under his house, where he occasionally invites the group, though they never go inside the big house only the cellar. 'Those of us who left home and now live here tend to get together once a year.' Other times, they party on Flappy's allotment, they barbequed there a few times but the sleeping arrangements aren't so good there. They definitely get together once a year. Wine cellar, allotment, guest house. Or at Tomi's, who now lives alone after his divorce.

Their other life is invisible. The life of family fathers who do the school run in the morning, work all day, paying off mortgages and loans, go on holidays, attend school concerts and take their kids to fencing. The gang doesn't go on holiday together, that's a family affair. Among the group there are diplomats, anaesthetists, advertising specialists, as well as holders of engineering degrees still earned back home, who started various businesses later on.

They are now drinking in another style, not like in the old days, Tomi points out. Everybody has settled down by now. 'We have grown up. Family, kids, such-like. We are getting on and can't handle the old pace.' Perhaps Yuri Mamleev is right: even alcohol has changed. In Moscow, both people and alcohol have changed an awful lot.

Tomi is the only divorcee among them. The boys have brought wives from back home, only Tomi married a woman from around here and there you go, they did obviously divorce, Csaba gives a bit of a context after they finish the call. 'These separate universes don't ever meet.'

Tomi talks for ages, he has unlimited calls: 'I can talk as long as I'm able.'

He actually has to be careful, ever since his operation he has to reduce his alcohol intake, only lay the foundation so to speak. Tomi explains it's because of his pancreas. The eternally slender guy had a hard ball-shaped belly the last time they met a couple of years ago. 'Now it's all good, they have fixed it. I can show you my wound if you like. You can even touch it, completely smooth.'

So, would she come? To the party. Maybe, she replies politely, she'll be able to tell when the exact date is known, as she has other stuff to do at the end of the summer. She has to travel to Finland, and there are some invitations to the countryside, too. This is also an invitation to the country, 'but this is in earnest,' Tomi interjects. 'It will be unbelievable, you'll see.'

'Of course, Tomi, of course I'd like to come.' Who wouldn't want to fly with you? Not in order to drink until unconscious, falling ill, throwing up or having eye-straining headaches, not a single cell in her body wants that, she also hates having a hangover as that's a lion's roar for her, not a simple katzenjammer. Only the flight that takes place in the moment is joyous. The soaring and hovering ecstasy. To drink lightly, as if dreams were taking flight from one's hand.

Her father had another approach to drinking. This sort of alcohol feast, a revelry holding everyone together, the shared release from reality was unknown to him. He may have never even got to experience bliss. In the secret police files, there isn't a single word about pleasure, which is another reason not to believe this fiction. It is of course possible that he never soared, and only knew invisible wounds which one cannot reach or ascertain.

She won't go to the party, she knows that already. This is another life. Hers is another wound; she doesn't yet know where it is and how it healed.

'Come, it will be a party like the ones we used to throw back home. I swear, isn't it right, Csabika?' Tomi's voice is echoing in the metal box, filling all ears, awake and asleep. 'Like in the olden days. You know how I miss those?'

'Tomi, you have phantom pains,' she tells him. 'It's easy to talk to people who are drunk. Drunkards turn into children. It's easy to have words with them, as if there was nothing at stake or serious consequences, words are simply taking flight from one's lips.'

'Tomi, do you know what phantom pain is? Shall I explain?'

There are very few cars on the two-lane road, so she has time to expand. They are driving on the new motorway.

'When pain is connected to something that doesn't exist. The odd thing is that phantom pains have a medical explanation. You know, on our cerebral map ...'

'Well, I have long guzzled away that,' Tomi interjects, giggling.

'You can't guzzle away a map. However, pain can get stuck in maps. Let's say that they amputate your arm because you had a bike accident, and the pain you experienced then persists in your brain, because the wound didn't heal but was chopped off, so as a result you are left with the idea that the wound didn't heal and there is an actual recollection of it in your brain. A phantom memory. It's not the soul being sore, because until then people thought that all this was only a matter of the soul. There is no body versus soul, these are not two separate things. Never two. These phantom pains and their healing on the mental map were described by an American doctor of Indian descent. A migrant, from India, you see, who else would have a clue about maps and phantom pain? Rama. Rama something, like the God. He was only interested in the map. He understood that all this wasn't pure flights of fancy. Until then, people would battle their phantom pains for decades, and nobody understood or was able to cure them. This Rama invented a mirror box. The essence of this therapy is that it doubles reality. You put your hand into the mirror box, but you only have one because the other is missing. In the mirror box, however, it looks as if you had two. You can stare at this, as long as you need, and you make your brain believe that you have another hand and you are now moving it. If you practice this a lot, you can persuade your brain that you have two hands and this puts an end to your phantom pain.'

'Listen, come to the party and explain it there, I didn't get it.'

'The essence is that our map is so mobile, so pliable, that it can rewrite itself. The map redraws itself. This is the main idea. The map is not forever.'

After a long silence, as she's overtaking a slow car, she adds:

'The map is the last thing that dies in us.'

'One could really have a philosophical discussion with you. We'll sit around and talk and drink and have a bite. As in a Chekhov play, okay? *Platonov*! What a great show! There was some proper drinking going on. Come on, join us and we'll carry on chatting into the small hours. You can't come up with a drink we won't be able to have there. That also rewrites the map, trust me. You don't have to bring anything, everybody will be thrilled to see you.'

He can't drink anymore, he adds wistfully. The time for alcohol is over. Okay, he's drinking a little, but not like that. 'Not to worry, we aren't drinking like that, we're getting old. Everybody is well behaved. We drink when we see each other,' Tomi explains, otherwise only at home at night, such small middle-class portions. Proper drinking only at major festivals and family events. You know, family, kids, and so on. The old life hasn't really carried on. Tomi is now a free man, divorced, with a grown-up daughter. He's at home everywhere, coming and going as he pleases. He lays as much foundation as he likes. He's even driving with such a 'foundation'. He had already caused a serious accident and almost lost an eye, Csaba tells her later. His license has been revoked, so he's meeting Csaba at the petrol station accompanied by someone else.

'How far are you? Come then, we are expecting you. We'll talk until the small hours. About the olden days.'

Well, if she happens to be in the middle of something then she won't go, when she's writing she goes to bed at ten, she muses but doesn't respond to Tomi. She gets up at dawn to write, she has become used to this routine, together with the light. She may well start something again. She can't write in the dark. As if she was a photographer, who doesn't have anything to capture in the dark. What she writes can only be seen in the daylight, even if it's about the dark.

'Come, it will be like it used to be back home.'

After they hang up, Csaba tells her that Tomi is dealing art, paintings and graphic arts, he's trying to discover young talent and 'sell it'. He hasn't had much luck yet, a proper outstanding discovery with which he could have made a lot of money. So he has another job, he's a freelance concert organiser. He used to drive a lot, but doesn't have a license at present.

Soon it's time to make a detour for the petrol station.

After they hang up, the dialogue continues in her. You have to make your brain believe that you have another hand, she tells Tomi, they say goodbye but they soon see each other at the petrol station and then again at class meeting in the evening. You have to persuade the map in your brain, using this method. A looking-glass land. Understand? You are looking at it and you believe that you have two countries. Two homes. Another country in the mirror. You have to believe this, and make your brain believe it. And then your hand grows back. It really does and everything's fine.

'I don't get this looking-glass land, I don't believe in such things,' Tomi replies in her imagination, while slapping her on the back. 'On my map, there is only one, this one. This is another country, another kind of people. It will never be like in the olden days. That's true love. The first love. So will you come? There will be an incredible party, with the whole gang. For me, you are the person you have always been. Come and we shall philosophise. Everyone will compare wounds. And you know what? I'll tell you what to write about. You'll laugh. Write about this, about home.'

'Good job that you aren't suggesting love of one's home as a topic, Tomi.'

When they meet at the petrol station, Tomi repeats in person that Gogo's guesthouse looks just like as if they were back home, with fir trees and freshly planted walnuts. Listen, even the toilets smell of fir trees. And there are deer. Proper deer roaming about! he shouts. 'Come, man, you'll love it. Just like back home. I won't labour the point,' he concludes. 'By the way, it's a hunting lodge, used mainly by Italians. So will you come?'

Tomi, what sort of a hopeless love is this? Perhaps she should really go to this party, to understand what people mean, Tomi and the others. 'I don't have another love, another home. I don't want to use big words but...'

'Maybe I'll go,' she changes her mind. 'I'll go to the party and find out. How did the grown-ups do this? I want to copy them. We have to copy the saints, right?' Home-sickness, home-love, home-malady, some people simply die of these.

She'll do what the contemporary English Painter did, who wanted to tap into the knowledge of his predecessors. In order to come up with a 'greater message', David Hockney digitally cleaned, using visual editing methods, Claude Lorrain's three century-old painting, *The Sermon on the Mount*, in other words, he created a cleaned-up digital version of it, a copy. Over time, the original painting got darker, and the figure of Jesus sitting among his disciples blended into the majestic landscape, he basically vanished into it. One could only see the dark mountain by the end. The viewer was looking for the protagonist, who'd bring the promise of happiness, in vain, and the sermon was left without an audience. The dark painting, that according to experts had even survived a major fire, is flooded by light, shade by shade, by Hockney. Following his intervention, the figure of the Saviour dressed in azure blue lights up the top of the mountain. His clothes are like the sky, the heavens on the edge of which he stands. Hockney's work is monumental, 180 × 288 cm, as if we only noticed things when they are blown-up to gigantic proportions. Have people gone blind? Or they have changed an awful lot, like in Moscow.

Underneath the words, dark and dangerous meanings are lying dormant, akin to five-hundred-year-old beings at the bottom of the sea, the silent and menacing whales. Words, slumbering predators, waiting to be awoken. The word darkened and turned alien, growing a crust and becoming unspeakable, moving to a distance from where the point and message of things, the 'greater message' has become unrecognisable for her. What's this longing? Mandatory loyalty? Instinct, akin to animals, who also have a place to live and sleep, a home and a homeland?

Immersing into a word, and scratching off whatever time has overlaid within it, time and space being one. To scratch off, clean with hard graft, with some sort of processing from depth and darkness. Then, she could catch a glimpse of azure blue salvation. Her own salvation from foreignness. From that thing that keeps giving birth over and over again to this coldness, this distance in her, which doesn't have a name, yet its walls are cold and closed-off. On top of the mountain, however, it's warm and safe.

The Painter said at the end, and it took him a lot of effort, as if it had caused him bodily pain, he said after she had read out loud her text written for the catalogue of his exhibition, that *PM, a Perennial Mourning* was a correct interpretation of the title, he could totally accept it, though he wouldn't have used it himself, perhaps he hadn't even thought about it, or at least not by way of words, only of his dreams and paintings. Yes, the interpretation is correct and he can agree with it. Perennial Mourning means that the home is lost. For him, in his personal history, in his dreams. She came up with a correct interpretation, therefore she deserves a –

'What is it that you always want? You always want something. Light or peace?'

Words are inaccessible. But perhaps paintings aren't.

Homelands, houses and abodes are represented in Egyptian hieroglyphs as bare walls, protective walls with an open door through which people can come and go, be they alive and dead, foreign and indigenous, human and divine, god-pharaohs and cats, this includes each person with a place of their own because everybody's got a home.

It's wide open.

It lets you go.

It lets you come back.

It makes you free.

In her case, one home let her go, the other let her in. This is what happened.

This is her story. This is the topic of her speech.

The Speech

She gives her speech on the morning of the day after their arrival, and it can't possibly be about anything other than her personal story.

It would have been possible to handle it with a single sigh, a deep breath in and a slow breath out. A simple breath, seeing that she agreed to do this address. Not as a stand-in for the form tutor who couldn't come, this former Maths teacher and form tutor who has been dead for a decade. Perhaps she should allude to his absence, to this Maths teacher who for her has completely gone to dust, and to numbers. She knows nothing about numbers, she has chosen letters, yet the talk will be about prime numbers.

'You'll stay seated, okay?,' she begins, in the restaurant where furniture has been pushed back and chairs laid out in a circle.

She had read the text out loud three times previously. An image, a thought, a funny comment – just as the teacher had taught her. This is what fits into the space of ten minutes. As always, she stuck to the allocated time: 9'56" when read out loud is 10 minutes in real time. Talking head. But not Orpheus, whose head is singing while swimming in the foam, capable of addressing trees, rocks and the dead with his songs.

Upbeat, effective and well-constructed, one can see the writer behind it, a true writer, Kathrin points out, seeing that this speech was initially her idea.

Well, this is precisely her tragedy, that it was written by a writer, who found refuge in ornament, in complicated sentences, juggling thoughts by way of a clever dramaturgy that captivated attention for ten minutes, exactly ten, especially in the middle part that tends to falter as a rule, she spruced it up with a mix of self-irony and cautious irony, and then ended it with an unexpected image. There were uplifting, outright sublime and playful elements, as well as sad and concrete aspects – she hinted, for instance, at the dinner about to be served and featuring a proper highlight, such as schnitzels most likely to be on the menu and brandy glasses fresh from the deep freezer. She alluded to the forthcoming starfall, when the revelation of big secrets is expected. To the lively children who can't be put to bed and teenagers smoking in secret. To local patriots and multiple identities.

In short, one can see the writerly touch. The impossibility of uttering the truth suffocatingly encroaches the speech, like some January city smog, when everybody is breathing cautiously and slowly even at the edge of town. You were expecting a moral, well, that's not available, either.

She concluded her speech by quoting a few lines on the topic of returning home, she would have liked to analyse this longer, but there was no time. The poem is about the fact that, according to the poet, the sea has grown during the return home, the road has played tricks on the traveller and it not only didn't get shorter but actually the opposite. This is what Odysseus feels:

> 'my homeward way has proved too long.
> While we were wasting time there, old Poseidon,
> It almost seems, stretched and extended space.'[30]

In the poem, Odysseus addresses his son: he must have left the war zone so long ago that he can't recall how the war ended. He can't even remember the age of his son. He doesn't remember anything, neither the starting, nor the departure point, all he can recall is the endless sea, some grimy islands, huts, thickets and pig grunts. As he's sailing towards home, one island is just like the other. He has no idea where he is, where East or West is, why he went away and whom he left behind. She took the opportunity to listen to the poem read by the poet, but this voice is foreign, odd, singing like some Greek minstrel. One shouldn't listen to masterpieces in the voice of their authors.

When Joseph Brodsky wrote these lines in 1972, he was already thousands of miles away from his homeland.

Odysseus set sail for the benefit of others, but returned home for his own sake, Brodsky, however, didn't want to be put to sea at all. He was given the opportunity to emigrate to Israel twice, but he didn't go, which irritated the authorities no end, so they summoned him to the Home Office and asked: what on earth are you thinking, why aren't you clearing out of here? Because he wants to live here, he said. Fine, всё ясно, if you're not going, we shall put you on the first plane, the Office announced, and indeed ten days' later, they broke into his home and airplane engines starting revving at once. According to the record, all Brodsky had to say was: '*Я русский литератор*, I am a Russian writer.' This sentence meant that he wanted to live there. In the Russian language.

Perhaps, he never left.

Physically, he had never returned to his homeland, not even after it would have been possible.

As for her personal goals behind her departure, they would be hard to sum up in a sentence, she concluded in her speech. Let's leave it at this: the boundary that has been crossed between must and may isn't barbed wire but a comfortable wide band, the unknowable no man's land with all sorts of directions, including leaving, staying, returning, East-West-North-South all at once, the whole human adventure. This is what happened to her. She will have to give an account to her own self as to whether this was a waste of time, as in the poem. In search of wasted time. Account. An account of everything.

After delivering her speech she has to withdraw to her room and remove herself from the group. At least for a quarter of an hour, so she can step away from this all-encompassing hot thing, this melting pot, this three-day-long communal melting and togetherness.

Despite delivering her speech, truth has been left untouched. It's black like the touchstone, with which they are testing gold. She is standing in the middle of the narrow, bare room, like an unattainable star who immediately vanishes from the scene after her performance in order to consolidate her mystery. After a long wait, she appears again and, with the help of this dramaturgy of absence, just draws added attention to herself.

Yet she's only gone to take a shower and cool down her hot and sweaty body. The speech was a great success, people laughed and clapped. They kept bringing it up during the evening, too. 'How did you put it?' Ha-ha-ha. Truth, however, remained silent. The truth is that Pilate has a headache. The moment spent in the stuffy room ended with a long cold shower. As if she was sweating all the time, the body working and the mouth talking in public, impossible to stop. The catastrophe has taken place. Yet catastrophe will only really occur from now on. She should perhaps write a story about prime numbers, which can give an account of themselves.

She often looks up during the speech. They are all sitting in a circle: Kati, that is Kathrin as she's now known, the well-dressed Bali, Csaba, Edina, Hilda, the quiet Gabi, the best in class, Tomi, Zsolt, known as Nemo, Kincső, Valentin, Laura, Péter, Bernát, nearly two dozen people. When she looks up, she can catch a glimpse of the back of Ágó's head. This is when she notices in her short hair the purple V-shape that she liked so much when she first saw her among the red brick buildings at Yale, it was this playful viper-sign that she noticed when they met, something trendy and upbeat but not intrusive – perfect for a tenured professor at Yale. Ágó explained back then that this V needs monthly attention in terms of colouring and cutting, better still if done every three weeks, so much time and 'human resources' which are the equivalent of time.

This V-shape instantly draws attention to Ágó's foreignness, around here it would be very difficult to be an academic or vice-chancellor with such a hair style and a purple stripe on one's head.

The V, the viper on the back of the head keeps those who are unbefitting away, chases them away, scares them as if it was protruding from some unconscious depth, seeing that Yale is not for everyone, it's for the very few and the very best. Or for the utterly wealthy, because graduating from its medical school costs the equivalent of over a hundred million in local money. The cheapest degree is offered by the Divinity School, capitalism seems to be a touch more timid and less greedy when it comes to the service of God, as it were, the science of God is the most affordable.

She's looking at this head, this round and clever head with the purple V-shaped stripe, as she's delivering her speech. She doesn't have that much to say in fact, she's talking about her story, her very own life and about why she came to the class meeting. Because she couldn't find enough reasons not to. While talking, every so often she looks up and around. 'Good to see you.' The morning light accentuates the magenta arc on the back of the head – a beautiful accessory to superfluity and futile human efforts. 'It's good to see it.'

She's talking about their shared story. Out of thirty-six students, twenty-three left and thirteen stayed. These are the statistics. These are only statistics. Prime numbers about which books have been written. The series of prime numbers is endless. Those of us who also appear in Euclid's *Elements* are in endless numbers, staying and leaving, in other words being scattered around the world. Yet we are only divisible by ourselves. Thirty-six stories, twenty-three went away, two died, four are unaccounted for, only seven didn't come to the meeting. See, I'm here, too. Sigh.

After her speech, they enumerate everyone, alive and dead, partners and children, present and absent.

They black out the room, and draw the electric blinds on the two huge windows. The sharp summer light still manages to penetrate along the edges and divides the space. They are projecting the images on the back wall.

Kathrin has prepared a password-protected website about the class, a ready-made *template*, she explained in her letter when she started to build it over a decade and a half ago. Everybody has their own page, which can be clicked on via their name, and this hosts photographs, short films, music and texts that people sent in. The aim of this is to allow those who are far away to see their classmates and to leave some proof of this shared experience behind. The landing page is a billowy, interconnected and knitted, somewhat irregular line, yet those who see it are tempted to create a kind of a system within it. The order of appearance has been randomised, as Kathrin explains the *random format*. She created most of the site but she gave permission to everybody she corresponded with to edit their own page and put up what they liked. She didn't leave any blanks or let anyone disappear without a trace. In the case of people where all she could find was a lone school photo, she uploaded some music and poems. From the page of classmates who vanished or died, a delicate bird, drawn with a fine pen in a single line, takes flight. The exquisite line of this ink bird, crafted by Kathrin herself, uncurls and disappears, like Chinese calligraphy.

'It's time for Rita to join us,' Kathrin begins but then there's a pause and the connection falters. 'We agreed initially that she'd be here in person. But then things suddenly changed,' she adds while Rita's page is loading.

Kathrin clicks on it, the opening photo is a smiling face in a nice office, decorated with family snapshots and an official photo of Rita in a green gown and gloves.

'Back in the spring the plan was to be there with you. But then everything fell apart. I can hear you,' Rita confirms.

And then the picture comes to life. Rita's face appears elongated and distorted during the time she's adjusting the camera, as if a large black mouth was crying out. Now she's sitting in front of a white wall with holes left by a shelf, the wounds of the house.

'I still can't see you,' she says and switches off her camera. We are back to the initial photo with the smiling face and large cup in hand.

The class is sitting in silence while the connection is re-established.

'I can see you now, though you seem to be sitting in the dark. You can see me, too, right?'

Rita couldn't come to the class meeting because they are moving house. They had to pack up stuff from a nearly hundred square metre home, and put them into boxes. But this isn't what she wanted to say. In short, she's been here for eighteen years, meaning that they decided to go there because they both got a job at the institute and hence settled there for good. They've been citizens for eleven years, have two children who are attending the local school, not the international one. She shows a picture with her daughter, seventeen, at an acrobatic competition, the girl is wearing a sparkly dress and is hooked into a ring with her foot.

'And he's a fifteen-year-old teenager who hates being photographed,' she shows another photo, of a boy in a hoodie, one can barely see him on the dark picture. 'We built our life on this. Sorry,' she stands up unexpectedly. A blank space in front of the camera. The sound of a door being shut. Eventually Rita is back, after a long silence.

'I would have never expected to have to move again.'

Rita looks into the camera. She can see unfamiliar faces sitting in a dark room several thousand miles away. Her eyes are looking for a focus on the screen in the empty space.

'My husband wanted to go, I didn't. I didn't want to go again. I don't want to go anywhere. We had a fabulous life here. But our institute moved away under these new circumstances. This is an international research institute, which couldn't remain here anymore. Our contracts stipulated that if we wanted to work for them, we had to follow the institute within two years. We had built our entire life around this. My husband wanted to go. You may know him, he was three years above us, in the Maths class. I'll show you a picture.'

On the blown-up photo, there are four people sitting on some terrace, huge ice-cream bowls in front of the children, a beer in front of the dark-haired man and water in front of Rita.

'So we are moving, we sold the house, we have to find new schools for the kids and another home. We also have a dog. I couldn't travel home this time, but I did on every other occasion. We now found a good school. This is very important,' she smiles, just like on the photo. 'We were also fortunate to attend a good school, right?'

A few people smile back at her in the dark but Rita can't see this.

'I was convinced that such a thing couldn't happen to us. We were safe. We had a great life here. We had a very different life. We weren't migrants here. You know what I mean. We had an entirely different life. And now it's as if we were some what-d'you-call-it. As if we were from, I don't know where. Sorry.'

She sobs and turns her head towards the light, where the unseen window must be. She's searching for words with which to describe safety. Kathrin is leaning against the teacher's desk and smiling encouragingly. Rita can't see her but Kathrin knows that it's her task to say something when the time is up. Because everybody has been allocated three to four minutes in the first round.

'This can't happen to us,' Rita continues. She's looking into the dark screen and talking to faraway and barely familiar people. 'I'm fifty. I don't want to move anywhere. We are fifty, aren't we?'

Long silence settles in the suffocatingly hot room. Kathrin slowly goes to the double door and opens it. Cool air pours in from the corridor, the school building is empty on a Saturday. One can hear a choir rehearsing among the polished pews of the nearby, recently renovated church.

'When are you moving?' Kathrin leans closer to the microphone to ask an encouraging question.

'Mid-August. That's when school starts.'

They have just enough time to clarify where the institute is moving exactly, and Kathrin observes that they hadn't had a war for five hundred years over there. Rita says goodbye and everyone responds in a loud voice: 'take care, have a safe journey!' they wave. Kathrin switches off the projector and the loudspeakers, but they don't open the blinds. The laptop, however, carries on as Rita is still online. One can hear a soft noise coming from the device. Only three people can see the screen, as everybody turns to Edina who introduces herself next.

Rita is still sitting behind her laptop, then lowers her head and starts crying. She conceals her face, as if one could hide a face covered in tears even if there's no one there to see. She then leans on the table and her short thick dark hair, neck and back of the head become visible from a close-up. As if she was leaning into a guillotine. Then there is a thumping sound, coming from very near. Rita is weeping in pain. The faraway device is shaking in the wake of the blow, as Rita just hit the table.

She's watching Rita, turning the laptop to herself and then literally taking it into her lap, while everyone is paying attention to Edina who's talking about her passion, which is language-teaching. A thousand miles away someone is crying for an unknown life, a lost sense of safety, a shattered world. She should close the lid of the device, but she's just holding it in her lap as if it were a cat or a baby. Let it end, she thinks. Let it end. 'Stop it, Rita.' She can see something she shouldn't. She can't behave as if she didn't see this. Her hand suddenly starts moving as if this was her own laptop, and finds the chat, as if she was unable to control her hand, her hand is the only thing she has never been able to control. 'Get well, Rita,' she writes and hits send. She's waiting for someone far away to notice that they had been sent a message. 'All will be well,' she continues. 'These fifty years were the tough part. What follows, is easier. Bye.'

She then turns her attention to Edina, who's now talking about her children. By the time she looks at the screen again, she can only see the bare wall. Rita has gone, she left the scene. On the walls, the holes left by the bookshelves are gaping like a bunch of a dark eye sockets.

The Sky May Well Be Different

There aren't many shooting stars where she lives. She hasn't seen any in twenty years. This may be due to the haze. The sky is different around there. As she promised in her speech, they will be taking a look at the shooting stars at night.

The sky is a giant tent, embroidered with gold, underneath the dark, thick and silent forest. The shooting star leaves a bright arc in its wake, like a beetle flaring up in the darkness. A huge secret story is about to duck right in front of our eyes. Doesn't this mean that a god is dying? They can wish for anything, right? When someone sees a shooting star and wishes for something, it comes true. Ágó could explain what's happening up there in such situations, but she's now standing next to her former desk mate. Ágó is inside with the teenagers who follow her everywhere.

They had to sit next to each other for two years, as some sort of punishment. Time has washed away what the nature of their sin was, which of them committed it, and also the issue as to who was actually punished by being made to sit together. Nemo I and Nemo II, these were their nicknames. Nemo got his name because he would invent tall tales and extended journeys. She ended up Nemo II after she was made to sit next to him, because she started to write stories.

'Where do you live now?'

During the so-called form meeting, from which the form tutor was conspicuously absent, she started to mix up the great many unfamiliar stories and country names, and all she could recall was that Nemo moved to somewhere in Scandinavia. Sweden? Denmark? Norway? Finland? Bloody geography. Bloody places one is unable to remember.

'So why did you choose this place?'

Nemo replies: 'We didn't. It wasn't a matter of deciding to go there and stay for good. What is for good anyway? We have no idea. It was this home that chose us, not the other way round.'

Nemo, aka Zsolt, is looking up to the sky. To the once familiar sky. They grabbed a couple of cold sodas and walked to the bottom of the garden, away from the guest house. They didn't bring any glasses, so they're drinking straight out of the can.

'We simply arrived here, meaning there,' Zsolt points out, who has long got rid of the nickname Nemo. 'I followed Einar who's from there but had moved for a few years to Scotland, where we met, and then he mentioned that there might be some work back home. The health system was on the verge of collapse, or rather some people thought that this was collapse, but those who knew anything about the future – and there were such people here – had a plan that they call future building while others call it collapse. In any case, they closed two thirds of the hospitals. I arrived at that point, because there was suddenly a demand for people to work in an alternative health care system, which isn't hospital but home-based. I don't have any qualifications other than care assistant, but that sufficed twenty years ago. So I thought I'd check this out and move on, in case it doesn't work out. Einar was on the verge of relocating back to his homeland. At that point, I had already been living abroad, in an English-speaking world, for ten years and dry for two years, Einar hadn't yet got there, he was still oscillating while attending an AA group.

'This country isn't officially one of the Scandinavian states, but since it doesn't have another group to join, it counts itself as such, so we consider ourselves Scandinavian for want of a better option. My wife was born here. Our children can communicate with Swedes and Norwegians alike. I, however, struggle to understand the Swedish and Norwegian children of our friends because this isn't our, meaning my mother tongue.

'This home has somehow managed to keep me here. I can't explain why. It's perhaps down to the sea. I've never wanted a family, but it had already been decided before having kids or marrying my wife that I'd stay here.

'You can go round this country by walking along the sea. Like a Viking. Einar told me this. You can walk for weeks, months even, and you can cover the whole area by following the coast. He invited me on a hike early on – all sorts of groups have emerged out of that dry group I attended, language learning was also great and there were all sorts of activity groups, from men's handywork to cycling, you name it. The point was not to continue what you had been doing before in terms of drugs. The only condition was that one couldn't attend events unless they had been dry for at least a day, aka for twenty-four hours. Or clean, because there were all sorts of people among us. There was a hiking group, too, Einar was a member and kept going on walking trips. For me, excursions used to mean something entirely different until then, you know, deciduous forests, home landscapes, dry rustling leaves, groves, streams, even in England we had always been visiting green spaces. After he persuaded me to go on such a trip, it turned out that we were meant to walk in the sand along the coast all day. This was a great disappointment for me. Our kind can get easily disappointed, you know. This is somehow part of our psyche.

'Here the clouds are low lying, I observed them, they are like some huge cushions or rollers full of water, because there is water all over – this is how I tried to explain this to myself. It feels as if the world was confining us, not to smother us but just to draw some boundaries, you know? The sky isn't so menacingly high and end-less as back home, but somehow more homely and smaller. The sky feels closer. I don't know why. Perhaps due to the clouds, that is the multitude of seas and the ocean that surrounds us. Einar wasn't a great talker so he just kept walking and every other hour would take a break for a few minutes, he'd drink, eat, piss and sweat, he was even shaking a bit, he said he'd start feeling dizzy and unwell after coming to a halt but he could walk perfectly well. His body was very hot. Like fire. Because a week before he was still drinking a fair amount and taking all sort of pills, too. We didn't discuss details. We'd always just talk about staying dry. This was a rule. People's previous shenanigans weren't a topic. That was reserved for the group, for those individuals who were game. So we just carried on walking around the country, the sea to our left, with huge cargo ships in the distance transporting fresh green lettuce to Greenland according to Einar.'

'Greenland? Lettuce?' she interrupts. 'I've always wanted to make it to Greenland.'

'Everybody does, for a while. Then they give up. One can't go there anymore.'

Zsolt is immersed in thought as he's spraying some soda into his mouth from the can.

'To the left, there are high cliffs, dunes, low-lying dark clouds, meaning that the bottom layer is greyer and darker, while the top is whiter and shinier. The sun had also come out, and the wind wasn't entirely unpleasant. As if the whole world had decided to show its best face, unable to offer more, but this is all ours, mine and Einar's. Einar said he had seen seals here before, but we couldn't spot any despite looking out for them really carefully. Einar wanted to walk around the country because he didn't believe it was possible to sail along the coast. He kept marking the locations he visited on a large map but many times he wouldn't make any progress for months because he was doing something else.

'Until then, the sea meant something entirely different for me: the urge to get going. Crossing seas. Facing the sea and looking at the seamen sailing to faraway lands and distant hopes. All this had suddenly turned into a grind, as if always reminding you of your limited options. Of being excluded from something great and unable to receive anything from the truly great things. Of the fact that this sea belonged to others and was fulfilling the wishes of others, while you were just standing there and waiting lamely. Yet this sea suddenly told me to just keep walking next to Einar. It told me that it would be here for all eternity, I can walk around the coast, and that this sea belongs to no one and everyone, it's yours and that of poor Einar, who two years later would most probably sit down on the shore, possibly grow cold and never get up again. It's very easy to grow cold. He was found naked. Perhaps he wanted to go for a swim. Or perhaps he just felt that it was time to face God the Judge.

'Legend has it that in the olden days people knew when their time was up, and they had to stand in front of the Judge while still alive, fully dressed and in pomp, revealing their ancestry and having their whole life considered, and the Judge also gave his sentence fully dressed. This had led to lots of unfair sentences, because clothes concealed true identities. When the gods realised this, they decided that they had to take away from people the knowledge about their exact hour of death, so they couldn't conceal their nakedness with full regalia and blue blood. Thereafter, we only have to face the Judge after our death, and apparently the Judge is naked, too.

'Temperatures never go down to freezing around here, not even in winter. It's impossible to freeze. Yet somehow, in Einar life grew cold. This guy was either hot or cold. He was a great guy. Simply just great. He didn't hurt anyone. Except for a single person, whom he killed.

'The kind of creaking frost, as in our childhood, when the fresh snow snaps under your feet and crackles, doesn't exist. When the cold bites your face that it almost hurts, burning your thighs through your trousers, when it's dry and fresh and blinding. I miss that.

'We often go to the seaside with the children, we have a wind tent, into which we nestle and then read and sleep. Our backs are to the sea. Before, I never had the courage to turn my back to the sea, it felt like an insult. As if you were pointing your arse at the altar. The sea wants you to admire it, to be amazed by it, but not to dare to turn your back to it. The tent is positioned with the opening facing the sea. One could place it the other way round, too. But in this way, it being open to the sea from the rear, you are turning your back safely to this roaring vastness, this eternal something, which has always been here for thousands of years. In such moments you aren't preoccupied with your own small problems, for example that first thing tomorrow you must be doing the shopping for such and such an old person, or that you have to pay in some fee that is due for the kid. The scale of things changes. It is as if someone loved you in this world. Maybe Einar should have slowed down to feel this. He was unable to stop. When he did try it nonetheless, he couldn't bear the love. He couldn't bear being loved.

'This sounds stupid as I'm explaining now. Somebody else had actually said this in our group when we were holding a memorial for Einar. You know, in our group those who stop, come back many times. People tend not to get this. I don't get it, either, and there's no need. It happens and that's that.

'I attend this group every now and then. When the kids are with my wife and I have more time. My ex-wife. We always have to be alert now. I later started to work at a health centre in a nearby village, recommended by one of our group members, you know, we are connected for good by visible and invisible threads, as you also are to your dad, I remember you talking about him in year seven when we sat next to each other. At our centre they were just about to set up the 'Stay at Home' programme, which advised people not to go to hospital with every little problem, but to attend the centre where lots of things previously done at hospital could be handled, you and your doctor would get the test results, discuss the relevant action and after this only go to hospital if necessary. I continued as a care assistant because I told them about my past, the things I'd done and the gear I'd taken, and they considered, or rather we considered together, that I shouldn't enrol for a higher qualification. It's not a good idea for me to have a key to the medicine cabinet.

'The essence of the health system is that whoever can stay at home should do so, and receive treatment there.

'Our children are Danish, of course. But I'll never entirely be a Dane.

'But as you know, Denmark is a prison. I don't think it will ever let me go. Perhaps because here I keep bouncing back somehow. I'd be afraid to start again.

'Will I be able to pull through, though?

'It's so weird to be back home. Not just the landscape. We came in a taxi with Csaba and Tomi. In a taxi, to come here. I had only taken a taxi twice since I left twenty-five years ago. Once when my wife was giving birth, and again when I had to accompany a patient to hospital.

'I miss this landscape from home. As you look out of a tent and everything is familiar. And you can say that this is my landscape. I can't get used to things over there in a way to find something easy. Self-explanatory. Natural. For it to be the first thing that comes to my mind when thinking about a landscape. Perhaps natural isn't the right word. Like an excursion with your parents when you were a kid, even though you actually hated excursions and would have much rather done something else, my parents were always going on day trips, every bloody weekend. I never understood this business with excursions when I was a kid. But I shall always marvel at the sea. The sea may well be something that even people who were born there marvel at. I tried to ask the kids about this, but they simply shrugged. It's cool, they said and that's that. Perhaps this is it. This is home for them. Cool and that's that. Perhaps it's not interesting for them. It's right there. Always at hand. It's theirs.'

By the time they return to the restaurant, the tables have been cleared but the drinks counter is well stocked. Unlimited beer, wine, soda and cordial. The old soda bottles are kept in large buckets until ten at night, the staff, reduced to two people, keep refreshing the ice cubes but then even they leave the class to their own devices, they can manage from then on without assistance. They splinter into small groups, pulling chairs next to one another. Bali is surrounded by a larger group. It's borderline impossible for someone not to have anything they could claim back. 'I haven't seen such a case,' he asserts with great confidence to those listening.

While introducing himself in the morning, Bali explained with a degree of amusement that he never wanted to pursue a career in law, at first, he simply studied what he had to study, like a sick patient studies the nature of their disease. He was already a father when he obtained a law degree.

He was able to win back his family's fortune in three instalments: 'I won't go through all the legal modifications which we'd never ever get to the bottom of.'

It wasn't for material gains that he embarked on recovering his family's inheritance, not at all. Who was interested in land twenty-five, thirty years ago. Especially those rubbish plots of land on the other side of town, by the industrial estate, some with a factory built on them, where would you be with those, you were unable to claim anything back, twenty years ago at least. 'So we didn't embark on this for material gains but for the sake of honour. So that things are in order.' His father died of this and his mother ended up an invalid. For the sake of honour – 'as a mark of respect for the forebears, for those in the grave, for their final rest, and mainly, because this was my father's wish.' His father spent seven years on the various documents, he even helped neighbours yet he didn't get anywhere, only getting back one plot of land, located far beyond the edge of town. 'Well, now they are extending the airport in that direction, so you can imagine...'

He doesn't finish his sentence about what people should imagine. Perhaps the significance and value of this piece of land, the astonishing turn of fate.

'Besides, my father was able to handle language quite well but not so much the hassle, and after the second modification of the law, he had a heart attack. This had to do with ...' he dismisses it with a wave of his hand and takes a deep breath. 'At that point, new obstacles emerged in the way of reclaiming property.'

Bali decided then that he wanted to carry this through. He collected their documents, and those of the neighbours, 'You know, lots of old people whose children left and who didn't know shit about fuck and the children couldn't care less. Everybody had chosen a different job, nobody believed in land anymore. This is pretty normal behaviour. Most people had owned land, but then it emerged that there were many other things out there, too.' At that time, one could do a law course by correspondence and he was almost thirty-five when he enrolled. 'You know what a good student I used to be.'

'I'm dyslexic, and so is my son,' Bali explains, so his wife helped him, reading stuff out loud to him, he repeating it, and his wife checking his answers. They went through the course together but only he obtained a doctoral title. 'By then, one could study law in several languages, including English, but I chose to study in the official language. We have to make our way in life here,' he said, deep in thought. Meanwhile, someone brings a fresh bottle of soda to the table. Bali prepares a long spritzer and drinks half. 'This term is just perfect: to make one's way in life,' he's savouring the word, though unable to read, he can talk really well. 'Well, this can't even be expressed in other languages, can it?' People around him offer up English, Swedish, Danish, German translations, suddenly everyone is a linguist, someone comes up with the Italian *prosperare*, bringing in the many forms of flourishment and development.

'Oh, no. I meant to make one's way in life. That's something else. We have to make our way in life here.'

The group surrounding Bali goes silent, the many languages they speak together yet separately come in handy, they utter words in some kind of an invisible competition in which everybody wants to win and prove themselves, by uttering the word and laying their cards on the table by way of the language they master. They want to prove that it is possible 'to make one's way in life' in any other language, too, they have done it and many understand the word and are making their own way in life. Flourishing, developing, prospering. *Prosperus*? Bali is proudly demonstrating that they did learn Latin, 'Prosperus, that's hope, right? Can you check, dear? Pro + spero. There you go. But here we don't just have to hope, that's not enough, we have to also make our way in life.'

'We got back three properties,' he points out, 'and then I took on the largest claim, the collective one. But they never give back what's most valuable. Never ever. They keep modifying the law until it can't be restituted. But we'll still go to the bitter end, whether it's possible or not. We are the winners on the back of losers. If they didn't take away our lands, houses and fortunes, we would have never studied. We had no other way. Our parents lost the land, so we were forced to study. This is called modernisation, both my father and mother finished their schooling after year seven, and here I am: Doctor Bali. Not to mention that I only studied to regain all this.'

Bali is going on about the fact that here every generation has to start anew. 'This is a kind of rollercoaster, you know? Your grandfather is a lawyer but your father a factory worker and you are a director of a large enterprise. One generation studies, the next is a manual worker, the third gets wealthy and the one after is brought to a morsel of bread. Okay, fair enough,' he addresses Hilda, 'your grandfather was a writer and you're a teacher. There are exceptions. But here, this is the modus vivendi. Everybody is reinventing themselves from scratch. As if there was nothing to inherit, you know.'

Someone asks a question in a subdued voice but Bali replies loudly, confidently, demanding attention and addressing everyone, this is everybody's cause and he is representing everyone. As if he was pontificating in a large courtroom, with wide gestures, both chairs next to him unoccupied and taking up all the space around him. 'These are not personal causes! These are community causes,' he concludes. 'You get it back but it is also a gain for the community, you know?'

He's not encouraging anyone with empty words. 'We have to look into it, we'll discuss, bring in your paperwork, we'll help you obtain the documents from the land registry. Restitution is possible, though *restitutio in integrum* less so, we've found this already. It's impossible to say how much a particular property or piece of land is worth until we take a look. It can well happen that next to nothing is worth a fortune. Indeed. It can emerge that they want to build something right there, in that area. As it happened to us with the airport. Twenty years ago, that small plot of land behind the yarn factory that my father got back was worth nothing. Nothing at all. Now – an entire estate has been built on it because people flee there from the town centre. By the way, we won't charge you the commission we usually take on the open market.'

'The more valuable a particular property, the harder it is. They are not working for religious organisations, they have their own people in power, besides that's a complicated business. They had always had their people,' Csaba whispers and adds, 'I hate them.'

Csaba was among the first for whom Bali handled such a restitution case. Edina, who's chatting to Ágó and the teenagers in front of a screen, on which Ágó is offering a demonstration about Little Baby, interjects that the case of the building they are renting has also been handled by Bali, and it now belongs to an elderly Jewish woman.

'We are no sharks, we haven't built our office on this,' Bali exhales deeply. 'There are law firms that purchase these reclamation rights and sign contracts whereby in case of success they receive eighty, even ninety percent of the amount received. All this is fully legit. These people are the actual winners on the back of losers, but even the losers may feel that this ten percent is a gain of some sort, they don't want to leave it to the state and this is all that matters. The gain can go to anyone, Gypsies included, except for the state.

Well, the Gypsies are the only category who don't receive compensation. They have never owned anything apart from being on the road. And nobody compensates for deportation. Nobody will ever compensate Gypsies because for that ... one would need a law that can convey the issues. But we do have Jewish clients. At first, none of them wanted to accept anything because the law was rather contradictory. What does it mean to be persecuted and to have one's life in danger? The law was talking about danger to life. Yet the law actually required proof of danger to life. Well, if somebody was Jewish, their life was immediately in danger, that's clear. But law is another matter. Yet when these Jewish people got older and needed help, then they accepted compensation from abroad. Or rather, they would have liked to accept. There is someone who has been waiting for a decision for thirteen years. Many people passed away during this process.

The compensation was from Germany. Not from here. Did anyone admit here that the state had persecuted its citizens? One should take whatever's given as long as the law makes it possible. One of my clients, who had been persecuted as a child, said that his grandfather mandated him that compensation is due. It's simply due. One has to take it.

But one has to prove being alive in order to receive such an allowance. You have to prove on a yearly basis that you're still alive. In legal terms. This doesn't mean that you have to turn up in person anywhere, only present documents. There's a lot of abuse to this system though.'

Csaba takes a deep breath before getting started. 'Hold on a minute. One shouldn't mix us up with the Gypsies. Or the Jews. The Jews should be left out of this. That's completely different. And the Gypsies should be left out, too.' Bali, however, having rolled up the sleeves of his pale pink and blue check shirt, is explaining that it is indeed different but still a compensation, and this happens to be his area of expertise. He's not looking at people's ancestry but the letter of the law. Moral compensation might well exist, but the law is struggling to find adequate terms. There will be no moral compensation for those who were under surveillance, harassment, or had their conversations tapped. These are very complex matters which law is unable to formulate.

Csaba takes the floor again and starts talking in a less loud voice.

Ágó looks at them, they exchange glances, and she nods lifting her eyebrows: 'talk to him'.

She leans over to Csaba, and puts her hand over his shoulders. 'Dear Csaba,' she tells him, 'we love you. But please, not here. Don't do this now.'

Bali stretches his legs and announces in a loud voice that he's happy to welcome anyone just let him know, but he's now going to take a walk because water is trickling down on him. One has to take on certain cases just to test the laws. He enjoys this a lot. To test that is. So, his door is wide open for everyone.

The group breaks up, but three people stay behind, they surround Csaba and lean in together.

Silent Rest

The room is much smaller than shown on the picture, the space between the two beds is so narrow that they are basically squeezed in together. The photos of the inner and outer spaces of the guest-house were taken with a most misleading lens. The space is greedily cramped and shrunk, the hills beyond the window are at arm's length, and the rooms, corridors and service spaces are so tiny that there isn't room to swing a cat. The furniture is made of cheap, untreated fir tree, creaking and snapping under people's weight.

They lie down on the beds in the afternoon scorcher. Silent rest. 'Will there be a silent rest?' the Son would ask in his eternally menacing voice. Stopping and resting is superfluous, wasted time, the invention of parents to be used against children. Sleeping, too. It took ages for the Son to learn to talk about his dreams. Only recently, on the verge of becoming an adult, did he start wondering about his dreams, previously, he'd just give a passionate and detailed account of them, as if he had visited an exciting world, without searching for meanings.

It's a Sunday afternoon. She's sharing the room with Ágó. They fall into deep sleep after the heavy lunch. The uncomfortable place nearly manages to soften into something home-like as the body relaxes. Ágó has a strong and arched dolphin body, sweating in the heat as the sun shines on her through the thin blackout curtains, perspiration is glowing on her skin as if she were swimming. *You are dolphin-like*, Ágó, capable of covering large distances, easily jumping across large waters. Her T-shirt rides up, her belly looks youthful and round as if she was still twenty, without a birthmark in sight, though slightly protruding after last night's copious dinner.

Everybody received three fried chicken thighs, of which people ate at least two as they were very juicy. Their classmate Valentin prepared the food, who's head chef at a hotel in town. He talks in a weird way, his mother tongue having fractured in him as he hardly ever uses it. The chicken thighs were crispy on the outside and tender on the inside. After the dinner, Valentin explains to those gathering around him how to prepare chicken in this way. She exchanges a complicit glance with Ágó and Zsolt, as all three of them have helped themselves to an extra chicken thigh from the large platter. Kincső was sitting with her back to them along the U-shaped table with the other young people and children, as she put it, in the animal-free zone: 'I don't want to watch you stuff animals into your face.' The kids are vegan, but not all the parents. One can see Kincső's tattooed back under her vest – plants, imaginary animals, a girl reading. The tattoos cover the whole area and continue on her inner arms. 'You'll burn in hell,' she chides them grinning, and takes a picture of them chicken thighs in hand, the handling of which was made easy by paper grips so they could be eaten without plates and cutlery. They wash the food down with fresh beer they can pull on tap themselves, the on-site brewery is in fact a major attraction of the venue.

'What a shame we can no longer smoke', Zsolt observes as he pushes his plate to one side. 'Why can't we?' Ágó asks, laughing. 'Yuck!' they say in unison as they picture themselves smoking; the horrible taste, disgusting, pungent, no, never again. Rules and decisions are suspended over the fried chicken; Ágó wipes the corner of her mouth with the serviette laid out American style in her lap, then stands up in her purple suede high heel sandals in which she walks as if she was wearing a pair of slippers. She enjoys using the tap, pouring the strong light beer into one and a half decilitre wine glasses, so she can refill them more often. 'I have always wanted to be a waitress,' she announces dreamily, as if she had to give up on the biggest dream of her life.

Eventually it's time to dance. As long as only Kati and Hilda with her three kids suggested it, nobody wanted to join in, and soon the room emptied as people left to smoke and others to watch the stars or back to their rooms. But then something gets underway, perhaps Csaba asks the petite Kincső to dance; she who is constantly talking about her projects and wants to involve everyone into the improvement of the world. In no time, the dance draws everyone in one by one, like a slow vortex. Ágó stays in her high heels the whole night, only removing her necklace made of large round lava stones, because it hinders her while jumping. Tomi is the one to start jumping, he holds on to Kati standing next to him and, all of a sudden, everything is billowing. They work off the dinner and the beers in this heated, strenuous and sweat-inducing dance, only to start again after midnight on some devilled eggs. 'I can easily eat ten,' Ágó pants.

The kids have lined up to demonstrate the latest TikTok dance, and teach the parents how to gyrate from the hip and saw the air, but the arms of grown-ups get tangled, besides they want to put together the separate elements in their head first, the kids, however, can't explain the movements, they are simply doing them, billowing together like fish.

After midnight, while the pairs are immersed in slow dance and Kincső is dancing with Csaba, she goes to the kitchen with Ágó to eat meat rolls, standing by the large fridge where they help themselves to cucumber salad using only their hands. They are standing in front of the open fridge in the dark kitchen, Ágó's metallic dress glowing like a night star, along with her invincible smile. The cold pouring out of the fridge cools down their heated bodies.

Reclining sideways on the bed, the dolphin-shaped Ágó states that she hasn't slept this much in years.

'Last time it was during the pandemic, back home.' Her left breast makes a big strong bulge through the T-shirt. She's not wearing a bra. Her face also lets itself go in this position, none of the muscles are in tone, they can fall apart if they so wish.

'Perhaps it will get better from now on, won't it?' she asks as if expecting some reassurance, agreement or guarantee with regard to the impossible: the future.

Ágó is awakening from some dream, talking to another world and only voicing her conclusions.

'It no longer has to be a success at all costs. Everything has been perfectly good until now anyway,' she declares cheerfully. '*It was hard and great*,' she suddenly switches to English, as if addressing her speech to the New World. She lets out a laugh, narrowing her eyes. '*Arrived*!'

Her voice in this language is higher pitched, it can be heard from further away as she usually has to project to cover a wider space. Her mother tongue, on the other hand, is softer, more monotonous, words blur into one another and spread out, this language is for a smaller space addressing fewer people. In such cases, one has to pay closer attention to the speaker. As if two people were talking on two different voices in two separate spaces.

'Imagine,' she excitedly says after a long pause, 'I'm writing my first article in my mother tongue. For the publication of the academy from here. *Academy* as in a scientific academy not the university. Hilda has made the connection with them. It was extremely difficult. Like any other race. A further trial of strength. Almost as hard as my first articles in English. Those could do with some correction and editing to this day. My editor told me that the more I write, the worse it is! Because now I'm spending only half the time on issues of language, I keep assuming that everything is going swimmingly. So, this was the first time they asked me for an article. Madness, isn't it? A publication that comes out in three hundred copies or so. But it's not this that matters to me, but that we won! You can't understand this as you're a writer, you have a language of your own. You can't possibly get this.'

'Linguistic suicide you mean?'

Ágó casts a serious look at her. This is the first time she stops smiling.

'*Can I tell you my dream*?' she asks suddenly. And continues on the language of the ocean, of that distant land to which she's connected by each and every awakening. '*I don't have anybody there to share a dream with. There, over the ocean.*'

'You laugh when boys or women tell their dreams, don't you?' she replies. 'Of course, I'm listening.'

'Where is this quote from?'

'Shakespeare: *Antony and Cleopatra*. I've never understood this line. Why are we laughing at the dreams of women and boys? And not at the dreams of men. I don't know. I'll find you the original, maybe you can understand.'

Ágó smells like babies, she realizes when she sits next to her to check out the quote together. They are scrolling up and down, reading the lines in context.

> *'No matter, sir, what I have heard or known.*
> *You laugh when boys or women tell their dreams;*
> *Is't not your trick?'*

'My English isn't good enough for this. I work in an entirely different linguistic register,' she points out before she shares her dream.

'I dreamt about my grandmother. She had lung cancer in my dream, and we smoked a last cigarette together.

When I looked at her, I could see that her lung was glowing. Everything was extremely hot around her, almost burning. But I was happy that she was still alive. That I could see her. At least in my dream. I don't think I could ever love anybody this much again. It may well have been her heart that was ablaze, not her lung.' She then adds, deep in thought. 'I love the fire. I work with fire,' she demonstrates by forming a globe with her hands, as if she was a magician.

'I rarely dream about her these days, she has faded away. Had I not come back here, she may not have appeared this time, either. It is the place that brings her to the fore.'

She also had a dream, could it be that they had a shared experience? It took place at their house where they used to live. It turned out that new spaces appeared in the house, one had to go up to the attic on some dangerously steep and rickety stairs, everything was covered in dust up there and the only light source was a tiny round window. Up there it emerged that there was another room, or perhaps several, in any case some more space she was unaware of so far, it turned out that the house was much larger and more spacious than she had imagined. And that those spaces may have always been there without her knowledge. Except that the way leading to them was very unsafe and dangerous, even slippery like a slope or a gradient, as if covered in dry leaves in a deciduous forest, with moist soil underneath which makes climbing extremely challenging. The Son had no difficulty going up, as if he wasn't even climbing a slope, but she slipped back several times and had to sit down. The Son did look back but by then he was already far ahead. 'Did you fall on your arse, mum?' he chuckled while carrying on, sure of himself. She woke up to find herself laughing, too.

They are both lying on their backs in the narrow, coffin-shaped room. Their hands are placed under their heads, the room filled with fir tree-scented air freshener, the silence after the shared dream, the smell of babies and sweat. The only trees around here are from deciduous forests.

'Longing for one's home, *being homesick*, as you say in England and America. Good word, I envy it,' she says, still lying on her back.

'*Oh, yeah*,' Ágó sighs, smiling, 'but my roots over there are deep enough to hold me, no matter what might happen.'

One can convey anything in English, even she can do that. One can always flee from one's own linguistic prison, there's no battle with wild beasts around there. Should she tell her about the flight? She asks Ágó as they are awakening from the afternoon nap. And about Oleg Pavlovich.

Because Oleg Pavlovich didn't flee from his own language, instead he sucked the language of others in, like some giant hoover, and then spat them out. She once appeared alongside the drunken Russian writer at a so-called emigration identity conference. The much-awaited intervention of the Russian giant took place in the evening, after he had spent the day at the hotel bar, not even taking a peek at the presentations of other speakers, as he seemingly didn't speak any language apart from Russian. After his name was announced, he slowly and wearily got out of his chair and limped unsteadily to the microphone, addressing the audience in a 19th century fashion. The men in the audience that is. Gentlemen.

'*Господа*' – he said, lowering the intonation and holding for a long pause.

With his huge hands befitting a labourer, he started to search for his notes or something in his pocket, then changed his mind as if it wasn't so important to find that something because it wouldn't actually be of any use.

'*Я не знаю, что такое идентити*' – he groaned, 'I don't know what identity is.'

With this, he swept the very topic of the conference off the table, with the conclusion that he wasn't prepared to talk about it, he wasn't prepared to talk about identity, uttering the word as if it was some disease for which there was no adequate translation, it being such a foreign and alien concept dragged into this world. During his entire speech he utilised the term *идентити*, and the more often it came up, the more ridiculous it sounded. He refused to soften his 'D' or the 'T' sound, thus not pronouncing the word as 'idyentiti' but insisting to retain its foreignness by stressing its harshness. The writer gradually sobering up during his speech, eventually manages to produce his notes from his pocket, and in his presentation about Russianness, he babbles about spirit and soul, *дух, душа*, and God, simultaneously standing on the shoulders of his forebears and looking over the head of his contemporaries, while periodically uttering the ominous term – *идентити* – to lay emphasis on the ridiculous invitation to speak at the event with a theme such as identity. He refers to Russia as *Русь*, as it was known in the Middle Ages, and as *на Руси* when conjugated. His words generate displeasure and senseless appreciation among the audience, meanwhile, sat at the back, she is past her own speech presented in American English on multiple identities and the smallest minorities utilising 'well-considered and clever contemporary critical theories', and has a feeling that the unfathomable and untranslatable sentences of this patronising and arrogant growly Russian, in the facing of whom two interpreters occasionally exchange clueless glances, actually make an attempt at saying something personal. While she's only regurgitating a lesson that perfectly corresponds to the time and place where she happens to be, instead of courageously drinking cocktails all morning like the Russian while others are presenting their papers, and then, towards the evening, unconcerned about anything and after a swooning afternoon nap, talk about that impossible to fake self-pity and nostalgia, home-love and home-malady, using these exact personally coined terms that definitely can't be translated as *romantic love*, which is why she's using them in her mother tongue for want of a better option. This is her mother tongue. Instead of discussing the issue that *modernity* will swallow up, or rather has already started to swallow up *ethnicity*, just as her former classmate, that weird Bernát, who used to repel girls, pointed out in his very influential essay published in Heidelberg. Instead of this, she could have said something personal, as if sobering up from a state of drunkenness like Oleg Pavlovich, who will only say in the end, in lieu of a convincing argument, 'look at me, I'm right here, am I not Russian? Could I be anything else?' he asks his rubbish baggy suit, in vain did he buy it in Germany or France, it still looks as if it had been made in Taganrog.

'Ladies and gentlemen. Alas, we may really vanish in an instant.'

In the end, close to the finish, she did indeed say this or rather whispered it, disregarding her carefully considered English words, from which she had kept everything away, and which also had kept her away from her own self. She said this under the influence of the Russian writer, during the closing round table discussion. In response to an auxiliary question that she barely understood, and she felt again as she did when travelling with Mark, that she could talk but not understand. Eventually she responded in her mother tongue, to the tune of a sentence that she had to translate herself at once, not having an interpreter. Even though, as she had already mentioned, *modernity* swallows up *ethnicity*, there are fewer and fewer people where she comes from, half a million people have vanished, scattered around the world, merged in with another landscape during the thirty years when she had also moved away. She is one of this half-a-million, and this is the only story she knows. From where she comes from. But for how long are we being seen as coming from somewhere, she continued wrathfully, frowning like the Son and making a fist under the table. Those of us who had left ages ago will never ever arrive anywhere, we are still just coming, *coming from* somewhere. Even if they have arrived in a sociological sense, have been integrated, adapted to local conditions and ended up as fine improvements to their new home, how long does this in-between state amidst worlds last, this *coming from*.

She wanted to write something about this once, she tells Ágó, 'I wanted to write about these things,' she says, still irate like Oleg Pavlovich, who was irate about the stupid request of the organisers, he was irate about *identity*, whereas she was angry about talking in English instead of struggling with words in her mother tongue. Home-malady. Home-love.

Because she concluded that love is the most fitting word. It may well be that affection and love, desire and yearning and wishfulness were one and the same at the beginning of time, until they spread out in many directions in as many languages, from love in chains to love freely chosen. Love, and it can only be love, because it draws the most from that meaningless and unexplainable passion towards space and landscape. Because love is that shy and fugitive animal that immediately tries to escape as soon as you get closer, that is in hiding and then suddenly jumps up triumphantly standing in front of you – but only in your dreams.

'Are you longing for home?'

'Yeah. My mum is really expecting me, I'll finally see her to-morrow. Mamsie. We meet once a year.'

'It's great to be expected by one's mother back home. It's great to be expected. It's also great to wait for someone.'

'I no longer have a room of my own, but still keep some pyjamas here. And there will be another helping of fried chicken. When I go back, I'll have to carve seven pounds off my body. At least seven. My mum keeps telling me that I'm not coming home to be on a diet. But we'll dance it off tonight.'

In the end, the wheel of time starts rolling back and they turn around in the one-way street. Through Kati, the Teacher's daughter requests the class visit her mother after the meeting. Kati urged them, appealing to their soul – she says heart by accident – to go without fail, whoever possibly can. In case too many people were to attend and not fit into the two-bedroom apartment where the Teacher lives with her daughter, they could gather at the large play-ground opposite the block, there are some stone tables and people often hold children's parties in the area. They picture a group of middle-aged people hanging out at a safe playground, suitable for all ages, in the company of an elderly Teacher who has mobility issues. On the stone table, there are a few disposable plates with salty sticks, biscuits, peanuts, apple and carrot sticks, and lukewarm raspberry cordial served in plastic cups. She even receives a personal message from the Teacher, transmitted by Kati in a precatory-authoritative tone, that she should definitely come as she has to sign another book, her very first publication. By now, the Teacher can only be in possession of books, like a child unable to read as yet. Words can no longer get to her.

In the end, eight of them will pay her a visit in the dim flat, blacked out in order to reduce the scorching heat.

The eight former students are greeted by the daughter, who is the same age as them. She's dressed in her long skirt and matronly blouse, as if she was still an awkward teenager who has never grown up, yet aged childlessly in an odd way while remaining a child none-theless.

She offers them a seat in the room packed with embroideries and folk saucers and weaves. On the table, there is a tablecloth embroidered in colourful floral motifs, as seen in airport souvenir shops. The Teacher's daughter offers them some cherry brandy in shot glasses, thinking that grown-ups always drink when visiting someone, but in this heat, nobody wants to accept. A group photo, taken in year four, is on the table and the daughter asks them to talk about the protagonists while the Teacher casts her glance around the room in silence. She looks either at the students and her daughter or the star and moon-shaped biscuits laid out on the table. She grabs a glass of raspberry cordial with soda, checking it out, sniffing it. 'Drink, mum, you like this. It's sweet.' She tastes it and suddenly her face twitches as if she sampled vinegar. She puts it back.

'Look how cute,' the daughter shows the photo taken at the class meeting to her mother. Hilda's triplets, dressed in colourful blouses with patterns similar to the ones on the embroidered tablecloth, sing some funny school songs. The Teacher points at three children on the forty-year-old photo.

'Here they are, I remember.'

When Gabi returns from the bathroom, the Teacher seems startled and turns to her daughter.

'Who's this?'

'You remember Gabi. She was the best student in class, you used to be so proud of her,' she points at the spectacled girl standing in the middle row.

'I don't know her,' the Teacher replies confidently. They continue with a recording from the class meeting. They are listening to the speech for nearly ten minutes. The daughter turns the screen towards her mother, who stares at it, then scans the room and finally rests her gaze on the speaker amidst the many foreign faces. She recognizes her and nods. The speech feels distant and meaningless, like a whale washed up on the shore. They maintain a polite silence, laugh when required and then leaf through some photos.

Next up, it's the presentation of the gift on behalf of the whole class, an album with the photos of everybody who could be contacted. This has also been put together by Kathrin, with an awful lot of work, correspondence and research. The large-format album opens with the same class photo that has been awaiting them on the coffee table. Then there is a page with everybody's signature and best wishes, followed by the protagonists in alphabetical order.

Grown-up people, families, kids, dogs, a snake, trips and homes, countless foreign countries, three continents. Four in fact, because Ari has been snapped in front of a huge water-spitting stone lion in Singapore. For those who vanished without a trace, passed away, couldn't or didn't want to come to the class meeting, failed to answer letters or rejected their former home, a careful hand included their names on a separate page in exquisite calligraphy. Kati uses deep saturated colours and chooses a unique shade and calligraphic style for everyone. Nobody has been missed out, there are no blank pages, in lieu of the menacing void there are pages and pages embroidered in colour.

The Teacher's daughter is slowly turning the pages, showing pictures to her mother, commenting on the kids, distant fairy tale lands or a dog with silky coat.

'I want to go home,' the Teacher indicates.

Her daughter continues to leaf through the album. She gets to Alex who died under unusual circumstances in a forest. The teenage boy doesn't smile on the photo. Kathrin cropped this picture from a blown-up class photo, under it there are two dates listed in small black print and connected by a thin line – the duration of his life. Among the many grown-up faces, Alex is frozen into the time of childhood.

On the opposite page, there is Csaba among his goats. Advertising for this cheese shop.

'I want to go home,' the Teacher insists.

While the daughter leafs through the album and tries to make her mother turn her attention to the photos, the others are engaged in subdued conversation. They have barely arrived half an hour ago but can't wait for the moment to be able to leave.

'I want to go home. They aren't letting me go,' the Teacher looks around the room imploringly, and starts to cry.

Meanwhile her daughter still keeps browsing the album, she's nearly done.

'You are at home, mum. This is your home.'

Her voice is reassuring, yet she doesn't even look her mother in the face.

The visitors stand up all at once, thanking for the hospitality. The Teacher also struggles to stand up, as though she was about to also take her leave.

She's not taking anyone with her on the way back. Departure is difficult and troublesome as always, as if she wasn't actually keen on leaving. She meets up with Edina one more time, and they take the dog for a walk in the woods. She makes her way early in the afternoon, by which point leaving the town is a trying experience in the heavy outbound traffic. This is when the Son's message arrives.

'Are we still going at the weekend?'

'Which week, where to?' She's yet again stuck between spaces and times. She's inching forward in a neighbourhood that has grown together with the town. Once upon a time in her childhood, they came here to visit so she can 'get to know village life'. There was a spare room they never used, a cow and strange smells in the house.

She only replies to the Son fifty kilometres later.

The Son arrived from obscurity, from swirling darkness, from his own unknown story personally reserved for him. He lays claims to his story and asks her not to tell others. When he's a grown-up, once he gets to know it, he will tell his story himself. This is their agreement.

This Son is conceived in their hearts during the years spent under the bright Spanish sky. His foreignness is striking at first, especially in his young age. He has dark skin, as if he were the son of the Spanish sun. But then the world gets used to him, and he to the world.

The Son arrived to remind her of the infinite magnificence and complexity of things. As well as the continuous changeability and curiosity of things. Together they will get to know the world again and catch up with missing yet indispensable knowledge. 'Is this 'F' really written in such longhand?', she marvels when the Son isn't prepared to recognize her own handwritten letters. The Son's questions after he learns to speak shower down on everyone like a siege. As if he'd never accept that there might be no answers. They are hoping he'll give up. But he won't, only get less loud. It seems as if he didn't even catch his breath in-between the avalanche of questions, and he either doesn't hear or doesn't consider the answer. 'Will you wait for the answer?' they nudge him a thousand times. Who could he have inherited his restlessness from?

As he keeps growing and turns into a teenager, his questions are getting shorter and more speculative. Thereafter, he'll ask his questions in increasingly limited confines.

'How many people died in the world between five and six pm tonight?'

For the majority of these questions the answer is: 'I don't know.'

'On the Moon, there is an answer for every single question', he points out proudly.

He is a born melancholic, hailing from that mysterious dawn. His best friend lives on the Moon, and visits him regularly. The friend from the Moon knows everything and tells him about the Moon, the cold, the loneliness, the big mountains and deep craters, the dark and the visitors with a strange head, not to mention the journey lasting a year to make it to Earth in order to visit a friend. The parents are delighted to present their child about to learn to read a knowledge book entitled *The Friends of the Moon*. He'll read it out loud to them after he learns the alphabet. The letters, dreams and adventures of his 'friends from the Moon' are all present in the book. The erupting volcanoes, the giant fish and sandstorms, the pies piled up high. Eventually, he announces that his home is on the Moon.

'This is your permanent home,' they tell him in a velvety reassuring voice.

'How do you know?' he asks sternly, because he still refers to them as 'you in the plural'. 'Us' only appears in rare moments. You, who are handling my affairs, organising my fate even though you don't have the faintest idea about my future.

He then asks with the same scepticism:

'Will you always live here?'

The answer takes forever and starts vaguely, because his parents simultaneously want to offer him a sense of safety and the pleasure of arrival, and to chart the distant future, the independent and vastly unfamiliar life of the grown-up, when everybody is operating on their own terms in the world.

'Always, if you want to,' they reply in the end, having found a roundabout way to handle this pedagogical task.

'I don't,' he concludes. 'I want to live on the Moon.' The parents then promise him to try to fling him up to the Moon. The child lies in the middle of the old blanket, in which the parents have once smuggled through customs some family portraits of unknown ancestors from a faraway country, and the parents grab the four corners and lift it high up in the air. The Son doesn't laugh, waiting for arrival instead.

'How do you want to fling me up to the Moon? Through the roof?' They wearily lower the blanket containing the almost twenty-kilo weight.

'We'll try again tomorrow.'

'You're lame. Besides, it's cruel not to fulfil the wishes of a small child if he wants to go to the Moon,' he states on a peeved and contented tone, seeing that he managed to cleverly weave in a new word: cruelty. He's lying on the blanket, looking at them. He grins. 'By the way, I can go there by myself whenever I want,' he states, sure of himself.

After this, he asks them to keep flinging him up some more. They continue until their arms go numb.

As the Son continues to grow, he expects an answer to his questions less and less. He's sixteen, paying close attention to the cars that drive past them every now and then. They have been standing in the torrid sun for an hour, trying to hitchhike.

He still formulates his questions but has got used to the fact that there aren't any valid answers. The words that are said out-loud only serve to make things less easy. For them. 'For you.' He's getting answers that the parents are only patching up with great effort, so they can utter them in earnest, in a loud voice – but these are only momentary truths that wither in an instant. He's looking at the occasional car that drives past them without slowing down.

'Since when have you become so cruel?' the Son asks in a soft voice, staring ahead.

He has stopped reminding them of what he said after the initial twenty minutes of disappointment: 'You promised me that hitchhiking would be great fun.'

At first, he looks at the cars indifferently, his one-time loves, the large dark vehicles swishing by, at the sight of which he concludes: 'Such cars won't stop. Audi, Mercedes, Volkswagen, Volvo.' As for the shabby old cars, he won't want to get into those anyway. Words are in vain, nobody is stopping. Couples sitting in cars turn their heads away, as if they suddenly spotted something untoward on the other side of the road, beyond the fields and the horizon. Fawns, awesome natural phenomena, huge seed-trees, shepherds minding their flock.

'They turn their heads not to feel remorse,' she sombrely explains to the Son.

'Why?' the Son asks flabbergasted, 'if they looked at us, they'd feel any?'

'This way they are at least pre-empting the possibility of allowing their hearts of stone to be touched by anything,' and she should say a bit more about these hearts of stone for the benefit of the Son. They are not putting their hearts at risk. She knows what she knows. For a very long time, she wouldn't have taken any risks, either. Their hearts aren't at risk.

'One has to wear one's heart on one's sleeve,' the Son replies.

He doesn't even admonish his mother for missing the bus because she had to stroke a cat. Seeing the departing bus, his mother cheerfully promises that they'll hitchhike instead, she used to hitchhike a lot, for summers on end, and it was great fun. Besides, they gain an opportunity to revert to the past in this way.

The cat was lying in front of the shop on a towering wooden box, meant to conceal some electronic device. The grey striped beast with a wide muzzle was stretching out in the sun, an old, muscular creature with lacerated ears and sticky snout-like substance in its inflamed eyes. It rolled over a couple of times, preening itself. The shop assistant was busy picking out the tufts of grass from in-between the pavement tiles, as there were no customers at present.

'The cat has an eye problem,' the Son pointed out cautiously, to which the woman replied, without as much as looking up, that she had already administered some drops to cure it.

'Is it yours?' he continued to quiz the woman even though the cat in front of the shop didn't

exactly appear to be anyone's pet.

'It's the village cat,' the woman replied, still without looking up from the pavement. 'One of its owners died, the other returned to England and couldn't take the cat. Since then, it has become the village cat.'

The Son is listening to all this, arms a-kimbo.

'They wanted to take the cat but it wasn't possible?' he snapped, a touch too loud considering how close they were standing to each other. By this point, she also came up to the cat, not waiting for the answer, which failed to materialize anyway. The cat had become much more interesting since it emerged that its English owner left and couldn't take it with them, whether this was deliberate or not. People who leave their homes behind only take their cats with them in books, in important books, these are exceptionally rare events so they have to be recorded. She used to know a woman who returned from America after seven years and brought her cat along. She paid three hundred dollars to be able to bring the cat, and everybody laughed at her.

'Shall we save it?' the Son asks after scratching the blinking cat with the sticky eyes behind the ear, despite his mother warning him not to touch the sick animal.

The Son already knows that one has to scratch animals behind the ear if one wants them to be happy. The cat isn't mistrustful, there is no need to get to know, smell, weigh up or get used to one another or look into each other's eyes in order to express one's intentions. The long and muscular animal yields at once, as if it was still prepared to put its trust into the world. As for the Son, he only asks the question to create an opportunity for her to look into the cat's eyes and thus make her see clearly her own cruelty in them.

They understand each other, needing no words or to receive an answer.

They miss the bus and after an hour of trying to hitchhike they manage to board the next service. Nobody offered them a lift. For a while, they keep waving at the cars passing by, then they sit down in the grass, still waving, but the drivers are unable to figure out what these two people could possibly want. Eventually, they recline in grass. The Son wants to know what they did in the past when nobody stopped. They did stop, she replies. If that's the case, what should they do now?

'Should we pray perhaps?' he asks, in shock yet reproachfully. As if it was always his mother's fault that things didn't work out. Summer sky, with clouds' racks hovering high above. The Son is staring up as if the answer was to be found right there.

Apparently, anybody can pray, including those who don't believe in God. Looking at the sky, she remembers to talk to the Son about prayer. She should have told him about purgatory while watching the cars indifferently racing past.

'There's no correlation between faith and prayer, she starts her reasoning. You can still have a go despite not knowing or not believing that there is someone who can hear. The existence of someone who can hear doesn't depend on whether you believe in it or not. If someone is there, they exist. This doesn't depend on us. In case this someone exists; they can hear anyway.'

It's easier to talk about prayer while observing the sky above with the cumulus clouds than watching the road with cars dashing past. 'Writing is a bit like praying,' she adds still lying on her back in the grass. 'When you write, you can't be sure whether anyone actually hears you. There's no one there, yet you keep talking. If someone is there, they exist. This doesn't depend on you'.

'It's worth engaging even with the things you are unsure of ...'she doesn't finish her sentence. 'Shall I explain or draw this?'

'You can't really draw,' the Son observes, grinning. 'I'm bored of stories, so draw it.'

This is a system of coordinates. She passed her Philosophy exam with this. It's called Pascal's Gambit. It's very simple, from which she

concluded that it's worth engaging even with things that are uncertain. That said, at the exam the young lecturer told her that this
wasn't relevant and didn't logically derive from where she started.
So she got a C in the end.

God Faith	Exists	Doesn't Exist
You believe You do it, e.g. you pray	Infinite reward	Finite loss Wasted time for prayer
You don't believe You don't do it	Finite reward	Finite gain Saved time

After she has sketched out and explained this figure while lying
on their tummies – the Infinite Reward according to Pascal – they
revert to their backs. They are staring at the narrow jet stream left
behind the planes criss-crossing the sky. This jet stream is in fact
artificial cloud, the Son explains, who knows everything there is to
know about planes.

As a kid, he'd always be restless and keep asking: 'Where is this
plane going?' The grown-ups did their best to explain that nobody
could know such a thing, as this wasn't possible to tell from down
below. But the Son insisted that he wanted to find out. To Berlin,
they told him, or to Bucharest. Abu-Dhabi. The Moon. – 'How do you
know?', he'd then frown, suspiciously.

'Where is that bird flying to?' he's asking now. They can see a crow,
and then its mate with a nut in its beak. They are taking flight from
the banks of a dried-out creek by the roadside. Then they notice
an entire murder of crows, a mix of hooded crows and rooks, black
and greyish-black. Among them, there is a bird in shades of black
and white.

'Magpie!' the Son observes. But it doesn't have the long tail typical for magpies and it looks just like a crow.

They fly over to a nearby group of trees. Minutes later, the birds fly back again, right above them. The crows are searching for nuts by the roadside tree. Soon, one of them drops the nut held in its beak. Several of them try to grab the broken nut, but its original owner chases away the others – they should put in work for their own, too. The black and white crow is flying alongside the others, gathering nuts from last year's harvest and breaking them by dropping them onto the ground. 'Neither crow, nor magpie,' the Son concludes after a thorough observation. The bird returns with a new nut, and then a few more, again and again. The son lies on his belly, photographs the bird and checks his phone. A few minutes later he announces:

'Australian magpie.'

'Cracticus tibicen,' he's reading out loud. A black and white crow they have never seen before.

They stare at the nut-gathering magpie for a long time, a bird reminiscent of crows, busy at work alongside the hooded crows and rooks. Judging by its looks and habits it's like a crow, but has a strikingly different colour.

'How did it get here?' she mumbles to herself, looking at the clear, cloudless sky and not expecting an answer. How did it get here, how did it find its way here, did it want to come here or it simply got lost in the world?

'According to the Ornithological Association, the Australian magpie can be found only in Australia,' he reads. The story of this bird is unknowable.

Her phone screen lights up – a message from him. It will be great to see the Son, they haven't met since she returned home. The wallpaper shows the son jumping into the water from the edge of a village swimming pool, on a picture taken just as he jumps up and is in mid-air. The photo was taken by the Son's father, and the ten-year-old had to jump many times and even slipped, 'I fell on my arse!' he shouted but was unable to stop even after the picture was taken. Photos are the father's job, this is the way they divided the different tasks between them: her share were words and letters, the father's were images. On the photo, the Son's arms are stretched out, one knee pulled up, joy and excitement on his face. Mid-flight, he'd cast a quick glance at his parents: can they see him? Are they encouraging him with their gaze? He's now flying.

Have You Survived It?

'Have you survived it?' the Son asks in a message accompanied by a gif he must have found while searching for the word survive. A person vanishes and then emerges from among the waves: a desperate human face, caught between drowning and hope, perhaps at the very least breath. There doesn't seem to be a body attached to the head, continuing to swim and submerge until people click on the next thing and put an end to this endless drowning. It will remain a secret forever whether these images are real or fake, an animation or the story of an actual drowning.

She had read out loud her speech to him prior to leaving for the class meeting. 'Good,' the Son observed. He wasn't prepared to add anything. Good. It will be just good for them. After some consideration, he flippantly added:

'Why are you going if you're so afraid? What are you afraid of?'

'I have no idea what I shall find there. And whom. I barely remember anyone, except for those I meet or hear about every now and then. These people are total strangers. And the town, too. It has changed.'

'Shall I come with you?' he asked at long last. He'd have had to cancel a trip with his former classmates, but he would have been prepared for this sacrifice. In the end, they agreed that his company wasn't necessary.

So now comes the laconic message: 'Have you survived it?'

'No', she replies after some consideration. 'And I no longer want to' – she talks into the phone, still in dictating mode, using their shared language with the Son.

'I can give you details if you want,' she switches to voicemail. 'I can't write this much at the moment.'

'Great, I'll listen to it,' the Son sends a curt reply. He has something else to do. The Son always has something to do, a lot of personal business.

'I met new people, not those they used to be thirty and forty years ago but the ones they had become. I can barely recall the world in which we used to exist, and I'm not familiar with the new ones. We are bringing these new selves of ours, which are unfamiliar, and show them to one another. We had a few great conversations. Proper, genuine conversations. And we danced, imagine! Twice. To Dancing Queen. And to Gimme, Gimme. I met Peter with whom we snogged once at a party during the summer we graduated from school, and we kissed to this very tune. We had no idea that a kissing competition had just been announced, and everyone else was also kissing in the hall, but the song ended and we carried on for ages. There was nothing at stake with that kiss, Peter was about to leave in a few weeks as he married someone from abroad and was ready to leave. This may well have been the reason why we could kiss for so long. As there was nothing at stake. I used to travel abroad a lot, to festivals and conferences: everyone is very well-behaved at first but on the last night... So it would have been helpful if my mother had warned me about the frenzy of these last few nights, but she hadn't, so I have you know that one always has to be extra vigilant on the final day, that's when something insurmountable comes to the fore which can only be curbed with discipline and the awareness that things can have consequences, so one shouldn't really go ahead.

I have such a story about a last night, I'll tell you about it one day. It happened before I met your father. This time, nothing happened on the final night. We are past that age. But a good thirty years ago we won the kissing competition, despite not even knowing about it. Peter left the country that very summer and I hadn't seen him since, except for once. He lives in the countryside. Now he's a chubby fifty-year-old man, who enjoys his food and fills out his shirts. We all enjoy our food in fact. He is excellent at talking about the different kinds of taxes. One morning he told us that taxes were his passion, so I wanted to ask him about royalties but didn't understand his response, even though he talked about taxes with as much delight as if he had been talking about Creation. Peter no longer wants to dance; his figure isn't really cut out for dancing. He's fat. To be fair, everybody has put on weight. He promised though that he'd help me with royalty issues, he'll look into the various allowances, as they exist. He really encouraged me to use his services.

In the morning, I went for a jog with the Scandinavians. I haven't done this for a long time. They are very fit but are struggling to cope with the heat. There is hardly ever such a heat around there to make it impossible to run. I was able to handle the heat, not so much the jogging. Susan and Kati held a yoga class, more like an acrobatics class where they were standing on top of each other, and only the kids joined in. We were watching them from the veranda.

We listened to Ágó talk about the *Little Baby* project. To date, I've only heard men improvise a forty-minute presentation. Forty people were listening to her, even the kitchen staff came in, and everybody felt as if she was explaining things to each and every member of the audience in part.

Hilda's children tried to teach some dances, they all have a different name and are very fast, requiring body parts to move at a separate pace, so nobody was able to imitate. I talked to people a lot. Many people have read my books, so they asked me when I write and how, how many years I need to write a book. Somehow this is always of most interest, the issue of technique. At times, they told me strange stories that I 'should write about' in their view. And then they'll be furious if I do. I have already missed the mark with that scientist, you know. So, I'd better be cautious.

Our chef Valentin, who prepared all the food with two local aides and showed us a couple of recipe tricks, is working at a golf paradise at present. You know how I enjoy cooking. He showed us for example what to do to prevent omelettes from drying out. Would you have guessed? The most insignificant and ordinary things can gain a new dimension if you are an expert. Things are hellishly complicated in fact. Even a humble omelette. So, it doesn't dry out. What could possibly dry out in an omelette? Well, I can relate to this because I have eaten dry omelette and have prepared some for you, too. It would have been good to learn about this twenty years ago. This omelette we made was truly yummy. I broke sixty eggs. It was so enjoyable. We prepared it in four instalments.

That morning we found some left over ladyfingers in the kitchen, also made by Valentin, so we asked him, or rather Hilda did, how come they were so fluffy. Asked him to share his tricks with us. This is also a situation where technique is interesting, as it is with novels. He dismissed this with a wave of his hand: it's a matter of luck, but then corrected himself, saying that sponge cake biscuits are basically an act of grace.

'Great,' Hilda replied, she loves baking so she'd just pray next time, but Valentin made it clear that this wasn't about prayer! 'Grace. *Gracie*. This isn't a matter of making a request. It will simply come about. You'll either have it or not. Does this make sense? This is the nature of spongefingers.'

As far as I know, Valentin is Pentecostal.

At this point Bernát comes into the kitchen, you know the guy with the books published in German, a philosopher, very quiet, barely talks to anyone, somehow he's unable to engage in a conversation or connect to things. Yet he's a great star, but this is something only I know and Ágó, his publisher is the very best. Bernát tells us when he appears in the kitchen to grab a coffee that in some theological view, can't remember which one, there is cheap and expensive grace.

To this Valentin replies that there is only a single form of grace. And he just keeps baking: 'I baked this for you.'

If you listen from afar, it sounds as if Valentin had a foreign accent.

I ate an awful lot. And drank, too. All sorts of things I shouldn't have. We are all chubby fifty-somethings. And I signed lots of books.

The weirdest thing was that everybody was nice to everyone else. We were simply too nice to one another. Perhaps those who know each other better or meet more often or live in the same place compete, critique or fight more. Many of us hadn't seen each other since we had left home. So there's nothing to compete over and we can get along. We offer the opportunity to be nice to each other.

It's incredible how much Kathrin had worked to make this class meeting possible. She visited us once, remember. She wrote personal letters and called everyone she could reach. She has been toiling for two years. I would have liked to ask her why she wanted to do this. In the end, the question didn't come naturally to me. From afar, it was impossible to understand why she wanted this so much, it would have come across as a vulgar question. It was simply great to be there.

I also learned a new thing from Laura. I'll teach it to you, too. Laura works at an Italian hotel and changes on average two hundred bedsheets a day. Kathrin begged her to come, despite this being high season for them, as they had barely recovered after the crisis. In the end, she agreed as she hadn't been back home for at least six years. One morning, Ágó brought some tea up to her room and accidentally spilt it on her bed. She went down to reception to ask for the sheets to be changed, and Laura came up with clean sheets and changed them in about ten seconds. We watched it as if we had been witnessing some rare celestial phenomenon. So we asked her to show us what she did. You turn the duvet cover inside out, grab it together with the corner of the duvet and flip it over. In a single move it's all in place. I was able to follow the technique when she slowed it down, but this isn't quite enough.

You remember what I said about our Teacher. I was afraid of her. She was someone I was truly afraid of.

After the class meeting, we visited her at home, as she was unable to attend. The others have already left and I stayed behind to sign the copies of my books she owned. Her daughter bought the first edition of my first novel from a book dealer, you know the one I'm not so proud of as it still contains lots of stupid things. We saw the others off and she joined us thinking that she'd now go home. She wanted to go home at all costs. She was unable to tell where she lived. She said she lived by the church. Their childhood house doesn't exist anymore, her daughter pointed out. 'Which church?' I asked. She thought about it for a while and then said, 'Sebastian. Saint Sebastian.'

Yet this town has never erected a church in the honour of Saint Sebastian. This saint hasn't been honoured here. There are churches dedicated to him in Rome and Madrid, also Manila as I found out later. Had she ever been there? She may have wanted to go somewhere she had never been. Hilda had sent her a postcard from Manila, where she had gone with the local choir. It features the inside and outside of a Neo-gothic church, a card that looks like a triptych. This postcard is on display in their home, Manila and the cathedral of Saint Sebastian. On one side of the postcard, there is the saint himself as angels are pulling arrows out of his body. How odd to see this Gothic image with a caption that indicates it is in the Philippines. The neo-gothic is pure nostalgia. Perhaps it was this very nostalgia that made the Teacher establish a connection with her home. She may well be craving for a dream. Something that she'd never have access to in the real world.

We all went down to the playground in front of the block. I wrote in the book, as her daughter put it, you've been so kind to write in it for us, meaning that I signed it for them and then would have wanted to leave. The Teacher said she'd come with me because she was now ready to go home. I said I'd accompany her. I signalled to the daughter that I'd take her for a walk and then bring her back. She's limping slightly but she can still walk really well, she's surprisingly agile in fact. She was struggling much more in the flat. She has stiff legs, like pillars, but she walks fast as if she was in a hurry. We take a long walk; the river is close so we cross two bridges and have a rest on a bench. Every so often she'd ask who I was. I told her that you and I used to play a game whereby we'd try to guess the riddle of the clouds. In the sense that we'd guess what they really were, such as a piano, a dinosaur, a rabbit with large ears. I showed her a cloud that obviously looked like a trumpet and asked what she thought it looked like.

'What do you mean?'

'The cloud.'

'What cloud?'

'The one up in the sky.'

'Whatever is that?'

'That cloud,' I pointed out. 'That large white thing on the sky. All those are clouds.'

'Cloud,' she repeated, unsure of herself. She then said that she wished I was her daughter.

'Or son,' this is what she said the second time round when I put on my sunglasses, the one you told me looked as if I was straight out of a Soviet war film. We walked up to the next bridge, after which she got tired and told me that she'd really like to go home and could I please accompany her.

We headed back on the opposite bank, where I filled my flask at a well and drank some water. In the park we bumped into Edina who was walking her dog. We said hello, chatted a bit and agreed that I'd call her the next day and go for another walk. When we said goodbye, the Teacher lowered her voice and asked me:

'Do they allow Hungarians in this town?'

'Of course they do, and others, too, Saracens. French, Dacians, Vends as well as Americans.'

'That's good,' she noted.

When we got back to their house and I buzzed her daughter, the Teacher appeared confused and asked:

'I live here?'

'Here indeed,' I said, 'and your daughter is at home.'

'My daughter? Aren't you my daughter?'

'No, but I could be. Would you like me to be your daughter?'

'Okay,' she replied, laughing and winking.

This was the first time she laughed. As if her face had forgotten every expression. Its only feature was a sort of ultimate blankness. I walked her up to their flat.

'Are mum and dad at home?,' she asked after I knocked.

I hugged her, she was the same height as my mother so I squeezed her, like a cloud vanishing in my hands. 'Don't strangle me!' she screamed. The old rigour I remembered so well was still present in her voice. 'When are you coming home?' she asked. I told her not to worry and just go to bed because I'd be late as I had stuff to do in town. She won't go to bed until I come home. 'Okay,' I said, 'I'll try to be quick but it won't be before midnight.' Yet another hug and we parted. 'Bye,' I said. 'Mum!,' she snapped. 'Don't you call me mum?,' I replied that I'd call her as she pleases from now on.

Her daughter hugged me, too, for the first time. Anxiously, with the stiff body of a teenage girl who's embraced for the first time by a boy. She barely dared to touch me.

One wound less. This is good, isn't it? It was worth it for this alone. And anyways.'

The Son will listen to the long voicemail. Parents think that their children never read their long letters or listen to their long messages, that they don't care anymore. But they do. Except that their attention is invisible. And their replies are reduced to a word or two. Was it worth it? Yes. No. It was. Or they channel the conversation to something else, more immediate.

'So will you come to Somlyó?' he asks because their former teacher promised that he'd check out the ground for their start of the year excursion and put up some markings. Meanwhile, the teacher twisted his ankle and is now in need of help.

'Yes,' she says.

She then adds that she dislikes driving in the dark. The Son promises that in this case he'll also come home and drive at dawn. He'll bring the retriever, too.

As soon as he gets home, he discards his shoes and bag the exact same way he used to when coming back from school as a kid, having something urgent to do: playing, eating, drinking water, playing the piano as loud as possible. He puts the light jacket on the coatrack but it slips down and he doesn't even notice. The hallway is covered in discarded shoes, coats and a half-open bag from which an English book is about to slip out. The retriever keeps jumping up and down, jumping on everyone, looking happy. The Son walks around the house, the dog tailing him, carpets and rugs crumpled in their wake. After surveying the field, he comes to a halt in the kitchen, checks out the kitchen counter, taking note of the preparations for the next meal, and asks, frowning and looking dissatisfied:

'Is this for dinner?'

His presence fills up the space and he sucks in all the attention. The Son is of a gaseous substance, this is his home where he reigns supreme. He throws himself fully clothed on the parental bed and occupies it completely. From this bed, he resounds the entire house. 'The sun rises at 5.53, we'll shoot off at 5.10.' These days, he only uses his room for sleeping.

This early hour means a wasted day for her, when she can't write at all. Or perhaps after they come back, she imagines stubbornly. The Son announces that they'll come back together and he'll stay for lunch. With the Son present, there's no writing. Had the Son never existed, would there have been any writing? He'll only leave in the afternoon. And would like to take some food with him, for two or three days. Fine, they reply. This means there will be cooking all day. By the time the Son leaves, equipped with boxes he'd never bring back, to embark on his exciting missions, the parents exhaustedly fall into a chair and barely have strength for the evening dog walk. This is because the Son announces that he'll leave the dog for some time, because he's going on an excursion with his friends. The young retriever fills up the space just as much as the Son, who had never had a dog before so as soon as he moved out had acquired this pet. As it turned out, the parents ended up looking after the dog about half the time. When the Son is absent, there is the dog, its hair is falling out, constantly drawing attention to itself and wanting something.

According to plans, they'll go up to Somlyó and look at the sunrise – the school group will follow the same route without parents in the dark – and on the way back, put up the markings.

Five fifty-three. The sun is rising a minute or two later every day.

They leave in the pitch dark, dressed in warm clothes and equipped with food and drink. They have been admiring the sunrise at the start of every single school year for eight years. 'A Solemn start to the school year', according to the Son's teacher. The parents had to bake a sort of brioche known as *kalács*.

'I hated it,' she remembers in a loud voice.

'Really?' the Son marvels, having tasted everyone's brioche. They are struggling to make their way up the hillside, the grass is still dewy and slippery. It's cold at dawn.

'We've always brought tons of clothes, which we then had to carry back home,' she states. 'Really?' the Son marvels again, not remembering any of this. He didn't carry them after all.

But he remembers rolling down the hill. The hill previously tidied up by parents, who removed all the pebbles...

'Really?'

The sky is covered with clouds, so the sunrise may not be visible at all. They are at Somlyó, and as the Son announces, the great show will begin in five minutes. Yet the sky is dark, concealed by thick clouds. But then, as if the world changed its mind, darkness ruptures, light slowly breaks the sky open from below, from the direction of the presumed town. She hated baking just as much as rising at dawn, but she's grateful to the teacher for rushing them out of bed. The sun climbs up the sky at a dazzling speed, like someone who modestly turns down being admired and just wants to get to the end of all this.

'Did you bring the ribbon?' the Son asks.

He frowns and stares at her, but doesn't say a word, only communicating with his gaze: you offered to do this, so it's your job. The son hastens to open the large bag, finding a ribbon and a pair of scissors at the bottom.

The aim is to put up markings for the children along the track, while parents stay behind. 'And lay the tables,' she reminds the Son. The smaller kids go in pairs, the older ones go alone and do larger and larger rounds. In certain places, there are guardian angels, a parent watching out at the bottom of the larger slopes. The Son loves these tracks, being very competitive he wanted to arrive first, often losing his way because of not paying attention only dashing forward, ignoring the ribbon-markings, then running back, sliding down on his bottom and knees, his trousers looking like hell and his nails breaking off as he'd try to clamber up. They begin to put up the markings. The Son is the one to show the route.

'Here we'll introduce a twist,' he announces and goes off the path.

She stops at some distance at the back, her task being to check whether the kids can actually see from one ribbon to the next. 'Not good, one can barely see!,' she shouts.

'Don't be a sissy,' the Son replies. 'They'll have to look for it, this isn't a walk in the park, but a learning curve.' What's more, he introduces further twists. 'They'll go back if they go wrong,' the Son announces, it's out of the question not to go back and look for the markings. The teacher reassured the parents on their first meeting that nobody had ever been left behind in the woods, and everybody from every single class of his had always returned.

The Son suddenly changes the direction of the route from the slope upwards to the left, with the aim of going round the rock and then going down where it's the steepest. She can barely keep up with him, despite wearing hiking boots. She has always found going upwards easier, the slope seems particularly hard. The Son is already at the bottom, he looks up, they can see each other and he can sense that his mother is squatting and trying to gather some strength. The Son is waiting, perhaps she'll make a start again. Well? But she's just crouching, pebbles rolling down as she makes a move and starts to slide, there's nothing to hold on to, the thin dry branches are unable to hold her back. 'Shall I go up?' the Son offers his help from below. 'Wait!' he shouts.

She didn't remove her many layers of clothing, so started sweating as the sun crawled to the zenith and there were suddenly ten degrees more. The forest is making music in silence, the birds have taken possession of the world. The Son is still waiting patiently, he has already completed his task and marked the route on which everyone will have to proceed on their own. He produces an apple from his backpack, breaks it in two and offers half to his mother.

'Want some?' he shouts. He has always loved shouting.

As she's sitting, she looks down, the forest seemingly safe and friendly, yet she can't go down the slope.

'Shall we go home today?' the forest is resounding with the voice of the Son. He's encouraging her not to try to solve the problem in her head but to get going. Not to keep thinking but to get started as the kids will also get started and run down without overthinking it, just making a move and getting started. He'll catch her at the end if need be.

In the end, she'll be the one driving on the way back. The Son asks whether she had really left to take on the world aged eighteen, as his grandmother told him. He's staring at her, trying to get a sense of the unfamiliar person within her. Meanwhile, she's just staring ahead, to the road and then into the rear-view mirror, but it's not the barren morning landscape that she sees behind the car but her current face. And the invisible age rings.

Endnotes

1   This is a reference to the peregrinations of Abel (Ábel), the protagonist of a trilogy by Transylvanian–Hungarian author Áron Tamási. The
volumes include *Ábel a rengetegben/Abel in the vast forest* (1932),
translated as *Abel Alone* by Mari Kuttna (Budapest: Corvina, 1966);
Ábel az országban/Abel in the Country and *Ábel Amerikában/Abel in
America*.

2   Homer: *Odyssey*, Book V, lines 207–208, trans. A.T. Murray.
Cambridge, MA: Harvard University Press; London, William
Heinemann, Ltd. 1919.
data.perseus.org/citations/urn:cts:greekLit:tlg0012.tlg002
.perseus-eng1:5.192-5.227

3   This is a reference to the (abbreviation of the) Hungarian Protestant
greeting 'áldás, békesség' (blessings and peace).

4   Homer: *Iliad*, Book 1, l. 1, trans. Ian Johnston.

5   Homer: *Odyssey*, Book 5, ll.82–85, trans. A.T. Murray. Cambridge,
MA: Harvard University Press; London, William Heinemann, Ltd. 1919.
data.perseus.org/citations/urn:cts:greekLit:tlg0012.tlg002
.perseus-eng1:5.50-5.91

6   *оказаться без социума* = Without society (Russian)

7   *русская тоска* = Russian melancholy (Russian)

8   *дежурная* = *Dezhurnaya:* steward, usually a female attendant in
colleges, art galleries and museums, epitomising customer service in
the Soviet era.

9   *А можно посмотреть* = May we take a look? (Russian)

10 *лавка* = Shop (Russian)

11 *Можно* = You may (Russian)

12 *А вот это?* = How about this?

13 *Что* = What? (Russian)

14 *Вы про что* = What are you talking about?

15 *Прорубь* = Ice hole

16 *стажировка* = Internship

17 *Причем тут Набоков?* = Why should we need Nabokov?

18 *Эмигранты такие* = Kind of emigrants (Russian)

19 *Надо читать Пушкина* = Read Pushkin (Russian).

20 Fragment from Tatiana's letter to Onegin, *Eugene Onegin* by Pushkin, trans. Rosa Newmarch.

21 Anna Akhmatova: 'For the last time, we met…', trans. A.S. Kline. ruverses.com/anna-akhmatova/for-the-last-time-we-met/2121/

22 *взаимосведение* = Cooperation, mutual understanding (Russian)

23 *Мы выше любви!* = *We are above love!*
    Chekhov: *The Cherry Orchard,* trans. Ronald Hingley.

24 Chekhov: *The Cherry Orchard*, trans. Ronald Hingley.

25 *свет* = Light (Russian)

26 Dostoevsky: *White Nights*, trans. Constance Garnett, www.gutenberg.org/files/36034/36034-h/36034-h.htm

27 Brodsky: 'At the edge of the lake'. brodskiy.su/korotkie-stihi/v-ozernom-krayu/?lang=en

28 *от нечего делать* = Nothing to do (Russian)

29 Paraphrasing Frida Vigdorova: 'The Trial of Joseph Brodsky', *NER* 34.3–4 *Translated from the Russian by Michael R. Katz.* www.nereview.com/2014/02/18/the-trial-of-joseph-brodsky-frida-vigdorova/

30 Brodsky: 'Odysseus to Telemachus', trans. George L. Kline. ruverses.com/joseph-brodsky/odysseus-to-telemachus/1278/

Andrea Tompa is a multi-award-winning Hungarian novelist and theatre critic, former editor of Színház/Theatre and a member of the prestigiousSzéchenyi Literary and Arts Academy. Tompa is author of the novels *A hóhér háza/The Hangman's House* (translated into English by Bernard Adams, Seagull Books, 2021) and shortlisted for the Oxford-Weidenfeld Prize, *Fejtől és lábtól/Top to Tail* (2013), Omerta (2017, translated into German by Terezia Mora, Suhrkamp, 2022, Omerta in English by Bernard Adams coming out in fall 2024, Seagull Books), *Haza/Home* (2020, translated by Jozefina Komporaly, Istros Books, 2024) and *Sokszor nem halunk meg/Often We Don't Die* (2023). She lives and works in Budapest. She is an academic at Babeş-Bolyai University, Cluj, Romania, Hungarian Theater Department.

Jozefina Komporaly is a London-based academic and translator from Hungarian and Romanian, specializing in theatre and contemporary literature. She is editor and co-translator of the drama collections *How to Explain the History of Communism to Mental Patients and Other Plays* (Seagull, 2015), András Visky's *Barrack Dramaturgy* (Intellect, 2017) and *Plays from Romania: Dramaturgies of Subversion* (Bloomsbury, 2021), and author of numerous publications on translation, adaptation and theatre. Her translations appeared in Asymptote, The Baffler, Columbia Journal, Los Angeles Review, Modern Poetry in Translation, Poet Lore, Words without Borders, World Literature Today, and were produced by Foreign Affairs, Trap Door, Theatre Y, Trafika Europe. Recent work includes *Mr K Released* by Matéi Visniec (finalist for the 2021 EBRD Literature Prize), *Story of a Stammer* by Gábor Vida (Seagull Books, 2022), *MyLifeandMyLife* by Melinda Mátyus (Ugly Duckling Presse, 2023). She is a member of the UK Translators Association.